PENGUIN BOOKS

MARCH

Geraldine Brooks is the Pulitzer Prize-winning author of *March* and *Year of Wonders* and the nonfiction works *Nine Parts of Desire* and *Foreign Correspondence*. Previously, Brooks was a correspondent for *The Wall Street Journal* in Bosnia, Somalia, and the Middle East. Born and raised in Australia, she lives in rural Virginia with her husband, Tony Horwitz, their son Nathaniel, and three dogs.

Praise for *March*

"*March* is a beautifully wrought story about how war dashes ideals, unhinges moral certainties and drives a wedge of bitter experience and unspeakable memories between husband and wife."
—*Los Angeles Times Book Review*

"Clarity of vision, fine, meticulous prose, the unexpected historical detail, a life-sized protagonist caught inside an unimaginably huge event. [*March*] shows the same seamless marriage of research and imagination. . . . Brooks's version of March's story is both harrowing and moving . . . *March* is an altogether successful book, casting a spell that lasts much longer than the reading of it." —Karen Joy Fowler, *The Washington Post Book World*

"Pitch-perfect writing." —*USA Today*

"Researched with great historical thoroughness, *March* hews faithfully to the spirit of Alcott's original. . . . [*March*] enhances rather than appropriates its sister work from 1868. Louisa May Alcott would be well pleased."
—*The Economist*

"It is harder, sometimes, to review a glorious book—to convey its power and influence without relying on suspicious adjectives. Good books can be slotted, characterized, explained; great books often cannot. I believe Geraldine Brooks' new novel, *March*, is a very great book. I believe it breathes new life into the historical fiction genre, the borrowing-a-character-from-the-deep-past phenomenon, the old I-shall-tell-you-a-story-through-letters tradition. I believe it honors the best of the imagination. I give it a hero's welcome." —*Chicago Tribune*

"Powerful" —*The Boston Globe*

"*March* is a first-rate historical novel. . . . It feels honorable, elegant and true, an adult coda to the plangent idealism of *Little Women*."
—*The Dallas Morning News*

"The pictures that Brooks paints of the war-ravaged South, particularly on the liberated plantation, are haunting. This richness, of time and place and of March's unrelenting struggle to live up to the man he thinks he should be, makes *March* a spellbinder. The picture is not simple, neither in terms of the life nor in the emotions of its principals. It is, however, compellingly honest. It is the feeling that the reader is witness to truth that elevates *March* beyond a gimmick to an engrossing, thought-provoking tale."
—*The Denver Post*

"Brilliant . . . It is this disconnection between the inner self (what one knows and feels) and outward presentation (what one allows others to see and know of oneself) that provides this wonderful novel with dazzling narrative tension. . . . It is this struggle for balance—between being human and being principled—that is Brooks' brilliant creative stroke. From the intimidating virtues of the March sisters, it's clear that Alcott favored principles. But thank goodness for Geraldine Brooks: She allows her characters to be human. And in the end, they have more to teach us."
—*The Atlanta Journal-Constitution*

"Brooks has written a gripping story of an impossible time, and simultaneously a neat deconstruction and reconstruction of one of American literature's best-known families." —*The Oregonian* (Portland)

"Richly imagined . . . This meticulously researched and well-crafted book reveals that atrocities occur on both sides in war, leaving countless innocent victims, and that even the most seemingly dedicated often have feet of clay." —*Rocky Mountain News*

"When I learned the subject of this novel, I felt a twinge of envy. How inspired to fill out Mr. March, absent from nearly all of *Little Women* but, as a chaplain in the Civil War, probably up to something quite as interesting as the tribulations of his four daughters at home. . . . [I]n *March*, Brooks dares to create a man of his times, who believes that curbing his wife is among his proper duties as a husband. She also allows him to be as self-righteous as might be expected of someone with his fervent, high-minded convictions." —Christina Schwarz, *The Atlantic Monthly*

MARCH

A NOVEL

Geraldine Brooks

PENGUIN BOOKS

PENGUIN BOOKS

Published by the Penguin Group

Penguin Group (USA) Inc., 375 Hudson Street, New York, New York 10014, U.S.A.

Penguin Group (Canada), 90 Eglinton Avenue East, Suite 700, Toronto, Ontario,
Canada M4P 2Y3 (a division of Pearson Penguin Canada Inc.)

Penguin Books Ltd, 80 Strand, London WC2R 0RL, England

Penguin Ireland, 25 St Stephen's Green, Dublin 2, Ireland (a division of Penguin Books Ltd)

Penguin Group (Australia), 250 Camberwell Road, Camberwell, Victoria 3124,
Australia (a division of Pearson Australia Group Pty Ltd)

Penguin Books India Pvt Ltd, 11 Community Centre, Panchsheel Park, New Delhi – 110 017, India

Penguin Group (NZ), 67 Apollo Drive, Rosedale, North Shore 0632, New Zealand
(a division of Pearson New Zealand Ltd)

Penguin Books (South Africa) (Pty) Ltd, 24 Sturdee Avenue, Rosebank,
Johannesburg 2196, South Africa

Penguin Books Ltd, Registered Offices: 80 Strand, London WC2R 0RL, England

First published in the United States of America by Viking Penguin,
a member of Penguin Group (USA) Inc. 2005
Published in Penguin Books 2006

15 17 19 20 18 16 14

PUBLISHER'S NOTE

This is a work of fiction. Names, characters, places, and incidents either are the product
of the author's imagination or are used fictitiously, and any resemblance to actual persons,
living or dead, business establishments, events, or locales is entirely coincidental.

THE LIBRARY OF CONGRESS HAS CATALOGED THE HARDCOVER EDITION AS FOLLOWS:

Brooks, Geraldine.
March / Geraldine Brooks.
p. cm.
ISBN 0-670-03335-9 (hc.)
ISBN 978-0-14-303666-1 (pbk.)
1. United States—History—Civil War, 1861–1865—Fiction.   2. March family (Fictitious
characters)—Fiction.   3. Fathers and daughters—Fiction.   4. Soldiers—Fiction.   I. Title.
PR9619.3B7153M37 2004
823'.914—dc22   2004049496

Printed in the United States of America
Set in Caslon Book   Designed by Francesca Belanger

For Darleen and Cassie—
by no means little women.

PART ONE

Jo said sadly,

"We haven't got father, and shall not have him for a long time." She didn't say "perhaps never," but each silently added it, thinking of father far away, where the fighting was.

–Louisa May Alcott, *Little Women*

CHAPTER ONE

Virginia Is a Hard Road

October 21, 1861

This is what I write to her: *The clouds tonight embossed the sky. A dipping sun gilded and brazed each raveling edge as if the firmament were threaded through with precious filaments.* I pause there to mop my aching eye, which will not stop tearing. The line I have set down is, perhaps, on the florid side of fine, but no matter: she is a gentle critic. My hand, which I note is flecked with traces of dried phlegm, has the tremor of exhaustion. *Forgive my unlovely script, for an army on the march provides no tranquil place for reflection and correspondence. (I hope my dear young author is finding time amid all her many good works to make some use of my little den, and that her friendly rats will not grudge a short absence from her accustomed aerie.) And yet to sit here under the shelter of a great tree as the men make their cook fires and banter together provides a measure of peace. I write on the lap desk that you and the girls so thoughtfully provided me, and though I spilled my store of ink you need not trouble to send more, as one of the men has shown me an ingenious receipt for a serviceable substitute made from the season's last blackberries. So am I able to send "sweet words" to you!*

Do you recall the marbled endpapers in the Spenser that I used to read to you on crisp fall evenings just such as this? If so, then you, my dearest one, can see the sky as I saw it here tonight, for the colors swirled across the heavens in just such a happy profusion.

And the blood that perfused the silted eddies of the boot-stirred

3

river also formed a design that is not unlike those fine endpapers. Or—better—like that spill of carmine ink when the impatient hand of our little artist overturned the well upon our floorboards. But these lines, of course, I do not set down. I promised her that I would write something every day, and I find myself turning to this obligation when my mind is most troubled. For it is as if she were here with me for a moment, her calming hand resting lightly upon my shoulder. Yet I am thankful that she is *not* here, to see what I must see, to know what I am come to know. And with this thought I exculpate my censorship: I never promised I would write the truth.

I compose a few rote words of spousal longing, and follow these with some professions of fatherly tenderness: *All and each of you I have in my mind, in parlor, study, chambers, lawn; with book or with pen, or hand in hand with sister dear, or holding talk the while of father, a long way off, and wondering where he is and how he does. Know that I can never leave you quite; for while my body is far away my mind is near and my best comfort is in your affection* . . . Then I plead the press of my duties, closing with a promise soon to send more news.

My duties, to be sure, are pressing enough. There are needful men all around me. But I do not immediately close my lap desk. I let it lie across my knees and continue to watch the clouds, their knopped masses blackened now in the almost lightless sky. No wonder simple men have always had their gods dwell in the high places. For as soon as a man lets his eye drop from the heavens to the horizon, he risks setting it on some scene of desolation.

Downriver, men of the burial party wade chest deep to retrieve bodies snagged on fallen branches. Contrary to what I have written, there is no banter tonight, and the fires are few and ill tended, so that the stinging smoke troubles my still-weeping eye. There is a turkey vulture staring at me from a limb of sycamore. They have been with us all day, these massive birds. Just this morning, I had thought them stately, in the pearly predawn light, perched still as gargoyles, wings widespread, waiting for the rising sun. They did not move through all the long hours of our Potomac crossing, first to our muster on this island, which sits like a giant barge in the midstream, splicing the wide water into rushing narrows. They watched, motionless still, as we crossed to the farther shore and made our silent ascent up the slippery cow path on the face of the bluff. Later, I noticed them again. They had taken wing at last, inscribing high, graceful arcs over the field. From up there, at least, our predicament must have been plain: the enemy in control of the knoll before us, laying down a withering fire, while through the woods to our left more troops moved in stealthy file to flank us. As chaplain, I had no orders, and so placed myself where I believed I could do most good. I was in the rear, praying with the wounded, when the cry went up: Great God, they are upon us!

I called for bearers to carry off the wounded men. One private, running, called to me that any who tried it would be shot full of more bullets than he had fingers and toes. Silas Stone, but lightly injured then, was stumbling on a twisted knee, so I gave him my arm and together we plunged into the woods, joining the chaos of the rout. We were trying to recover the top of the cow path—the only plain way down to the river—when we came upon another turkey vulture, close enough to touch it. It was perched on the chest of a fallen man and turned its head sharply at our intrusion. A length of organ, glossy and brown, dangled from its beak. Stone raised his musket, but he was already so spent that his hands shook violently. I had to remind him that if we didn't find the river and get across it, we, too, would be vulture food.

We thrashed our way out of the thicket atop a promontory many rods short of the cow path. From there, we could see a mass of our men, pushed by advancing fire to the very brow of the bluff. They hesitated there, and then, of a sudden, seemed to move as one, like a herd of beasts stampeded. Men rolled, leaped, stumbled over the edge. The drop is steep: some ninety feet of staggered scarps plunging to the river. There were screams as men, bereft of reason, flung themselves upon the heads and bayonets of their fellows below. I saw the heavy boot of one stout soldier land with sickening force onto the skull of a slight youth, mashing the bone against rock. There was no point now in trying to reach the path, since any footholds it might once have afforded were worn slick by the frenzied descent. I crawled to the edge of the promontory and dangled from my hands before dropping hard onto a narrow ledge, all covered with black walnuts. These sent me skidding. Silas Stone rolled and fell after me. It wasn't until we reached the water-laved bank that he told me he could not swim.

The enemy was firing from the cliff top by then. Some few of our men commenced tying white rags to sticks and climbing back up to surrender. Most flung themselves into the river; many, in their panic, forgetting to shed their cartridge boxes and other gear, the weight of which quickly dragged them under. The only boats were the two mud scows that had ferried us across. For these, men flung themselves until they were clinging as a cluster of bees dangling from a hive, and slipping off in clumps, four or five together. Those that held on were plain targets and did not last long.

I dragged off my boots and made Stone do the same, and bade him hurl his musket far out, to the deepest channel, so as to put it from reach of our enemies. Then we plunged into the chill water and struck out toward the island. I thought we could wade most of the way, for crossing at dawn, the poles had seemed to go down no significant depth. But I had not accounted for the strength of the current, nor the cold. "I will get you across," I had promised him, and I might have done, if the bullet hadn't found him, and if he hadn't thrashed so, and if his coat, where I clutched it, hadn't been shoddily woven. I could hear the rip of thread from thread, even over the tumbling water and the yelling. His right hand was on my throat, his fingers–callused tradesman's fingers–depressing the soft, small bones around my wind-pipe. His left hand clutched for my head. I ducked, trying vainly to refuse him a grip, knowing he would push me under in his panic. He managed to snatch a handful of my hair, his thumb, as he did so, jabbing into my left eye. I went under, and the mass of him pushed me down, deep. I jerked my head back, felt a burn in my scalp as a handful of hair ripped free, and my knee came up, hard, into something that gave like marrow. His hand slid from my throat, the jagged nail of his middle finger tearing away a piece of my skin.

We broke the surface, spewing red-brown water. I still had a grip on his tearing jacket, and if he had stopped his thrashing, even then, I might have seized a stouter handful of cloth. But the current was too fast there, and it tugged apart the last few straining threads. His eyes changed when he realized. The panic just seemed to drain away, so that his last look was a blank, unfocused thing–the kind of stare a newborn baby gives you. He stopped yelling. His final sound was more of a long sigh, only it came out as a gargle because his throat was filling with water. The current bore him away from me feet first. He was prone on the surface for a moment, his arms stretched out to me. I swam hard, but just as I came within reach a wave, turning back upon a sunken rock, caught his legs and pushed the lower half of his body under, so that it seemed he stood upright in the river for a moment. The current spun him round, a full turn, his arms thrown upward with the abandon of a Gypsy dancer. The firing, high on the bluff, had loosed showers of foliage, so that he swirled in concert with the sunshine-colored leaves. He was face to face with me again when the water sucked him under. A ribbon of scarlet unfurled to mark his going, widening out like a sash as the current carried him, down and away. When I dragged myself ashore, I still had the torn fragment of wet wool clutched in my fist.

I have it now: a rough circle of blue cloth, a scant six inches across. Perhaps the sum total of the mortal remains of Silas Stone, wood turner and scholar, twenty years old, who grew up by the Blackstone River and yet never learned to swim. I resolved to send it to his mother. He was her only son.

I wonder where he lies. Wedged under a rock, with a thousand small mouths already sucking on his spongy flesh. Or floating still, on and down, on and down, to wider, calmer reaches of the river. I see them gathering: the drowned, the shot. Their hands float out to touch each other, fingertip to fingertip. In a day, two days, they will glide on, a funeral flotilla, past the unfinished white dome rising out of its scaffolds on a muddy hill in Washington. Will the citizens recognize them, the brave fallen, and uncover in a gesture of respect? Or will they turn away, disgusted by the bloated mass of human rot?

I should go now and find out where upon this island they are tending to the wounded. Naturally, the surgeon has not seen fit to send me word. The surgeon is a Calvinist, and a grim man, impatient with unlabeled brands of inchoate faith. In his view, a man should be a master of his craft, so that a smith should know his forge, a farmer his plow, and a chaplain his creed. He has made plain his disregard for me and my ministry. The first time I preached to the company, he observed that in his view a sermon that did not dwell on damnation was scant service to men daily facing death, and that if he wanted to hear a love poem he would apply to his wife.

I dragged a hand through my hair, which has dried out in tangled mats, like discarded corn silks at a husking. Even to raise my arm for that slight effort is a misery. Every muscle aches. My aunt was right, perhaps, in her bitter denunciation of my coming here: the cusp of a man's fortieth year is no season for such an enterprise as this. And yet what manner of man would I be, who has had so much to say in the contest of words, if now I shirked this contest of blood? So I will stand here with those who stand in arms, as long as my legs can support me. But, as a private from Millbury observed to me today, "Virginia is a hard road, reckon."

I stowed the lap desk in my rucksack. We had left the main part of our gear here on the island, but my blanket was sodden from the use of it to dry myself and to blot my soaking clothes. Still, there is some warmth in wool, wet or no. I carried it to a youth who lay, curled and keening, on the riverbank. The boy was dripping wet and shivering. I expected he would be on fire with fever by morning. "Will you not come up the bank with me to some drier ground?" I asked. He made no reply, so I tucked the blanket around him where he lay. We will both sleep cold tonight. And yet not, I think, as cold as Silas Stone.

I made my way a few rods through the mud and then, where the bank dipped a little, scrambled with some difficulty into a mown field. In the flicker of firelight I discerned a small band of walking wounded sitting listless in the hollows of a haystack where they would shiver out the night. I inquired from them where the hospital tents had been established. "There ain't no tents: they're using some old secesh house," said a private, nursing a bandaged arm. "Strange place it is, with big white statues all nekked, and rooms filled up with old books. There's an old secesh lives there, cracked as a clay pot dropped on rock, seemingly, with just one slave doing for him. She's helping our surgeon, if you'd credit it. She probed out my wound for me and bound it up fine, like you see," he said, proudly raising his sling, then wincing as he did so. "She tol' me they was more than a dozen slaves on the place before, and she the only one ain't ran off."

I don't think the private knew his left from right, for his directions to the house were less than coherent, and his friend, whose neck was bandaged and who couldn't speak, kept waving his hands in objection at every turn the other man described. So I blundered on in the dark, finding myself at the riverbank again, uncertain whether the farther shore was Maryland or Virginia. I turned back and found a line of snake-rail fence that led past the ruins of what must have once been a gristmill. I continued following the fence line until it turned in at a gate. Beyond stretched a drive lined with dogwoods, and a gravel of river stone that was hard on my bootless feet.

And then I knew I was on the right path, for I smelled it. If only field hospitals did not always have the selfsame reek as latrine trenches. But so it is when metal lays open the bowels of living men and the wastes of digestion spill about. And there is, too, the lesser stink, of fresh-butchered meat, which to me is almost equally rank. I stopped, and turned aside into the bushes, and heaved up bitter fluid. Something about my state just then, bent double and weak, brought to my mind the recollection of my father, caning me, for refusing my share of salt pork. He believed a meatless diet such as mine made me listless at my chores. But what I shirked were the tasks themselves, foul and cruel. No soul should be asked to toil all day with the yellow oxen yoked up, unwilling, their hide worn raw by the harness, their big blank eyes empty of hope. It drains the spirit, to trudge sunup till sundown at the arse-end of beasts, sinking into piles of their steaming ordure. And the pigs! How could anyone eat pork who has heard the screams at slaughter when the black blood spurts?

Perhaps it was the darkness, or the different season. Perhaps my biliousness and grief and exhaustion. Perhaps simply that twenty years is a very long time for an active mind to retain any memory, much less one with dark and troubled edges, begging to be forgot. Whatever the case, I was halfway up the wide stone steps before I recognized the house. I had been there before.

CHAPTER TWO

A Wooden Nutmeg

I had been there, on a spring morning, when the fog stood so thick on the river that it looked as though the bowl of the sky had spilled all its milky clouds into the valley. I was eighteen years old, and I had walked, in stages, the long way from the port at Norfolk. I was lean and strong, with sun-bleached hair that stuck out near-white from under the brim of my straw hat.

There was a little barge-ferry then, that would stop on request, at a jetty on the island's northern tip. I had alighted there on a whim and walked the mile and a half to the house, whistling the song of the boatman who had poled the crossing. The white dogwoods were in flower all the way up the drive, and the air seemed viscous and honey-fragrant, unlike the mud-scent of a chill May morning on Spindle Hill. I had two heavy trunks tied to the pole across my shoulder, and so I was defenseless when a brace of mastiffs came baying after me, sending the stones flying under their thick, swift paws. It was, you might say, a typical welcome for a Connecticut peddler, our reputation being less than luminous. Too many of us, in the quest for gain, had forsaken honesty for cunning, decency for coarseness. But I knew dogs: at home we'd had a collie that was like an extra pair of arms when you needed the sheep gathered in. And I'd learned a thing or two more on my way north from Norfolk, the most useful being that if a Cerberus comes at you barking and snarling, call him to you with a joyous enthusiasm. Nine dogs in ten will greet fear with aggression, and friendship with fine humor. By the time I reached the big house those two beasts were gamboling beside me, nuzzling their big drooly muzzles against my thighs.

A young servant stood atop the steps, looking surprised and perhaps a trifle annoyed by this. She whistled sharply, and the dogs' ears flattened as they sidled off. "Those two would more likely have a chunk each out of your hams before you'd got a halfway up the drive than be fawning like that." Her voice was unexpected: refined, and resonant as a bell. She stood with arms akimbo, her long-fingered hands, dark brown on top and pale pink under–which contrast still surprised me–resting on the waistband of a starched skirt striped cream and gray, which she wore with a spotless, high-necked bodice. Around her head was knotted a rigolette, dyed the color of beet, that made a handsome effect against her copper-colored brow. Her appearance was an excellent omen: a household that got its slaves up so neatly was likely to be liberal-handed.

As she came down the steps to where I stood, I set down my tin trunks, swept off my hat, and affected what I hoped was my most ingratiating smile. Manners matter in the South; I had met even field hands, half-naked and barefoot, who comported themselves with more grace than the average educated New Englander. I had learned, too, that winning over the upper servants was the first object for a gentleman of the road in pursuit of a sale. It was they, after all, who presented one's suit for admission to the master–or, of keener interest to me, to the mistress–and they could do that in any number of more or less helpful ways.

Since I stand more than six feet in my stockings, being eye to eye with a woman is not something that I have grown much used to. But that day, my pale blue eyes gazed into her dark ones, which were lit with a faint amusement. Even now I remember that I was the first to look away.

"Thinking to charm me, as well as the dogs," she said, in that silvery voice. "Yankee, are you? From Connecticut?" She raised her chin sharply and made a slight clicking sound with her tongue. "The last peddler through here was a Connecticut boy, too. Sold the cook a jar of wooden nutmegs."

"For shame!" I said, and meant it, though I'd seen many a likely fake whittled in the idle campfire hours of my competitors.

"I don't believe the household will be interested to see your notions, but we'd be remiss if we did not offer you a cold draught on a warm morning."

There you are, I thought. A Negro slave, probably not even as old as I, yet with a style of address that would not shame a great peer. No one I knew at home talked like that, not even the minister. Spindle Hill, a thousand feet high and with only one narrow road leading up to it, was a terse place, where people spoke a spare dialect that even the folk in Hartford, not twenty miles distant, could not readily understand. I was, at home, a "loping nimshi," rather than an idling fool. The plural of "house" in our thinly settled hamlet was "housen" and my father, when he wished to assert something, would end his declaration with the words "I snore." Not even a century separated me from the great-grandparents who had wrested our fields out of pine and stone and oaken wilderness; our home, built by my father in a clearing made by an Indian deerhunter's fire circle, was just three rooms of wide, unpainted board already falling into ruin. I hoped to help my father find the funds to build a new house, and I had used to look forward to the day I would return with profits from my peddling in hand. But somewhere along the York or the James, I had ceased to long for that day. Now, to my shame, I would find myself gazing at the planters' idle, silken wives and blushing at the memory of my work-worn mother, her clay pipe perched on a chin that bristled with errant hairs, her hands engaged in ceaseless toil, from the time they touched the cow's udder in the dim predawn to the time they set down the shuttle of the flax loom late at night.

"I would be most grateful for that kindness," I replied, thinking that the great thing about being always among people of noble manners was the inevitable elevation of one's own. The young woman led the way around to the side of the stone-walled house, through a low gate, and into an orderly kitchen garden, where the nobbly purple tips of asparagus stood straight as sentries and low strawberry beds hung heavy with early green fruit. They would be feasting on berries here before the ground at home had thawed. I followed, noting the way she walked: perfectly erect, yet perfectly at ease.

Inside the kitchen, wholesome morning smells of toasting hoe cake and good, rich coffee made my stomach contract with longing. "What you drugged in, Grace?" said the cook, a wide-hipped woman with a flattened, sweat-glistening face. My hunger must have been evident, for the cook, without even asking, laid a tin plate piled high with hoe cakes in front of me, even as she hectored me about the wicked ways of my kind, and how she didn't cotton to those who made a fool of her. I nodded vigorously while spooning the food into my mouth.

"No nutmegs of any kind in my kit, ma'am," I said. "Just a lot of useful and pretty things for the betterment of the body and the mind."

"Is that right?" she said, her broad mouth turned down in an exaggerated attempt at a scowl. "Better show Annie you Yankee notions then, and be quick about it, for I ain't got no time for dawdlin'."

When I first set out from Norfolk, I had been proud of my beautifully japanned trunks with their interior nooks and shelves and clever fastenings for holding stock in place. The contents I had selected myself, with much thought, and I believed my stock, then, to be very fine. I had invested most heavily in goods likely to appeal to women, since I am easier in their company than among those of my own sex. I had combs of tortoiseshell which the fancy-goods dealer had assured me were the latest fashion; jewelry and amulets and garnets and pearls, reticule-clasps and rouge papers; essences and oils and fine soaps and pomatums; silver thimbles and gold and silver spectacles with shagreen cases; sewing silks and cottons and threads and buttons and needles with silver and gold eyes; pencil cases, pen knives, scissors (of Rogers' make, at the dealer's recommendation), playing cards, and wafers; fans and fiddle strings; and many diverting picture bricks and puzzles for children. At the floor of each case I had books. These I had not got from the Norfolk dealer, but traded for on my journey, anywhere I could. I would devour them, mastering all their contents, before I bartered them into new hands.

I had, as I said, been proud of these things when I set out so many long months earlier, but I now knew that most of what I had was tawdry. I had learned this slowly, for the planters' wives had been courteous in their expressions of interest, exclaiming over the jewelry, but buying only utilitarian trifles like the sewing silks or games for the children. It wasn't their words but my own eyes that had taught me the shortcomings of my wares, for many of the homes in which I had been received were temples of elegance, where even a small item such as a salt dish might be the work of a quattrocento silversmith from Florence or Bruges. And the jewelry! From the luster of the pearls that wrapped slender, unwattled necks and the luminous gems in ancient, heirloom settings, I soon learned to see my bits of paste for what they were.

But the books were another matter. Of these, at least, I did not need to be ashamed. I remember what I had with me that day in some detail, as these proved both the means of securing my place in that beautiful home and the cause of my abrupt departure. I had old favorites, such as *A Pilgrim's Progress,* but also newer acquisitions such as the poems and prefaces of Wordsworth, Marsh's edition of

Coleridge's *Aids to Reflection,* Cowper's *Life and Letters,* Lavater's *Physiognomy,* Johnson's *Rasselas,* Goldsmith's *Vicar of Wakefield,* and John Locke's *An Essay Concerning Human Understanding.* For children, I had *Noah Webster's American Spelling Book* and nicely illustrated little books of moral fables such as *The Fox and Grapes* and the tale of the milkmaid who spilled the milk.

When she saw the books the tall slave named Grace straightened and asked if I would like a ewer of warm water for my toilet before she showed me to the master's room. I had shaved by the river that morning before I'd made my crossing, but I was pleased at the chance for a hot wash. When Grace returned, she said the master bade me to bring the books and leave the rest. She led the way through the narrow hall that joined the kitchen, warming room, and buttery to the cool expanse of the main house. The house was not especially large, nor by any means the grandest I had been in—some of the plantation homes along the James were more like palaces—but it was perfect in proportion and exquisite in appointments. White walls soared to high ceilings plastered with elaborate swags and rosettes. Turkey carpets in jewel colors warmed the dark wood floors. In the center of the house a sinuous staircase with acanthus leaf carving swept up from an oval entry hall. Grace gestured with her long-fingered hand—hands that did not appear accustomed to heavy chores, I noted—indicating I should sit upon a marble bench that fit the curve of the south wall, directly opposite a faux-grained door flanked by marbles of Apollo and Daphne and Prometheus Bound. "That is the master's library. He will be with you presently," Grace said, and swept away to her duties.

The home's massive entrance was to my right, the wide door surrounded by lights of beveled glass, and I sat there, watching the golden morning sunshine fracture into tiny rainbows. Because I had been staring into the bright light, I could not see him well when he at last opened the library door, for he stood in its shadow. There was an impression only; of great height, very erect bearing, and a mellow voice.

"Good day to you, sir. Would you kindly come in?"

I entered and I stopped and twirled as if I were on a pivot. It was a double-height room, with a narrow gallery at the midpoint. Books lined every inch of it. A very large, plain, and beautiful rosewood desk stood in the center.

"Augustus Clement," he said, holding out his hand. I shifted the weight of the books into the crook of my left arm and shook his hand absently, for I was transfixed by the magnitude of his collection. "I've always imagined paradise as something like a library. Now I know what it looks like." I barely realized I had spoken aloud, but Mr. Clement laughed and clapped me on the shoulder.

"We get a few of you men through here, or we used to, before my daughter married. I think the word went out that she was–what do you call it? A mark? A touch? In any regards, she bought a bushel of worthless notions from your colleagues over the years; I think she just liked to talk to young men, actually. But I've never come across one of you with an interest in books. Set them down there, would you?"

I placed them on the rosewood desk, and he worked briskly through the pile. Now that I had seen the magnitude of his library, I doubted he would find anything of interest to him. But the Lavater *Phyisognomy* caught his eye. "This is a later edition than the one I have; I am curious to see his revisions. Tell Grace what you require for it and she will see to your payment."

"Sir, I don't sell the books for cash."

"Oh?"

"I trade for them–barter–a book for a book, you know. That way I keep myself in something fresh to read along the journey."

"Do you so! Capital idea!" he said. "Though no way to make a profit."

"I am interested in money, of course sir; it is necessary for a young man in my circumstances to be so. But I trust you will not think me irresponsible if I tell you I am more interested in laying up the riches of the mind."

"Well said, young Mr.–March, was it? Well, as it happens I have business elsewhere this day, so why don't you make yourself free of the library. Do us the honor of taking dinner here, and you can tell me then what volume you would consider in barter for the Lavater."

"Sir, I could not impose upon you–"

"Mr. March, you would be doing me a great kindness. My household is reduced, at present. My son is away with my manager on business. Solitude is no friend to science. You must know that we in the South suffer from a certain malnourishment of the mind: we value the art of conversation over literary pursuits, so that when we gather together it is all for gallantries and pleasure parties. There is much to be said for our agrarian way of life. But sometimes I envy your bustling Northern cities, where men of genius are thrown together thick as bees, and the honey of intellectual accomplishment is produced. I would like to talk about books with you; do be kind enough to spare me an evening."

"Mr. Clement, sir, it would be my very great pleasure."

"Very good, then. I shall look forward." He paused at the door, and turned. "Grace mentioned you had some notions for children. Whatever you have in picture puzzles or games for the illiterate, I will take—presents for the slaves' little ones, you know. Just let Grace know what compensation you think fair."

I realize that lust stands high in the list of deadly sins. And yet lust—the tightening throat, the flushed cheeks, the raging appetite—is the only word accurate to describe the sensation I felt that morning, as the painted door closed and I was left with the liberty of all those books. By afternoon, I could say I was ready to love Mr. Clement. For to know a man's library is, in some measure, to know his mind.

And this mind was noble in its reach, wide in its interests, discerning in its tastes.

Grace knocked on the door at some point and brought me a cold collation on a tray, but even had it not been meat I would not have paused to eat it. I did not want to take even a moment from my perusal of the books. About an hour before dinnertime, she came again, clucked at the uneaten food, and offered to show me to my quarters—I was to use the absent estate manager's cottage. There I attempted to make myself presentable within the very severe limits of my wardrobe. Not for the first time since I set out, I was mortified to have to present myself at a civilized table clad in a suit of linen, harvested from our own flax fields, spun and sewn by my mother. I resolved that I would reserve some part of my profits for a decent suit from a New York tailor when I returned north.

Mr. Clement was waiting in the drawing room when I presented myself. He was alone. I had hoped to meet the lady of the house. My face must have registered surprise.

"Mrs. Clement bids you welcome and sends her apologies. She is not well, Mr. March: she does not dine down. However, she said she would like very much to make your acquaintance tomorrow, if you would be kind enough to visit her. She would like to hear your impressions of Virginia, as they have been informed by your travels."

I have never been in the habit of consuming alcohol, but out of politeness I took the glass of champagne Mr. Clement held out to me. My mood was elevated enough by the joys of my day, and by the time we sat down in the handsome dining room, the bitter little bubbles seemed to be bearing me aloft. A Negro glided in with a silver salver, upon which stood a slab of sanguinary beef swaddled in a blanket of glistening yellow fat. The drippings from this joint had contaminated the potatoes so as to render them inedible to me. Next, he proffered a dish of greens, and I accepted a liberal serving.

But as I brought a forkful to my mouth I caught the stench of pork grease and had to lay it down.

Still, I barely noticed my hunger, engrossed as I was in the conversation. I cannot say now all the topics upon which we alighted, only that we moved from the ancient world to the modern, from Rome's Cato to our revolutionary Catos, from Kant on apperception to Coleridge on Kant, to Coleridge's unacknowledged debts to Schelling. Clement led the way and I followed, the wine on my empty stomach providing volatile fuel for my flight. I hardly noted the translation from dining room to drawing room and do not know what time it was when Clement finally drew a hand, on which a handsome signet ring gleamed, across a brow which I suddenly noted was gray with fatigue.

"You must forgive me, but I am not accustomed to attending to estate matters, as I had to do today. Usually my son and the manager between them handle the business of the farm, deferring to me on only the most consequential issues. Since they are away, I must concern myself, and as a result I find myself weary. But I don't know when I've enjoyed a young man's company so. You have a supple mind, Mr. March. It's clear that you have read widely for such a youth, whose circumstances, forgive me, could not have made this easy. If your plans allow for it, you are welcome here for as long as you would care to remain."

There was a saying among the Connecticut peddlers: beware the hospitality of the planters. Many a young man had been turned from the road and its profits by just such an offer as was now extended to me, and had ended his journey in idle dissipation. And yet I was hungry for knowledge in those days, and the prospect of spending more time exploring the library and the intellect of Mr. Clement was more than I could withstand.

The next day, I paid a call upon Mrs. Clement. I found her reclining on a chaise in a sunlit sitting room, a, huge-eyed beauty clad in a froth of white lace and *broderie anglaise*. Grace sat in a high-backed chair at her side, reading poetry, with a surprising delicacy of expression. "Thank you, Grace, my dear. That was lovely, as usual. Why don't you take a little break now, while this fine-looking young man is here to amuse me?" Hearing Mrs. Clement speak, I realized that Grace's voice had been schooled in imitation of her mistress, and yet the slave, having a naturally lower register, had the richer and more resonant timbre.

Mrs. Clement held out a hand to greet me. The touch of her skin—hot, dry, papery—was a shock. I did my best to hide my recoil. "My husband said you were a very conversible young man, but he did not mention that you were so handsome. Quite 'the golden lad' the poet speaks of, indeed. Why, you must have the belles of Virginia casting themselves at your feet!" She tittered girlishly. I coughed with embarrassment. Grace shot me a cool look as she slipped a silk bookmark into the slim volume and slid from the room. Mrs. Clement saw my eyes following her silent exit. She sighed. "Sometimes, I believe I am more fond of that girl than of my own daughter. Do you think that very wicked of me, Mr. March?" She did not expect an answer, and I gave none. "One's son is so much in the world, and a daughter marries young and leaves. My daughter was married last year, and only fifteen. Can you imagine? Such a little girl, to be mistress of her own great estate. Though I warned her. Oh yes, I tried. But she stamped her dainty foot and would accept the young gentleman's proposal, for all her father and I counseled her to wait. The young are willful, Mr. March, as you should know, being so very young yourself. Why, you can't be much more than a boy . . ."

"I shall be nineteen in November, ma'am."

"You see? A boy, as I said . . . but a very well-grown boy . . ." The large, dark eyes appraised me. "What are you? Six feet?"

"A little over, ma'am."

"Good for you. And broad-shouldered, too. I do like a tall, broad-shouldered man. My husband is six feet, but he *will* sit all day in his library and I am afraid he has not the manly figure he could have, if he would only ride out more . . ." She gave another mannered, musical little laugh, and then she frowned as her fluttering thoughts alit once more upon her absent daughter. "I said, 'Marianne, they might call you "mistress," but one thing you must know: on most great plantations the mistress is the most complete slave on the place.'" She tittered again. "I tell you, Mr. March, my Grace has a great deal more freedom than my daughter now enjoys. Not freedom to leave me, no; that she will never have. Grace is mine, here with me forever. She was born right here, you know. Mr. Clement gave her to me as a wedding gift. Such a pretty infant. I suppose he thought I could practice my mothering skills upon her until our own children came. Who could guess that one's first essay would be the most eloquent? I taught her to read, you know. It was no effort, no effort at all. She picked up her letters better than I had as a child, and much better than Marianne. I do not know what I would do now, ill as I am, without my Grace to read to me. My daughter never cared for books. No poetry in the girl at all. I can't think why that is. Can you, Mr. March? No, how could you have an opinion? You haven't met her, have you? My mind wanders, forgive me. It's the illness. My son is a busy man. He never comes to see me. Hasn't been for days . . ."

"I believe he is away on estate business, ma'am."

"So he is. Mr. Clement did say something about that. It's the illness, you see? I forget things. When you go down, do send my son to me, would you? A boy should visit his mama, do you not think? I think it is not so very much to ask. My daughter, now, you would think she at least would come. But no, she married, didn't she? Where was it she went off to? I can't recall the name of the estate. Brilliant match, I recollect that everyone said so. Most brilliant match of her season. But I can't recall now who it was she married . . ."

Grace will know." She turned her head. "Grace, who was that gentleman?" She swiveled, looking all about for the absent slave. Her expression became frantic. "Where is Grace?" Her voice scraped like a knife on pewter.

"You sent her out, ma'am."

"Fetch her back! Fetch her back! I can't be alone with a gentleman caller! What would Mr. Clement say? Grace!" The effort of crying out set her coughing, horrible wracking spasms that raised blood onto her lace handkin. Grace, who must have been hovering, slid into the room, carrying a pitcher of minted lemon water, which she poured and offered her mistress. Mrs. Clement took the glass in a trembling hand and drank thirstily. Grace gently lifted a lock of pale hair that had fallen from the lace cap, tucked it away, and stroked the parchment brow.

"I think Mrs. Clement is tired now. I am sure she would like you to visit her again, another time, perhaps."

I nodded and withdrew with relief. Later, in the cool of the afternoon, I walked out into the fields. The light slanted on the brightly clad field hands, who sang as they planted out vivid green tobacco seedlings. I breathed the scented air and thought how lovely the scene was, compared to the spare fields of Spindle Hill. I had not been wont to sing at my labors. I had cursed rather, as the stony soil dulled the shares and the refractory beasts stood stubborn in their traces. Turning back toward the house, I came across Grace, picking early roses in the cutting garden.

I held her basket for her, so she could reach some blooms high on an arch of braided locust boughs. As she reached up, she looked like a young bough herself, supple and slender. "Mr. Clement did not tell you what to expect of Mrs. Clement's condition, did he? I thought not. He finds it hard to accept her decline. She has never been entirely well, but two years ago there was an accident. She was riding, coming out of the shadow of the woods into sunlight, and her mare shied and threw her. Since then, she has had no sure sense of balance, and keeps to her couch. The cough and fever seem to grow worse from the lack of exercise and outside air. She is terrified of the world, Mr. March. If she stands her head spins, and she feels that she is falling from the horse all over again. She sleeps a great deal nowadays, which is a blessing."

"It must be; I mean, to give you some respite."

"It is a blessing for *her*, Mr. March. She is the one who requires respite–from her fears, her confusion."

I felt the force of her rebuke. "She loves you like a mother," I blurted.

She turned and placed the roses carefully in the basket, then regarded me with a steady gaze. I could not read her expression. When she spoke, her voice was low, her words clipped. "Does she so? I wouldn't know. My mother was sold south by Mr. Clement before I was one year old." She took the basket from me and walked, erect, swaying, up the path to the house.

That evening, Mr. Clement was full of his reading in Lavater, and from there we progressed to Samuel Morton's book on human crania– a handsome new volume, to which I had been drawn by virtue of its elegant plates. Mr. Clement, in his generosity, had offered it as barter– a most unfavorable one for him. It was inevitable that we should move from there to the science of "Niggerology," as Mr. Clement called it, and from there, by easy stages, to the matter of slavery. I thought to begin by praising the smooth management of the estate, and the relations of affection and trust I had observed between master and servant.

"Trust!" He laughed, dabbing at his chin with a heavy damask napkin. "The only way to keep slaves honest is *not* to trust them!" He must have seen me wince. "Does that seem to you a harsh assessment, Mr. March? I daresay it is, and yet it is unfortunately too true. Why, I had a neighbor, a capital fellow, lived just west of here.

Never known to punish his slaves. Boy became insolent one day, and when my friend reluctantly raised the lash to him, why, the boy grabbed a white-oak branch and beat my friend's head to a pomace." He grimaced and put down his food-laden fork, signaling to the hovering slave to take the plate away. The man was barely through the door, and hardly out of earshot, when he continued. "Name a vice, Mr. March: laziness, deceit, debauchery, theft. Place your trust in a slave and soon, very soon, you will see how proficient he is in any and all of them."

"But, sir, surely the very condition of enslavement, not the slaves' inherent nature, must account for such lapses of honor. The heart is a crimson organ, be it within white breast or in black, and surely wickedness may dwell alike in either . . ."

"But I do not speak of wickedness!" Clement said, almost glee-fully, bringing his hand down upon the table. "You have touched upon the sinew of the matter! Does one speak of wickedness in a child of four or five, a child who has not reached the age of reason? Not at all. For the child knows not the distinction between honesty and falsehood, nor does it think of future nor of consequence, but only of the desire of the moment and how to gratify it. So it is with the African. They, too, are children, morally speaking, and it is for us to guide and guard them until their race matures. And I believe it will, Mr. March. Oh yes. I am not one of Morton's skull-spanning acolytes. I do not think the current order immutable. Don't judge a book by its cover, March, nor by its plates. You take with you a handsome volume, but you will soon see that Morton's methods are flawed, very flawed. Why, even the great Aristotle was wrong in this: he held that no race other than the Hellenes could be elevated to civilization." He placed his glass on the damask cloth and gestured at his finely appointed room, its gleaming crystal and bone china. "And yet here we are, you and I, whose forebears were blue-painted savages gnawing on bones when Aristotle's city flowered." He flourished his napkin, dabbing delicately at his lips. The candlelight flared on his signet ring.

"Slavery *will* wither, in time. Not my time. Not my son's. Yet wither it will, as the African grows morally in each succeeding generation. His mere residence among us has already wrought a great and happy change in his condition. We have raised him out of the night, and into the light, Mr. March. But the work is far from complete. It is our place to act the role of stern father. We should not rush them out of their childhood, as it were. And if sometimes that means a resort to punishment, so be it, as the father must punish the wayward child. But never in anger." He leaned back in his chair, draining the wine in his glass. His tone, when he continued, was reflective, as if he were speaking to himself, rather than instructing me. "To manage the Negro without an excess of passion, this is the Christian challenge. In this way no one mistakes personal malice for what is mere necessity of good husbandry."

"Forgive me, sir," I interrupted, "but surely you do not speak of the lash?"

"I do not speak of the lash as it appears in the fevered imagination of your would-be Northern philanthropists," he replied, leaning forward, once again declamatory. "A great deal of whipping is *never* necessary. But *some* is. For their good, as well as ours."

He lay down his napkin in a neatly folded triangle and pushed back from the table. I rose with him, and we retired to the drawing room. We let the subject lie as the liveried slave returned to hand a crystal decanter of brandy, which Mr. Clement poured liberally. As the boy withdrew, Mr. Clement picked up his own thread. "You may think that slavery is for the sole benefit of the master, Mr. March, and there are benefits, I grant; the institution frees one from the routine toils which interrupt the unfettered life of the mind. But it is not so simple as that." Clement swirled the amber liquid in his glass, brought it to his nose, and inhaled deeply. I imitated him. The fumes seared my sinuses and brought tears to my eyes. "As the slave benefits from the moral example of the master, and the glimpse of what a superior human condition is, so the master suffers from the exigencies of providing apt example. I believe that the holding of bondsmen subjects a man's temper to a true test; it will be either ruined or perfected by the disciplines required."

My limbs had grown warm and heavy. I smiled and nodded, thinking what an apt example he made, how fortunate his slaves. I, too, felt fortunate: flattered by his attention, overcome by his wisdom, and thrilled to be, even briefly, a part of this higher way of life.

And so my days passed in the most pleasant combination of study and society. My place in the household remained fluid. Though I took my dinner with Mr. Clement and had the freedom of his library during the day, I did not sleep in the house, but in the staff cottage, and I breakfasted, as on the first day, in the kitchen. In some ways, I came to enjoy this meal as much as my evenings of talk with Mr. Clement. The cook, Annie, proved to have a very thin crust. Underneath it, she was a warm, soft soul, full of earthy humor and motherly affection. Her children she kept as close to her as she could. Her lively daughter of seven years, a merry little soul named Prudence, shined shoes or shelled peas, generally busying herself, treating chores as play. There was also Justice, a fine-looking boy of about ten, whose task it was to haul wood and water, to scrub blackened cooking pans, and occasionally to help serve at table. Annie told me proudly that Justice had been selected for house service, unlike his father, who had been a field hand till he died in a lumbering accident. "I ain't a-sayin' he weren't a good man, no sir, Louis a fine good man all right." Annie was stirring a batter as she talked, and her spoon slowed down in the mixture as she thought back on her past. A shy half-smile lit up her wide face. "I was a nursery maid when the young marse was born; my mama was the cook here dem days. I recall I was out with the young marse in the yard, and it was summertime and the flowers git be a-blooming and the honeysuckle smelling so sweet. And up come Louis, and makes a big show of talking away to the babe, and making funny faces for him an' all. And I says, 'Ain't he a pretty baby?' And he says, 'Surely is, but not as pretty as you is, Annie,' and out of that kind of foolishness by and by we comes to be asking the marse's leave for a wedding. For he lets us marry here on dis place, yes sir; he and the mistress say it's proper so. They doan hold with marrying in blankets. Mistress say to the marse, 'You kill a beef for the feastin',' and the whole day before she kept me shut up in the nursery room, sayin' a bride ought not be seen. It was a fine wedding we had, for sure, and the good Lord done left me these two fine chillun to remember Louis by. Justice favors his daddy," she said, looking proudly at her handsome, silent son. What Justice thought, I never learned. Unlike his sister, who chattered away, the boy said little. But sometimes he sang, in a sweet and clear soprano.

The children were disposed to like me, as I was the source of the playthings Mr. Clement had purchased for them, and I encouraged their affections by showing them the workings of the puzzles and teaching them some simple games. Sometimes, I read to them from the children's books I had on hand, though Grace had made it clear that none of these were to be purchased.

I noticed that Prudence liked to stand at my shoulder as I read, and one morning it came to me that she was trying to follow the words on the page. I commenced then to trace my way under the text with my forefinger, and before long I noticed that she mouthed the sounds of short words such as *to* and *at*. The next day, I saw that she was trying to form letters in the hearth ash with a piece of kindling. I took up a second twig and reformed some for her, showing how a downstroke usually preceded the curve when making letters such as *b* or *d*. Annie had her back to us, kneading a trough of dough, when Grace came in to fetch something for Mrs. Clement.

When Grace saw what we were about, she sucked her breath in sharply, seized the hearth brush, and commenced sweeping the letters away. Annie turned then from her kneading, scolding. "Now, Grace, what you be soiling your hands for–" but then, seeing the traces of some letters in the ash, she stopped abruptly. The cook's wide face darkened and she bore down on Prudence, snatching the twig as if the child held a burning brand. She turned on me, thunderous.

"What you thinking to do to my chile?"

I looked at her, baffled, and spread my hands to signify that I did not understand the question.

"*How* long you done say you been in Virginia?"

"Almost a year now . . ."

"Almost a year, and you don't know it's a crime to teach a slave her letters?"

"But Grace knows how to read." I turned to Grace, seeking support. "I heard you reading to your mistress. She herself remarked on the pleasure it gives her . . ."

Grace closed her eyes, as if asking for patience. "Yes, I read. Slaves my age, some of us, some lucky few, read. But for almost ten years now it has become a crime to teach us."

Annie had turned back to her trough, pummeling the dough with fierce blows. "You set sunup till sundown reading in them big ol' books dat could stun a bullock, and yet you ain't learned nothing. What kind of fool puts a little chile in risk of a whupping?"

"A whipping? Prudence? For wanting to learn her ABCs?"

"Why doan you ask Marse Clement all 'bout dat?" Annie said, turning the dough with an angry thwack. "But doan you be telling him what you been up to with my chile."

Grace inclined her head toward the door. "Mr. March, perhaps you might help me gather some berries for Mrs. Clement's tea cake?"

I patted Prudence's head, noting with chagrin that her eyes were brimming, and followed Grace into the garden. She did not stop until we were well clear of the kitchen, hidden from view by a line of espaliered apple trees. Then she turned, her lips compressed.

"Mr. March, will you help me to teach the child? She longs to learn so badly. Annie wants the best for her, but she doesn't see . . . For her, the future means tomorrow, nothing more. She doesn't look beyond. The girl might need . . . that is . . . it would be better if she had the means . . ." Grace, so astonishingly eloquent, for the first time seemed tongue-tied. She took a deep breath. "None of us knows the future, Mr. March. But Prudence is an uncommonly quick child; she'd learn in a few weeks what others struggle on for a year or more . . ."

"Why don't you teach her yourself?"

"I'm not permitted to bring any books or writing things from the house, and in any case, there is no private place in the slave cabins, and the risk of discovery elsewhere is too great. But I could fetch Prudence to you—just for an hour, in the evenings, after Annie falls asleep."

Grace had no way of knowing how her request touched me. When I had left Connecticut, it wasn't with the ambition of peddling. I had yearned to be a teacher. It seemed to me that most schools went about the work of instruction entirely backward, crushing children's natural curiosity and deafening them to the wisdom of their own internal voice. I did not have sufficient qualifications to do such work up north, where even distant settlements had their pick of fresh-minted graduates from our many universities and seminaries. So I had come south, thinking that this population might be less nice about such matters. But I'd soon discovered that even here, communities well set enough to have a school wanted credentials, or at least maturity in years, neither of which I could claim, while the poor in the remote places didn't care to have their children schooled at all.

"Why don't I do as Annie suggested and ask Mr. Clement? He is a scholar and loves learning; I am sure he will see that this is a good thing for all the children, not just Prudence . . ."

Grace pulled angrily at an apple bough, stripping the new leaves. "You don't know him! Perhaps Annie is right, after all; for all your reading you-you . . ." She did not complete the sentence. Whatever unflattering thing she had been about to say, she evidently thought better of it. But she gave me another of her unnerving stares, this time letting her gaze pass from my head to my toes and back again. Then, as if she'd noted nothing worth looking at, she turned and marched off. I stared at her retreating back, gaping like the loping nimshi my father had so often called me.

As it happened, Mr. Clement himself provided the opening by which I was able to sound him on the matter. He sought me out before the dinner hour, apologizing that he would not be dining down that night on account of a most painful headache.

"In truth, Mr. March, though my son can vex me at times with his mercantile obsessions, I am ill fixed to do without him. I have been forced to spend the better part of this day in the soul-deadening occupation of calculating gristmill accounts. Of what possible consequence is it if Mrs. Carter's grain weighed in at six bushels or sixty?"

I thought it better to resist the obvious reply: that it was of great consequence to Mrs. Carter. Instead, I asked, rather disingenuously: "Cannot one of your slaves be trained to do such routine factoring?"

Mr. Clement shot me a reproachful glare. "And have him forging papers for every passing runaway?" He rubbed his brow. "Are you not familiar with the history of the Tidewater insurrection, Mr. March? The women and children butchered in their beds? The simple farmers, rewarded for their indulgence to their slaves with a pickax through the skull? That butcher, Turner, was a literate man. You should study that tragedy. I must say that we in these parts have not ceased from doing so, though it is now a decade gone. What great moral reasoning dictates that I should risk having my wife slaughtered in consequence of my slave reading some incendiary tract? Your Yankee pamphleteers have much to answer for. I'll not have anyone on this place reading those foul, intemperate, slanderous rags!"

I had never heard him raise his voice before. Now he pressed the tips of his fingers to his forehead and winced. "Forgive me for my own intemperance. I am not myself. I did not mean to offend you." He made a bow then, wished me a pleasant evening, and withdrew. I went to the kitchen, begged a brace of apples, and retired to a lonely supper, accompanied by my own confusion.

By morning, I had made my decision, and so they came that night. Grace waited till she saw my lantern passing across the lawn that divided the house from the manager's cottage. I had barely splashed some water from the ewer on my face when I heard a scratch on the door. She stood there in the dark, Prudence at her side. The child did not look in the least as if she had just been roused from sleep. She kept shifting her weight from one small foot to the other in a skip of excitement.

"You managed it, then? Annie did not notice you rousing the child?"

Prudence gave a giggle. "Mama snores too loud to notice nothin'!"

"Your mama is up before the birds," said Grace gently, "making the marse's cook fires and warming his bathing water. That's why she falls dead asleep as soon as ever she lays her head down."

I had trimmed and mended a goose quill and ruled up a sheet of foolscap, so we opened the Webster's and set to work. She was, as

Grace had predicted, an apt pupil. Tell her a thing but one time and it stuck like clay to a boot. I believe she would have worked at the letters all night if I had not stifled a yawn and Grace called a halt to the lesson. Prudence turned to her, with a disappointed, "Oh!"

"We must not impose too much upon Mr. March's kindness, and you, my little one, need *some* sleep, after all."

"You may come again," I said. "You are a good girl and have done well." We agreed that if it were possible, and conditions seemed safe, we would meet for an hour every other evening, as long as my stay with the Clements lasted. At the door, Grace turned. She smiled at me, and I realized I had not seen her smile, not fully, since I had arrived there. "Thank you!" she said, and her voice was so warm I wanted to wrap myself up in it, like a quilt.

For the next two weeks, I felt my life more complete than during any period I had known until that time. I had my studies by day, enriching conversation in the evening, and at night, a work that I found uplifting. On the nights they did not come, I stayed up in any case, planning how best to instruct the girl at our next lesson. I looked forward to each part of my day with equal pleasure at first, and then, as Prudence progressed more quickly than I could have imagined, I found that it was the secret schoolroom that most inspired me.

I had grown to like the rich clarets that Mr. Clement poured, but on the evenings of our lessons I held back at dinner so as to better stay alert. One night, Clement noticed my abstinence, and commented upon it; so I laughed and let him pour liberally for the duration of the dinner.

As a result, my judgment was impaired that night, for I let the lesson go longer than usual, and was waxing on some point of no doubt critical pedagogic importance when I noticed that my pupil, for the first time, had dropped off to sleep, her little chin cupped in her hand. I glanced up at Grace, who smiled at the drooping head. "I will carry her," she whispered, rising.

"Surely she's too heavy for you . . ."

"No, no. Not at all. I have grown strong from lifting Mrs. Clement. Oftentimes she is too faint to, well, to ease herself unassisted . . ."

She glanced away. I felt the heat in my own cheeks, half embarrassment, half anger at the thought of Grace, as refined as any gentlewoman, required to hold the buttocks of demented Mrs. Clement and to clean her stinking chamber pots.

"It's not right!" I said, forgetting to modulate my voice.

Grace smiled then, not one of the rare, sunshine smiles, but a sad smile of resignation. "If you live with your head in the lion's mouth, it's best to stroke it some," she said.

It was, perhaps, the beauty of her curved lips. Perhaps it was pity, or admiration for her dignity or her patience. Or perhaps just the extra glasses of claret. I stood, reached out a hand, and touched her cheek. And then I kissed her.

I was eighteen and I had never kissed a woman before. The taste of her mouth was like cool spring water. The sweetness of it made me dizzy, and I wondered if I would be able to keep my feet. I felt the softness of her tongue in my mouth for a moment, then she raised her fingers, laid them lightly on my face, and gently pushed me away.

"It's not wise," she whispered. "Not for either of us."

I was overcome with a rush of confused emotion: delight at the sensation of my first kiss, mortification at my lack of restraint, desire to touch her again, to touch her all over, to lose myself in her. Alarm at the potency of my lust. And guilty awarness that I had an obscene power here. That if lust mastered me, this woman would be in no position to gainsay my desire.

"Forgive me!" I said, but my voice came out like a bat squeak, barely audible.

She smiled again and scooped up the child as if she weighed nothing. "Don't be a fool," she murmured. I opened the door and she slipped out into the night.

I lay awake a long time, pondering the nature of desire, and why God would endow man with such unbridled passions. And if, indeed, we are created in his image, what part of the divine Nature is mirrored in this? No answers came, nor any prospect of rest. Finally, when the birds had begun their loud dawn chorus, I gave way to temptation. There was a warm shudder, followed instantly by a hot shame, and then sleep claimed me at last.

I awoke to a bright band of sunlight shafting through the opening door. I had overslept. I could tell by the heat of the sun that it was late morning. I scrambled to my feet as a small, sparrowlike man entered the cabin and peered at me through a pair of horn-rimmed spectacles.

"March, is it?" said the man, sweeping off a travel-stained hat to reveal an almost bald head. "I'm Harris, Augustus Clement's manager. He told me you'd been staying here, but I didn't expect to find you still abed. Be grateful if you'd be good enough to, ah, afford me the use of my rooms. On the road for more than a week now, you know. Tired out, filthy, and a lot to do this day."

I muttered apologies and turned to gather up my things. I saw the quill, the ink, the Webster's, and the pages of childish writing, scrawled all over with my corrections. I moved, abrupt, awkward, putting my large frame between Harris and the table, hoping to block his view. I began to speak, rapidly, in an effort to distract him. "I do hope your venture was successful? That your road was not too difficult?" Harris, who looked utterly done in, drew a hand through his dusty hair.

"Yes, yes. As good as we could have expected . . ."

"What route did you take? I have an interest, you know, in Virginia's likely byways . . ." I was holding my clothes in a bundle before me. With an awkward flick of my wrist, I tried to fling my shirt over the pages. "Would love to go over a map with you . . ." I missed, and the garment fell in a heap by the table. Harris, impatient to get me moving, bent to retrieve it. Seizing that second, I spun around and swept the child's pages under my jacket. He rose and handed me my shirt. I was edging for the door. As I reached to take the shirt from him, one of the pages slipped from my fingers and fluttered to the floor. It landed facedown. Quickly, I moved to snatch it up. Harris, his attention arrested by my odd behavior, was just as nimble. Our skulls met with a crack. We each had hold of the paper. I tugged, and it tore. Harris turned his fragment of foolscap over, his brow furrowed. "What the devil . . ."

He straightened, his small face pulled into a fretwork of lines. It was clear that he grasped the whole. "This is a fine sight to come home to! And a fine reward to the Clements for their hospitality! Damned interfering Northern poltroon! What are you? Abolitionist? Quaker?"

I shook my head. My mouth was filled with cotton from the wine and the lack of sleep, and I felt a wave of bile rise from a sour stomach.

"Whose writing is this?"

I didn't reply.

"By the light, you'll answer to Mr. Clement. I think your visit here is over."

Still wearing his muddy travel clothes, Harris strode out, slamming the door behind him. I watched him through the window, strutting like a bantam cock across the lawn to the house. I sank into a chair, uncertain what to do. I wanted to warn Grace, but since she would already be attending on Mrs. Clement, I could think of no way to do so. I don't think I have ever felt so low as I did that morning, making my way, heavyhearted, to the house. Word had preceded me. Annie, in the kitchen, was slumped over the deal table, her head buried in the crook of one arm, the other wrapped protectively around Prudence, whose little face was wet with tears. Annie looked up at me as I entered, her eyes filled with reproach, hurt, fear.

"I'm so sorry!" I said. She glared at me, her mute rebuke more eloquent than the most scathing excoriation. I made my way to the library. Mr. Clement had the fragment of foolscap in his hand. He tossed it onto the rosewood desk. Beside him stood a well-grown youth, his face a windburned version of his father's. The manager perched between them, his diminutive stature emphasized by the tallness of the Clements.

When Clement spoke, I felt as if he were emptying a glass of cold well water down my collar. "Since you have betrayed my hospitality and flagrantly disregarded my express wishes, perhaps you will not think it unreasonable if I inquire which of my property you have contaminated with your instruction."

I had felt guilt until that moment. But his use of the word *property* in connection with the vivid person of Prudence and the dignity of Grace suddenly swept that sentiment away. "I am sorry I flouted your wishes," I began, "but you yourself said that providing instruction for the African is part of the duty and burden of your system. Surely . . ."

"How dare you, sir!" barked Clement's son. He took a step toward me, his face florid. He reminded me of a pup mimicking a grown dog's menace. His father raised a restraining hand.

At that moment, there was a light tap upon the door. Mr. Clement said, "Come!" and Grace glided into the room, her eyes, cast down, avoiding mine.

"What is it, girl?" Mr. Clement barked impatiently.

She raised her head then and looked him straight in the eye. "Sir, it was my doing entirely," she said. "I asked Mr. March to instruct Prudence. I urged him to do it, against his own judgment and inclination. Annie knew nothing of this. I acted expressly against her wishes."

"Thank you, Grace. I'm much obliged to you for your candor. You may return to attend Mrs. Clement now." She nodded and went out. I was unable to catch her eye for even an instant. But my relief at the mildness of Mr. Clement's reaction was immense.

"I expect it will not take you above one half hour to gather your belongings and depart from my property. Forgive me if I do not see you out." He gave me his back then, and I crept, like a chastised child, toward the door.

It was not gone a quarter of an hour when I set off down the long dogwood-lined drive. While I had been Mr. Clement's guest, May had given way to June and now that month was waning. The dogwood petals had fallen and the trees leafed out, offering some protection from a midday sun that already burned with the heat of full summer. I had gone only a little way toward the gate when I heard Mr. Clement's voice, calling to me.

"A moment, Mr. March, if you wouldn't mind. There is something you need to see before you leave us, if you would do me the kindness of one last indulgence."

I felt relief at his words. I hoped they signaled that we might part on some terms, after all. I set down my trunks and followed. He turned toward the north path that led to the high-roofed tobacco barn where last year's cured leaves had recently been hanging. Inside, I was surprised to see that all the slaves, house servants and field hands, had been gathered. Then I saw Grace.

They had laid her facedown upon a bench, her arms stretched out above her head, her two thumbs bound together and fastened to a rope that then passed the full length underneath the table and came up to bind her ankles. A wide leather strap passed over the small of her slender back and pressed her flat against the table. Below the strap, the lower part of her body was exposed, in a complete state of nature.

"Surely there is no need for this violation?" I said, my voice coming out high and cracked. Clement merely lifted his chin and turned to Mr. Harris. From a burlap sack the man drew out a braided leather whip almost as tall as he was. Then, moving to a spot about six feet from where Grace lay, he made a swift, running skip, raising the lash and bringing it down with a crack. The stroke peeled away a narrow strip of skin, which lifted on the whip, dangled for a moment, and then fell to the leaf-littered floor. A bright band of blood sprang up in its place. Her whole body quivered.

"For pity's sake, man!" I exclaimed. Clement's face was as cold and immobile as one of his sculptures. It was—though I grudge the sense of fairness which bids me set this down—almost as white.

The whip fell, again, with an almost delicate precision, the second strip taken just one inch lower on the buttocks, in perfect parallel to the first. Prudence was howling and had buried her face in Annie's skirt. Clement raised his hand then, and I felt my body go limp with relief at the end to this terrible proceeding.

"Turn the child," he said. "She must watch the punishment." The cook untangled her daughter's fingers from her pinafore, placed a hand on her wet cheek, and turned her face around.

"Proceed," said Clement. Strip by strip the lash carved into Grace's shuddering flesh. My tears were falling by then, heavy drops, joining in the leaf dust with the blood that had begun to trickle from the table. My limbs were so weak that I could not even raise a hand to wipe the mucus that dripped from my nose.

Finally, Clement raised his hand again. A column of sunlight from a missing board in the barn roof glanced off his signet ring. "Thank you, Mr. Harris. That will be all." The man ran a gray cloth along the whip to clean the blood off it and replaced it in the bag. The women had rushed forward, one unbinding and kneading Grace's hands as the others brought ewers of water to bathe her wounds. She had been lying with her head faced away from me. She lifted it then, and turned, so that we looked at one another. If an anvil had fallen from the sky at that moment and landed upon me, I could not have felt more crushed.

CHAPTER THREE

Scars

November 1, 1861

My dear,

Your very admirable letter and the welcome contents of your parcel came straight to hand. Many thanks to you for the warm wishes of the former and the warm wool of the latter. I rejoice to hear that you and my girls continue well as the cold season creeps onward; tell my dear Jo that she must not despise her knitting, but see her needles as jousting lances, for her fine blue socks are marching now into the fray. I wish there were some better returns for so much, than these lines I send in haste, for word comes that we are to move from this place shortly and there is much to be done in consequence. I for one will not be sorry to venture forth from here, and yet even in such a place as this, there may be found much uplift.

If anyone should continue to doubt, my dearest, the Negro's fitness for emancipation, then let him come and stand by me in the field hospital, established in this house whose aged owner once used to boast of his descent from the Cavaliers. Indeed, "descent" is an apt word, for he is descended now, through a combination of caducity and destitution, to a very low condition. Most of his slaves ran off before the battle for this island, which preceded by a fortnight our ill-fated assault on the Virginia shore. There was but one slave who remained and, having volunteered to help our surgeon, worked tirelessly, with such deftness and dedication as seemed set to *put him to the blush. In the days since then I have kept some note of the men she tended and most of them seem to mend better and more rapid than those under his care. The colonel acknowledges as much; he has offered to determine her "contraband of war" and to secure a place for her at a hospital in the capital–a wages-paying position, and this for a woman who has been a chattel slave since birth. But here is the cloth of gold from which her character is spun: she refuses to leave her frail master, stating that he is incapable of surviving without her. And yet I know that this very man once had her whipped for some most trivial transgression of his authority. What an example of Christian forgiveness! Some call them less than human; I call her more than saintly–a model, indeed, for our own little women. Who of course need no pattern more than their dear mother, she who radiates perfection, and to whom I happily proclaim my constant devotion . . .*

I knew that I should snuff out my candle, in case its light troubled those injured men with whom I share floor space here, in what used to be Mrs. Clement's sitting room. But I took a moment, before I did so, and drew out from my blouse pocket the small silk envelope I kept there. Carefully, I drew forth the locks and laid them in the circle of candlelight. One fat curl in gleaming yellow, tied with a bow of pink satin: my little Amy's glory. A mouse brown wisp from my tranquil Beth. A chestnut swirl from Meg. And last, two thick locks, dark and lustrous. Even though the hair color and texture of mother and daughter were identical, I had no trouble lifting out Jo's and setting it alongside her sisters'. My wild girl had hacked at her hair, so that the ends were all jagged, and tied it with a practical piece of string. I gazed at the girls' locks for a long minute, imagining the four beloved heads, sleeping peacefully on their pillows in Concord. I placed them back in their envelope then and blew out the candle. The last lock I kept out. I held it against my cheek as I waited for sleep. But lying on the hard boards amid groans and snores, I found sleep elusive. And so I had time to consider why, among all that I had shared with her, I had never yet confided in my wife the tale of that unhappy Virginia spring.

To be sure, those events were several years behind me by the time we met. The guilt I felt, for having let myself be seduced by Clement's wealth and decieved by his false nobility had eased, in time, from an acute pain to a dull ache. By then, I had little wish to recall the callow peddler who would turn over any dank stone in his quest for knowledge. Certainly, I was reluctant to admit to her—to her, of all people, for I soon saw the hot wrath with which she dealt with like cases—that I had suffered, even fleetingly, from moral blindness on the matter of slavery; that I had averted my young eyes in order to partake in a small share of that system's tempting fruits.

After my eviction from the Clement estate, I went on peddling, though I ceased averting my eyes. From my youth, I have been unorthodox in my faith. I could never reconcile the Calvinists' stern preachments that we are all of us, even radiant babes, sin-saturated. Nor could I bring myself to believe in a deity whose finger touched every man's slightest doing. To me, the divine is that immanence which is apparent in the great glories of Nature and in the small kindnesses of the human heart. And yet, for a few moments, in a little church on the outskirts of Petersburg, I did feel as if a Power revealed itself to me and made known how I was meant to go on.

I had noted a Bible study under way and, with no pressing business, on a whim decided to join it. Why I did so I will never rightly know, as I had long since given up an expectation of gaining any spiritual sustenance in churches, finding within only stale and pompous ritual in the North, and primitive superstition in the South. Nevertheless, I entered the small clapboard building, unremarkable, except that it happened to be set down in that part of the square adjacent to a courtyard where slaves, from time to time, were put up for auction. It happened that just such a sale commenced in the course of the Bible study hour.

So as, with one ear, we heard the good tidings of great joy that shall be to all people, with the other we heard the resonant voice of the auctioneer cry out: "Bring up the niggers!" As we contemplated the teachings to be drawn from the greatest life ever lived, the voice without was crying up the lot in hand: two children without the mother, who had been kidnapped therefrom. My thoughts flew to the verse "suffer the little children to come unto me," and had I then the means, I would have marched out and bought those children their freedom. What was most striking to me was that no one else in the church seemed to mark what was going on without, and when the pastor asked for subscriptions to aid in sending the scriptures into Africa, I could bear this no longer, but stood in my place and asked how it was that the Good News could not be sent more cheaply to the beings on the auction block next door? This was greeted with hisses and tuttings and a cold request that I leave, which I did, speedily and without regret.

Outside, the two children had already been sold, and bidding was vigorous for a fit-looking man of about thirty. The auctioneer cried out that the man was a free black, now put up for sale for non-payment of his city taxes. The man was weeping and I did not wonder at it. How intolerable to have once earned freedom and then to have it snatched away.

The next lot was a youth whom I judged to be about fourteen years of age with straight brown hair whose skin was as white as any in the crowd of buyers. A few of the men called out coarse jests alluding to the youth's parentage, and the boy's freckled face flushed. The bidding was desultory, and when the auctioneer, citing the youth's soundness, exhorted the crowd to higher offers, a cry came forth that he "wouldn't have those goods as a gift." A man standing by me shook his head, and when our eyes met, I thought that I had a companion in my anguish at the scene. "It's wrong," he said.

"Shockingly so," I assented.

"White niggers are more trouble than they're worth."

The boy was knocked down for $250, and as he was handed off, I saw a very young woman penned among the unsold lots, reaching out her arms in the boy's direction, crying out farewells to the son she would likely never see again. I left the place, being able to stand no more. I could not help but wonder how the scene might have gone if the pastor had led his people of faith out from that little church to stand in that square with their Bibles raised in protest. From that day, I was convinced that the pulpit was the place from which to decry this barbarous system. But how I was to find my way there was, at that time, unclear to me.

And so I went on, tramping in summer, the roads dusty and the weather sultry, and likewise through winter, the snowfalls knee-deep and the ways icy. At times, searching for new markets, I pushed through trackless wastes such as the Dismal Swamp. It was there that I lost myself, at night, in the midst of a tempest so terrifying that I believed I was meant to die, running, in the illumination of the lightning flashes, amid falling branches and drenching torrents. But I lived, and at 33 percent on each small sale, my profits accumulated, until I had enough put by for a horse and trap, and could expand both my inventory and my territory. By the end of the second year, as my receipts increased, I took on Connecticut lads just off the sloops to work for me on commission, and when I sold out the concern to the brightest and most industrious among them, it was for a tidy little sum.

I traveled home through the city of New York, where I stopped on the Broadway to bespeak the suit of clothes I had promised myself, and returned to Spindle Hill in triumph and a vest of Marseilles. I bought my parents their new house, then chanced a like sum on a silver speculation that paid out handsomely enough to afford me an interest in a half dozen factories on the Naugatuck. Poverty, they say, is the philosopher's ornament and the worldling's plague. Yet, though I like to think of myself as a philosopher, this did not deter me from gathering most gratefully what came honestly into my hands. In short, by my early twenties I found myself rich: enough to afford a set of tasteful rooms within easy walking distance of the great libraries of Boston. There I commenced to apply myself to study, reflection, and, by stages, to the quill driving and lecturing that brought me a small measure of notice among those whose good opinion I most valued. Through the intercession of one of them, the estimable Unitarian Reverend Daniel Day, I was approbated to give sermons, and became a preacher of no fixed pulpit. It is to Reverend Day, also, that I am indebted for the introduction to that remarkable person, his sister, who is now my wife.

As I lie in the dark, thinking over the words I have just written to her, I recall that I have said I will not be sorry to leave here. Contemplating those words, I realize that they are not altogether true. I will be sorry indeed on one account: that is, to leave Grace, for this a second time, in bondage. Although this time, the choice to stay is hers.

I had stood for a very long time, that night after the battle of the bluff, trying to gather the strength to once again enter this house. I cannot say how long it was that I stood with my head pressed against the chipped white pillar. Despite the chill, sweat formed scalding rivulets down my back. I could hear the cries of the wounded men coming from inside, and knew I should be with them. For their pain was real, and present, and mine was just an old memory from a past that no one could change.

I straightened, finally, took a last deep breath of outside air, and laid my hand against the great door. There were bits of board nailed up where the beveled lights had been. I supposed they had been shot out or shattered in the battle for possession of the island. Inside, in what had been the elegant oval reception hall, men huddled, wounded and wet. Some lay flat upon the floor, some half-propped against the walls. One man's head was pillowed on the plinth that held the Bound Prometheus, and his face had the same wracked expression as the carved countenance above him.

No one, it seemed, had got across the river with a full kit. Some had pants, but were missing shirts; others were attired the opposite way, having lost the lower half of their costume, but retained a coat. Some were entirely nude. Of these, a few shared Turkey rugs pulled up to cover them. Others, without such comfort, shivered so hard that it seemed likely they would shake the house off its foundations. I gave my own black frock to one of these wretches.

Because cries issued from the room that had been Mr. Clement's library, I expected that the worst cases were within, and that I would find our surgeon there. Dr. McKillop is a short, stocky man with muscled forearms as hairy as a Barbary ape's. He was turned away from me, working on the wrecked arm of Seth Millbrake, a wheelwright from Cambridge. I noted that even the back of McKillop's coat was blood-spattered, indicating the work he had accomplished whilst I'd tarried to wallow in my own exhaustion and despair. I resolved to think better of him. At his feet lay a forearm, a foot, and a leg, sheared off at the knee. McKillop lifted his boot from this gore-slicked floor and commenced to use its sole as a strop for his scalpel.

Seth was pleading with the surgeon, as such men always do, to save his limb. But the missile had shattered the bone near the elbow, splintering it into a score of white needles now sewn all through the shredded muscle.

My resolution regarding McKillop was tested within an instant when the surgeon, turning to wipe his knife on a piece of rag, noticed me. "March! About time! Get over here!" he barked, as one might call to an errant dog. "Hold his shoulders," he instructed, and I did, concentrating on Millbrake's face so that I would not have to watch McKillop's ferreting. Millbrake's eyes were all pupil—black with agony and fear. His tremors shook the table he lay upon. I brought my head close to his ear and whispered the words of the psalm: *"Then they cried to the Lord in their trouble, and he delivered them from their distress . . ."* Just then, McKillop's instrument hit a vessel and a spurt of warm liquid flew into my eye. I could not let go my grip on the writhing body to wipe it away, so I went on: *"He sent forth his word and healed them . . ."* I tasted iron as the blood trickled down the side of my nose and found my lips. Millbrake went limp under my hands then, and I thought that he had fallen into merciful unconsciousness. But when McKillop lifted his hand from where he had pressed it down upon the spurting vessel, I saw that the fluid flowed without pulse, and realized that the man's life had ended. McKillop grunted and turned to his next patient, who had taken a ball in the stomach. He plunged a finger into the wound and felt around in a desultory manner for a few moments. Then he withdrew his hand, shrugging. "When balls are lost in the capacity of the belly one need not amuse himself by hunting for them." Fortunately, the wounded man was unconscious and did not hear the grim sentence the surgeon had just passed. As McKillop moved on to attend to a man whose skull was stove in like a crushed tin mug, I lifted Millbrake's half-severed limb, which was twisted most unnaturally, and arranged it on his breast, then set the other arm across it. "Philbride, over in the corner there," McKillop said without raising his eyes from his work. "Shrapnel in his breast. Nothing I can do. He was calling for a chaplain. Better make it quick."

A farm boy would never have mistaken haystacks for tents. But they hadn't sent a farm boy to scout the Virginia shore. Philbride was a mill-town lad, accustomed to made roads and brick walls and a vista no wider than a street. At night, in thick fog, his fear had filled a harvested field with an enemy company; sentryless, seemingly, set there as if in answer to our general's desire for an easy victory. Poor Philbride. He knew that his erroneous report was the crumbled footing on which our whole day's edifice had collapsed. But it was not the only mistake, nor even the gravest. And that was what I whispered to the youth, who could scarce draw a breath and whose sweat, despite the cold night air, pearled on his pale skin.

I wish his eyes had grown less desperate, his shallow breathing deeper as I spoke. But I cannot say so. "Will of God," "bosom of our Saviour," perhaps these were the words he wanted. Perhaps it was in the hope of such preachments that he had called out for a chaplain. Instead, what I told him was the plain truth: that today's business was neither God's work nor his will, but a human shambles, merely. I would have gone on to say that it was no matter, that one botched battle did not make a war, and that the cause we served was worth the price paid, here and in perhaps a hundred other places in the days to come. But all I had done that day had gone ill, and my ministrations to that boy were no different. He sat up suddenly, desperate for breath. His pierced lungs, it seemed, couldn't draw air for him, so I just held him there, his mouth gaping like a landed fish, while his skin turned slowly to the color of oatmeal.

Afterward, I went in search of some container to haul away the litter of amputated limbs, the presence of which, I judged, could only work on the fears of the wounded. That chore accomplished, I looked for water to clean off the blood. Finding the ewers empty, I gathered as many as I could carry and, picking my way through the ruined men, made my way to the well house.

Even in candlelight, even after twenty years, even with her back turned, I recognized her. She was bending to fill pitchers from the well bucket, and there was something in the curve of her back, the sway at the waist, and the way she came slowly erect. As I had stood outside on the steps, gathering my courage to enter this place, it had fallen into my mind that Grace might be the slave the private had mentioned. I wanted it to be so. I dreaded it be so. At the moment I recognized her, longing and dread collided with a force that made me clumsy, so that a ewer slipped in my hand and I fumbled to keep hold of it. She, of course, could not have entertained the possibility of seeing me. So that when she turned, all she saw was yet another in the roll of the wounded, a coatless soldier without token of rank, whose blood-spattered visage spoke of some grievous hurt.

"Let me take those, soldier," she said, reaching for the ewers. That silvery voice, so distinctive. "You are kind to try to help, but you shouldn't be walking about with your wound untended."

"I'm not wounded, Miss Grace. I was helping the surgeon with an amputation."

Her head, tied just as I remembered in an elaborate rigolette, went up like an animal, scenting. She raised the lantern that held her candle and looked at me, hard. "Do I know you, sir?"

"You probably wouldn't remember me–" Even as I said the words I realized how ridiculously they rang. How would she not remember the foolish youth who had been the source of her agony?

"My name is March . . . I was here in forty-one . . ."

"Mr. March! The teacher!"

I could not tell, in the dark, if she intended irony by addressing me so, or whether the warmth in her voice was genuine. "Forgive me, I did not expect to see you a soldier."

"I am serving as a chaplain."

She raised her chin in a slight nod, as if that fit her memory of me, and held out her hand. I took it, noting as I did so that it was chapped and calloused.

Something must have shown in my face, for when she drew back her hand, she looked down at it self-consciously. "So many things have changed here, Mr. March. Some of them you see for yourself. Others are less evident. Perhaps we will have time to speak of it, if you would care to, but now the wounded men are thirsty . . ."

"Of course," I said. "We both have much to do." I let her go and went to my own duty, which was to bring comfort where I could. I was sitting in the oval entrance hall sometime toward dawn, my back propped against the stairwell, when exhaustion finally claimed me. I had taken the hand of a gravely injured man, and I held it still when I awoke. But it was cold by then, and rigid.

Grace was standing over me, pouring from a jorum of coffee. I closed the eyes of the dead man and stood stiffly, every fiber of my body complaining. As I steadied myself on the stair rail, I noted that the wood was rough under my hand. Grace ran a finger over the ruined banister. "My doing, I fear: I brought Mr. Clement's horse in here, during the fighting," she said. "He chewed the banister, as you see, and then of course the army found him anyway, and took him as contraband . . ."

She looked away then, and I wondered if she was aware that her own status was not unlike that of the horse: she, too, might be considered contraband of war. I accepted the tin mug she held out to me, drank the scalding contents, and passed it back to her so that she could serve another man. In the gray light—for it had rained hard all through the night, adding to the misery of the many men without a shelter even as cheerless as this house—I studied Grace's features. She had aged in twenty years, certainly; there were fine lines etched around her eyes and mouth, and hard times had robbed her skin of its bloom. But she was handsome, still, and I could see the eyes of the men following her as she moved from one to another.

There was much to do that morning. We buried those we had recovered from the toll of the battle's dead, laying them side by side in a shallow grave, each man with his name and unit inscribed on a scrap of paper placed in a bottle and tucked under his blouse, if indeed he still wore one. Before noon, the ambulances arrived on the Maryland side to fetch the wounded to Washington, so I lent my hand as stretcher bearer to move the men down to the boats, over the protests of my aching muscles. It was a labor of many hours, made miserable by the incessant rain and mud. I had no boots, so the viscous stuff tugged at my bare feet with a thirsty suck, and soon the skin was rubbed red raw. Across the river, as the day wore on, the hungry mules pulled in their traces, wrenching the wagons back and forth. The moans told the effect on those lying within. When the train finally set out, we had left with us only the walking wounded and those so gravely injured that McKillop had deemed they wouldn't last the journey to Washington.

By daylight, some things were evident that darkness had concealed. It was clear that the ruined state of the house was not a matter of a few weeks at war. The signs of long decay were everywhere. The tobacco fields were overrun by tare and thistleweed; the plants, which should have been harvested for drying, stood blackened by frost. The pollarded fruit trees that had hedged the kitchen garden were sprouting unpruned; the long-stretching bean rows, once trim as a parade line, were leggy scraggles, while many beds stood unsown. I realized that the ruined gristmill I had passed in the darkness was the selfsame structure that as a going concern had so vexed Mr. Clement. Some calamity, clearly, had overtaken this place. I longed to learn more. But I was pressed hard all that day and into evening, and when I glimpsed Grace, she, too, was about myriad duties so that we had no chance to speak. The next day, our colonel came to make an assessment of our condition, and told us that we were left with no more than 350 effectives in a unit that had numbered more than 600.

McKillop proved himself a good judge of the men's condition, as most of those he had marked for death were indeed gone within those two days. In the afternoons I helped to bury them with what ceremony conditions allowed.

I was coming from the corner of the field we had staked out for a burial ground when I saw Grace, walking on the terrace with a frail old man on her arm. I say walking, but in fact the progress the pair made was achieved in an odd gait for which there is no name. Augustus Clement—I cannot say I recognized him, but rather knew that it must be he—no longer had the posture of a man. His head was cocked forward and to one side, like a rooster's, his ear almost set down upon his collarbone. Grace held his left arm in a firm grip and supported him further with a hand around his waist. His right arm seemed fixed to his side from shoulder to elbow, but the lower arm flapped wildly, his fingers fanning the air. He progressed by raising one knee almost waist high, swaying there for a long moment, then placing the toe tentatively onto the ground before letting the heel follow it, deliberate as a dancer.

Because they could make no very rapid progress, I soon came abreast of them and offered a greeting. Mr. Clement could not raise his head, but turned his body sidelong, his cloudy eyes groping to see who it was that spoke to him. There was a blankness to his expression, for it seemed that the muscles of his face were as palsied as the rest of him. Grace leaned down to his ear and spoke soothingly. A strange sound, a kind of donkey bray, issued from his slack lips. A bubble of saliva formed itself into a thread and dribbled down his chin. The flapping of his hand became more violent. Grace drew forth a handkin and wiped his face. "Mr. Clement is very agitated because of all the confusion here," she said. "Forgive me, Mr. March, but I believe I had best return him to his room."

"Can I help you? He seems so very frail."

"I would be obliged," she said, and so I took my place on the other side of the trembling body, and together we brought him within. She had made up a bed for him in the breakfast room, for it was long since he could negotiate the stairs. When we got there, after our tortuous progress, and Grace eased him down upon his couch, he gave a ragged sigh of relief. I held the basin as Grace bathed his face, and by the time she was done he seemed to have fallen into a doze.

Grace took the cloths and basin and withdrew to what had been a small butler's pantry. There was a narrow pallet upon the floor, and this, I thought, must be where she now spent her nights. When she was done arranging his toilet things, she straightened and stared out a small casement window. The light was fading on the neglected fields, and the thistleweeds threw long shadows.

"Nothing beside remains. Round the decay of that colossal wreck . . ." She gave a deep sigh. "Mrs. Clement loved that poem, Mr. March. She had me read it until I had it by heart. I am glad she is not here to see what a wreck we are become."

Grace turned from the window and came back into the breakfast room. "She died, you know, the autumn of the year you were with us. The mourning was very correct, but really, I was the only one for whom her death changed anything." She sat then, upon a ladder-back chair. I imagine she often sat so, keeping vigil over the old man. Her back was very straight. She gazed at the hands folded in her lap, turning them over, as if their workworn condition still surprised her. It seemed that she wanted to say more, so I sat down also, in an armchair that I assumed was Mr. Clement's accustomed place. It must have been months since she had had anyone to whom she could speak freely, for once she began on the tale, it poured out, a litany of loss.

"It all went on, just as it always had. I know that Mr. Clement's daughter begged him to give me to her, to work at her plantation on the James. She claimed, quite rightly, that there would now be too few duties for me in this house. But Mr. Clement refused her and she departed here in a great huff. I expected to take up the duties of one of our house servants and have that unfortunate relegated to the fields, but nothing of the kind happened. If Mr. Harris suggested it, Mr. Clement did not heed him. I was left alone, to fill my hours as I wished. So I did what I always had done. I read, Mr. March, but with the difference that I chose volumes according to my own desires rather than Mrs. Clement's. So it was for more than a year, until the following fall. Mr. Clement had gone ahead to his daughter's plantation, where a family celebration was to be observed. His son was to follow on the eve of the gathering, and he decided he would bring a brace of wild turkey for the occasion. He went out alone, and did not come back. It was Mr. Harris who found him. Apparently, he had got his boot tangled in some honeysuckle thicket and his fowling piece discharged into his face. Mr. Harris carried the body home here and I tried to tell him that it would be best to get it in its box before the master returned. But he said he wouldn't do anything until he knew Mr. Clement's wishes. Well, of course Mr. Clement rode back here in a distraught state and insisted on seeing his boy. I had done my best, but that didn't amount to much." She looked at me then, and I could see the condition of the corpse just from the memory of it in her eyes. "He sat up all night by the body. The next morning, I noticed a tremor in his hand. I thought it was exhaustion, merely. But it was the beginning of his long decline.

"Mr. Harris did not stay here long after. He got a better offer and he took it. His ties had been to the young master. I think he really loved the boy, in his way. He certainly spent more time with him than Mr. Clement, who made it cruelly plain that his own son bored him. It was Mr. Harris who praised the boy when he mastered some aspect of farm work. I think you know that Mr. Clement never troubled to conceal his contempt for estate matters or those whose minds they occupied. You could not have known how it galled Mr. Harris, that morning of his return, when he came into the kitchen for refreshment and learned from Annie that you had been dining with Mr. Clement every day. He himself had never been invited to do so. Not once, in nine long years of service. So, I suppose you could say that Mr. Clement had no right to the man's loyalty.

"In any case, the place has never been well run since the day he left. The replacement Mr. Clement hired was a swindler: he made off with a year's profit. The next man was a brute–" She stopped for a moment, dealing with memories that were evidently so bitter she could not give them voice. "Mr. Clement dismissed him after two of our best hands, Mose and Asa, ran off. Until that time the Clements had never had a runaway. By then, the place had a name for mismanagement, and the only person Mr. Clement could find to take it on was a man who spent all night drinking applejack and all day sleeping it off. That was the year Mr. Clement started selling people, to make ends meet. The speculator wanted to sell me: I overheard him say that a "yaller girl" like me would be worth more than any other three hands down in New Orleans. But Mr. Clement wouldn't hear of it. He sold Justice and Prudence instead. The day the speculator took them, Annie went to the river. Mr. Clement always maintained that she slipped on the rocks, but it wasn't so. She just walked out into the channel until the water closed over her head." I felt a hard lump form suddenly in my throat. Grace stood, abruptly, and busied herself lighting the lamp against the gathering dark. Before the wick flared, I dashed the tears from my eyes with the back of my hand. "As soon as we got word that the Union army was camped across the river in Poolesville, half the remaining hands ran off. That left but three of us, and the other two left here a fortnight ago, during the battle for the island. "

"Grace," I said, standing and taking a step toward her. "Why do you not go, too? The colonel told me he had offered you a place in a hospital in Georgetown . . . You could begin again there . . ."

In answer, she turned and looked down upon the sunken face of Mr. Clement. She bent over him to adjust his coverlid. He was snoring now; great shuddering sounds like a beast makes. "Just because he refrained from selling you to a bordello hardly means you owe him this kind of loyalty. He has a daughter, after all," I went on. "Why cannot she have the care of him?"

She straightened, and looked at me, that direct gaze I remembered so clearly.

"He has two daughters, Mr. March."

For a moment, I did not grasp her meaning. Then, as I did so, I put a hand out to the chair back to steady myself. It was so obvious, after all; her status in the household, the light tone of her skin, the resemblance she bore to Clement in her height and bearing. If I had not been such an innocent when I first came here, I must have seen it at once. She had told me that her mother had been sold at the time of Clement's marriage. Surely it often went just so.

"But do not think I deceive myself. That is not the reason I was kept from the speculator." She turned, in the dim lamplight, and I perceived that she was untying the lacings of her skirt.

"Grace," I said, but she raised a hand to her lips to hush me.

"What is the point of modesty, between you and me?" she said, her silvery voice suddenly hoarse. "You have seen me this way before." Her gaze was unflinching, even though her eyes brimmed. She pushed the fabric down below her right hip. The scars stood, puckered and pale, against the smooth sheen of the uninjured skin above them. Twenty years, and there it was: the evidence of the great crime I had witnessed. That I had caused to be committed.

"The fancy-girl merchants don't pay for spoiled goods, Mr. March."

I moved toward her and pulled the fabric up to cover the obscene marks. As I did so, my fingertip brushed against the place. The scar was hard as rind. I dropped to my knees then, overcome with grief and pity. "I am so sorry," I whispered. But as I tried to rise, she laid her hands on my shoulders and gently, firmly held me. Then she drew my head against her.

There are many things I have told myself since, in exculpation for what I felt at that moment. I have tried to plead that fatigue had blurred my judgment; that amid so much death the body's compulsion to reach for life, to the very act of generation, could not be gainsaid. This much is true: at that moment I believed that the most moral act I could perform would be the one that would unite us, completely. I wanted to give the lie to every claim of difference save the God-ordained one of Genesis: man and woman created he them.

But this, also, is true: I wanted her. The thought of her—arched, shuddering, abandoned—thrilled me to the core.

CHAPTER FOUR

A Little Hell

Outside Harper's Ferry, January 15, 1862

My dear,

 This morning, at last, everything is quiet along our lines, and so I take the opportunity to thaw my frozen fingers with the exercise of writing these lines. By the time you receive this, whatever festivities the Christmas season may have afforded will be memories. I hope my girls were able, even in these hard times, to find some merriment and some meaning. Knowing you, my dearest, I do not doubt the latter; I imagine you all about some great Good Work. How I long for a letter from your own hand to tell me if I see you aright from this distance; I pray that some account of your doings will yet manage to reach me.

 While I imagine Meg and Jo have long had recourse to Hannah's hot morning "muffs" as they make their snowy way to their honorable employment, here the season's first white cloak descended just this past night, and today's sun rose in a clear sky to reveal the remarkable natural beauties of these ridges. They are etched out now in a black-and-white clarity such as our Amy could capture, were she here with pen to make a drawing of their loveliness.

 The ridges, though picturesque, made for hard marching, and we had every kind of precipitation to contend with. The new recruits joined us before we marched, fresh-faced New England boys, and not a few of them fell out with exhaustion attempting to carry packs and equipment weighing more than fifty pounds. Despite the hardships, the newcomers are in good spirits and spoiling for a fight (simply because they have not yet had one), and that in itself cheers the veterans.

I find it suits me, this job of chaplain. I am, indeed, a "chapel man," who carries within himself all that's needed for worship. At last, it is possible to have a part in faith without carved pulpit or Gothic arch, without lace altar cloth and without robes, save my suit of unornamented black.

It is true that some of the men of strict denomination are perplexed by me, and I in my turn by them. I will share with you one tale which has, I think, an amusing ending. A private came daily to my tent over the past week, falling to his knees and crying out upon the heavens over his sins and his corruptions, begging all the saints to intercede for him that he not die so stained and be thrown into the Everlasting Fire. As a rule I would not presume to question a man's beliefs, but this boy seemed so distraught that I began to lead his thought a little, sharing with him my conviction that since there were neither saints, nor a literal hell, he need not torment himself so over past failures, but simply try to do better in the future. At which point, he got up off his knees, swore, and pulled on his forage cap with a most disgusted expression. I was chastened, and feared I had offended him by casting doubt on his cherished creed. "It ain't that," he said. "It's just I see I been wasting my time here. All I wanted was a furlough and I figured you'd help me git one if I could convince you I been saved!"

It seems clear from the disposition of the artillery that we are poised for an attempt on that little river town so sacred to the history of our struggle. Last night, I conducted a service; the lieutenant colonel, a shouting Methodist with a fine pair of bellows, sang a gathering hymn. We could not have a light for it might attract the *fire of the enemy, so we prayed in the dark, and I sermonized about grizzled old John Brown and his band of boys, black and white, who came to this very place in an attempt to liberate the slaves, and how our efforts soon might secure the ends that had eluded them. Because it was dark, I could not read the men's faces, but all listened in respectful silence until the snow brought down a white curtain on our service.*

When I stepped out of my cloth house this morning and into this sparkling world, my thoughts flew northward, for you will recall that it was on just such a crisp and luminous day that I first saw you . . .

I lifted my head, and she was there before me: seated in the second pew of her brother's chapel in Connecticut. The Reverend Day had called on me to reinforce his own message; he had grown, he confessed, somewhat dispirited, after toiling for six of his best years in that place with so little visible effect. The village remained a forest of wagging fingers whose citizens were content to condemn, yet unprepared to do anything material against the system that provided their mills with cotton. He had invited me to speak, and I was in full flight, denouncing, as I recollect, the lamentable exclusion of the president's slave from the state funeral that had taken place earlier in that week. Six men, including our secretary of state, had perished together when the test firing of a heralded new weapon had gone awry. Five of them had been accorded the rites of national mourning. For the sixth, the black man, there had been no public grief. "This man," I said, "was held equal by the shrapnel that tore his body. He was human enough to die beside them, yet not human enough to be mourned with them. Thus does the minister who led that service turn religion, which should be our pole star, into a beacon of intolerance!"

She had been sitting with her head bowed, her face obscured by the brim of her bonnet. She was wearing a simple gown in a shade of palest lemon, so that she seemed to amplify the bright, snow-refracted sunlight that poured down from the chapel's high transoms. Suddenly, she looked up, directing her gaze right at me. Her hair was glossy black, and her eyes—her intelligent, expressive eyes—were dark and shining as a Spaniard's. When I met those eyes, my words flew away, as if they had risen up through the window panes and taken wing on the cold air. I faltered, fumbled with my notes, felt the flush begin to rise. As is ever true, the mortification of realizing one is about to blush only made the blood throb harder. I was twenty-two, and vexed at myself that I still colored as easily as a guilty schoolboy. I stood in that maghogany pulpit, and I must have glowed brighter than a jar of pickled beets. Helpless, I offered a silent prayer for self-command, which by grace was answered, so that I was able to go on. But I took care not to glance again in that dangerous direction until I reached the end of my text. When I dared to allow my eyes to seek her, she was looking down again, the radiance safely quenched once more beneath the armor of her hat brim.

After the service, her brother presented Miss Margaret Marie Day, whom everyone in the family called by the affectionate childhood name of Marmee. I was invited to dine, of course, and I had to call on a lifetime's discipline to keep myself from staring fixedly at her face. It was not by any means a face that the conventional world would label *beautiful*, and certainly the word *pretty* had no part in it; her skin was olive-gold rather than society's preferred pallor, the cheekbones were set rather high and wide, the nose rather long, the chin decided rather than delicate. But the effect was such that the word which kept presenting itself to me was *noble*—she resembled an aristocrat rendered by the brush of some Iberian court painter.

During the dinner, she acted the part of hostess, as Mrs. Day was recuperating from a difficult lying in with her second child. Miss Day did not have a large share in the conversation, but neither did she radiate shyness or indifference. She was, rather, an active listener, seeming to drink in the words of her brother and his other guests, including, I was flattered to note, myself. It was a family alive with good feeling, their zeal for reform matched by a zest for life. There was lively discussion of serious subjects, but there was also laughter, and in this Miss Day participated with an unstudied naturalness that filled me with warmth toward her. The meal was unpretentious and hearty—I took bread, cheese, and apples, bountifully served up in a cloth-lined orchard basket.

I was invited to spend the night at the parsonage, and I woke the next morning to the most astonishing sound. In fact, even before it wakened me, the music penetrated my dreams, and somewhere between sleep and consiousness, I had a vision of a lark in full-throated song. In my dream, I did not marvel that a bird should have the gift of language, but only that it should be so well schooled in the repertoire of *bel canto*. When I came to full consciousness, I realized that the sweet soprano must belong to Miss Day. She sang as she went about her morning duties. Lying in my bed, I envied my colleague such a reveille. I pictured the generous lips giving shape to the lyrics, the throat from which the music issued. I imagined my fingers lying lightly there, feeling the glorious vibration. I saw the rise and fall of her breast as she gave breath to each sweet note.

The consequences of these thoughts meant that I was a little delayed before I was able to present myself at breakfast. When finally I felt able to come downstairs, I learned that Mr. Day was unexpectedly called out on a pastoral emergency. "The person is not, strictly speaking, a member of his flock," confided Miss Day, as she pressed a basket of fragrant, steaming muffins upon me, "but a horrid, stiff-shirted old Calvinist." I smiled at her frank expression. "But for my brother, to hear of a hurt is to seek to heal it. He has ever been thus, even as a small boy, bringing in every waif and stray that crossed his path. Once, he even brought home an injured dog whose only thanks for his succour was a series of very savage bites." She wore a tender expression as she spoke of this much beloved older brother, and for the second time that day, I felt a stab of envy.

Miss Day did not retire after the meal with some slight excuse, as other young ladies of that time might have felt obliged to do, on finding themselves alone with a bachelor stranger. Instead, she led me into the parlor and commenced to converse with an open manner and a lack of affectation that I found remarkable and refreshing. We had spoken, the evening before, of her brother's views of education. While he had enumerated what he saw as the deficiencies of the Connecticut common schools, she had said little. But now she expressed herself freely, and fiercely, on the particular deficiencies in female education.

"It is bad enough that so few, so *pathetically* few of us are advanced an education worth the name at all," she said. "But worse that we, the fortunate ones, whose families seek out the best for us, are subjected to a course of study that is stultifying, oppressive, crippling rather than enhancing to our moral integrity and intellectual growth."

I asked her to enumerate specific areas in which she found flaws, and it was like tapping a wellspring. She jumped up from her chair. She was wearing another unadorned gown, this one the color of rich caramel that looked well against the tones of her skin. It rustled as she paced, her stride as wide as a man's.

"What do they teach us?" She held out a graceful hand and began checking off subjects. "Music, yes, but music of the *most* banal kind–" She tossed back her head: "Tra-la-la, fa-di-da," she trilled mockingly. "Little airs and dances for drawing-room entertainment. Nothing that one might have to sweat over." She touched a second finger. "Drawing—decorative landscapes in quiet pastels. But may we learn to hack life out of stone like a Michelangelo? Or push juicy oil paint around canvas to portray human agony, like a Goya? 'Oh, draw, by all means, little girl, but please, don't aspire to be an artist.' And what else may we learn? Languages? Very good; to gain another language can be to see into another soul, do you not think?"

I raised my chin in a little gesture of assent. I did not want to risk her negative opinion in confessing that I had not mastered any other language. But she was launched: she did not need any wind from me to fill her sails.

"So, we are drilled in foreign grammars and vocabulary. But in how we apply this knowledge, we are censored. Show me the French class where girls are given to read the passionate poems of a Ronsard. Oh no. This is not for us. We must not corrupt our delicate minds. Neither may we read the essays of the French revolutionaries; we, who are the daughters of revolutionaries! No, there must be no argument, no strong emotion. A little vapid romance perhaps, but not love. Not passion. Not that which beats at the very heart of women's being!" She was pulled tight as a wire, standing almost on her toes, her hands drawn up now, clenched together under her chin.

"Perhaps you yourself should teach young women?" I interjected. "I'm sure your ardor for the subject would suit you to the profession."

She laughed, the tension going suddenly out of her, and shook her head. "Who would hire me to corrupt their daughters' minds? And even if they did, I have not mastered that which I would wish to teach. I have not scaled the cliffs of knowledge, only meandered in the foothills. If I have reached any heights at all in learning, it is as a sparrow-hawk who encountered a favorable breeze that bore it briefly aloft." She flopped down onto the chaise in a flutter of skirt, as unself-conscious as a little girl. "You have unmasked me! I am one of those who knows how I wish the world were; I lack the discipline to make it so."

"You are severe upon yourself."

"Quite the opposite, I assure you. If I were more severe I should be more accomplished. But perhaps one day I will be entrusted with daughters of my own, and if so, I swear I will not see their minds molded into society's simpering ideal of womanhood. Oh, how I would like to raise writers and artists who would make the world acknowlege what women can do!" She gave a light laugh. "Of course, I will first have to find a partner willing to share his life with such an opinionated termagant."

There was an awkward silence. I do not honestly know how I might have filled it, if the Reverend Day had not returned at that exact moment. I should have proposed to her then and there, and spared us both an agony of pointless waiting. But return he did, and the moment passed, and she withdrew to see to the recovering invalid and to be useful in the nursery.

Generally, I relished the chance for conversation with Daniel Day: he was a great reader whose quick intelligence and large heart always illuminated every argument. That morning, he wanted to discuss the works of Dr. Channing, whom we both admired. Daniel was expounding at some length on the doctor's masterly categorization of greatness, which he made to exist in descending ranks, depending on its essential roots in the moral, the intellectual, or the realm of action. I remember arguing that moral greatness had little meaning without action to effect the moral end. It was, I see now, the rehearsal of the great argument that would animate my life; the selfsame argument that has brought me to these wintery ridges, at this grim time. But that morning, as we walked in Daniel Day's garden, our scarves drawn up to our chins and the frost crunching underfoot, I had difficulty erecting the scaffolding to shore up my views. My eyes drifted often to an upper dormer. Even through the closed window, it was possible to hear snatches of a sweet voice, crooning a lullaby to a fortunate newborn.

How often it is that an idea that seems bright bossed and gleaming in its clarity when examined in a church, or argued over with a friend in a frosty garden, becomes clouded and murk-stained when dragged out into the field of actual endeavor.

If war can ever be said to be just, then this war is so; it is action for a moral cause, with the most rigorous of intellectual underpinnings. And yet everywhere I turn, I see injustice done in the waging of it. And every day, as I turn to what should be the happy obligation of opening my mind to my wife, I grope in vain for words with which to convey to her even a part of what I have witnessed, what I have felt. As for what I have done, and the consequences of my actions, these I do not even attempt to convey.

Many ill things happened in those weeks of waiting, encamped on the outskirts of Harper's Ferry. Our side made several small harassing actions. Townsfolk loyal to the North crossed the river to come to us, and spies and scouts from our side ventured into the town. When one of ours, a man widely liked, was killed in an exchange of fire, the major ordered a retaliation which, in my view, went too far. He ordered a party to burn down all the town buildings that stood between the armory and the railroad bridge. Most of these were civilians' homes or businesses, and since their charred ruins made excellent cover for the Confederates' sharpshooters, I cannot see that any military purpose was served by their destruction. When I expressed that to him, he turned livid and refused thereafter to attend my services, or even exchange a greeting with me. Later, I learned that this very major, Hector Tyndale, had been detailed to escort Mrs. Brown, two years earlier, when she brought her executed husband's body home from Virginia to New York. Brown had prophesied that Harper's Ferry would be destroyed, and now much of it had been. A part of me wondered if the Old Man's spirit hadn't somehow possessed Hector Tyndale and caused him to act so. Who knew better than I the power of that man to possess? For him, I had been a tool, to be used with no more thought than a blacksmith gives to a pair of tongs when he thrusts it in the fire. It was a source of equal parts pride and mortification that Brown had used me, as he used every man that came to his hand, to rid our land of its abomination.

When we finally occupied the town toward the end of February, it was a scene of utmost desolation. Many of the inhabitants had fled. Those who stayed had done so only in the hope of securing their property, a hope that in many cases proved vain.

As soon as we took the town, I resolved to make a small pilgrimage to the Engine House where Captain Brown's attempt to capture the federal armory and incite a slave rebellion had ended in bloody failure. Finding myself at last with an hour's leisure, I made my way down to that haunted little building. I stood before it, my feelings on a seesaw between repulsion and admiration. Was ever a course of action more reckless and savage? Was ever one so justifiable, so self-sacrificing? My mind was as confounded as it had been the day I heard the news. I had been with Beth and Amy about an afternoon's chestnut gathering in the autumn woods. Tom Higginson, another who had welcomed Brown as a guest in Concord, came up to us, all grave looks, with the news of Brown's attempted insurrection, and his capture. He wrung his hands as he described Brown's saber wounds and the young followers shot dead. I told Higginson then and there that I thought the deed would give impulse to freedom, no matter what became of its instigator and no matter how the states howled over it. But I hurried my youngest ones home, with my heart pounding, and made a fire in my study grate. I fed to it all the papers that documented my dealings with Brown, even though most of them had only to do with land surveys.

Some weeks later, on a mild winter's day, it seemed that all Concord came out to mark the hour of Brown's execution. There were no bells, no speeches; only readings. Emerson read, as did Thoreau. Sanborn, the schoolmaster, had composed a dirge and the assembled sang it. I read from the Song of Solomon, and a passage from Plato. And now? What would Brown say now, I wondered, of this *guilty land* and the purge of blood he had so accurately predicted?

My reflections were disturbed by the uncouth behavior of some of our enlisted around the tiny building, which was, it seemed, being used as a holding cell. How distasteful, I thought, to use as a prison a place that should better be respected as a shrine. It appeared that there were some three or four rebels detained therein, and our men were taking it by turns to climb upon barrels and peer down through the high windows, offering coarse taunts to the unhappy souls within. I had a few words with the men about their conduct, but found them sullen and unreceptive.

I was making my way back up the steep streets, reviewing the painful history of my acquaintance with Brown. My melancholy thoughts were interrupted once again; this time, by the loud cry of a woman coming from within a fine house just a little up the hill beyond me. Of course, I hastened to see if I could be of assistance. The door was ajar and so I entered, just in time to be almost crushed by the sound board of a pianoforte as it came tumbling end over end down the stairs. Fortunately for my skull's sake, the heavier part listed leftward, proved too massive for the banister, and plowed through it, landing with a crashing discord atop what had been, until that moment, the dining-room table. From above came the sound of shattering glass, and as I turned back toward the street I saw the remains of the upper windows falling in a glittering shower.

At that point the woman cried out again and I bounded up the stairs two and three at a time, tripping over broken piano legs as I went. The scene that greeted me on my arrival at the top beggars description. There were three soldiers, two of whom I recognized from my unit, the other either a new recruit or a transfer, and all of them from the very patrol that was meant to forestall disturbances of the peace. They were flushed and laughing, as a woman and a girl of about thirteen years, whom I took to be mother and daughter, cowered, their faces tear-streaked and terrified. The men were playing catch across the ruins of the room with a Chinese vase of some apparent antiquity. The woman was crying out that it was all she had left to her of her grandmother's possessions, and begging them to stop. The girl ran between them, trying to grasp the vase in midair. The third soldier grabbed her around the waist and pulled her away. When I saw him place his hand most lewdly between her thighs, my thoughts flew to my own daughters, and the bellow of rage that escaped me was a ferocious thing, so loud as to freeze the actions of everyone in that room.

"Who is in command here?"

Five faces—the soldiers', florid, slack-jawed with surprise; the womens', pale and blotched with emotion—turned suddenly toward me.

I lowered my voice and repeated my question: "Who is in command?"

"I am, sir," said the corporal, wiping the sweat off his brow.

"Then kindly explain this outrage."

"Why, sir, we was just raising a little hell with the secesh. Don't the Bible say Sodom and Gomorrah was destroyed because they was wicked? Why not this rebel nest?"

"Corporal, your orders were to take anything of which the men have actual need. You were expressly forbidden from acts of theft or wanton destruction. What you have done here is contemptible."

The corporal gave me a dark look, then hawked and spat right on the Turkey carpet. "'Bout as contemptible as shooting all those good men in cold blood under the bluff, would you say, chaplain, sir?" I felt the blood draining from my face under the force of his insolent stare. "The men ain't forgot it, even if you has."

"A gentleman–no, say, rather, a *man*–would take his just anger to the field of battle," I replied coldly. "You may not visit it on innocent civilian women. Kindly clean up as much of this mess as you can and accompany me to the colonel." I turned to the woman and her daughter. She had drawn the girl close, and was smoothing her hair with a tenderness of gesture that brought my Marmee and little Beth before me. "Madam," I said gently. "You have my most profound apologies. These men do not represent the army of the Union, and do no credit to our cause."

She drew herself up, cowering no longer. Her gray eyes were lit with rage. "Your men, sir, are scum. As is your 'cause.'"

I heard the corporal give a snort, whose meaning was clearly "I told you so." I turned and glared at him, and he went about a perfunctory cleanup, which consisted merely in kicking some splintered pieces of furniture toward the fire grate. I was anxious to be gone from that house, so I did not trouble to exhort him to more particular efforts, and very soon we were marching in a cold silence to the house where the colonel had set up his command post.

When we arrived he was taking a conference in regard to the pontoon bridge, and so we were obliged to wait above an hour for an audience, and when we were admitted he was still poring over engineer's drawings and seemed to listen to my complaint with only half an ear.

"Very well," he said when I had concluded. He turned to the offending soldiers. "The chaplain is quite right. I won't have civilian women molested, even if they are the wives and spawn of rebels. I understand why you felt driven to do it, but don't be doing it again. Dismissed."

The soldiers left, their relief propelling them swiftly from the room. Only the corporal paused, to give me a swift grin of contempt. The colonel had taken up a compass and commenced measuring distances on the engineer's drawings.

"Sir–" I began, but he cut me off.

"March, I think you should reconsider your place with this regiment."

"Sir?"

"You can't seem to get on with anyone. You've irritated the other officers . . . Even Tyndale can't abide you–and he's as much of an abolitionist as you are. Surgeon McKillop ruins my mess more often than not, ranting about your latest outrage. The night before last you'd put him beside himself with some preachment you gave that a Christian needn't worship Christ as God. I've got him in one ear complaining that you don't preach against sin, and yet here you are sowing discord in the ranks by seeing a great sin in harmless soldierly pranks . . ."

"Sir, such wanton destruction is hardly–"

"Keep your peace, would you, March, for once in your life?" He jabbed the compass so hard that it passed right through the chart and lodged in the fine mahogany of the desk beneath. He came around the desk then and laid a hand on my arm. "I like you all right; I know you mean well, but the thing of it is, you're too radical for these mill-town lads. I knew your views when my old friend Day recommended you to this service, and personally I have no love for slavery. But most of these boys aren't down here fighting for the nig– for the slaves. You *must* see it, man. Be frank with yourself for once. Why, there're about as many genuine abolitionists in Lincoln's army as there are in Jeff Davis's. When the boys in this unit listen to you preach emancipation, all they hear is that a pack of ragged baboons is going to be heading north to take their jobs away . . ."

"Sir! I hardly think . . ."

He shot me a hard look. I held my tongue, with the greatest difficulty, and wondered again how a man like this ever came to be counted a friend by Daniel Day. He went on, as if speaking to himself. "Why do we have chaplains? The book of army regulations has little to say on the matter. Odd, isn't it? In that one institution where order is everything, where every man has a place and a duty, the chaplain alone has no defined place and no prescribed duty. Well, in my view your duty is to bring the men comfort." Then he glared at me and raised his voice. "That's your role, March, damn it. And yet all you seem to do is make people *un*comfortable." He plucked the compass out of the desk and rapped it impatiently against the chair back. When he resumed speaking, it was in a more civil tone. "Don't you think you'd do better with the big thinkers in the Harvard unit?"

"Sir, the Harvard unit has famous ministers even in its rank and file—men from its own divinity school. They hardly need . . ."

He raised his big, meaty hand, as if conceding my point, and, turning away from me, waved it in a vaguely southern direction. "Well, then, since you like the Negroes so very much, have you thought about assisting the army with the problem of the contraband? The need is plain. Ever since Butler opened the gates at Fortress Monroe to these people, we've had hundreds streaming into our lines, and more still falling under our care on the liberated plantations. Someone has to make dispositions for them. The labor of the men is useful enough—better they be employed building our breastworks than the enemy's—but they *will* come trailing their bedmates and their brats. They are upon our hands by the fortunes of war, and yet, with war to wage, officers can't be playing wet nurse. If something is not done, why, the army will be drowned in a black tide . . ."

"But, Colonel," I interrupted, taking a pace forward and putting myself back in his line of sight. "I know the men in this regiment. I was with them at the camp of instruction; we drilled together. I prayed with them when we got the news of the defeat at Bull Run and when we traveled south in the rush to the front lines that followed it . . ."

"Good God, man, I don't need to hear a recitation of your entire service . . ."

I kept talking, right over the top of him. I was beside myself with the need to make my case: I did not see that I was vexing him beyond measure. "I've been through defeat with these men, I've been covered in their blood. No other chaplain–"

"Silence!" he shouted. He walked over to the window, which opened onto a remarkable prospect of faceted cliffs falling sharply to the crotch of the merging rivers. The light was failing and a red glow burnished the surface of the water. He spoke with his face turned toward the view so that he wouldn't have to look at me.

"March, I tried to put this kindly, but if you insist on the blunt truth, then you shall have it. I have to tell you that McKillop is lodging a complaint against you, and some of what he plans to put in it is rather . . . indelicate. I'm not about to pry into your personal affairs. You may be chaplain, but you're a soldier at war, and a man, and these things happen . . ."

"Colonel, if Captain McKillop has implied . . ."

"March, let me do you a kindness. Do yourself one. Request reassignment to the superintendent of contraband. Who knows? You may be able to do a deal of good there."

I left that makeshift office in a ferment of rage, mortification, and, yes, shame. For the surgeon's complaint was not groundless. He had come looking for Grace to assist him and found us together in Mr. Clement's chamber. I had pulled the rigolette off Grace's beautiful head, buried my face in her hair, and tasted again the cool sweetness of her mouth. But then I felt the tears on her cheeks, and suddenly I was transported in memory to another time, another cheek wet with tears, and the thought of Marmee and what I owed to her fell upon me like a cold mist. I took Grace's face in my hands and looked into her brimming eyes. She broke away from me.

"What is it?" I whispered.

"It's too late," she said, her voice trembling. "You are not the beautiful, innocent vagabond walking toward me under the dogwood blossoms, with his trunks and his head full of worthless notions. And I am not the beloved, cherished ladies' maid . . ."

I stepped toward her and embraced her again, but this time as one embraces a suffering friend. And so when McKillop came upon us a short time after, he found us so: Grace, with her hair all loose, her face buried against my shoulder. For a man like McKillop, who saw sin everywhere, it was enough.

To me, it was a grave transgression to have entertained those longings, and to have acted upon them even so far as I did. To that extent, I deserved this. But what greater punishment would it be if whispers of my momentary weakness should come to the ears of my dear wife, or scandal touch my daughters in their youthful innocence? Accordingly, I made my way back through the slippery streets to the tent camp on the town's outskirts, took out my lap desk, and wrote up my request for transfer of service. And now that is done, and I have turned to this sheet, bound for the eyes of my wife—eyes whose wise luster is no less beautiful to me now than that day in her brother's church so many years ago. When I had imagined this correspondence, I had thought to leave nothing in reserve that came gracefully into words. I thought I would commit to these leaves even those things which could not be easily spoken, and that at the end of my service it would endure as a loving record preserving an honest record of both our lives.

But today's epistle is shrouded in words meant to mislead. After much reflection, I have decided to cast the matter of my transfer in an entirely positive light. Leave aside that which cannot be confessed. I also find I can write no word to her of my lesser failures. Of my inability to win the minds of the officers or the hearts of the common soldiers she must not know. For how can I justify the sacrifice she has made in letting me come here to minister to these men, if she learns that none of them want me, that my service is, in fact, despised?

I shall say, rather, that my decision to seek a ministry with the contraband came to me as an inspiration brought on by walking these streets in the steps of Captain Brown. I shall say, like the hymn, that his truth is marching on, and I feel called to march with it. And even as I write this, I know that between me and my beloved, truth recedes with every word I set down.

CHAPTER FIVE

A Better Pencil

There was a time, not so very many years distant, when my mind possessed no thought I did not share with her. I had returned to my rooms in Boston after my sabbath at Daniel Day's Connecticut church, but thoughts of dark hair and darker eyes returned with me. I found I could not apply myself to writing or reflection, unless it was writing verses to the beauty of her voice, and reflecting upon the vibrancy of her mind. She was the woman who had haunted my imagination, noble yet unpretentious, serious yet lively. It took no very vast period of time for me to realize that I was in love.

Since I was already on terms with her brother, it wasn't a large matter to find a pretext for a return visit, and another one after. We conversed on the widest range of subjects. And yet, on the subject upon which, above all others, I most wished to speak, I found myself entirely tongue-tied. I came back to Boston after our second encounter frustrated by my own reticence, and poured my yearnings into the pages of my journal. The thaw had swollen the Charles, the trees on the common had leafed full out, and still I had not spoken. So when I received a communication from Reverend Day to the effect that his sister would be returning for a time to her father I could not have been more delighted. The senior Mr. Day had been a widower for some half dozen years, and was grown frail and required his daughter's care. I happened to know the village in which he lived; it was not twenty miles from my rooms. It was now in my own hands to bring matters to a point, and if I could not find a way in such a case, then, I told myself, I did not deserve to be happy.

Some years earlier, my uncle had settled in the very same village and made a tidy fortune there in the lead sheeting business. He was a kindly man, and I might have applied to him for an invitation had his wife and I been on better terms. He had married late to a woman from an old Boston family, far above the claims of our Spindle Hill connections, a woman whose lameness and captious nature had kept her single past the prospect of any match more equal in situation. Her peppery wit somehow attracted my quiet uncle, setting her, as it did, aside from the bland manners of the day. Others did not find it so appealing, and I confess I was among them. When their one child, an infant girl, was taken from them, it soured her temper still further. She became a wasp, ever ready to sink her sting into any person foolish enough to expose to her a vulnerable place. And so I did not think it prudent to conduct a courtship from under her roof. Instead I wrote to my uncle on the pretext of business, to ask him if he knew of any likely local interests in want of capital. He replied with news of a mechanic in the village whose son had developed a scheme for the manufacture of a better pencil. I was inclined to find this rather ordinary proposal of immediate interest. And so I wrote, and obtained by return post an enthusiastic invitation from the mechanic.

It is a tedious journey by stage, and I found myself thinking along the way that I could walk the distance more profitably. My first impression of that place I have come so much to love was rather mixed: it seemed to me scant of trees and overserved by taverns. Yet I was struck, even on that first approach, by the handsome array of ponds edged by woods that stood to the south of the village. Walking those woods, by that water, I thought, would afford a man a great refreshment, and so it has proved these many years.

There were some two thousand industrious souls settled in the village and its surrounds, engaged predominately in agriculture but also in manufacture and commerce, while the many inns profited from the teamsters' patronage. I had thought to stay in one of these, but the pencil-maker would not hear of it. Greeting me at the stage with a horse and trap, he told me that his wife let rooms in their own house, where I would be most welcome. The house was more elegant than I had expected: a handsome foursquare yellow clapboard structure set in grounds planted out with many saplings of hemlock and balsam. Someone other than myself, I thought, had taken note of the village's want of trees.

I had not expected any form of agreeable society in the pursuit of my ruse: I believed that putting up with tedious dissertations on the better milling of plumbago and the inferior quality of spermacetti as binding agent were the price I should have to pay to secure my proximity to Miss Day. But there I was much mistaken. I was barely inside the door when the mechanic's wife launched into an encomium on a sermon I had but recently preached on the internment of Massachusetts's Negro seamen in Southern ports. She was, it seemed, one of the leaders of the Concord antislavery women, and, on learning this, I could not help but blurt out an inquiry as to whether she was acquainted with Miss Day. She shot me a look that was at once piercing, intuitive, and kind. Why, yes, she said. That young lady was a very great friend of her daughters, Sophia and Cynthia. In fact, she and Sophia had been speaking that very morning of Miss Day's return, and of their obligation to invite her to dine. I blushed when she said this, confirming her instinct, and went gleefully upstairs with the mechanic, ready to hear all about his notions for the improvement of the pencil.

His son, it appeared, was the family innovator. That young man was about my age, or perhaps a little older. We found him at work on the third floor, packing pencils for shipment. There was a greasy feel to the air in the workshop, and a strong scent of cut cedar. Motes of sawdust and a dirty gray mist danced together in the bands of light from the attic transoms. Henry Thoreau was unhandsome in physique, with short legs and long arms. But his face, framed by an untidy thicket of hair, was very striking. His features were large–the nose a vast hooked thing, the mouth full-lipped, and the eyes enormous–pale, deep-set, and prodigiously intelligent. He nodded curtly as his father made the introduction, and I noted the wonderful economy of his gesture, clutching up an exact dozen pencils at each grasp of his hairy hand, not falling short or overreaching by a single unit, but sliding the green bands around the bundle with the exactitude of a machine.

John Thoreau was as voluble as his son was taciturn. "I have been making pencils, Mr. March, since my brother-in-law discovered a seam of plumbago–or graphite, as some like to name it, from the Greek, *graphein*, 'to write'–back in, ah, I think it was 1824." It was all I could do to stifle a yawn as he went on. "The pencils we made were nothing special then, nowhere near as good as the European. But young Henry here, while he was at Harvard, used the library to study the matter, and learned the Europeans' secret: mixing clay with the plumbago as a binder. But he wasn't satisfied with that, were you, son?"

The old man turned to his son, who shook his unruly head without an upward glance and did not pause in his packing. "Henry has an idea for an improved mill that will make the graphite less gritty, and he also has an idea–quite brilliant, I think–for a drill the same size as the leads, so that we shan't have to saw and glue the cedars anymore." As Mr. Thoreau rambled on about his son's notion of manufacturing leads in varied grades of hardness, which he thought would find favor among both artists and technicians, my mind drifted. I could readily see the virtues in these proposed improvements, and the amount of capital required to implement them was really very little. Yet, since coming to any hasty agreement would thwart my own purposes, I pretended to be unconvinced, advancing a number of rather dull questions until the young man, weary of my apparent obtuseness, flung a last bundle of pencils into a gross box, wiped his hands on a piece of rag, tossed that down impatiently, and marched out of the workshop. As he brushed past me, he looked right into my face—a penetrating look from those remarkable gray eyes: a look cold enough to blast the foliage off an oak tree.

John Thoreau sighed as his son's boots thumped down the stairs. "He'll be off now, to the woods, and I don't know when we'll see him again. You must not mind Henry's want of conventional manners, Mr. March. His brother died but recently; they were close, and Henry feels it. He has withdrawn into himself a good deal, since."

"Indeed; I am sorry for your loss."

He passed a hand over his bald pate and rubbed his eyes. They were kind, intelligent eyes, pale blue and watery. "Young John was a sunny boy, very different from Henry. Henry would always prefer a solitary walk in the woods to an evening at a salon, but John loved society, and Henry would go about with him, for his brother's sake, and so be drawn out in spite of his natural reserve. Now he embraces his loneliness, and becomes unfit, sometimes, for the company of others."

I tried to reassure the old gentleman that I had taken no offense, and that I was inclined toward favorable consideration of the investment. In fact, I said, a walk in the woods sounded like a refreshing aid to reflection, after being pressed like a salt herring in a crowded stage all morning. I had brought some old clothes for this purpose, so Mr. Thoreau showed me to my room, where I changed my attire, and then was set courteously on my path.

How one longs, when in love, for a glimpse of the beloved. As I walked through the village on my way to the woods, I imagined Miss Day's feet falling on the very same ground that mine trod. I indulged my fancy even so far as to let myself think that the air I inhaled might have contained a particle of her breath. Such is the folly of the young! Every glimpse of a woman in the distance made me check my stride, as I tried the height and figure against the ideal I held in my mind. Yet none was she, and so I passed on into the woods, chiding myself for my foolishness.

At first, these woods seemed neither as lush and humming with life as the Southern forests I had come so well to know, nor yet as wild and unyielding as the woods that pressed in around my childhood home on Spindle Hill. These were tamed woods, logged over time and again, cleared in broad patches for farms, dotted with the wretched shanties of the Irish, tracked through by hunters and fishers and aimless amblers such as myself. Yet as I pressed deeper, I saw spiraling cedars that had escaped the ax, their wide fronds fingering the high air, and old spruce festooned with webs of lichen. This was wholesome, inviting, unintimidating Nature. I walked on, listening with delight to the lisping voices of the leaves and when, thirsty, I reached the pond edge, the water I drew into my cupped hands was of a purity and sweetness I think few places so close to human settlement could match.

That day, I made my first acquaintance with sights and smells that would become dear and familiar to me. After I had strode out the restlessness in my limbs, I began to make my way more slowly, stopping to study a vivid fungus painting a beech trunk, and to note the delicate cutwork of the ferns. I bent and peered, got prone in the leaf litter to seek burrows or to admire the tiny, delicate star-flowers in bloom on a pillow of emerald moss.

I was about this, breathing deep the scent of crushed herbiage and rich wood rot, when Henry Thoreau came up behind me, silent as an Indian. He must have observed me for some while, for when I raised my head, he was leaning at his ease against a tall alder, smiling. His arms were folded across his chest. A flute protruded from the pocket of his coat.

"I did not take you for a natural historian," he said.

"A country lad who settles in the city sometimes yearns for the scent of wild earth," I said, returning his smile and getting to my feet, dusting the twigs from my well-patched coat. Henry eyed my attire with approbation. "Come fish with me!"

He kept a small skiff pulled up on the shore of a pond about half a mile distant. I tried to keep pace with him as he moved through the woods with the ease of a deer. Eventually, we broke out of the thicket onto a sheet of water more like a lake than a pond, its sedgy shore giving way to rank upon rank of rushes, waving gently in time with the waves. We were on the wild shore; the farther bank was groomed farmland. He found his boat and pushed off, handling the craft as dexterously as he had the pencils, with a grace belied by his gangly form. "This is not the most beautiful of the ponds," he said, "For beauty I choose White Pond, the gem of the woods; for purity, Walden, but this is the pond I find most fertile in fish."

"What is it called?"

His countenance, which had been benign, shaped itself into a scowl. "It is called Flint's Pond–though not by me!" His oars slapped the water, hard. "*Flint's* Pond! What right has that stupid farmer, whose farm abuts this luminous sky water–to give his name to it?"

"Our nomenclature seems impoverished, at such times," I agreed.

Henry tossed his head back in a gesture of assent. He was agitated, impassioned. "Rather let it be named from the fishes that swim in it, the wildflowers which grow by its shores. Not from him who could show no title to it but the deed which a like-minded neighbor or legislature gave him–him who thinks only of its money value and lays its shores all bare."

He rowed on into the center of the pond and lay back in the bow, letting the boat transcribe a lazy arc. "Flint's Pond!" he said again. "Mr. Flint, who never loved it, who never protected it, who never spoke a good word of it, nor thanked God that he had made it. Why, that man would have drained and sold it for the mud at its bottom. He'd carry the landscape, he would carry his God, to market, if he could get anything for him." His agitation brought him upright, so that the boat wobbled and I clutched an oarlock.

"I know I am extreme."

"Not at all," I said. "You are eloquent. It is the habit of our species to despoil all we touch. Yet few see it so."

"Few, indeed; yet I am glad to know another." He squared his shoulders, but did not reach for his line. Instead, he took his flute, and as the lowering sun turned the water scarlet, he played sweet airs, till the perch, charmed, rose all around us, beating the skin of the pond so that we stood in a circle of shimmer.

Over breakfast the next morning, Mrs. Thoreau mentioned that she had invited some friends of Henry's to dine that day. "They are the Emersons—Henry lived with them for a time last year and they have shown him much kindness." I feigned a polite enthusiasm, mentioning that I had heard Mr. Emerson speak in Cambridge, but my face must have betrayed disappointment. For I had hoped that the daughters' friend, rather than the son's, might have been applied to. Mrs. Thoreau rose from her seat and was almost out of the room when she turned, with a barely suppressed half smile, and added as an afterthought: "Miss Day also will join us. I think you said you were acquainted, Mr. March?"

I coughed and wielded my napkin, hoping to hide the flush racing up my neck. I could barely contain myself through the following hours, wishing the day away so as to get to the appointed time for dinner. I tried to read some published articles by Mr. Emerson in the hopes of being able to intelligently contribute to the conversation. But my thoughts flew about, hectic as hummingbirds, and could not settle.

We were to dine at the Thoreaus' generous table, round, of black walnut, with unusual spool-turned legs. I was wondering if Henry had crafted the piece himself, and was on the point of asking him when Waldo and Lidian Emerson arrived. Henry cut off our conversation as suddenly as a fisherman might cut his line. He almost ran to the side of the Emersons, made a curt good day to the husband, and then drew off the wife to the far side of the room, where the two of them began to converse with an intensity that quite excluded the rest of the party. And so, rather awkwardly, I was introduced only to Mr. Emerson. While he radiated a calm poise that seemed admirable, his manner toward me was reserved; his mind clearly was engaged elsewhere. It was plain that nothing I might have the power to say could compete for his interest with his own thoughts. But then the arrival of Miss Day drew him into the discourse in a most unexpected manner.

She was the last to join us, and arrived with a rather high color born of hastening too quickly from her father's house. The blush of her cheeks looked remarkably well against the white of her simple dress. The sight of her, so longed for, struck me speechless. After yearning for a glimpse of her, I now found myself unable to meet her eyes. She, it seemed, did not suffer so. She hailed me with a composed, "Mr. March! What an unexpected pleasure to find you here in Concord," and then turned to her hostess to apologize for her lateness, explaining rather obliquely that she had been detained by the arrival of an unexpected package. Sophia Thoreau shot her a glance full of warmth and meaning. "Is your father quite equal to managing it? You might have brought it here, you know, without any reservation."

Miss Day gave a radiant smile of gratitude and embraced her friend. "Thank you, my dear. I know I can always count on you and your family in these matters."

Mr. Emerson looked grave. "I hope you will not mind my venturing to express a concern, Miss Day, that you do not involve your father in this beyond his wishes or capacity. For you know the extent of your influence with him, and you also know his frail state at present. It is upon him, after all, and not upon *you*, that the weight of adverse consequences would fall."

Her color, already high, rose to an even deeper blush that I mistook for mortification, until she commenced to speak. "Mr. Emerson," she uttered the name like a hiss. "If *some* in this town would take up the mantle of leadership that their positions warranted, these obligations would not be left to young women and frail old men."

"My dear Miss Day, a man can only extend his active attention to a certain finite amount of claims. Yet wherever I hear the black man spoken ill of, or whenever I see a Negro person mistreated, I always feel obliged to speak in his behalf. More than that I do not think it is presently in my power to do."

"Not in your power!" She seemed unaware that she had raised her voice. Henry and Lidian broke off their intense tête-à-tête and looked across the room. Sophia and Cynthia had each drawn close to Miss Day. Standing one on either side, they half patted, half held her, as one would both soothe and restrain a lunging, growling dog.

"Not in your power! You, who command great crowds at the Lyceum, who may write for any of a dozen eminent journals . . . to say that you can do no more is a sham! It is a disgrace! Worse, it is a lie!"

The intemperance of her attack left me breathless. Angry women generally cannot be said to show to advantage, and to see that lovely face so distorted by such a scowl as it now wore was immensely shocking to me. Who could have imagined this gently bred young woman to be so entirely bereft of the powers of self-government? I had never seen such an outburst, not even from a market wife.

Mr. Emerson, too, seemed stunned. He had blanched whiter than the table linen. He answered her unseemly shouting with a voice so low it was almost a whisper. "I am deeply sorry to find myself sunk so low in your esteem, Miss Day. I regret that I spoke in question of your judgment. I will consider what you have said."

She was trembling with uncontained rage, and I feared that she would continue her assault. Instead she turned her head and looked at me as I stood staring. I saw that the black eyes were swimming with angry tears.

"Come with me, my dear," said Sophia. "It is too close in here. I want to show you my roses before we sit down to dine." Sophia did not wait for an answer but simply threaded her arm through her friend's, which was trembling, and drew her from the room. The rest of us all let out our breath. Poor Mr. Thoreau, so gentle and amiable, looked as pained as if someone were driving an auger through his toe. Somehow, Mrs. Thoreau managed to address Mrs. Emerson on some light matter, but no one truly relaxed until Sophia returned, alone, from the garden. Miss Day, she said, apologized, but she had developed a headache and thought it best if she return to her home.

I drew Sophia aside. "Do I understand correctly, that Miss Day has involved herself with the Underground Railroad?"

Sophia's intelligent eyes scanned my face. She lowered her voice. "Miss Day and her brother have been conductors for some time," she murmured. "She told me that tonight's package will be making a brief stop of some hours only, but at times she has harbored fugitives for many days. She is a resolute woman, Mr. March. Although some"– she shot her eyes in the direction of Mr. Emerson–"say she is reckless." We were forced to separate then, as we were called to be seated. I could take no pleasure in the dinner, though Mrs. Thoreau had troubled to order wholesome vegetable fare in deference to my scruples. The party never really recovered, breaking up early, to my great relief.

It was hot that night, the air stubbornly refusing to cool, so after tossing and turning I rose, dressed in my walking clothes, and took my restless thoughts outside. A full moon lit my way through the village, and seemed to lead me on, to take the now familiar wooded path that wound toward the ponds. Under the trees, the air felt cooler, and the haze in my head began to lift. Long before I gained sight of the moonlit water, I realized I was not the only one there. Sound carries by night. The notes of a flute told that Henry, too, was out. He was somewhere in the middle of the pond, in his boat, serenading the perch. I walked around the pond shore, the smooth white stones glowing clear enough to make the way easy. My thoughts were all on Miss Day. I imagined her, mortified by her outburst, sleepless and fretful. I could not conceive her insensible of her fault, nor of the need to conquer it. I did not know Mr. Emerson and therefore was not in a position to judge the fairness or otherwise of her attack. Certainly, if any cause merited heat in argument, this one did. But it was the manner of the attack, the scorching flare of temper . . . Perhaps, I mused, a husband's gentle guidance could assist her in the battle against such a dangerous bosom enemy. But what if she *were* insensible, after all: what if the ungoverned tongue and the impulse to wound with it were so deeply ingrained as to be ineradicable? What sort of wife, what sort of mother . . .

And at that moment, my eye was caught by a glimmer of white, flickering through the woods farther up the shore. As if I had conjured her, there she was: walking through the trees like a wood sprite. At the mere glimpse of her, my mental reservations were swept aside by my bodily longing. I called to her. She started, and turned, and as she recognized me, replied to my greeting with a laugh. "Is all of Concord here tonight, then?" Changing her direction, she made her way through the forest fringe to join me on the stones. She passed her foot lightly back and forth over the smooth flat disks, so that they clattered.

"My brother and I used to come here on summer nights like this, when we were children. We'd make a fire and catch fish with worms strung on a thread. They made me give it up when I got older. They would keep me instead in their stifling parlors, making polite conversation—"

She broke off. I wondered if she were thinking, as I was, of an exchange in a parlor that had been in no wise polite. "Well," she continued in the same light tone. "Now I am older still, and can choose for myself, so I choose to come here. Although Father does not know of it; he could not approve that I come alone."

She sat down then and commenced work upon the lacings of her boots. These she stood upon the white shingles, and then set about peeling off her stockings. She looked up at me. "Do you think it very shocking, Mr. March?" The whites of her dark eyes gleamed. She jumped up, lifting the hem of her dress so that the pale curve of one bare calf was exposed. She skipped down the beach, dipping her toe in the lapping water. An animal sound escaped me. She must have taken it for a snort of disapproval. "You do!" she exclaimed. "In but a single evening I have exposed myself to you as both a Harpy and a Helen!" She tossed her head back and gave what I thought at first was a soft laugh. But then her shoulders shook and I realized she wept. A long strand of her hair escaped its pins and came tumbling, a dark skein unspooling over the white of her dress. "They branded him, Mr. March, the man I helped tonight. A human being, and they shoved a red-hot iron into the flesh of his face . . . And we sit in our parlors, and talk, and do nothing, and tell ourselves that is enough . . ." She gulped, and the weeping overtook her ability to go on. Crunching the stones, I was beside her. I reached for her, pushing back the fall of hair—it was heavy and thick and smooth to the touch—and tilted her chin so that the moonlight shone on her wet face.

It was fortunate for both of us that she had such long practice in these illicit evening outings, for some hours later, when we made our clandestine way back to the village, neither of us was in any state that could have been easily explained. I have no idea what she did with that white dress, stained as it was with mud and, yes, blood. For we married each other that night, there on a bed of fallen pine needles—

even today, the scent of pitch-pine stirs me–with Henry's distant flute for a wedding march and the arching white birch boughs for our basilica. At first, she quivered like an aspen, and I was ashamed at my lack of continence, yet I could not let go of her. I felt like Peleus on the beach, clinging to Thetis, only to find that, suddenly, it was *she* who held *me;* that same furnace in her nature that had flared up in anger blazed again, in passion.

I did not sleep that night. Too early for a seemly morning call, I was at her house, admitted by the housekeeper, Mrs. Mullet, who was surly–she may have known something of the ruined dress–and, in due course, shown to her father's study, where I went through the formality of asking for what I had already taken. The old man fretted and complained when I said we would have a simple ceremony, right there in the parlor, and as soon as could be, rather than the large and formal church wedding he had always wanted for his daughter. But I could brook no delay that would keep us apart for one unnecessary night, and so we were lawfully joined there by her brother within the fortnight, with only her father, my uncle and aunt, and the Thoreaus as witnesses.

It was well I insisted, for on the full moon exactly nine months later I held our first child in my hands. The babe emerged into the world with a countenance and coloring that were a tiny miniature of my own. We had jested privately that if it were a man-child, the circumstances of his conception would oblige us to name him Achilles. But we had a little woman, and so I was free to call her by the name that had become dearest in the world to me: her mother's. I named our firstborn Margaret.

CHAPTER SIX

Yankee Leavening

Aboard the Hetty G., *March 10, 1862*

My dearest,

How much this month I have felt like one of the Magi, setting out on a journey in a bleak season, yet knowing in my heart that the goal of the going will reward every hardship of the way. I lie down this night upon our vessel's rough deck in the hope that tomorrow I will be better housed in one of the great white mansions vacated by the chevaliers of this rebellion. You, who have been so busy about scraping lint, rolling bandages, and sewing gaiters, know better than most how dire is the need for the cotton that grows here, weed-choked from neglect, or rots unpicked, or worse, is wantonly destroyed simply to deny it us. At times I have espied rising curls of smoke that I must think mark the firing of fields by retreating rebels. At other times, we have steamed through waters strewn with cotton spilled from bales broken open and rolled into the river.

Tomorrow should see me at last arrived at my assigned destination: a thousand liberated acres where the Negros now under our protection are learning the sweet savor of toil performed for the reward of wages. My heart is light tonight, as I think about my part in this first great experiment of equality.

I have now traveled so far south that I find myself come to a place where our common expression "white as snow" has no useful meaning. Here, one who wishes his words to make plain sense had

*better say "white as cotton." I will not say that I find the landscape
lovely. We go up through Nature to God, and my Northern eye
misses the grandeur that eases that ascent. I yearn for mountains, or
at least for the gentle ridges of Massachusetts; the sweet folds and
furrows that offer the refreshment of a new vista as each gap or
summit is obtained. Here all is obvious, a song upon a single note.
One wakes and falls asleep to a green sameness, the sun like a pale
egg yolk, peering down from a white sky.*

*And the river! Water as unlike our clear fast-flowing freshets as a
fat broody hen to a hummingbird. Brown as treacle, wider than a
harbor, this is water sans sparkle or shimmer. In places, it roils as if
heated below by a hidden furnace. In others, it sucks the light down
and gives back naught but an inscrutable sheen that conceals both
depth and shallows. It is a mountebank, this river. It feigns a gentle
lassitude, yet coiled beneath are currents that have crushed the
trunks of mighty trees, and swept men to swift drownings . . .*

I looked up from my page, over the ship's rail, to the thing itself,
and the scene was again before me: the federal ram-boat steaming
into the enemy's vessel, staving its side like crumpled paper so that
it sank in less than three minutes, with the loss of all hands. I did not
tell her I had witnessed this. Neither did I tell her of the silent gloom
aboard the *Hetty G.* the night before that engagement; the surgeon
flinging down sawdust to receive the blood that was yet to flow,
each man on board left to reflect on whether it would be his own or
his companion's. And how it flowed. That day, I moved from man
to wounded man, loosening a bandage on a swollen limb, holding
cones of chloroform for the surgeon, bathing the wounds of men
blistered with steam burns from a shell-ruptured pipe. One of these,
who was clearly dying, said he was a Catholic and asked if I was a
priest. Knowing full well that there was no priest to bring to him, I

looked around to see if we were overheard, and then I whispered to him that I was. I let him make his confession, and gave him absolution as I had seen the Fathers do it. I have wondered, since then, if I did wrong. I cannot think that even the exacting God of Rome would find so.

The deck remained stained dark from that grim morning, despite a week of hard swabbing. Still, I rested content upon those bloodied boards, because I believed that the letter I had penned would bring an end to the necessity for dissembling. Of my new duties, I felt sure, there would at last be nothing unfit to share with my wife. Finally, I would be about work that had as its object the betterment of life rather than the ending of it.

All the next day, from sunup, I was by the bow, impatient for the first glimpse of the landing that would mark my new home. There was little wind and the air was inconceivably mild for the season. How strange it seemed to be passing by banks where the high green grasses grew on, insensible of the browning blight of frost.

I had been assigned to an estate named Oak Landing, now in the hands of one Ethan Canning, an Illinois attorney. He had secured a year's lease from the owner, the widow of a Confederate colonel named Croft. That lady, a Northerner by birth, had removed herself to the city after her lands fell under Union occupation and had readily taken the loyalty oath. In consequence, her property was now afforded Union protection, and she was free to lease it, which she had done, for small payment plus a half share in whatever profit Mr. Canning might be able to wrest from it.

The intention of leasing to such men as Mr. Canning was, as I understood it, threefold: to save what could be of the sorely needed cotton, to introduce a certain Yankee leaven into the Southern loaf, and to provide direction for the slaves fallen under our protection. These would now work for the first time willingly, rather than from fear of the lash. Adult male hands were to be paid ten dollars a month, less some small amount retained for the provision of clothing and other essential supplies.

My part was to help in establishing schools for the colored children and those among their parents who had the desire to learn their letters. I had occupied my idle hours aboard the steamer in drawing up lesson plans and making alphabets that could be hung in the ginning room, the cookhouse, or the smithy, so that adults might learn even as they labored. Busying myself about this work had acted like a salve on the sting of the colonel's decision to send me hence. Indeed, as my enthusiasm mounted, my true feelings began to reflect the fair face I had put upon the change in my letters home. I did most sincerely look forward to this new calling.

I suppose I had expected Canning himself to meet me at the landing, word of my arrival having been sent ahead with the patrol. So I was surprised to see no one but a ragged, skinny Negro who could not have been more than twelve years old, waiting with a spavined mule that cropped the river grass in the slanting light of late afternoon. Upbraiding myself for my pridefulness in expecting any larger reception, I arranged my face into a cheerful expression and greeted the boy, who I assumed would soon be one of my scholars, with an enthusiastic salute. The boy neither returned my smile nor raised his eyes. I introduced myself and asked him his name. His answer was inaudible, so I was obliged to ask again, leaning down to catch his reply.

"Josiah, marse," he said, his chin tucked into his chest and his eyes on the pebble he rotated under a bare and calloused toe. He tugged on the mule's headstall to bring it round, seemingly expecting me to mount, and when I said I would walk alongside him so that he could more easily tell me about the place, he shot me a swift, scared glance. I spoke brightly to him, but failed to extract more than a mumbled word or two in reply to any of my queries. His eyes were crusted with some pussy discharge, and before we had walked any distance at all he was wheezing and laboring for his breath. We went along the yellow clay track in silence for a while, past trees mottled with lichens and swagged with Spanish moss. I had to slow my step to accommodate the boy, who nonetheless fell behind even my slowest pace. When his brow became damp from fatigue I could bear it no longer. I stopped on the path and waited until he drew level with me.

"Get up on the mule, Josiah," I said in a kindly voice. He shook his lowered head sharply and gave a grim ebony frown.

"Go on," I urged. "You're too ill to walk."

"No sir, marse. S'not allow."

"Josiah," I said. "Look at me."

Slowly the boy raised his rheumy eyes. "I know it must be hard to get used to such a vast change in your condition, but you are going to be a free boy directly. Get up on the mule. No one is going to beat you anymore."

"Go in dat hole be worse than beating."

"What hole?"

"Place for bad niggers."

He would say no more than this, though I pressed him gently. He turned his face away from me and would not meet my eyes. I reasoned that he spoke about some barbarity of the former regime, the subject of which distressed him, and so I ceased my inquiries and simply walked on, as slowly as I could. I hoped that the boy's listlessness was the product of his ill health merely, and not a harbinger of some shared trait to be overcome with all my pupils.

The ground began to rise gently, signaling our approach to the house. I had noted from the bow of the *Hetty G.* that the buildings of the gentry always occupied any slight elevation that might be had above the flats and swamps. It was dusk when the track took a sharp turn and widened suddenly into a grand avenue, shaded by the curvaceous boughs of live oaks. The house gave only a glimpse of itself, a flash of white amid the shadows cast by the trees. Only when the trees gave way to gardens of crape myrtle and azalea did the mansion materialize: a two-and-a-half-story brick house with eight plain Tuscan columns forming its portico and supporting an entablature in the temple style. At either end of the portico, sets of moss green shutters promised shady respite. I could see that every room on the first two floors had a doorway to the porch. My imagination ran to visions of languid ladies, their silken skirts swishing through those doors in the early evening, as they came out to catch the breezes from the river.

The vision dissolved as I crossed the plaited brick patio and a slight young man opened the paneled door. Inside, the house had been stripped bare of its former luxuries. I stepped into a hall innocent of any carpet, the floorboards wearing instead a mantle of dust that spoke of neglected housekeeping. Ethan Canning held out his hand and grasped mine in a vigorous shake. Though his was the soft hand of a man unacquainted with physical labor, his grip was almost painfully firm, as if he wished to leave me in no doubt of his power. It was, I thought, the overzealous handshake of a boy playing at being a man. Indeed, I was astonished at his youthfulness. He was a sharp-featured, intelligent-looking fellow, but I doubt he had reached his mid-twenties. His smooth skin was puckered with a harassed expression, and as he turned to lead the way inside, he walked with a limp that spoke of clubfoot and explained why a man of his age was not in uniform. He was not particularly tall, his stature bringing him barely to my shoulder. He had to peer up at me through a pair of gold half glasses he wore perched on the end of his nose.

"I thought we would sup directly, if you don't mind, Mr. March. I expect you are hungry from your journey and we keep early hours here."

He led me into what must once have been a considerable dining room, the paneled walls painted with frothy scenes of French fops at play upon flower-decked meadows. The Southern chivalry who designed this room might once have enjoyed a similar life of pleasant idleness. Now, however, the painting's beribboned ladies turned their gaze of amusement upon a hollow, echoing space. A small utility table had been pressed into service instead of whatever fine piece had once held pride of place. Upon it were a few dishes of chipped and mismatched china. As I seated myself gingerly on a rickety stool, an elderly black manservant made to serve me a greasy piece of pork. I declined this, contenting myself with a watery dollop of sweet potato. It was not the dinner I had conjured for myself.

Since the dusk was gathering, Canning asked the servant to bring light. The old man shuffled in with a pair of candles mounted in a hollowed-out potato. "Thank you, Ptolemy," he said, then chuckled as the flare of the kindled flame illuminated my expression.

"Not what you imagined, eh, March? Not quite what I had in mind, either." He chewed diligently upon his gristly meat. "First the federals went through the place, when the late owner was still alive. What they didn't take the rebel irregulars made off with, soon as they heard that the mistress had taken the loyalty oath. I've found one or two things in the slave quarters, and you can be sure plenty more left with the slaves that ran off–which was more than half of them, from what I can figure. Some of those came back; and we have forty people–including that clapped-out old house servant–assigned here from the contraband camp the Union army had to set up at Darwin's Bend, to accommodate all the runaways coming into their lines. At least, having been comprehensively robbed means we're marginally safer from raids now, since word has gone about that we don't have anything left worth looting. Although once news gets out that there's a fresh Yankee arrived here, they may come sniffing . . ."

"But I understood there was a garrison at Waterbank to protect the Northern lessees in this area?"

Canning gave a dry laugh. "There is a post at Waterbank, yes, but what they call cavalry is laughably insufficient for the making of patrols between that town and the next garrison, or for the hunting down of irregulars. I've never seen such an indifferently mounted force. Why, some are even on mules or cart horses confiscated from the citizenry. You can imagine their effectiveness in any kind of hot pursuit. No, Mr. March, the garrison's protection extends no farther than whatever the fact of its presence affords. I do not expect that they would venture any heroic effort on our behalf."

For the rest of that cheerless dinner, Canning enumerated the woes of the enterprise known as Oak Landing. The picking season in this region generally began in September but in any case no later than November, so as to be concluded by Christmas. But Canning had arrived to find the place in utter disarray. Those slaves who remained had—quite sensibly, it seemed to me—turned their hands to raising food crops that would stave off their own hunger. Before Canning could get workers assigned to him by the superintendent of contraband who ran the camp at Darwin's Bend, and then reorganize everyone into work gangs, the crop was months delayed. As a result, winter rains had washed almost half the bolls from the stalks, and the late picking, still under way, was yielding disappointment. "Mrs. Croft gave me to understand—and showed me the factor's accounts to support it—that the yield per hand would be above a hundred pounds of cotton a day. We are lucky to get fifty, and that from the best hands. The children and the old folk bring in much less. Still, we must use every hand we have."

This news was dispiriting, for it meant my classroom would stand empty until the picking was complete. I wondered aloud if I might in the meantime make myself useful among slaves such as Josiah, who were too ill to toil.

Canning's narrow face flushed. "That boy is *not* too ill to toil." He gave a sigh and, after fumbling in his lap for a napkin that did not in fact rest there, rubbed the pork grease from his chin with the back of his hand. "Whatever you may have heard said, Mr. March, about the evil exploitations of the plantation system–and I heard and believed such things, too, I'll not deny it–a great many slave owners must have been gullible beyond the reach of folly, if this place is any measure of the matter. Why, the hands here think they can lie all day in their huts on account of the slightest ache or sniffle. My view is that any man who can stand to make his water must go to the fields and do his share of work–or else forgo his share of corn."

My face must have told the emotion that was mounting in my breast, for Canning glared. "If you think that harsh, wait till you've been here a week. You will see what I am presented with. Colonel Croft and his lady wife had a slave's lifetime in which to defray the expenses of illness, real or feigned. My lease here runs a single year, and I mean to make something at the end of it, in return for all the danger and discomfort I've undertaken. I don't claim to be an evangel of abolition like you, Mr. March. I'm a businessman, simple as that. Yet we both have a role to play in the betterment of the Negro's condition. I came here with more than an ordinary interest in the free labor enterprise. I believe that the production of cotton and sugar by free labor must be both possible and profitable . . . for *them* as well as us. If we cannot prove our point, what future will these people have? A *dark* one, wouldn't you say?" Canning smirked at his own wit, pushed away from the table, and checked his pocket watch. "And now, if you like, I will show you your quarters. I need to make the nightly check of the slave cabins–make sure everyone is where he is supposed to be, and at his rest, rather than squandering strength at some savage rollick or another. The drivers must have the gangs in the fields a quarter hour before sunrise."

I followed as he led the way from the dining room, holding the potato candlestick before him. Tired and downcast, I looked forward to my bed—the first real bed I would have enjoyed since setting out from Concord so many months earlier. But Canning did not ascend the large staircase that swept to the upper floors. He led the way to the cookhouse, where the old slave Ptolemy handed him a parcel wrapped in a cloth blooming with grease stains, then held out another, similar packet to me. "Corn bread for the morning," explained Canning. "We can't spare the time or the manpower to be preparing breakfast." I thought, but did not say, that if palsied old Ptolemy, who appeared to be both cook and butler, was classed as indispensable field labor, then the situation must be grave indeed.

Canning turned then to the door leading to the yard, and ushered me outside. "You are free, of course, to sleep in the house, but I don't advocate it. I recommend you do as I have and choose one of the outbuildings. If the guerrillas *do* return, it will likely be by night, and they have a reputation for untender behavior to abolitionists such as yourself."

There was a full moon, so we made our way easily across the yards toward a cluster of looming shapes that resolved itself, as we approached, into the industrial hub of the plantation. The chimney of a large steam engine towered over a collection of low-slung huts and workshops. The tang of wood sap told that one was a sawmill. Another disclosed itself as the smithy, while what I assumed must be the gin house stood at the far extent of the yard. Canning tugged one of the candles from the potato and handed it to me. "Be sparing with this—I'm rationing myself one half candle a week. I sleep in the corn mill. Recommend you try the storehouse. There are bags of cotton seed there. You'll find they make a fair mattress. Oh, and don't take that candle anywhere near the gin house. The lint flares up like a lit wick."

I pushed open the balky door to the building Canning had indicated. A huge pile of cotton seed—many hundreds of bushels, I estimated—rose almost to the roof beam. Much of the seed had been stuffed into hessian sacks, and so I arranged a pair of these for my bedding and used my army greatcoat for a blanket.

I awoke in the dark to the sound of a great clanging. I had slept heavily, the cotton seed indeed making a yielding sort of a bed, and so had to lie for a moment staring at the rafters, trying to recall just where I was. Eventually, I understood that the clanging must be the slaves' waking bell. Anxious to meet my future pupils, I rose, throwing my coat around my shoulders, and went searching for water with which to make some kind of morning toilet.

It was, as Canning had warned, still some time before sunrise. The predawn air was cold, and I pulled my coat tight about me. So accustomed had I become to the mildness of the region, I had to remind myself that a chill morn was no great oddity for this time of year. I stumbled around in the dark for some time before I could make out a well house. Inside, the damp cold was penetrating. There was no bucket attached to the rope wound around the turntree, so I fumbled around, feeling along the wall brackets, to see if I could find one. Losing my footing on the slick stone floor, I skidded, landing hard on my buttocks. I let out a curse at my own clumsiness.

A quavering voice, coming from somewhere under the floor, made me jump almost out of my skin.

"Marse? Dat you, suh?"

"Who is that?" I cried. "Where are you?"

"'T's Zeke, marse. Don't you 'member? I's been down here since before two days, and I is real sorry for what I done. Please, suh, I is powerful hungry an' cold. Please let me come on out."

I lay down on my belly on that cold damp stone and peered over the lip of the well, which was sunk into the floor to a depth of some twenty feet. At first I could see nothing but blackness, but as my eyes adjusted I made out the light color of a smock, and the whites of two frightened eyes. The well, I perceived, was dry save for a few inches of water at the bottom, in which the poor wretched man was standing.

"Good heavens, man! If I lower the rope will you have the strength to climb out?"

"Yessuh, I reckon I can, but you's not the marse after all, and if he ain't give me leave to git out, I don't rightly know as I should."

"Zeke," I said, "I am working with Mr. Canning. I will make it right with him. Come on, now, and take the rope and I'll help pull you up." Zeke was a tall man, but spare to the point of wasted, so it took me no very significant effort to hoist him over the lip of the well. He lay there for a minute, panting and shivering. I wrapped my coat around him and assisted him outside, where the temperature was at least a couple of degrees less chill. He stumbled, and I saw that his bare feet, withered and blue from standing in the water, were shedding slabs of sodden flesh. We sat down with our backs to the wall of the well house as a pale sun eased up over the lush horizon. I opened the cloth holding the corn bread, and passed it to Zeke. He took it in trembling hands that were knotted all over with snaking veins. He ate with the desperation of the starving until every crumb was consumed. He leaned back then and closed his eyes with a sigh. It must have been a handsome face once, but now the cheeks were sunken.

"Why were you in there, Zeke?"

His eyelids flickered. "Best you ax Marse Canning."

"No," I said firmly. "I am asking you. Please give me your account."

"I done butchered a hog and fed it to my chillun," he said. "The marse got in a temper 'cause I say I never stole the hog. Way I figure, that weren't no lie. The marse own the corn and the marse own the mule, and I spose to give the corn to the mule and that called looking after the marse's property. Well, I and my chilluns the marse's property, and the hog is the marse's property, so what mind if we eats the hog? The hog part of us now and the marse still own it, 'cause he still own us."

"But, Zeke," I remonstrated. "Mr. Canning does *not* own you. You are contraband of war. You are his employee, not his slave."

"'S that so? Sure enough still feel like I's his slave." He pointed a trembling finger up to the horizon, where a pale moon still lingered. "That there moon done wax and wane and wax again, and we's promise we be paid and more than a month done gone and we ain't seen a cent. Old Marse Croft time, he say, 'Work you stint, git done, then go dig you taters to feed you chilluns.' Young Marse Canning, he say, 'Work you stint and then go work some mo'.' But if you works a man from black to black, there ain't no daylight for plantin' greens and our taters all run over with weeds and the chilluns' bellies aching."

I did not know what the truth of this account might be, so I kept mum, but resolved to go directly to find Canning. How could the young man sanction such cruelty? To let his people go hungry, and to put them in a hole for the crime of feeding themselves! Such a punishment might not flout the letter of the army's directive, which specifically banned only flogging, but it most certainly flouted the spirit of the leasing experiment.

Accordingly, I took instruction from Zeke with regard to my direction, and set off for the cotton field. Soon, I came up with a little water carrier—a girl not yet as old, I judged, as my Amy, and similar to her in delicacy of movement and grace of build, except that the large water bucket sat upon dark fuzz rather than that tumble of golden curls of which my little one has a tendency to be a trifle vain. I greeted the girl, and she replied with a cheerful openness of manner that came as a relief after the reticence of Josiah the day before. When I told her I would be her teacher presently, she clapped her hands together, somehow managing to keep the bucket upon her head even without the benefit of a steadying arm. "I wants to learn *too* bad," she exclaimed. I wished my Amy, who whined incessantly about the trials of her schoolroom, shared this little one's enthusiasm. Cilla, as she introduced herself, was happy to lead me to the field, chattering all the way about the progress of the pickers, the prospects for continued dry weather, and quizzing me about the lessons and when they might begin.

The field, when we reached it, was an impressive sight. I judged that it stretched over more than a mile of country, yet the whole looked as carefully wrought as a Boston gardener's tiny pea patch. The plants stood in serried ranks, grown tall on the river's rich alluvium. While some showed the clear ravages of the wet weather of which Mr. Canning had spoken—their highest stalks stripped or broken, or foliage blighted brown with rust—a good part still stood in large-leaved luxuriance, the whole expanse luminous in the early light, awash in a sweet green freshness.

The pickers looked to have moved through about half of this field. I did not know how many such large expanses of planting the estate afforded. As I drew closer to the work gangs I noted the economy of the pickers' movements. The best of them, it seemed, could pick with two hands simultaneously, somehow twisting and plucking so that the staple fell readily into their grip. Less skillful pickers had to grasp the boll with one hand and pluck the staple with the other. Canning had said that every hand had been pressed into service, and I soon saw the truth of it. Even very young children were gathering low-growing staple, while elderly men and women, bent with age and the weight of their sacks, struggled with trembling hands to add their mite to the massing clouds of cotton.

Canning limped briskly up and down the long rows, exhorting the laborers to greater effort, hurrying them along to the telltale, and carefully scrutinizing what weight the scale disclosed. He had a ledger with him, in which he noted a running tally of each hand's pickings, apparently comparing it with previous days. He barked at one man, whose bag's weight displeased him, and praised another who must have been running ahead of his stint.

Canning wore the same rumpled camel waistcoat and trousers as he had the prior evening, but he had forsaken his jacket, and sweat stains already had begun to darken his shirt. He looked sallow in the bright light of morning, and I wondered if his bluff manner covered an incipient illness. On his head was the same broad palmetto hat the Negroes wore, and from time to time he swept it off impatiently to mop his brow.

I watched for a while, suddenly abashed at interrupting this scene of industry. The Negroes seemed intent on their task, few raising their heads even to note my presence, which seemed odd, since strangers could not have been very frequent in the fields. Canning perhaps provided the lead in this, for though he could not have missed me where I stood, he made no sign of greeting or acknowledgment.

As the hour wore on I saw not a few individuals in the gang who were clearly tiring. Several had the same hacking cough as young Josiah. None of them looked robust. Many, especially among the children and the elderly, were emaciated. Almost every piece of clothing was patched, torn, or threadbare.

When Canning called for the water carrier, I took the chance to plant myself before him. I thought to start on a positive note, so praised the scene of diligent toil. Canning took a swig of water, swilled it around his mouth, and spat without troubling to make me any reply. Affronted by his rudeness, I bluntly spoke my dismay at his ill usage of the man Zeke.

Canning grabbed my arm roughly and marched me briskly away from the telltale. When we were well out of earshot of the workers, he launched himself into a lacerating rebuke.

"How dare you, sir! How dare you arrive here with the very barest notion of the difficulties I am confronted with, and have the effrontery to rebuke me, to rebuke *me!* Ill usage? I assure you, I am the one being ill used here—by the lessor, by the army, by the Negroes! And to raise such matters in front of my hands! Have you no sense of order? Have you no sense, period?" His grip on my arm had tightened like a claw, and his voice had risen to a shout. He threw my arm down with a gesture that was almost violent, and opened his mouth to continue his tirade, then seemed to think better of it. He gathered control of himself, and lowered his voice. "I don't have time for this. If you have inquiries to make to me regarding my management, kindly reserve them until this evening, at which time I will endeavor to answer your concerns in full. Now you will excuse me. I have work to do. It would be advisable if you found some practical task to set your own hand to. Don't you have a schoolroom to be preparing?"

"I don't know exactly–" I was about to say that I didn't know what building might be available, but Canning cut me off.

"No: you don't know. You know exactly nothing." With that, he turned his back on me and marched off toward the work gang. He was, I thought, the rudest and most arrogant young man I had ever encountered.

I spent the rest of the day walking the estate to become more familiar with its layout and buildings. At noon, I took from the cookhouse a heel of bread, which I dipped in a jar of honey that had been kept so negligently I had to pick corpses of dead flies from it. After that undistinguished luncheon, I went in search of the slave quarters. These, I discovered, were a village-sized array of tidily made cottages, built of poles lapped with clay, set out in parallel, like a street. The place at first looked deserted, everyone being off at his work, but from one cottage rose the mewling of infants. When I approached and peered inside, I saw an old, hunchbacked woman, brown and wizened, sitting in the corner of the room, whose rafters were strung with eight or nine small hammocks, each of which contained a baby, some newborn, some a few months old, all quite naked. There were also ambulatory infants of one or two years old, also naked, scrambling like dogs around a pile of cooked peas that had been turned out of the cook pot directly onto the earthen floor. The old woman had a long staff with which she could reach each hammock and gently prod it into swinging without rising from her stool. She alternated this with a switch of reeds, which she flicked smartly at one infant who had snatched an extra handful of the terrible gray peas. He pulled back his tiny hand and howled.

"There now, Mother," I remonstrated. "Surely it's not necessary to strike such a small child?"

She squinted up at me through opaque eyes. "And who be tellin' me that, then?"

I introduced myself. She cackled. "Well, you being a minister, you tell me now; what the good Lord go make switches for, if it ain't for lickin' boy chilluns?"

She rose then and hobbled to the doorway. "Doan none of you move an inch, hear?" she croaked loudly at the poor little black lambs, who shrank back from the terrible crone and looked completely fearful. "I's got to manage these newcomers," she explained, "and I's also got to nurse the ones who's leaving us shortly." She extended a boney claw to me as she said this, and I took her hand, reluctantly. Leaning on me and on her staff, she made her unsteady way out of the infants' cottage along the packed earth path to an adjacent one. As she opened the door, a stink of sickness greeted us. This, then, was what passed for an infirmary. Some dozen souls lay on filthy floor mats. Roaches ran over those too weak to swat them or too ill to care. It was not necessary to be a physician in order to perceive that every one of them was most gravely ill.

There was a bucket of water near the door and the woman drew a wet cloth from it and went from one prostrate figure to the next, bathing each sweaty brow. A second pail contained a ladle, so I dipped this and followed her, offering water to those who could drink, and dribbling a few drops on the parched lips of those too weak to make that effort.

"What illnesses are they suffering?" I asked.

She shrugged her hunched shoulders. "Fevers, fluxes. Some's got the yellow sickness. Some's got the white flux. That girl there, she got childbed fever."

"Has a doctor seen to these people?"

The woman gave a snort. "Ain't no doctors in these parts, not for such as we."

I thought it odd that Canning had not summoned a Union medic. "What used to happen here, Mother, when people became ill?"

"Why, every spring the old marse done give molasses and sulfur and sassafras tea to purify they blood. He give the same spring clean medicine to every mule and pig and slave on the whole place. It worked good. Time the old marse, not so many people get so much sick as now. If they gets a little sick, they take a little this, little that, herb and root medicine that the Missus Croft knew 'bout. Someone done git fever, she say wash 'em in strong pokeroot, and vinegar and salt, but we doan have no salt nor no vinegar nowadays. But mainly she and de old marse says to the sick uns, just set a little, and they be better by an' by. Young marse say no, make the sick ones get up and work till they cain't get up no mo'."

I made my way back to the house with a fury at Canning and his cruelties fomenting in my breast. I waited for him, formulating my complaints, pacing the dusty drawing room so that the motes leapt and sparkled in the slanting light. When I heard his irregular tread I hurled myself out into the hallway, ready to accost him. But the sight of him gave me a check. The man was ashen. His limp was far more pronounced, so that he seemed to be dragging his left leg like a deadweight behind him. I calculated then that he must have been driving the laborers for a full sixteen hours. This further enraged me. Army directives said contraband labor should be worked not more than ten hours of a summer's day and nine in winter. My temper must have shown in my face, for Canning raised a hand when he saw me, and murmured, "Soon, not now. Give me just some little time, chaplain, before you subject me to your terrible, swift sword." He climbed the stairs, with some difficulty, pulling himself upward with the aid of the banister. Ptolemy followed him, bearing ewers and a square of ill-laundered linen.

A half hour later, Canning descended, looking somewhat restored. I had waited by the black marble mantel of the drawing room, my hands, in their agitation, tapping a tattoo on the cool stone. The drawing room's wide, high windows offered a sweeping prospect of the gardens, which must have been very fine when they were properly maintained. But the boxwood hedges were shaggy now and what must have been the cutting garden was brown and dead and untended. I turned from the fireplace when Canning entered. He drew up a spindle-back chair and sat down heavily. "Now," he said. "Now you may do your worst."

I began with the "infirmary" and the criminal neglect of the gravely ill. "To have that old woman—who looks almost dead herself—as the only comfort for those people is appalling."

"Mr. March," he said with an exaggerated courtesy. "Almost the first thing I did when I got here was to apply to the Union surgeon at Waterbank. That good doctor at first demurred on the grounds that the needs of the soldiery were too pressing. When I remonstrated with him, detailing the plight of the human beings under my charge, he replied that 'niggers were only animals, and not half as valuable as cattle.' After that, I ceased my pursuit, for what healing could come from a man of such monstrous convictions?"

"Well," I said, "but what of the sicknesses that old woman carries back to the infants she neglects and abuses. Is it worth a few more bags of cotton to put those infants at such risk? Could you not spare one of the mothers to the task?"

"The mothers are not always the Madonnas you conceive them, Mr. March. Have you heard the way they speak to their children?" He gave a thin smile. "In these times the infants' fates are uncertain, whatever I do. But I will consider sparing a half hand, yes: it does seem an unnecessary risk to expose infants to the miasma that the crone brings from the sick-house."

"How could you not have thought of this?" I said, disarmed by his ready assent on the point.

He ran a hand through his sandy hair. "There are things, a myriad things, every day, that I wish that I had thought of. I came here to see a cotton crop to market, not to be a politician, a doctor, and a wet nurse. I am an attorney, Mr. March. A bachelor attorney. I have had to learn how to farm and factor with only the assistance—contrary to the romantic nonsense that has been bruited about them—of a very abject and unpromising class of beings. How can I be expected to master medicine and midwifery as well? I am doing my best, March, damn it."

"Your best?" I said, freshly incensed. "How can you call it so, when you cast a human being into a sodden hole for the crime of being hungry?"

"Ah," he said. "We come to the matter of Zeke."

"Yes," I snapped, "and the poor man was in a most wretched—"

He cut me off. "I suppose he told you he stole the hog to feed his children?"

"Are you saying that is false?"

"No, it is true. What he neglected to tell you is that those 'children' are youths well grown, who wear butternut and ride with the rebels." My face must have been blank with confusion. His tone became testy. "Don't be a simpleton, March. There are Negroes who serve the secessionist side. You must know this."

"Yes, of course. But only under duress . . ."

Canning shook his head. I was clearly trying his patience now. "Zeke's wife was the overseer's house servant, so her boys grew up as servants and companions to the overseer's sons. By all accounts they were quite privileged—spared field work, trained in crafts such as smithying and saddlery, allowed to earn a little cash on their own account hiring out these skills. When the overseer's boys joined the army, Zeke's sons went along as their servants. One of the white youths died in the engagement that killed Croft. The surviving son joined the irregulars. Zeke's boys drifted back here, but ran off directly they learned that I expected them to work in the fields alongside everyone else. It seems they'd rather be slaves living off plunder than contraband working for their keep. But you will, I trust, forgive me if take exception to this plantation's depleted livestock being used to feed the very men who harass and threaten my existence."

"Well," I said, "perhaps they would not have run off if you did not drive everyone so cruelly."

"I came here to get cotton picked for the Union cause that is so dear to you, Mr. March, and getting it picked—this late in the season, in these conditions—requires sacrifices, yes, from everyone. To do it I have to wrest the maximum amount of labor from the sinews of every man, woman, and child on this place, including myself. And I will not apologize for that!" He had jumped up, in the course of this speech, his voice rising. Then he staggered slightly and rubbed at his chest.

I took an involuntary step toward him, thinking he might be about to faint, but he waved me away and sat again, sighing. When he resumed speaking, his tone was level and calm. "What I have had to contend with here is not just foul weather and murderous rebels, but an attitude of mind, Mr. March. It will take some considerable time to make the Negro understand that to be emancipated does not mean to be liberated from toil, which has been the lot of all the children of God since Adam and Eve were cast from Eden. Why, some of them here seemed to apprehend that Mr. Lincoln meant to carry them all in state on up to Boston, and give them white men for *their* slaves!"

"How can you expect them to feel emancipated when you tyrannize them in every way short of the lash, and meanwhile pay them nothing?"

"Why, I am paying hands eight dollars a month, and half hands—children, the elderly—according to their stint."

"But they say they have received nothing."

"Well, of course they've received nothing yet. I will pay them from the factor's funds, when we receive these after the harvest."

I thought it no great surprise that men like Zeke doubted such promises, when every white had always lied to them as a matter of policy. I knew the kind of "facts" slaves were taught; that those who fled to Canada would be caught by the British, who would have their eyes put out and set them to toil in underground mines till death overtook them.

I thought of the women I had seen that day in the fields, their shifts shot through with holes, not an undergarment in evidence. I thought of the naked, crying infants in their urine-soaked hammocks. "Is there no way that in the meantime you could do something to increase their rations, improve their clothing?" Canning looked up then and raised his hands in a gesture of despair. "You tell me, March! You tell me a way. I have racked my brains on this. I was not a rich man when I came down here. I spent every penny I'd managed to save from my practice and put myself in debt to buy the lease from Mrs. Croft and pay for those few scraggly mules you see, to replace the ones that had been stolen. Now I find that I have a lease that likely will yield but half of what I expected. I will be very lucky to leave here without being ruined. And that is if fever or a rebel raiding party doesn't kill me first. How, then, am I to feed and clothe 167 people? I don't suppose you have a private fortune on which you'd like to draw?"

I thought, but did not say, that not a decade earlier I would have had just such a fortune. But I did not wish to canvas to Canning the whole tangled history of my swift journey from plenty to poverty. Still, the young man's words had inspired me. There *were* men of fortune—in Concord, in Boston, and in New York—to whom we might apply for help.

"Loaves and fishes, Mr. Canning. That is what we need."

"I suppose a belief in miracles is a requirement of your calling?"

"Indeed, Mr. Canning. And I intend to convert you. I don't suppose I might have the use of your horse tomorrow?"

"If Aster can help you work a miracle, then by all means. But may I ask what you propose?"

We went in to dinner then, and over a supper much more agreeable than I had expected (both for my finding reason to hope that Mr. Canning might not be quite the young ogre I had conceived him, but also for the cook's managing to make some tolerable beans without the inevitable inclusion of swine fat) I set out for him the outline of my scheme.

At the end of it, he shook his head, but he was smiling as he spoke. "A miracle indeed, if you can make it happen, Mr. March. But I wish you all success." We rose then, he to his nightly rounds, I to my bed, on which I lay much of the night wakeful. I began by going over the details of the next day's tasks, many of which had to do with the penning and dispatch of various begging letters to wealthy abolitionist acquaintances. As I mentally composed these letters, it was inevitable that my mind would turn to the days when it was myself to whom such epistles had been directed. From there, my thoughts traveled in easy stages to the unraveling of my fortune, and to the exigencies of a current situation so threadbare that even my daughters are forced to toil for wages. None of them blames me, I know that. But it is a hard thing when a man is ruined by the very idea that most animates him. And that night, when I found myself tossing sleeplessly, I could not help but blame myself.

CHAPTER SEVEN

Bread and Shelter

If a man is to lose his fortune, it is a good thing if he were poor before he acquired it, for poverty requires aptitude. Lucky for me that I knew how to wield an adz and a hoe long before I learned to read a ledger book or negotiate a contract.

While it was true that as newlyweds we lived without ostentation in the home I established in Concord, it is also true that we lived entirely without want. My mission was to provide Marmee with complete liberty of mind so that she might tend to her twin passions—the education of our little women and the cause of abolition—without having to trouble about the least detail of housekeeping. For we had not long passed a year of blissful absorption in our golden Meg than our dark, lusty little Josephine—the image of her mother—arrived to join her.

Marmee's father had moved in with us, bringing with him his long-time housekeeper, Hannah Mullet. She was a capable soul but crude in her perceptions of what a home might be. I imagined a seminary of society, a place of calm, beauty, and order. At first, Hannah saw the chef, the valet, and the nursery maid I employed as usurpers in her realm, but her grumbling ebbed as Mr. Day's decline demanded more of her, and she was glad to have the extra time to devote to his care.

Marmee, for her part, chided me that the large staff left her little more to do in a practical way than "tend her pocket handkerchief." Sometimes, when I came upon her by Jo's crib, humming some movement from a Beethoven symphony that was by no means a soothing lullaby, or rolling on the grass in some wild tussling play with little Meg, I recalled our first private conversation in her brother's house and teased her, asking if she had determined yet which of the girls was to be the famous author and which the renowned artist.

In the months that had followed our marriage I quietly conspired to build beauty into our daily life. The house I had purchased was large but charmless. By ordering the removal of a partition here and a set of folding doors there, a pair of boxy sitting rooms became a generous parlor through which light spilled even on the grayest of days. Old ovens and ash holes I had converted into graceful arched alcoves; gradually, and with not a little tact, I replaced the conventional and undistinguished furniture that Mr. Day had gifted us with items of more elegance and lineage. A table of polished elm found its way into the dining room; a set of sofas covered in French silk graced the parlor. I also put in place an ambitious scheme for the garden. It is a pleasure to complete the design of Nature by adding something to the landscape, rather than merely denuding it for the production of fuel and fodder. I extended the stables and added a ring so that our daughters might learn to ride at the earliest opportunity. Along our boundary walls I started espaliered fruit trees–apple, plum, and pear. Because we stood at the foot of a steep slope, I had this terraced and created upon the levels a number of different styles of planting. Some acres I left quite wild, a refuge for the birds and small beasts and pollinating insects. Upon others I devised parterres of a classic formality. I started climbing roses over bowers and devised a pleasance for the children by the brookside. Under the cover of all these improvements made for enjoyment and elegance, I also undertook, in secret, the conversion of an attic stairway to something resembling a "priest's hole" of medieval times. When it was completed, I brought Marmee upstairs and showed her how an innocent-seeming wainscot concealed our new "railway station," where a fugitive could rest, in comfort and safety, for as many days as might be needed. Her delight in this exceeded her pleasure in all my other improvements combined.

Freed from the quotidian, Marmee and I spent our first years together most profitably: she would lead me through the hidden paths and byways around Concord that had been her childhood haunts, teaching me to know my new place. In turn, I tried to teach her something about *her* new place, giving her to understand, with gentle hints and loving guidance, that what might be considered lapses born of high spirits in a young maiden were in no way proper in one who was now a mother and a wife. And just as some of the ways she showed me were stony and bramble-thatched, so, too, did we stumble, from time to time, in our progress upon that other difficult road. But we pressed on, growing in intimacy with each other, and then with those others whom we were most fortunate to call neighbors.

Waldo Emerson was by no means the closed and aloof figure I had conceived him upon our first meeting. At the risk of self-flattery, I can say that he came to value my opinions upon the ideas of our time. Before very long it was unusual if we did not spend part of every other day in company and close discussion. Marmee was delighted when Mr. Emerson began to be more outspoken, indeed, passionately eloquent, on the subject of emancipation, and was inclined to take a little credit for the change. But I think the Thoreaus had a greater, if quieter, share of influence there, especially Henry, through his unusual intimacy with Lidian Emerson. Waldo's wife was the one adult with whom Henry was never awkward or reserved, and to her children he could not have been more affectionate if they had been his own. With my girls, too, he was considerate and interested, and as soon as they were conversible, he elected himself their unofficial tutor in the ways of the natural world and became, perforce, our daily intimate. He delighted to take Meg and Jo into the woods to observe the life within. It was not all science with him: a row of orange fungus was an elven staircase, a cobweb the fairies' lace handkin.

It was a constant wonder to me that a man who could be abrupt to the point of unkindness with adults had nothing but gentleness and patience for children. One day, he arrived at the door, suggesting to the girls a huckleberry-gathering expedition. I, restless from a morning of quill pushing, decided to accompany them. Henry was a master for such a mission, for he knew with an unerring sense exactly where every variety of the berry might be found, and so could give the little ones swift success in their hunt. Jo had amassed quite a creditable harvest when she tripped on a tree root and fell, spilling the entire contents of her basket. She set up such a howling as would have driven beasts to ground and set the birds aflight throughout the wood. Even then, Jo was showing signs of her mother's volatile temper, and Marmee absolutely refused to bridle Jo's outbursts, saying that the world would crush her spirit soon enough. We had exchanged sharp words on the matter, and I was glad that Marmee was not there when I chided Jo and asked her to control herself. My words, however, were to no avail. Meg tried her sisterly best, kindly offered her a share of her own gathered berries, but Jo would have none of it. *Her* berries were lost, and no other berry might replace them.

Thoreau knelt down then and put his massive arm around the tiny heaving shoulders. "Dear little Jo, you could not help but fall just here: Nature's own fairy folk tripped you up a-purpose. They want little girls to stumble now and then to sow the berries for the next crop. Next year when we come here we will find a grand garth of bushes laden with berries on this very spot, and we will owe them all to you." At this, Jo's little mouth ceased trembling and the lips turned upward again in a smile of pride and pleasure.

When Marmee confided that a third child would soon join us, I rejoiced in the news, all the more so as her poor ailing father was finally released from his suffering within a month of the confinement, and it seemed apt that the sweet spirit who is our Elizabeth should arrive from heaven as our consolation.

If Marmee had been ardent in her abolitionism before the birth of her children, their coming into our lives set her on fire. I came upon her one day, nursing little Beth, with Jo curled up asleep, pressed against her lap, and Meg making an imaginary tea party at her feet. It was a delightful scene of maternal tranquillity, except that my wife's shoulders shook and her face was wet with tears. I came up to her and gently inquired as to the source of her distress, thinking that the fatigue of the new mother and the death of her dear father perhaps had combined to oppress her spirit.

"No," she sobbed, when I probed her. "I am thinking of the slave mother. How can I sit here, enjoying the comfort of my babes, when somewhere in this wicked land *her* child is being torn from her arms?"

My passionate wife had an uncommon ability to feel within herself what others must be feeling. Sometimes, harsh upon her own nature, she would refer disparagingly to this trait as her "morbid sympathy with human suffering." At other times, she would use the power of her emotion as a spur to good works. But always she felt that what we did—the speeches, the occasional provision of overnight refuge to a runaway—was none of it enough. Sometimes, the ferocity of her views burst out in that same intemperate rage I had witnessed unleashed upon Mr. Emerson. It was the only cloud marring the amity of our union. I liked it very little when I was the object; even less when it was aimed at one of our intimates.

My wasp of an aunt was, understandably, no great favorite with Marmee, but for my sake she bore a certain amount of forced intimacy. I required this of her because my dear uncle was, that winter, in the last stages of a long illness, and I felt—correctly, as it happened—that he would not be with us come the spring. There was something poignant in watching the old man, who had not had children of his own, sporting with our young ones. Jo, especially, took his fancy, for even before she could read, our writer-to-be was drawn to books. My uncle had a fine library, and he allowed Jo great liberty, letting her build railways and bridges even with his rare volumes. When she wearied of this, he would fetch down an interesting old folio with lavish plates and beckon her onto his lap. It was a pleasure to see Jo perched in the crook of his arm, her dark head nestling against his wattled neck as he turned each page.

It was just such a convivial scene that Marmee's temper marred one Sunday's teatime very near to the end of my uncle's life. I had mentioned that we planned to attend a lecture that same evening, to be addressed by John Brown, who was visiting Concord for the first time. Aunt March, always forthright in her opinions, stated that she found Mr. Brown's views extreme, and that she herself would never think of attending an address by one so radical. She was not alone in Concord in viewing Brown so; rumors about wild Old Brown had him sleeping with a dagger in his teeth and a pistol for a pillow. "I have always considered," Aunt March said, in the proud Boston accent she affected, "that slavery is more a matter for prayer than protest. Preferably," she intoned, peering meaningfully over her half glasses at my voluble wife, "silent prayer."

Marmee's anger unsheathed itself. Her voice became cutting. "Why, I believe you would decline to keep company with that notorious radical, Jesus, were he to appear in Concord!"

My teacup rattled in my hand. Aunt March's eyes narrowed. I placed my index finger on my lips—a signal we had agreed upon—when Marmee, remorseful after just such another outburst, had asked me to help her curb her temper. Though she looked straight at me, and could not have missed the gesture, she chose to ignore it.

"You are," she hissed at my aunt, "incapable of appreciating a moral argument." It was not her words—though these were hostile enough—but the manner in which she uttered them. I cannot recount all she said—my own nature is such that I would repress all memory of such exchanges—but insult followed slur, leaving no room for the attacked party to answer. At such times I thought I would rather live in the midst of a crashing thunderhead than with this Fury of a wife. Aunt March, who had herself no great claims upon an even temper, had turned quite purple.

My uncle, who had many more years of experience than I in averting such scenes, clapped a hand to his breast. Jo slid from his lap, looking up at him anxiously. "I am unwell," he said, rising unsteadily. "Would you excuse me?" He was, in fact, quite gray in the face, and I felt a stab of my own real anger at my wife, that her outburst should add to his afflictions. Uncle March reached for his wife's mottled hand, which was trembling with rage. "My dear, would you mind? I need your assistance." Much against her own inclination, for she was never one to shirk a skirmish, Aunt March gave her husband her arm and the two made unsteady progress toward the door. I did not wait for any further hint, but swept an arm around my own wife's waist and propelled her from the premises. My idea was to walk off her temper, thinking that the brisk winter air would cool her. But I thought we might have to march to Boston and back before she managed to regain her self-command.

Eventually, she calmed, and we made our way to the town hall to hear the divisive speaker. There were more than one hundred citizens gathered there, no doubt interested, as I was, to lay eyes on the man of whom we had read so much. The hall was ill lit; a few oil lanterns cast sharp shadows on Brown's severe visage as he made his way to the podium. He was, in type, a true frontiersman. I assumed that this must be an impression he deliberately cultivated, since he wore, upon his arrival at the hall, a coonskin cap. Later, I learned that he was entirely unaware of his own person, and that the cap, made from furs his sons had hunted and his daughters had sewn, was a product of his necessitous circumstances. He shrugged off a heavy woolen military overcoat, revealing square shoulders and sinewy arms formed by long days of land clearing and the other physical toil necessary to establishing himself and his large brood in the harsh landscape of the Adirondacks.

He must have been approaching his fifties. But he had a younger man's energy, all held in tight reserve. The word that occurred to me was *couchant:* ready to spring at the least rustle in the grass. To continue the predator analogy, his nose was huge and beaked like a raptor's. His eyes, too, were eaglelike; his rufous hair, silvering at the temples, shot backward from a low point on a large brow deeply scored with lines.

Brown knew his audience. He began his oration with a nod to the town's proud history, commenting on the great justice of what had been done here in 1776; not only, indeed, its justice, but also its inevitability. His argument proceeded then in easy steps to assert that a war to end slavery was equally inevitable. "I tell you this," he declaimed, "the two most sacred documents known to man are the Bible and the Declaration of Independence. Better that a whole generation of men, women, and children should pass away by violent death than that a word of either should be violated in this country!" This drew a scattering of applause, although not from me. I was not so profligate with the lives of women and children as he. I glanced at Marmee, but instead of the disapprobation I expected, her black eyes were warm and approving. Here, then, was a man intemperate as she, a man whose measure matched her own. Lifting up his voice, Brown proclaimed that he had *no doubt* it would be right, in opposing slavery, not only to accept a violent death, but also to kill. I felt my face settle into a scowl at this. If there is one class of person I have never quite trusted, it is a man who knows no doubt.

I do not think I was jealous of Brown, exactly, for finding approval in my wife's fine eyes. And yet I was uneasy, as we left the hall, and were invited by our girls' teacher, Mr. Sanborn, to an impromptu reception for the speaker. The Emersons and the Thoreaus were attending, Sanborn assured us. Marmee assented even without waiting for a word from me, and at that I felt my gloom settle a little deeper upon me, rolling in like a damp fog.

We got to Sanborn's rooms a little before Brown, who, when he arrived, seemed ill at ease. I judged him a man unused to refined interiors. The young man introduced him to those he had not yet met, coming at last to us. Up close, I noted that Brown's corduroy suit was frayed at the sleeve. His hand, when I took it, was calloused, as you would expect, and there was dirt trapped under his fingernails.

Marmee addressed him with great animation, inquiring about every particular of his Adirondack project, which, with the largess of a wealthy Quaker benefactor, aimed to turn indigent blacks into landowning farmers—and voters. Brown and his boys had surveyed and registered the freedmen's land titles so that unscrupulous whites could not lay claim to them, and now they were helping the settlers master the rudiments of farming in a harsh landscape with a short growing season. Brown spoke kindly but tersely in answer to her queries, only becoming animated when Marmee asked if such a settlement was not a boon to the enterprise of assisting runaways on to Canada, as the border was not very distant and a black community must offer better opportunities for concealment. Brown's eyes bored into hers as he recounted the flight of a couple he had but recently assisted under pursuit from a bounty hunter who, he remarked coldly, he had been obliged at last to shoot. Marmee's lips, as he said this last, were parted. Her face wore an expression I could only describe as avid. I could see that Brown ignited the very part of my wife's spirit I wished to quench; the lawless, gypsy elements of her nature.

She was congratulating him on his works and wishing him even greater success in the future. "I could do so much more, madam, had I only the means. But I am dogged by debts and lawsuits."

I had heard something of Brown's business history: how he had been most unfortunate in certain well-meaning efforts to sell American wool to the English mills. But I had no idea, until he began to enumerate his woes to my wife, of the extent of his indebtedness and his legal worries. Marmee turned to me, and I saw the question framed in her eyes. I had seen the way our girls jostled for her gaze, and I felt myself that moment like a child in want of her approval. I realized then that I *was* jealous. She saw Brown as a heroic figure; I wanted her to see *me* that way. And yet I did not have it in me to make wild rides to the border, shooting over my shoulder at bounty hunters. Even in speech, my most stirring sermon paled beside the blood-dipped oratory of Brown.

Well, then. If I could not earn my wife's esteem, perhaps at least I had the means with which to purchase it. I had, for some time since, been quietly divesting myself of my industrial interests, as the repulsive effects of the factory system had become clear to me. I had come to the conclusion that I could not, in conscience, profit from the degradation of human toil and the despoilation of water and air, once I began to grasp how very much the returns on my investments were married to these consequences. So I had sold out of my shares in this factory and that, as opportunity presented, and I had a large store of capital awaiting a worthy use. Although I had not spoken of it to anyone, I had it in my mind to found a Utopian community one day, when the girls were older; a "place just right" where men and women of learning could live with Nature, but without its exploitation. But that was a dream for the future. It need not preclude some use of my capital in the present.

"If you have some time tomorrow to call on me, Mr. Brown, perhaps we could discuss this further?" Marmee's smile when I said this last was, I deemed, worth whatever sum Brown asked of me.

spoke to me of slave labor, worm slaughter, and sheep theft–for is not fleece the rightful property of the sheep? And why should the humble silkworm be sentenced to death for our finery? The one suit I kept was my humblest linen homespun.

Our bread we could raise, thanks to my familiarity with the rites of the soil. Shelter, too, we had, although our lives within the large house had to undergo some substantial alteration. For the servants, we had to find other situations–all but the loyal Hannah, who insisted that she would stay with us no matter how paltry the amount we could now pay. We sold the horses and carriage, and went instead on foot or by the public conveyance. The elegant elm-wood dining table went elsewhere, replaced with a simple piece I fashioned myself. The French sofas, likewise, departed to new homes, as did the silver service and the porcelain plate. Yet each loss was somehow compensated by Marmee's genius and industry. When we let go a beloved painted screen, she dressed the place instead with yellow branches of maple or twists of scarlet woodbine. Her busy needle embroidered colorful cushions for the simple stools that had replaced our silken upholstery. And so we were rescued from deformity and dreariness by her graceful plainkeeping. If she lamented the end of her leisure, she did not let me see it: she sang those days more often than she ever had, and found time for merry play with the girls. The sound of their laughter was sweetened when, in the waning days of summer, it was seasoned with the piquancy of our newborn Amy's cries.

We had been very quiet about our reduced circumstances, partly out of a natural reticence and partly out of anxiety for Brown, whom neither of us wished to expose to public opprobrium. But friends could not help but notice the carts coming to take our belongings. And despite our best economies, before very long I became behindhand with my debts. Tradesmen *will* talk in the taverns, and so eventually all Concord knew that we were in a most depleted state. Good

The mild-mannered man of business who presented himself at my study the following morning was a very different cast of being from the wild-eyed orator of the night before. Brown bearing his cashbook was almost irreconcilable with Brown bearing his broad sword. It was a transformation so complete as to be quite disarming. He seemed humble, diffident, almost embarrassed by his errand. I tried to set him at his ease. It would be an odd thing, in a former peddler, if I were to suddenly conceive that trade was somehow a base occupation for a crusading idealist. Brown had sought wealth for the highest reasons: so that he might support his large family and underwrite his antislavery struggle. That he had not amassed a fortune was largely, it seemed to me, the result of ill luck. Certainly, as he laid out his affairs, I saw a history of diligent, even backbreaking, effort. He had toiled and he had failed, and I couldn't find it in my heart to blame him for it. He did not come to me, he said, asking for charity, but for an investment in land that would be, also, an investment in human liberty. He had a new scheme that, if it prospered, would relieve his indebtedness and then fund what he described as a vast magnification of the Underground Railroad. I was captured by the vision he laid out: of brave escorts, well armed and amply supported, who would risk all to shepherd not just individuals to freedom but, working plantation by plantation, liberate dozens, scores, perhaps even hundreds of escapees at a time.

The business venture that was to fund this enterprise seemed sound enough–Brown clearly knew both land and livestock. He pulled out his maps and pointed to tracts in Ohio that had jumped in worth from eleven dollars to a staggering seven hundred dollars an acre. The land he proposed to buy would likewise soar, he said, as the same canal system pushed west. These were dazzling projections, but even if he were wrong, and the potential profit was not so vast as he calculated, then my capital at least would be secured in the land itself. Once I had agreed, his demeanor reverted immediately to that of the passionate evangel. He shook my hand vigorously. I rang for tea and Marmee came to pour it. It was a felicitous moment, for she entered the study in time to hear Brown declaiming: "Mr. March, know that one good, believing, strong-minded man such as yourself is worth a hundred, nay, twenty thousand, men of weak character." I could not help adding a little flourish to this. "I can take no credit, Mr. Brown. What is it that Heine says? 'We do not have ideas. The idea has us . . . and drives us into the arena to fight for it like gladiators, who combat whether they will or no.'" It was a pompous little utterance, in retrospect, and, recollecting the blank face Brown showed me, it was plain enough that he had little time for German poets, no matter that they described his character with precision. Indeed, I think he had little time for reading of any kind, save the Old Testament, which he seemed to have by heart, and which, I came to realize over the course of our acquaintance, he relied on as a military manual as much as a spiritual guidebook.

For about a year, I allowed myself to bask in his approval and, even more, in the approval from my wife that came as its by-product. The initial sum he had asked was itself large; and in the months after I had advanced it, he wrote to me of further expenses which must needs be met to secure the earlier outlays. The town that would grow up on our land would need a hotel; it would need a warehouse. Soon, the skeletons of these large buildings loomed large on the bare prairie, yet the promised canal and the town itself remained mere dreams. Somehow, Brown's confidence always stanched my skepticism and carried me along. Always, he was certain that just a little further investment would assure our vast return. I considered each request, and I assented, for by then I was in the stream so deep that rowing back to shore looked more arduous than pushing on. What I did not know—and where Brown was culpable—was that I was not, as I thought, his sole financier. Brown had borrowed against the very same tracts time and time again, spending the money, I learned

much later, on secret arms caches that were not destined for the facilitation of escapes, but for the mounting of insurrection.

Now, when I can view the matter at some emotional remove, I don't think he saw himself as misleading any one of us. He truly believed—he had completely convinced himself—that there would be profit enough to cover all he had spent. When the canal was routed elsewhere and the land was sold as nearly worthless, my claim was only one of several of equal merit, none of which could be satisfied. In the end, I used the last of my wealth to pay off his other creditors, rather than see him jailed for fraud and his work for abolition ended.

"But must it have been our entire capital?" Marmee asked, the day I unfolded to her the desperate state of our fortune. She was standing half turned away from me at the parlor window. Her hand stroked her swollen belly, for the news of my ruin had come as we awaited the birth of our fourth child. I moved to her, and embraced her, letting my hands rest on top of her own. I could not say that I had done it entirely to win her approbation. It would have been too cruel, and in any case, it was not, by then, entirely true. For if Brown had in some way seduced her, then he had seduced me, also. "He gives himself, entire." I laid my face alongside hers and whispered my words in her ear. "He risks his very life. I was asked to risk only money. How then offer any less than all?" We stood there for some time, silent. I felt her body shuddering, and I knew that she wept. "The ravens feed the prophets," I said. She turned her face then, and gave a crooked smile. "Do they so? Well, I hope someone has instructed them the way to Concord." I kissed her tears away. We did not speak of it again.

What does a man really need, after all, in a material way? Bread, shelter, a little raiment. The latter we had, even to being able to sell some excess cottons, silks, and woolens. What man can wear two coats, after all? I was glad to give up the garments on the peg rail that

friends such as the Emersons and the Thoreaus helped us, with tact, inviting us more often to dine at their table, pleading surfeit of some produce or other and sending baskets to our door.

I did note this, and set it down as yet one more of life's injustices: that the man who has been wealthy is dunned more civilly than the fellow who has ever been poor. My creditors would come to me most graciously, diffident, if not downright apologetic, for asking what was theirs. It was as if I would be doing them a great, unlooked for kindness if only I would pay them a trifling sum on my outstanding debts. I would give them tea, and polite conversation, and, even when my answer to their just entreaty had to be a regretful, "Nothing, sir," my mortification was always entirely self-inflicted, for *their* civility never failed.

You might wonder that I did not start again and build a second fortune. But one must have seed capital to grow wealth and I was not a footloose youth anymore, who could take to the Virginia byways for as long as it took to earn an honest nest egg. What I could make with my pen and my preachments was spent before it was earned, servicing our debt and that one luxury that neither I nor Marmee could forswear; giving our mite to those unfortunates even poorer than we.

And this, also: I had come in stages to a different belief about how one should be in this life. I now felt convinced that the greater part of a man's duty consists in abstaining from much that he is in the habit of consuming. If I prolong my dark hours by the consumption of costly oil, then I waste both the life of the beast slaughtered for the purpose, and the clarity of mind which comes from timely sleep. If I indulge in coffee then I pay to pollute myself, when instead I could have a cleansing draught of water at no charge at all. None in our household ate meat, but now we learned to do without milk and cheese also, for why should the calf be deprived of its mother's milk? Further, we found that by limiting our own consumption to two meals a day, we were able to set aside a basket of provisions from which the girls were able to exact a pleasure far greater than sating an animal appetite. Once a week, they carried the fruits of their sacrifice as a gift to a destitute brood of German immigrants.

My aunt, who might have been liberal in our misfortune, chose instead to offer only a kind of assistance that she must have known would be entirely unwelcome. My uncle had died thinking me amply situated, and had quite reasonably therefore not made any provision for myself or my girls. Apart from some bequests to various Spindle Hill relations, that good man had left his entire estate in the bejeweled hands of his already wealthy wife. When she became apprised of my descent into poverty, she arrived at our home, unannounced and uninvited, and proceeded to hector me in the most scathing terms imaginable. She took no note of the fact that my two eldest, Meg and Jo, were present in the drawing room (our little Beth, even then, would flee at the mere rumor of company, and the baby was at her nap). I saw Marmee's color rising, and planted my finger across my lips with the most meaning look I could muster. I saw her slight nod of acknowledgment, and the struggle in her face as she strove for self-mastery.

But then, having done at last with berating me, Aunt March turned to her true object. She waved a lace-clad arm in the direction of our darling Meg. "I am willing to take her," she declared with an exaggerated sigh of resignation. "I will adopt her forthwith, thus relieving you of the burden of at least one mouth to feed."

I glanced at my wife. No gesture from me would gainsay her now. The hand on my lips raised itself, instinctively, as a man would raise an arm to fend off a weight about to crash down upon his head.

"Burden? You dare to call my darling girl a *burden?*" She was on her feet as if the chair had a spring which had propelled her upward, and was advancing on Aunt March most menacingly. I, too, was affronted, but I could not have my wife behave so. Not to an elderly relative who, whatever her conduct, had a claim on our respect. And not, certainly, in front of our impressionable little women.

"Girls," I said, low but urgent, "go outside now and play." Meg, moist-eyed, mouth trembling, scuttled from the room. Jo, however, rose slowly, her brows drawn low over a pair of brown eyes that glinted—not with tears, but anger. She was glaring at her aunt, the very mirror of her mother's fierce, wild face. "Go!" I said, raising my voice. The last thing I wanted was for her, especially, to witness her mother's behavior, or the means by which I now felt compelled to curb it.

For the first time in such a case, I asserted myself, moving quickly toward Marmee and wrapping my arms around her as if she were one of the children, in the thrall of a childish tantrum. Yet she was no tiny girl, but a woman, and a strong one. She turned on me, swiveling in my arms, her face twisted in rage, and began to abuse me. I truly thought she might strike me. I tightened the grip of my right arm around her and clapped my left hand over her mouth. Using brute strength, I pushed her to the door and thrust her through it. As I let go my grip she wheeled around to face me, and I saw with dismay that the pressure of my hand had left a red mark on her cheek. As she began to push her way back into the room I had no alternative but to slam the door in her furious face. She pounded upon it with an angry fist. "Go into the garden, I beg you, my dear, and compose yourself," I said, as calmly as I was able. "I will join you there directly."

"Don't trouble!" came the terse, wrathful response from the other side of the door. I heard the quick tread of her step as she retreated, and then Hannah's earthy, soothing voice, and I knew she was in safe hands. Hannah had long experience with the management of that temper.

When I turned from the door and met my aunt's eye, I saw a look of vindictive triumph. My affront at her want of tact turned then to an anger of my own. "We don't give up our girls for a dozen fortunes, Aunt. Rich or poor, we will keep this family together and find a happiness in true affection that some will never know, because all the wealth in the world cannot buy it."

Aunt March's lips thinned. She stood and limped past me, letting her silver-handled cane land heavily on floorboards laid bare by the sale of our Turkey carpet. At the door, she paused and turned. "Affection? From that serpent-tongued harridan? I wish you joy of her." And with that, she left our home, and our lives, for ten long years.

I am not, as I have said, in the habit of imbibing ardents. But after that exchange I found myself in pursuit of the dregs of the portwine that I had been used, in better days, to offer to my guests. The chiffonier where I had stored such things was gone, and I was obliged to call on Hannah to find where the decanter might have been relocated. "Decanter?" She laughed. "We sold that a fortnight ago." She handed me a preserve jar containing a finger-depth of fluid. Thus, only slightly fortified, I went in quest of Marmee.

I found her in the pleasance, pacing the muddy brookside, ruining what I knew to be her last pair of decent boots. I saw to my dismay that the storm had not yet broken. I had learned the meteorology of Marmee's temper: the plunging air pressure as a black cloud gathered, blotting out the radiance of her true nature; the noisy thunder of her rage; and finally the relief of a wild and heavy rain—tears, in copious cataracts, followed by a slew of resolutions to reform. But the dark cast of her expression told me we were still within the thunderhead, and as I approached she confirmed this by raising her voice to me.

"You stifle me! You crush me! You preach emancipation, and yet you enslave me, in the most fundamental way. Am I not to have the freedom to express myself, in my own home? In the face of *such* insult? You call our girls your 'little women'; well, I am your belittled woman, and I am tired of it. Tired of suppressing my true feelings, tired of schooling my heart to order, as if I were some errant pupil and you the schoolmaster. I will *not* be degraded in this way."

"It is you," I said, trying to keep my voice even, though my pulse beat in my head. "It is you who degrade yourself, when you forgo self-mastery."

At this, she stooped, picked up a clod of mud, and flung it at me. I tasted dirt. I did not move to wipe my face, but just stood there, letting the silt slide down my cheek, and turned my palms toward her in a speaking gesture. Then I reached for a switch from the weeping birch tree, and handed it to her. "Go ahead," I said.

She took the switch. It whipped through the air with a whistle. I felt the burn where it sliced against my cheek.

Then the cloudburst. She ran toward me, the tears falling, and touched my bleeding face. I took the muddy fingers into my own hands and kissed them, was obliged to turn aside and spit a slimy fragment of leaf mold from my mouth. We laughed, and embraced, and as so often happened, the ardor of her anger turned to a more welcome sort of ardor, and we had to make our way privily back to the house so that Hannah and the girls would not see our disarray. From that day, her struggle for self-mastery took a more serious turn. "It might have been one of the children I struck," she said, looking ill at the thought. The work was not accomplished in a month, or even a year. Perhaps it is still not done, entirely. But never since that day have the storms threatened to so completely engulf us.

Effecting a reconciliation with my aunt also was not the work of a week. I thought it unseemly, in such a small town as ours, to be shunned by a near relation. As part of her penance, and her new resolution with regard to her conduct, Marmee called early on my Aunt March to offer an apology. But my aunt repulsed that, and every subsequent overture, maintaining an embittered silence. And so I could not go to her when it became necessary to mortgage the large house; even less when I was forced to sell it. Fortunately, the Emersons knew of a small brown cottage close to their home which was available for a trifling rental. To fund the sum, I chopped wood, and earned the princely figure of a dollar a day. By such measures we were able to remain in our beloved Concord. Meg and Jo wept bitterly on the day we left the only home they had known, but Jo soon found herself a writer's aerie in the attic, and, using the skills I had learned as a boy on Spindle Hill, where all we had we made, I built her a drop-leaf table to use as a desk in the confined space. Marmee involved Meg in schemes for covering the shabby walls with rose bowers outside and pretty curtains within, and the girls helped in the design of our home's first necessity, a safe place for our runaways. In doing this, their sense of their own misfortune fell into perspective and we saw no more tears.

Not long after this move, Aunt March came to visit our neighbor, one James Laurence, a man of substance who had made his fortune in the India trade. The man was reclusive, and often abroad, and we had not come to know him. Aunt March, however, had known his wife, and kept up a slight acquaintance with the widower. As she was leaving our neighbor's grand stone house, she was almost toppled over by Jo, racketing homeward with her head in a book. In her usual comical, blunt way, our wild girl cracked through ten years of ice. Those years had seen Aunt March become enfeebled, her lameness a real obstacle to her daily routines. And she was, I think, lonely in her large and dusty house; in any case, she offered Jo a paid position as her companion for part of each day. Since Meg had already gone out as a governess to help ease the family finances, Jo, too, was eager to find some way to contribute. But while Jo was widely liked by the families of our town, no one seemed to want a governess who was more disheveled, fey, and reckless than her young charges. So Jo took the position with my aunt, and to general surprise the seemingly ill-matched pair did remarkably well together.

Jo was thick-skinned enough to brush off Aunt March's barbs, and cheerful enough to brighten the old lady's dull days.

As well as the money, which was welcome, Jo's compensation was the freedom she had of my uncle's library. For some period each day, when my aunt napped or was occupied by company, she availed herself of the opportunity to read. If she had loved the place as a child, it was bliss to her now. Had I retained my fortune, I would have provided her tutors as fine as could be found, in this country or even abroad. Instead, she was left to scramble herself into whatever learning she could, with only her mother and myself for guidance. That room, full of its neglected books, became her university.

For my Meg, I would have afforded leisure and the refinements of life, for which I know she pined, seeing them every day in the wealthy home of the King family. The elder sisters of the children for whom she cared were close to her in age, and just out. My Margaret saw the ball gowns and the hair ornaments that she could not have, and had to listen to merry chatter of theater parties and concerts that she could not join. It was a trial for her indeed, for she was old enough to have formed expectations based on her privileged childhood, and could make a picture in her mind of what her life ought to have been.

But would it have been better so? I am not convinced of it. For instead of idleness, vanity, or an intellect formed by the spoon-feeding of others, my girls have acquired energy, industry, and independence. In times as hard as these are now become, I cannot think this an unfortunate barter.

CHAPTER EIGHT

Learning's Altar

Oak Landing, March 30, 1862

My dearest,

Today, at last, began the ginning of the cotton harvest. The apartment known as the lint room resembles nothing so much as Concord in a snowstorm, the fibers swirling like flakes, with a most wondrous lightness, and piling in a soft blanket on the floor. I was obliged to speak sternly to any number of the boys, who make a game of stealing into the lint room, to tumble in the soft cotton, their shiny faces standing out like lumps of coal. While the young ones love to play so, the work of supervising the ginning is not a task much sought after, as the cotton dust is inevitably drawn into one's nostrils and from thence into the lungs. The men tie cloths about their faces to work in this unwholesome space.

Now that our late harvest is in, I am hopeful that Mr. Canning may relax his stern regime. He already proves himself amenable to hints and suggestions which lighten the lot of our laborers. I must thank you in advance for your work in securing those goods of which we stand so much in need. I know your powers of persuasion, and I look forward every day to a boat bearing the fruits of your offices. I have now written to all those I hope hold me still in some esteem, explaining the exigent situation here.

Meanwhile, I have chosen my "schoolroom." It is to be in the *building that once served as the carriage house. It stands empty now. One carriage took the mistress of this place hence to the city, where it remains at her service. The other, Mr. Canning reports, was driven off by looters, no doubt happy to find themselves so finely conveyed. I have swept the cobwebs out and have had the children gather boughs of greenery and festoons of spring blossoms for its decoration. I have made a banner for the door bearing our favorite verse:*

"The hills are reared, the seas are scooped in vain,
If learning's altar vanish from the plain."

Both children and adults alike seem hungry for instruction and many ask me each day when classes may begin. It is hard to fathom how a people kept so long in the darkest ignorance can have such a keen desire for mastery of the written word. Some of them, it is true, have been so degraded by slavery that they do not know the usages of civilized life; these are hands innocent of pen or quill, having touched little else than the ax helve, the plow handle, and the cotton boll. Yet even these are by no means unintelligent. Many of them, it seems, have acquired the habit of veiling any brilliance of mind under a thick coverlet of blank idiocy. I can only speculate that life was easier for them so: a supposed simpleton threatens little, nor promises much. Mr. Canning calls them dull and lazy, but where he looks to find evidence for this, I see instead evidence of wit. Example: he bemoans the fact that they are forever slipping off from cotton chores to tend their corn patch. Why shouldn't they prefer to work a crop that can sustain them, when they have seen no evidence that a penny profit from the inedible one will flow back into their hands?

We are so used to judge a man's mind by how lettered he is; yet here I have already seen that there are many other measures. With book-learning so long denied them, they have, perforce, cultivated diverse other skills. Their visual acuity is remarkable, and their memories prodigious. For example, should a steamboat be plying the river, the Negroes can identify the vessel long before it approaches close enough to read the name on her side. When a new boat approaches they inquire as to her name and take careful note of how she is configured, so that even a year later they will be able to say, from a very great distance off, what vessel she is.

I hope to start lessons after tomorrow, which is Sunday, and the occasion of my first sermon. The Negroes have a "praise house" in which they perform their own heartfelt devotions. I have invited the troops from a scouting party presently encamped here, such as care to come, to join us in prayer, and so I hope to continue my work of ministry to the soldiery as I advance in my new tasks with the coloreds. Think of me, if you will, and send me your prayers and good wishes . . .

That afternoon I wandered to the riverbank, to a spot I had come to know, where a giant, deformed sycamore twisted and leveled itself out over the lazy brown water. It was an old tree; the survivor, I think, of some long ago lightning strike. Part of the trunk was blackened, dead, and hollowed out; the remainder pale, vigorous, and full of life-sustaining sap. There was a place where the dead met the living wood in a gently curved depression, which made a most comfortable seat. I perched there, thinking out the content of my sermon, for which I had decided to take as my text: "*Work* out your own salvation with fear and trembling, for God worketh in you both to will and to do of his good pleasure."

When I had some pages that seemed good to me I gathered them up and, instead of walking back to a cheerless dinner with Canning, decided to detour to the campsite of the scouts from Waterbank, to see if I could glean any news from them of the wider world. Unlike Canning, who would dine in the town anytime he found a moment's liberty to do so, I did not like to go there. The Union troops garrisoned there were, by and large, a rough sort: conscripts, many of them Irish, serving with ill grace and no fervor for the cause, and infamous for their depredations on the property of the surrounding civilians. They took the people's chickens or their pigs, and if some old man tried to defend his property their answer was a beating, or worse. The women they insulted with their inappropriate attentions. No wonder, then, when any Yankee appeared, the townspeople were surly. The wives and mothers of the fighting men were especially cold, and turned their backs if one offered a good day. So, since Waterbank held no prospect of agreeable society, I was content to wait for what news came to me.

There were ten in the scouting party, and when I approached they hailed me with good cheer and bade me sit with them. They had a cook fire under way at a little distance, and on it a kettle of molasses beans bubbled, rich and brown. My mouth watered. As a private ladled steaming portions into the tin cups of his brothers in arms and carried them up to distribute, the men passed about a big stone jar of corn liquor. It went from hand to hand and, when it came to me, I passed it on without, I hope, any show of disapprobation, though I noted that the contents were more than two-thirds gone. I asked if they had come upon anything untoward in their scouting forays, and they reported an exchange, two days earlier, with a party of guerrillas, which they had chased to within range of their garrisons' artillery. Once fired upon, the guerrillas had retreated, deliquescing like dew, as was their unnerving capacity, into what hidden burrows no one had yet been able to determine.

"It's that store in Waterbank," said one fair-bearded, pale-eyed corporal. "Why, if the wives and sisters of the marauders weren't free to go and come there, buyin' supplies as much as they can carry off, and payin' for it all with money their menfolk stole, we could clear these here woods out in no time."

"Why doesn't the general ban the store's proprietor from such trade?" I asked.

The pale youth laughed so hard a spray of corn liquor came out of his mouth. The others joined him. "Chaplain, you sure is an innocent man!"

"The general's best and oldest friend bought hisself a big interest in that there store," said another scout. "The general ain't going to upset his friend, is he? Specially when the store must be taking in something like a thousand dollars a day."

"It ain't just that, and it ain't just here, neither," said a jowly, hound-faced man, much older than the others, pushing back his forage cap to reveal a shock of grizzled hair. "Same thing up and down the river. The reb leader makes it plain to the garrison commander that his post won't be menaced too bad so long as the store stays open to the womenfolk. Southern chivalry, is how they dress it up. But the result is, the amount of supplies that gets into the rebs' hands is more than they need to keep harassing and bothering our pickets, as well as the kind of nigger business such as you got here."

If what the men said was true—and I had no particular reason to doubt it—what an inducement to the guerrillas to keep within our vicinity. I was so engrossed in digesting this bothersome news that I didn't notice what was going on by the cook fire until I heard the cry—a ragged thing, like a crow calling. A gaggle of scrawny children—infants, really—who must have been hiding in the brush, crouched wide-eyed around one who was clutching at his hand and howling. I ran down and gathered him up in my arms. His palm and fingertips were burned, the blisters already forming on the tender flesh. I turned to the scout who, with total disregard for the crying boy, was scattering and stamping on the cooking coals.

"What happened?" I demanded.

"I was just after having a bit of fun with the baby sambos. They was standin' round droolin' like starvin' cur dogs so I tol' them, go ahead, clean the pot," he said with a shrug. With a callousness I cannot fathom, he had not warned the ravenous children to beware the heat of the iron kettle, which had been sitting some hours on the coals. The burned child's sobs were pitiful, as the scalding molasses clung to his tender palm.

"Give me your canteen," I snapped, and when he did not immediately hand it over I snatched it from him and poured cold water on the child's hand. "Could you not have given him a spoon to use?"

The man grimaced. "You think I'd let a nigger brat eat off of my spoon?"

I strode away, furious, carrying the boy in my arms. Behind me, I heard the man's indignant voice, and then the other men's mocking laughter.

At the house, I searched in vain for salves and cursed our many wants and the distance between us and the friends I hoped were even now trying to supply them. In the end, all I found was some cool water in a stone crock, and a scrap of linen, and so I bathed and bound up the little hand. The child's wrist was so thin that my awkward effort resembled a ball of yarn with a knitting needle protruding from it. I took him out to the loggia in search of a cool breeze, sat him on my knee, and asked him what his name was.

"Jimse," he said in a squeaky little voice.

I fed him the watery greens, boiled gray, and the congealed hominy the cook had prepared for my dinner, and Jimse ate as if the grim fare were delicious. I held him, still, singing to him songs such as my little girls had liked, until the pain subsided enough to let him fall to sleep in my arms. He weighed next to nothing. I rested my cheek on his soft head. His hair had been allowed to grow out long, in tight, heavy little ringlets, so that he looked, asleep, like a dark cherub. I played with one of the springy curls, thinking about my family and how very much I missed them.

I must have drowsed in my chair, for it was full dark when the child moved in his sleep and wakened me with a start. There was a half-moon, which sent its pale yellow gleam through the slats of the green shutters and made patterns against the plaited brick. The thought had just entered my head that the child's parents must be missing him, and anxious, when I saw her.

She was standing in the garden, still as a tree, staring at me. Her skin was very dark, so that I couldn't make out her features. I have no idea how long she had stood like that, nor how long she might have gone on standing so. I rose, with the child in my arms weighing little more than a puppy, and walked down the steps toward her. She was a tall girl, very young; I would have said too young to be the boy's mother if I had not known by then that the carnal life of these people sometimes began long before their childhood ended. She reached out her thin arms and took her son, bending over him a head of cropped curls in a gesture like a bird nestling. She turned then and loped away across the grass, her long bare feet leaving tracks through the dew. When I woke the next morning, there was a handwoven, broad-brimmed palmetto hat hanging from the doorknob of the storage shed. It was, I guessed, her way of saying thank you.

When I saw her again I was wearing the hat. I tipped it to her, and she smiled the swiftest hint of a smile I believe a human face can make–like a tic, almost–before her countenance returned to its accustomed wary gravity. She was crouched on the swept floor of my classroom, the soles of her bare feet pressed flat to the ground, her elbows on her bent knees. It looked an uncomfortable posture to me, but she and the others seemed to have no difficulty squatting so. Her smooth brow puckered with the effort of shaping the letter *M* with a stick in the soft earthen floor. I had determined to start the teaching of literacy by having all my pupils learn to write their own names. First, though, I thought to teach them to write mine.

The girl's name, I had learned, although not from her—reticence or fear rendering her absolutely mute in my presence—was Zannah. Her little boy, Jimse, sat as close beside her as he could, as if the two of them were joined at the ribs. The room was very full, and a kind of rich, musky scent wafted up from the close-packed bodies. The first days of lessons proved very trying. My scholars had no idea of sitting still, of giving prolonged attention, of ceasing to chatter and laugh together as the mood took them. Mr. Canning looked in briefly on the second day of classes, and quickly withdrew without pausing long enough to observe that something was being accomplished behind the apparent chaos. I expressed my disappointment about the brevity of his visit over supper that evening.

He murmured something about having had cotton baling to see to, and then wrinkled his face. "It is so close in there, I wonder you can stand it."

"It is a large group for such a confined space," I conceded. Even though I ran my school in two sessions, to accommodate the rhythm of the field chores, there were seldom fewer than fifty persons in the room. "Indeed, I am surprised how many come to me, given that they have to toil outdoors for many hours in addition to the work of learning. They try so hard, even the most backward of them. Truly, I find them, as the poet said, 'God's images cut in ebony.'"

Canning laughed. "I pray God has not so rank an odor! I find them ripe enough out of doors. I wouldn't last an hour packed in amongst them like you."

How to explain to him? And to what end, with such a man as he? I loved their eagerness and their high spirits, even if it would take some time to effect the kind of order I desired for learning. This was the school I had yearned for as a young wanderer. At last I would be able to test my theories on teaching. My objective was to awaken their hearts to the ideas dormant there, rather than to implant facts into their memory. Because of their circumstances, the minds of the adults were as suited to this approach as those of the children; equally malleable and just as likely to be informed by the passions of the heart rather than constrained by the prejudices of the head. The first hour of our work was dedicated to copying letters and learning their sounds. This we accomplished by scratching in the dirt with sticks, or on scraps of board with slivers of charcoal. Even though we had no paper, nor any real prospect of gaining any, I set them about making their own quills and steeping bark for ink against the day when they might need such skills.

Next, we spent some time discussing words and their true meanings. In this I tried to provoke them to a freer expression and a deeper mode of thought than they had heretofore been used. I would ask them the meaning of *meek* and then follow by asking them to think of any meek person they knew, and what were his qualities. When we had considered meekness in full, I would provoke them by asking for a definition of *brute* and examples of the behavior that went with the word. By such meandering paths I led them to reflect on their situation, and gave them a proper voice with which to speak of it. It was demanding work for them, and so afterward, we took a short break for recreation, to let the children run freely out of doors, and the adults ease the stress of concentration. Canning, when he came upon one of our recesses, as I called them, was all frowns, maintaining that I was wasting time. He threatened to shorten the hours he allowed liberty from field labor. I was obliged to remind him that education of contraband was sanctioned by the army as part of the mission of the free labor experiment, and that in how I chose to conduct this mission he was my subordinate.

When we gathered after recess to resume lessons, I moved my pupils away from the abstract realms. Geography we approached by making maps of the slave quarters; arithmetic, by counting corn cobs–how many already shelled, how many awaiting husking–and calculating the difference. Some, it seemed, would never grasp even the rudiments of cyphering; one woman, a leathery, snaggle-toothed crone whom I judged to be in her sixties, told me proudly that she had mastered counting to ten, then proceeded to demonstrate her skill: "One, two, three, five, eight, ten." I congratulated her on placing the numbers in the right order, then gently pointed out that if she noted the number of her fingers, she would see that her tally was still somewhat off from the full count. At this, she looked most downcast and did not come again to the classroom. When I sought her out and urged her to persevere, she shook her grizzled head sadly. "It's gone too late for me, marse. I believe I'll give up my space for the young uns." She would not be persuaded otherwise.

Others, such as Jesse, a powerfully built young man whom Mr. Canning used as one of the drivers, showed an aptitude which disclosed a high degree of native intelligence and a surprising degree of self-education, given the intellectually barren conditions in which he had been forced to live. Jesse's facility with mathematics was remarkable. With him I was able to embark on projects such as calculating the percentage increase in the value of cotton in its life cycle from seed to bale to finished garment. I had only to introduce him to a concept to find that with but little practice, he could arrive at the correct answer to a problem more quickly than I.

I found that my pupils knew little of their country and had been encouraged to think less. They loved geography, as this subject had been entirely taboo, linked as it was with runaways and routes northward. But history was a blank page to them, and at first my attempts to interest them bore no fruit. I tried to make them understand that they were, from now on, to consider themselves as part of the American story, and therefore must take pride in their nation's past. It wasn't until I mentioned that I came from Concord that I got anywhere at all. I learned that my pupils would respond most readily to what could be made personal, so that when I told them of *my* town and the great events that had occurred there in the bringing forth of our nation, I was able to win their interest. Eventually, I think they came to like this "story time," as they called it, best of all, so I would save it for lesson's end. They were a rapt audience, and reluctant to have any story brought to a close. Cilla always thrust her small hand in the air, pleading, "Tell us what happened next, marse . . ." and it was with difficulty that I sent them off to their chores, wearing long faces.

· To do justice to so many it would be necessary to have more teachers. Frequently, I yearned for assistance. And when I did, I thought of Marmee, but more often, I must confess, of Grace. How it would inflame my pupils' ambitions, I thought, to see one of their own so accomplished. But Grace was beyond my reach, shackled by her own high principles to a wretched old man who had begotten but in no way fathered her. So instead, I introduced my students to the autobiography of Frederick Douglass and the poems of Phillis Wheatley, of which I had a number by heart. I took delight in seeing their eyes open with amazement at the attainments of these two, the one a runaway slave, the other a barbarian-born African, kidnapped into bondage.

I don't believe I have ever been so tired as I was those evenings, not even in the aftermath of battle. Teaching the Negroes required a vast expenditure of physical energy, as I found that if I did not talk with a high degree of animation and an almost theatrical amount of gesture and expression, I could not hold their attention. I went to my sack bed spent, yet with my mind still spinning out the thread of the next day's instruction. I would fall asleep and dream of lessons. I had found the work I was born to do. It was this conviction, and not the fatigue or frustration of trying to teach so many at so many different levels of understanding, that I tried to communicate to my dear wife, when I scratched out some lines every night before sleep claimed me.

How often have I wished for some kind of magic telescope by which I could look from afar at you and my girls, and see how you do, and that you could turn from time to time to look in on me, and see how my ventures prosper. If you could, what a difference you would see. The passing of a season has wrought a wondrous change to the beings whose home is Oak Landing.

My pupils, the old and young, progress apace with their letters. They open their minds to me now, and are no longer reticent. Josiah, who still ails and has a wracking cough that breaks your heart to hear, has nevertheless become a regular chatterbox, so that I hardly can reconcile him with the sullen, silent boy who met my boat. He is now so open that I can tease him about that time. He explained that silence was born of fear and prudence. In these regions, one learned young, it seemed, that even innocent speech with a white person could be dangerous. Once, he told me, having some errand in the town, he offered a "Good day" to a white sutler, who laid open his cheek because Josiah had had the "nigger insolence" to address him.

I paused there, and pondered whether to tell her of Zannah, the one student who could not speak freely to me. For many days, I had taken her silence for some high degree of shyness, which crippled her ability to speak up in class or in private. But as days turned to weeks, and she continued to present herself for schooling at every opportunity, I began to wonder, and finally I pressed her, in the classroom, to participate. I did this kindly, saying that every pupil's thoughts were a valuable addition to our mutual journey of learning.

Still I extracted not a word, and the others seemed uncomfortable, shifting restlessly about.

Later, the man Jesse, who as well as being my most apt pupil was something of a natural leader among his own people, came up to me and asked for a word. He told me that Zannah did not speak because she could not. As a very young girl, she had been the victim of an outrage committed by two drunken whites from a passing steamer. When she protested their molestations, "a-screaming and a-cussing fit to rend the heavens," as Jesse put it, one of them held her while the other took out his pocket knife, pried open her mouth, and cut off her tongue. When the Crofts, to their credit, sought justice for this brutality, they were told that they could have no redress for "damage to their property" because the slave in question was unable to make a statement regarding the alleged assault.

I did not write of this, for while Marmee was under no illusion as to the degree of barbarity to which slaves were subjected, I did not think the ears of my little women should be sullied with such things. So, instead of writing about inhumanity, I turned my pen to a description of the natural world:

Spring here is not spring as we know it: the cool, wet promise of snowmelt and frozen ground yielding into mud. Here, a sudden heat falls out of the sky one day, and one breathes and moves as if deposited inside a kettle of soup. In response, vegetation shoots out of the ground with irresistible force. Just when the body wishes to slow down and give way to lassitude, it must instead accelerate, for the challenge is to keep human labor on a pace with the work of Nature, or else be overrun by the excesses of her abundance.

If there was something unnerving about this sudden and extreme fecundity, I did not write of it. I wrote of my hopes for a great future harvest at Oak Landing, of a season which would see ripening in both its vegetable and its human product. I needed, then, to portray this green and growing time as a period only of promise. Of the blights that might come—of worms or weeds, of weather or of war—I chose to think little and say less. I felt I had no choice then but to take the time on trust.

CHAPTER NINE

First Blossom

Oak Landing, May 10, 1862

My dear,

There was great celebration here today. It would have been a notable day in any case, for we were at last to see the ginned and baled cotton loaded safely aboard ship and headed to market. The bales had been hauled down to the landing more than a week ago, but too much gunboat activity on the river made it impossible for a steamer to fetch them away, and every day that passed we feared a visit from the irregulars, who love nothing more than to see the labor of months set swiftly alight, or else bales slashed and spilled into the river. But the boat came, and the cotton departed, and there was much merry making, which only became more intense with the unlooked for arrival of a second boat, the Mary Lou, which you will by now have guessed contained the cargo secured by your good offices. How I wish you and our generous donors could have seen the faces light with joy and disbelief as the kegs of molasses, the barrels of salt and herring, the soaps, the threads and yarns, the slates and copy books, the cases of dried herbs and simples, but especially the boxes of good used clothing. You would have blushed to see the women trying on skirts and prancing about like peacocks, as if these plain things were Paris gowns. I was gladdened to see such a good store of medicines, for the hot season grows increasingly unwholesome and agues are a constant threat. Every one of us had some

cause for smiles and exclamations as the cargo was unloaded from
the ship and the contents of each box disclosed.

I did not write to her of the one face not smiling. Mr. Canning stood
so glum throughout the whole proceeding that I could not fathom
his sour mood, and finally had to ask him. He answered through
tight lips, "This is an extravagant liberality. You do no kindness to
the Negroes."

"But, Ethan," I exclaimed (we had resorted to first names by now,
not out of any affection but simply from the necessary intimacies of
our proximity). "You sanctioned this. You encouraged me to seek
this charity . . ."

"Yes. But I did not expect you to succeed in this degree. These
people must learn that as they are paid, so, too, must they pay in
turn to satisfy their wants. Yes, yes; I sanctioned some small relief effort, since we are not yet in a position to pay their wages—but this is
beyond anything I imagined. No one I know in Illinois would give
quality goods like this—and in such abundance!—to Negroes, in
wartime, when there are whites in want."

"Well, perhaps you need to widen your acquaintance in Illinois,"
I replied, and walked off so as not to give way to my annoyance.
Some of my female pupils were beckoning me, in any case, wanting
me to admire how they looked in their new garments. In truth, the
clothes were serviceable cambrics and denims that any working
man or women might wear—hardly finery—and yet every garment
had been carefully laundered and mended before being packed up to
send. In that, I thought I saw the kind attentions of my own dear little women, led by their remarkable mother. Who but she would
have thought of such details?

If Ethan Canning thought this small easing of want would make
the Negroes profligate, he need only have seen how they husbanded
the most wretched tatter of a shirt or pair of kneeless pants as they

exchanged their old clothes for the new ones. Even the most ragged things were folded and tucked away, no doubt to be reborn at some later date as patches in a warming quilt.

Marmee had often remarked on the African love of color and bright pattern, for we had had to convince more than one female "package" passing through our station that a rutilant shawl was not perhaps the best choice for someone hoping to avoid notice. But in this shipment, among the workaday necessities, she had included a good number of kerchiefs made, it seemed, from retired ball gowns, in exactly the vibrant hues and coruscating fabrics that she knew would be most appreciated.

I chose one of these for Zannah, who was hanging back with her usual shyness, away to the side of the noisy, laughing group of women. I picked out a satin square in a rich turquoise, and walked it over to where she was standing. "This, I think, would look very well on you." She took it, and within seconds had tied it in an elaborate and very fetching topknot. Jimse was at her side, as usual, and now he clamored to be lifted for a better view of his fine mama. I scooped him up, enjoying the sweet sound of his laughter. He clapped his little hands, healed now save for a cobweb of white scar tissue that threaded across his palm, and held them out to his mother, who reached for him with that tic of a swift smile and embraced him with her usual nestling caress.

Canning had promised the Negroes a night's liberty to engage in what he called their "savage frolics" in celebration of the cotton shipment. And celebrate they did, long into the night. The trash gangs had cleared mounds of cotton stalks from the fields, and these they used for a great bonfire. I could see the sparks of it flying high into the sky from my place near the gin house. It was a still night, so their music carried all the long way from the slave cabins. From my lonely bed of cotton seed, I listened to the singing: one clear, resonant voice, and then another, rising and falling, being answered by a rich chorus. It was full of life and rhythm, but also full of longing. The sound of it awakened my own longings and I became lonely and unaccountably sad. When I finally drifted to sleep, they were singing still. The sound of it must have entered my dreams. I thought I was being hunted down by unseen pursuers, and when they caught up with me, I woke, my heart pounding, and the piece of sacking I used for my pillow wet with tears that I did not remember having shed.

Things changed, after that shipment. I had conducted a burial every week since my arrival—three in my second grim week, including a stillborn and the poor girl I had seen in the sick-house, aflame with childbed fever—and to this duty I did not expect to see any sudden end, for the agues increased with the warming weather. But draughts of jalap and chamomile tea, along with the slight improvements to their diet the goods had offered, worked on the bodies of the ill so that some few of the less grave cases began to experience a return of vigor.

The larger change was with the laborers. Having seen even a small return on their effort, they set to their tasks with a new willingness. The work in the field resembled a stately procession. Plow gangs led the march, tossing the soil to either side to make a long mound. Across its top, a mule-drawn bull-tongue followed. Zannah, one of the sowers, walked behind this, hauling a bag of seed as big as she was, and casting it liberally into the fresh trench. Behind the sowers, in turn, followed a small harrow, covering the seed with rich soil. By the time the last field was sown, the earliest planted already hazed the red earth with a green mist. The rate of growth was a small miracle to one who had farmed in the cool spare soils of the North.

And there were other little miracles. A silver candlestick replaced our potato light at dinner. Thomas, the beekeeper, had suddenly come upon it while robbing one of the hives. "Someone," he reported, must have cleverly concealed it there from the looting rebs, and then "forgot" having done so. The candelabrum, and our grateful and nonpunitive response to its emergence, seemed to jog other memories: the porcelain dinnerware, it seemed, had been guarded well under the nests of our broody hens, while two settings–oddly, only two–from the silver service were recovered from underneath the pigs' slop trough.

To my relief, Canning took this with good-humored amusement. The goods, after all, were not his own, and had been "hidden for safekeeping" long before he arrived here. Although a hard and ungenerous man, he was, at heart, a fair-minded one, and he saw and was grateful for the honest effort the workers were making as the cotton plants emerged.

Within a fortnight from the last seed going in, the ridges were a mass of solid greenery. There were hundreds, thousands, of plants. Cotton seed being considered of no great value, it is scattered thickly– more than twenty or thirty times, I judged, above what was necessary. And so came the scrapers, the most skillful piece of manual labor I think I have ever seen. Armed only with their indelicate hoes, these surgeons of the field moved through the thickets of growth, pausing every two feet, selecting just one delicate shoot, swishing and slashing away all others. By nightfall we could look down the ranks of young cotton plants, perfectly aligned, stretching as far as the eye could see.

Weeding now became the daily chore, and all hands were pressed into service to keep ahead of rampant grasses, vines, and wildflowers that daily threatened to choke the favored plants out of existence. With industry and a few more weeks, the cotton began to overtop its rivals, and cast enough shade to stall their growth. All we had to do was await July and the sighting of the first bloom. I say "all" but of course there were food crops always demanding attention, chief among these the corn, of which we hoped to have a surfeit to sell. So no one idled, and I had pupils who often came to me bone weary in body, but never in spirit.

I had become concerned about Canning, who never ceased to drive himself as relentlessly as he drove his workers. He was drawn and spare, his limp growing more pronounced day by day, so that he now resorted to a whittled stick to assist his movements up and down the rows. He was awaiting, I knew, the factor's report and the proceeds from our sold cotton. The yield had been appallingly low compared with expectations for the property. Too much had been lost to weather and neglect. Acres that could yield two hundred pounds of lint cotton had given only a quarter as much. Still, prices were driven higher by scarcity, and Canning's mood veered from hopefulness to despair, calculating and recalculating inputs and wages and subtracting these from his hypothetical takings. When the factor's payment finally arrived by steamer, Canning retreated to the parlor to make a true accounting. He emerged with his ledger, the cash bag, and a wan expression.

"Mrs. Croft will be obliged to make some economies this year," he said with a tight and cheerless smile. "After I distribute payments to the Negroes she will have a pittance, and I . . ." He trailed off. I followed him outside, where he instructed the house servant Ptolemy to ring the bell to bring the laborers to muster.

"Whatever disappointments you are feeling," I said, keeping pace with his swift limp through the yard and along the fence line of the field beyond, "I feel obliged to remind you that this is an extraordinary day for these men and women. It would be a good thing for future relations if you were able to bring yourself to an appearance of good humor as you make these payments, if only for the sake of the next harvest relations."

Canning scowled. "You're right, of course. I must." We had reached the rise above the largest cotton field. He spread out a hand to take in the vista of promised abundance. "All my hopes lie there. This is the crop that will make me or break me."

The Negroes were setting down tools and coming from all directions. We fell in with the weeding gang. The little girl Cilla, who reminded me of a dark image of my Amy, came charging along the rows crying out gleefully. When she drew up with us, panting, she reached into her wild fuzz of hair and drew out a delicate, creamy-petaled flower. "'S for you, marse," she said, suddenly shy, holding it out to Canning. "First blossom!" Canning gave a slight smile and extended a hand to give the little head a tentative pat.

When we reached the quarters, the crowd gathered there was abuzz with low chatter. Canning took a roll call, and then, to my surprise, called upon me to offer a prayer of thanksgiving. It was the kind of gesture I had not expected of him. My prayer was heartfelt. While emancipation was not yet the law of the land, I said, the people of Oak Landing were about to taste one of the fruits of liberty, and I prayed that the day of total freedom might be close at hand. The assembled cried out "Amen!" and "Praise the Lord!" and like expostulations. Then Canning set to, calling laborers by name and handing them greenbacks. Every man scraped his foot behind, and each woman dropped a curtsy as they took their wages from Canning's hand. Some kissed the money, others held it aloft and danced a little jig. By the time we reached the end of the disbursements, the sun was easing down.

There was a slight stir among the men. Jesse, my best pupil, an enormous man with a voice resonant as the deep notes of a pipe organ, came forward and stood before Canning and myself, his eyes downcast. "The folk is axing me to say that we got something we wants to give you now."

Canning looked confused. I smiled at Jesse reassuringly and said, "That's very kind. What is that?" He turned then and gestured to the assembled people. About half of them scattered into their cabins and came out dragging the fat hessian sacks they used as mattresses. Jesse's son dropped the first one at his father's feet and handed him a scythe. Jesse swept the blade against the string closure so that the roughly sewn seam split. Out foamed cotton: the best long staple the property produced. All down the row, people were dragging out similar fat mattresses.

"When the missus left us," Jesse said, "and the rebs got wind she done signed the Union 'tection papers, they come through an' ordered us to set a-fire to all the bales on the place. Well, we ain't got no choice on it. We done burned maybe a hunnerd bales of Mrs. Croft's cotton that time. But when they wasn't looking we threw the husks or the moss out of our bedding and stuffed in the best of the crop. I think we saved maybe six, eight bales here. Since you bin fair with us and done like you promise, we's giving it over to you."

I had never seen Canning's narrow, rodent face so full of emotion. He pulled off his glasses and worried at his eyes. I realized he was weeping, with gratitude or relief, I could not tell.

"Thank you," he said finally, when he had command of his voice. "Thank you all! Curfew is lifted tonight. You may celebrate as late as you wish." Canning was turning to go when Jesse spoke up again. "The folk is axing if you gentlemens would join us for the shout," he said. I looked at Canning. To my pleasure and relief he gave a slight smile and nodded. I answered with genuine enthusiasm. "I would be honored."

I did not know then that the night would transport me across the seas to some jungle clearing in western Africa, and back into a time beyond the reach of my own past, my own God. I know that what I saw and heard and felt in my body was stirring beyond measure. Yet try as I may, I cannot convey the fullness of the thing in words.

They had brought out a pair of rickety stools for Canning and me to sit upon. As the sun set, streaking the sky all golden and scarlet and indigo, they lit their bonfire and gathered in a wide circle. Someone picked up a pair of old broomsticks and began beating them, one upon the other, in an accelerating, complex rhythm. One by one, the people took up this rhythm in their stomping feet, and began to shuffle around the circle. A voice, Jesse's voice at first, then others, rose to lead the shout, and the crowd answered with the deep rumble of an assenting hum. It was, truly, a shout: ragged, raw, almost tuneless, as unlike as could be to their sweet-toned singing. There were phrases, some repeated many times. Hands began clapping in yet another fast rhythm, quite counter to the feet, and counter also to the fast-beating broomsticks. I did not know how they managed this—children, old people, and young, all of them in unison. I could not tell all the words that were shouted, but these few I caught:

"By myself . . . by myself . . . tonight . . . you know I got to go . . . chariot comin' down . . . oh my Lord . . . oh when when when . . ."

Something about the intense, rapid rhythm began to work inside me, making my heart seem to beat faster. I became excited, thrilled, so that I was on my feet and swaying rapidly without even the thought that I had meant to rise registering in my mind. My mind became hollow as a gourd, emptied of all thought. Somehow, I have no idea how, I found myself in the circle, shuffling, clapping, adding my voice to the other raised voices until my throat was raw. I have no idea how much time passed this way, but when I finally fell out of the dance, soaked in my own sweat, my muscles spent and trembling, I looked around for Canning. His stool was empty and he was nowhere to be seen.

CHAPTER TEN

Saddleback Fever

I woke, as usual, to the clanging of the work bell, but on this day the sound landed like a blow against my eardrums. I opened my eyes, and even the wan half-light through the cracks of the storehouse boards seemed too bright to bear. When I tried to turn over, away from the stabbing fingers of dawn, my muscles rebelled at the effort and I found I could not lift even my shoulder.

I felt foolish. The sinews of a forty-year-old chaplain clearly weren't made for all-night revels devised by the fit bodies of field hands. I began an inventory of the damage done. Head, aching. Eyes, smarting. Throat, raw as a rasp. I gathered my will and commanded my body to rise, but when I moved my joints it was as if the bone scraped in sockets filled with ground glass. And I was shivering, when usually I woke misted with sweat from the heat of these midsummer nights. There was nothing for it, I thought, grasping my coverlet about me with aching fingers. I would have to rest just a little longer until I could gather my strength . . .

I lay there, slipping in and out of an uncomfortable doze, until the shivering turned to a fever that rose so high it sent me delirious. For the details of what happened next I am obliged to the accounts of others.

When Canning heard I had not presented myself at the schoolroom, he laughed, thinking I was sleeping off nothing worse than my own foolish excess, and came to seek me out to make some jests at my expense. He was, according to all accounts, in unaccustomed high spirits, having calculated that the extra bales of fine cotton staple would be sufficient to cover his indebtedness. Whatever the fate of the crop now in the field, he no longer faced the prospect of slinking away from Oak Landing at the end of his lease financially ruined. Now he could look at the new crop, growing robustly, with equanimity. Whatever happened, it could not break him, and it might yet send him home to Illinois a wealthy young man. I saw in him, for the first time, an image of myself as the young peddler, returning home from the South in triumph.

He came to the storeroom at noontime, on his way from the fields to the house, and flung open the door with a hearty hello, deliberately letting the bright noon sunlight fall full across my face. When it revealed my state, the jests died on his lips. He strode quickly to my side, dropped to his haunches, and laid a hand on my brow, snatching it back immediately as if my flesh scorched him. "Bring cold water!" he cried. "Saddle Aster! Mr. March is most gravely ill!"

Instructing Ptolemy to bathe me and enlisting several children to wield fans that might help bring down my fever, Canning galloped all the way to Waterbank and demanded to see the Union medic. When told that the gentleman was not at home to him, he barged into the officers' mess and insisted that the surgeon attend me, arguing that as I still held the rank of captain in the Union army, he, as army surgeon, was responsible for my care. But the doctor apparently had as little time for "nigger lovers" as he had for the oppressed race itself, and would not budge from his repast. He opined that I had contracted river ague, the commonest of the region's summer afflictions. He sent Canning off with a bottle of turpentine and instructions to administer it in small doses. When Canning asked for how long, the medic shrugged. "Till he improves—or until it kills him," and turned back to his plate.

Apparently, the only effect of the turpentine was to induce violent vomiting. I lay delirious, moaning and thrashing, for two days, but during the second night the fever broke and I fell into a healthy sleep. When I woke the next morning, the child Cilla was crouched, asleep, in the corner. She woke with a start, and then a radiant smile, when I sat up on my pallet. It seemed that a roster of my pupils had sat watch over me, placing quilts when I had the chills, bathing me with tansy-infused well water when the fever rose. When I adjusted my coverlid, a sprinkling of small round seeds rolled to the floor. "They's mustard seed," she said, her eyes wide. "Zannah done scattered them on you, every night, to keep the witch hag 'way." She dropped her voice to a whisper. "She wait till Marse Canning leave you, late at night, for the marse doan hold with notions 'bout witches." Jesse confirmed that Canning had spent many hours at my bedside. I received this news, and its evidence of concerned affection, with the easy tears of the convalescent, embarrassing myself and Jesse both.

That first day, I reveled in my recovery, feeling fortunate that the ague, if fierce, had been but brief. Jesse had been obliged to carry me, so enfeebled was I, to a much-mended wicker chaise placed on the shady, shuttered loggia. I sat there, enjoying the simple pleasure of wellness, and the leisure of scratching out a few lines home.

You must not think, my dearest dear, that because my letters are not so frequent these last weeks, my thoughts of you are any less than constant. You are before me the first moment I awaken and the last before I sleep, and often you, or one or other of my little women, or all in merry concert, visit in my dreams. I am wearing the set of shirts made by the dear hands of our Meg, and each time I put them on I see the fine white hands that toiled so in their making, and if I could, I would place a tender kiss on each dear finger.

Will you think less of me if I lay the blame for my slowing correspondence not on any large matter of war or policy, but indeed upon a very small excuse?

I speak of the mosquito, which is become so horrible a plague here that I cannot generally write anything at all in the evening, when I have the leisure and was used to do it. I tried getting under the net I had fixed to the rafters to protect my sleep from these marauding fiends, but my candle set the thing aflame and you would have laughed to see me dancing a jig as I tried to stomp it out. You could say that my words to you on that occasion were warm ones!

So, while I have the rare pleasure of a daylight hour at my disposal, I want to give you an idea of what I see as I walk the fields here now. The cotton has come into full blossom. The shy flowers open in the night, a delicate creamy white that seems to emit its own light, or reflect the moon glow. The blooms are glorious through the morning, but by noon the relentless heat has proved too much, and the petals begin to wilt and decay. By the following day they are russet and by afternoon have fallen, leaving the tiny nugget they call a "form," which ripens to the boll. Very soon—too soon, it seems to those whose toil it is—we must begin to organize the gangs for picking. The extreme lateness of the prior crop has left the people with too little respite, I fear; they are not ready to be plunged so soon into another round of such relentless work. And we have many ill of ague. It is the season for it.

Since I was recovered, I saw no reason to alarm her with the news that I had been among its victims. Indeed, I was thinking whether to strike out the last two sentences, when a clattering on the drive distracted me. I raised a hand to greet Canning, who had taken the cart into Waterbank to fetch some few supplies—the poor imitation of coffee and some rusty bread and, for his sole consumption, the pickled beef he referred to disparagingly as "salt horse," and complained of, but said he must have, since there was only so much pork meat a Northern man could stomach.

Canning had been in fine spirits when he left, jubilant about my recovery and newly optimistic about the world at large. So I was surprised to see his face pinched again into its former frowns as he limped up the drive, kicking angrily at the weeds grown up between the gravel stones.

"Ethan, whatever is the matter?" I asked.

He pulled off his riding gloves and slapped them furiously against his palm. "They are drawing down the garrison at Waterbank. By month's end the Union presence will be reduced to company strength."

"But . . . are you sure of this? Perhaps it is only a feint to mislead the rebels?"

He shook his head. "I am perfectly sure," he replied.

"But what madness is this? There was little enough cavalry there already. We are not the only lessees in the area. What is the decision based upon?"

"What do you think it is based upon?" he snapped. "It is based upon the fact that this war is being lost, because Lincoln's generals are the most incompetent ever to lead an army on the field of battle!" Ptolemy had appeared at his side with a pitcher of water. Canning took the proffered cup with such an impatient gesture that the handle slid from his grip and the cup shattered on the bricks at his feet. He turned, about to abuse the stooped old man. I rose, with difficulty, and moved between them.

"Ethan," I said softly. "Please contain yourself. I know this is a disappointment . . ."

"Disappointment! It is utter ruin! How long do you think before the irregulars—or even the regular Confederate forces—set about retaking every inch of this rich country? They will know how to value it, I assure you, even if our side does not . . ."

Ptolemy was on his knees, picking up the broken shards. I could see his hands trembling beyond his usual palsy. I motioned my head toward him and raised a hand to my lips. The last thing we wanted to provoke was a general panic in the quarters. Canning caught my meaning. "Of course," he said quickly, "Union forces dominate the river. The Confederates will not dare to attack a property like this one, in range of the gunboats, whether Waterbank is fully garrisoned or no."

I assented warmly. "So there's really no cause for concern," I said. Ptolemy got up, creakily, the pieces of broken pottery rattling in his hands. He turned toward the house, but not before I saw his face, which was thatched with worry.

"Of course, I went to see the colonel, who counseled that we put an overseer in place here, rent premises in Waterbank, near the barracks of the rump force, and take counsel regarding enemy movements before hazarding a brief daily visit."

"Well," I said, "the risk of a raid is higher by night, and I am sure a man like Zeke, who you say has ties to the guerrillas, might be a safe choice for overseer—"

He cut me off angrily. "How long do you think these people would keep their hand to the plow under the direction of one of their own? How long do you think before my mules 'wandered off' to be profitably sold, or the hogs turned themselves into hams and vanished down greedy gullets? No; it is folly to leave, and yet imprudent to stay. You, however, may do as you like. Perhaps you can continue to scold these people into a little learning from a safe distance; I cannot run a plantation that way."

"Ethan," I said quietly. "Do not think I am any less committed to my crop than you are to yours. I am working for a harvest, too; did you not know? In any case, if you think I would abandon you here, to face danger alone, you have not come to know me very well these past months . . ."

Once again, my labile convalescent emotions betrayed me, and my voice broke. Canning's face softened. He gave me his arm. "You shouldn't be standing," he said, easing me back into the wicker chair, which groaned as I sat. "Has Ptolemy brought you anything to eat?" he asked. "You must get your strength back. I shall have him bring you something from our delicious 'fresh' supplies," he said, and managed a wan grin.

He limped off into the house. I listened to him giving orders for the cart to be unloaded. I turned to my lap desk, but I was too distracted to continue my letter in any meaningful way. The end of the month, Canning had said. Two weeks. And then we should see.

I was back in my schoolroom for an hour or two the following day, although I was obliged to ride a mule to and from, and to sit throughout the giving of lessons. My pupils were touchingly glad to see me back, and even more anxious than usual to do their best. At the end of the class, Jesse helped me onto the mule. One of the children had been instructed to walk with me, to bring the mule back to the fields when I had done with it, and a cluster of them was arguing over who should have this privilege, when Jesse shooed them all away and took the bridle himself. When we were a little distance from the others, he spoke in a low voice.

"I just wanted to ax you, is you and Marse Canning fixing to stay here . . . ?"

"Well of course, Jesse; why ever not?"

He looked at me then, his dark eyes very bloodshot. "I think you knows why not." I did not reply, and we plodded on. The heat of late afternoon closed in around us like an animate thing; you could feel it on your skin, warm and moist, like a great beast panting. The air was so dense it seemed to require a huge effort even to inhale it. It lay thick in the lungs and seemed to give no refreshment. The thrumming and buzz of insects filled the silence between us. When

I continued to say nothing, Jesse mumbled, his eyes on the ground. "If they come, they'll kill you, and that a fact."

"Is it?" I said. "I think that's a rather extreme assumption. First, the Union forces in Waterbank are not withdrawing completely. Second, the Union presence on the river is strong. And third, Mr. Canning and I are noncombatants—you know what that means?"

"Means you don't got no gun to 'tect youself."

"Jesse, the Confederate soldier is a hard and desperate fighter, but he is not a savage. There are rules, even in war . . ."

He stopped then and gave me a look of the kind I had become all too familiar with in the course of my life, a look that combined pity and exasperation. "Marse, them men round here what hides out in the woods—they's thicker'n fleas in there—they ain't even rightly in the army, and they sure enough don't follow no rules. The folk in the quarters, them ones what ain't from here—the folk what got sent on up here from that camp at Darwin's Bend—they's scared. For us who's from Oak Landing, we knows those boys and they knows us, and likely they'll just burn the cotton and let us be if we says we ain't a-plantin' no mo'. But those that ain't from here, well, some's talking 'bout running off from here 'fore they get sold on off someplace."

I did not know what to say to this. I had no way of knowing whether such fears were well founded. I could hardly counsel people to abandon Mr. Canning, but neither could I exhort them to stay if they were right to think their liberty imperiled. We had reached the garden. The mule brushed against an overhanging branch of crape myrtle and loosed a cascade of pink blossoms upon us. I managed to dismount unassisted and handed the bridle to Jesse.

He turned to take the mule back to the fields. The shaggy petals lay in his hair like a garland. He looked back over his shoulder and regarded me sadly. "I was you, Marse March, I'd git on aways from here, and take the young marse wit you."

I meant to raise the subject with Canning over dinner, but he came in looking gray and rubbing at his chest as if it pained him. Saying he had no appetite, he went to lie down. I ate my hominy and some salat leaves I'd plucked for myself, and went off to my bed still troubled by Jesse's words. That night I began a little project: scooping out a tunnel in the pile of cotton seed that stood mounded upon the storeroom floor, and shoring it up with filled sacks. Eventually, I had scraped out a retreat sufficient to hide me and my few effects. I placed a canteen full of water there, and a quantity of hardtack. I masked the small entryway with an empty molasses barrel. From the inside, I could shift a single sack, and a fall of loose seed in front of it would mask the way in entirely. If the guerrillas did come, I could hunt my hole.

As I mounted the mule to go to my classroom the next day, Canning, who was usually in the fields by that hour, limped up to me, his face as creased as a rumpled bed. He looked as though he hadn't slept. "I'm going into Waterbank again," he said. "I have to try and hire some kind of guards—perhaps I can get the mulattos who were working at the post—I can't have the Negroes getting it into their heads to run off."

"Ethan! You cannot be serious!"

He looked at me quizzically.

"What on earth are you thinking? For one thing, may I remind you that you have absolutely no right to hold these people here under some kind of arrest. You are not their master, no matter what they call you. And for another thing, if you want to provoke a mass flight, I can't think of a better way to do it than to show that you are so scared of what's coming that you've run out and hired guards. Do you seriously think that two or three lightly armed mulattos will be enough to hold upward of a hundred people here if they take it into their heads to flee? You must be sunstruck."

I had never spoken to him so harshly before, even at the height of our many disagreements. He looked at me, and the bantam cock arrogance seemed to drain right out of him.

"I hadn't thought of it like that . . . I mean to say, I see what you . . ." Suddenly, he looked very young.

I changed my tone and reached out to lay a hand on his shoulder. "What will come, will come," I said gently. "And we will face it together."

And so July waned, and the drawdown at the Waterbank post took place as expected, but the locality remained quiet, with no reports of pronounced increase in guerrilla activity. As day followed upon uneventful day, we went about our various tasks of pencil and plow, and tried not to think about our vulnerability. In the first week of August I lost three more days to fever delirium, and when I recovered it was to the grim realization that I might never be quite well again. For it was now clear that I had not the common river ague, but saddleback fever, named because a period of health is just a temporary respite between the spikes of recurring debility. Yet dejection need not always partner with despair. For me, the knowlege of my fragile state proved a prod to greater efforts in the classroom. If my time was to be shortened by ill health, then all the more need to impart some useful learning to my eager charges. I worked them hard, and they did not complain.

The Darwin's Bend Negroes had not, after all, run off: perhaps because they feared the uncertainties of the road more than the uncertainties of staying. Men and women who had been refugees once did not relish experiencing that state again. They knew firsthand the dangers that stood between them and any scant sanctuary they might find behind Union lines; they also knew the squalor and disorganization of the contraband camps that awaited them there. Or perhaps they stayed because they had liked the experience of earn-ing wages for their work, and were unwilling to abandon the monies due them at the nearing harvest. Perhaps they stayed because they had come to trust us and put their faith in our decision not to flee.

There is a vividness to seasons lived as we lived that summer. Even as we pursued our routines and went about our tasks, the medium in which we moved had been stirred. A rat's tooth of uneasiness gnawed at me, and at Canning, and I am certain that the field hands felt it, too.

I recognized the tokens of the time, because I had lived through just such another uneasy season, when every day was tainted by the foul breath of a fear that could not be faced forthrightly, yet could not be ignored.

CHAPTER ELEVEN

Tolling Bells

Are there any two words in all of the English language more closely twinned than *courage* and *cowardice?* I do not think there is a man alive who will not yearn to possess the former and dread to be accused of the latter. One is held to be the apogee of man's character, the other its nadir. And yet, to me, the two sit side by side on the circle of life, removed from each other by the merest degree of arc.

Who is the brave man—he who feels no fear? If so, then bravery is but a polite term for a mind devoid of rationality and imagination. The brave man, the real hero, quakes with terror, sweats, feels his very bowels betray him, and in spite of this moves forward to do the act he dreads. And yet I do not think it heroic to march into fields of fire, whipped on one's way only by fear of being called craven. Sometimes, true courage requires inaction; that one sit at home while war rages, if by doing so one satisfies the quiet voice of honorable conscience.

In Concord, because of our work in the Underground Railroad, we had come to know many who fit the latter description. Mostly they were Quakers, whose abolitionism and pacifism sprang from the selfsame core belief: there is that of God in every person, and therefore you may not enslave any man, and neither may you kill him, even to liberate the enslaved.

And then, in October of 1859, John Brown, supported wittingly or unwittingly by Quakers and others who deplored violence, killed to liberate. Brown had three of his sons among the twenty men he led in an attack on the federal arsenal at Harper's Ferry in Virginia. He expected the slaves in the surrounding area to rise up in rebellion as soon as they heard of his act. He had the weapons—a thousand spears, wagon loads of Sharps rifles and pistols—waiting for them. I felt ill when I learned that the first to be mortally wounded by Brown's men was no slave owner, but Hayward Shepherd, a free black man who worked as railway baggage master. But Brown's "bees," as he described the slaves he believed would flock to his banner, failed to swarm. Two of his sons and several other followers were killed; he was wounded and taken prisoner.

I had absolved Brown, long ago, for the loss of my fortune; I had schooled myself to look back on the episode without bitterness or blame. But I had advanced him money to free human beings, not to slaughter them. I knew I could not forgive, if my innocent ties to Brown implicated me in such killings, and proved the means of undoing the blessed bonds of my family.

I soon learned that I was not alone in my anxiety. Young Frank Sanborn, our Concord schoolmaster, had been more closely bound up in Brown's plans than I ever imagined. Sanborn had been about to lead his annual school chestnut hunt; instead, when a fugitive from the raid turned up unexpectedly at his door seeking sanctuary, he handed the man over to Henry Thoreau and fled the village in panic, saying there were a thousand better ways to continue the antislavery struggle than by risking arrest and extradition to Virginia.

Sanborn's assistance to Brown was recent, mine was years behind me. Still, I walked through my life warily, as a man might walk along a cliff edge in a fog. Someone's money had bought the crates of Sharps rifles for John Brown, and Southerners were baying to know whose.

In the evenings, with my family gathered in our parlor, fear soured what had been my sweetest hours. I could hardly give myself over to the pleasure of regarding the brown and golden heads bent over sketchbook or journal, Jo's lush hair tumbling from her snood in lawless strands, Amy's curls arranged self-consciously about her little shoulders; my kindly Mouse, Beth, talking softly to her kittens; Meg and Marmee collaborating on a piece of needlework. I would gaze on them all, then look away, feeling a premonition of separation. My imagination did not then compass the truth: that it would be I who would choose to sever those sacred ties and bring about a separation whose end none of us would be able to foresee.

Others in my predicament did more than simply fret. The wealthy Quaker Gerrit Smith, who had long been Brown's greatest benefactor, arranged to have his friends commit him to an insane asylum so as to be beyond the reach of the Southern inquisitors. Sanborn went to Canada; Frederick Douglass took ship for England. Did these men act the part of cowards? I did not think so, even though Douglass wrote self-deprecatingly that he had "always been more distinguished for running than fighting, and by the Harper's Ferry test, I am most miserably deficient in courage."

If the Southerners had killed Brown on the streets of Harper's Ferry, or hanged him expeditiously in the week after the raid, I am convinced he would have been but a footnote to history. *Mad, misguided:* these were among the kindest things first said about him, even in the abolitionist press. But Brown brilliantly used his final weeks on earth. By the time he reached his executioner in early December, his demeanor in captivity, his address in court, the kiss placed on the brow of the slave child as he walked to the gallows—all these had changed the world's view of him.

When the news of the raid first reached us, our town was as divided over it as the nation. Henry Thoreau, alone of all of us, was immedately prepared to articulate the case for Brown. Indeed, he became obsessed with it, and declared he would speak at the town hall. All of us, even Waldo, counseled him not to. His reply was typically terse: "I did not send to you for advice, but to announce I am to speak." When the town selectmen refused to ring the bell to signal commencement of his lecture, Henry tolled it himself. It was one of the most passionate orations I ever heard from him, and one he was asked to give at many venues in the following weeks, on each occasion shifting the ground beneath his audience. "Some eighteen hundred years ago Christ was crucified; this morning, perchance, Captain Brown was hung. These are two ends of a chain not without its links." Well, I thought, as I listened, Christ never killed anyone in order to earn his death sentence. But as I looked around at the rapt faces in the hall, I realized that the ardor of Henry's argument was carrying them past any such defects of logic. "He is not Old Brown any longer," Henry proclaimed. "He is an angel of light . . ." By the time we gathered again at the town hall, on the unseasonable, almost sultry day when Brown was actually executed, his transfiguration from madman to martyr had been effected, and Henry's characterization had become a commonplace view.

The view from the South was very different. If a Northerner such as Brown was prepared to kill fellow whites, regardless of whether they owned slaves or not, and was canonized for it, then war was as good as declared. Southerners began to vilify Northerners long settled amongst them; a mob took one itinerant young peddler such as I had been, cried out that "Northern nigger lovers should be painted nigger-color," covered the youth with tar, and drove him from their town. Slaves, meanwhile, found the noose of their captivity drawn even tighter around their necks; free Negroes lost their liberty of movement.

One immediate result was a slowdown in the number of "packages" reaching Concord via the Underground Railroad. I will be blunt: I was glad of it. I did not want to risk any brush with the law, at this time, for this cause. But I knew better than to voice my fears to Marmee. She fretted at this loss of our small work for freedom. Our "line" was one of almost half a dozen that ran from Boston Harbor, where a schooner, supposedly a fishing and pleasure vessel, actually served as transport for escaping slaves. Sometimes, too, stowaways found their own way north by ship. Several homes in our village served as stations, and hence conductors conveyed the packages west to Leominster and Fitchburg, where the trains ran to waiting friends in Canada. We were required only to supply a night of food, shelter, and safekeeping while the transportation could be arranged. In normal times, we might see two or three packages a month. My girls had grown accustomed to welcoming a strange black face at our table. From earliest childhood, they were schooled in the need for tact within the home and circumspection outside of it. Only once, when Amy was very little, had I caught her boasting to a small friend about the hidey-hole at the top of the stairs. That evening, when we gathered in the parlor for our reading, I set aside Spenser in favor of *Uncle Tom's Cabin; or Life Among the Lowly.* Before we were very few chapters into the book, my little one's hyacinth eyes brimmed with tears of compassion, and I had to say no more to her about guarding her tongue.

I suppose we had helped some threescore people, all told: mostly young men, a few couples, but only on two occasions a woman making the perilous journey alone. These, to me, were the most poignant. One's imagination reeled, conceiving what degree of barbarity would drive a woman to risk the terrors of solo flight.

It was a woman—a girl, rather—who came to us in the early darkness of an icy January evening; the first package since the raid of the previous October. We were gathered around the fire, glad of our ample woodpile, the product of my efforts in the fall forests. When we heard the shake of a harness and the cries of "Whoa!" outside our window, all the girls rushed to lift the curtain to see who could be calling on such a frigid night. They immediately recognized the cart of our friend Mr. Bingham from Boston Harbor, and each of them rushed to do her part. Meg and Beth hurried to the kitchen to warm bread and see if any remnant of the supper's baked apples yet remained. Jo clumped up the stairs, graceless as always, to tend to the bedding in the hidey-hole. Amy took it upon herself to stand with us and do the part of greeter.

Mr. Bingham, muffled to the eyeballs, declined to come in, saying that he would not keep the horse standing in such weather. He and I went out to the cart and pulled back the sacking which concealed our package. The figure that uncurled itself appeared to be a boy, but Mr. Bingham introduced her as Flora, and I realized that the male attire was merely a disguise. When I saw she had no shoes, but just some rags tied around her feet, I offered to carry her up the snowy path. She looked at me with huge dark eyes and then glanced away, embarrassed. I saw that she was shivering, so decided to take that for a yes, and swept her down from the dray. Mr. Bingham was already back up in his seat as we reached the door, and his cry of, "Fare thee well and good luck!" was all but lost under the grind of the cartwheels biting the icy gravel.

She weighed less than Amy, though she was as tall as Meg, and I judged, when I set her down by the fire and got a look at her, about the same age. She was wearing a man's coat several sizes too large, and I guessed that Bingham had provided it. She kept it clutched tight around her, even in the glow of the fire, but she did raise a hand to draw off a rather dirty kepi and a tightly wound muffler, which I imagined had helped in her disguise, for her face was anything but masculine, even framed by the frizz of coarsely barbered, boyish hair. Through drawn and smeared with the grime of her journey, it was a delicate, pretty face, lit by a pair of large, expressive eyes. As Marmee spoke quiet words of welcome and reassurance, Beth offered warmed washcloths, which Flora, giving a little sigh of pleasure, wielded vigorously over her face, hands, and throat. Then she took a glass of steaming chamomile tea, wrapping both hands around it as though embracing the warmth.

Marmee had already noted the deplorable condition of her feet, and quietly whispered to Beth to fetch the rest of the hot water in a basin. She began untying the filth-stiffened rags, only to gasp as a piece of flesh, adhering to the blackened cloth, peeled away from the girl's foot. "Oh my dear, I am so sorry!" Marmee cried. Flora showed no reaction, no sign of pain. She set down the tea and leaned forward, continuing the work of unwrapping the red-raw flesh of her blistered feet. She winced for a second as she eased them into the water, and then calmly accepted the plate of bread and baked apples Meg offered her.

We had all learned long ago not to interrogate our railroad travelers, for reasons pragmatic as well as kind. The people who came to us were often in a sort of trance, brought on by fear, exhaustion, and, I imagined, a kind of mourning for what they had left behind—family, perhaps; friends, likely, and the certainty of all that had ever been familiar. A home in bondage is a home, still, and it is no light matter to leave such a place, knowing that one's act is irrevocable. But Marmee had also explained to me, at the time of our marriage, that the less we knew, the less we could betray, and this was particularly important when our girls were young and details such as a route or a name might innocently have slipped from them, or been prised loose by clever questioning.

So Marmee continued her reassuring words that required no reply, as she dressed the feet with a cool mint salve and bound them in clean bandages. When she held out the fetid rags to be carried away and burned, Amy, who was nearest, took a step backward, her little white hands fluttering behind her back. Marmee cast her a look that could have iced a pond over, and Amy colored, and reached for the bundle, taking care to hold it well away from her spotless pinafore as she carried it from the room.

When Flora had eaten and warmed herself, Marmee and Meg between them supported her to the kitchen, where Hannah had prepared a bath, and from there they helped her up the stairs to her "hole," which Jo had made bright and cozy with candle, quilts, and a bed warmer. Since I could do nothing to help with these female rites, I retired. When Marmee joined me, her face was creased with anguish. She closed the door, then stood with her back pressed to it, her eyes closed. A great sigh shook her.

"Whatever is it, my dear? Is she not comfortable now?"

"Comfortable! I doubt she knows what that word means." She crossed to the bed and flopped down upon it, her fingers working angrily at the strings of her tippet. I reached across to help her, but she batted my hand away and turned to face me. There was something in her face—a trace of the old rage, like a cloud shadow passing swiftly over a sunlit field. "That girl is carrying a child," she said bluntly. "And it's a miracle she is, for her back is all marked with fresh . . ." And at this point her voice broke, and she stopped, and buried her head in my shoulder.

Marmee's great desire was to keep Flora with us through her confinement. She hated the thought of letting her go on, in her condition, to an uncertain future in a new country. Even though her welcome among the free blacks in Canada was assured, that community had few resources. I saw her point, but even setting my own selfish anxieties aside, I could not think it wise. The Fugitive Slave Act hung heavy over every escapee, even in Massachusetts, and I could not condone keeping the girl, and the infant she carried, at daily risk of their being returned to bondage. So we resolved that she should stay with us a fortnight, resting safely while her feet mended, and Marmee set about nursing the little mother-to-be with her own prodigious motherly skills.

In the days that followed, we tried to keep as close to our normal routines as possible so as to attract no unwelcome attention. Meg went to her work with the King children, and that week, for once, I didn't have to chide any overheard grumbles about the difficulties of "running after spoiled midgets all day." Likewise, Jo had no ill words for her aunt's crotchets, and even Amy managed to speak only cheerfully of her vexing schoolmates.

Flora I saw little: despite my soft words to her, she seemed shy of me to the point of fear, and I did not press myself upon her. Given her condition, I could imagine several reasons why she might associate only ill things with white men of my age. But Marmee, too, reported the girl impenetrably withdrawn.

It was our little Mouse, Beth, herself the embodiment of shyness, who was able to break through Flora's carapace and learn a little of what lay within. Beth's poor heath and delicate spirit made her unfit for the world's bustle, and so she went neither to school nor to work, but stayed home and diligently helped Hannah with the household chores, taking what schooling she needed from her mother and me. Flora was not able to leave the house, for fear of being noted by unfriendly eyes—feelings ran hot on this issue, even in Concord, and Brown's raid had raised the temperature. The village was, as well, a stopping place for teamsters, and who knew the opinions of the travelers who frequented the taverns?

Since the weather remained bitter and our visitor needed rest, it hardly seemed a penance for her to remain indoors, but little Beth, who loved Nature in all its seasons, brought fronds of tangy pine and bright holly clusters back with her from her daily walks, and decked Flora's hidey-hole with these reminders of the outdoor world. Sometimes during the day, as I passed by on the stairs, I would hear two soft voices speaking together: Beth's familiar, diffident whispers and then the unfamiliar Southern cadence in reply. I longed to know what they spoke of: Mouse, at eleven years old, had led a completely sheltered life, while this other poor girl, who could be no more than fifteen, had been exposed to the world's most miserable depravities. I feared for my little one's innocence and her peace of mind, and yet to have interfered in their communion would have been unconscionable. My little Miss Tranquillity had a giving soul, and our poor guest surely needed a friend.

In the afternoon, when Flora had been with us three days, I was in my study, reading with interest a new manuscript of Waldo's, on which he had asked me to comment. I barely heard the scratch upon my door, but when it came a second time I raised my head.

"Yes?"

"Father," squeaked Mouse. "May I come in?"

"Of course you may, my darling girl!" I said, setting aside my papers, rising. Such an interruption was most unlike my Beth, and as I didn't want her to feel it unwelcome to me, I moved toward my fireside armchair so that the great cliff of my desk did not stand between us, and gestured for her to sit on my knee.

Her little fist was balled up in her pinafore, worrying the fabric nervously. I took the tiny hand in mine, straightened out and kissed the little fingers, and smiled encouragingly. "What is it, my dear?"

"Well, I know we do not consume milk or cheese any longer, because these are the rightful property of the calf, but I was wondering if you think that the calf might not mind sparing just a little of its milk for Flora, for she is very thin. She has worked since childhood in a factory in Richmond—oh!" Her hand fluttered to her lips. "I wasn't supposed to say that."

"Never mind, my darling, the secret is safe with me. Go on."

She looked at me trustingly. "I know it is, Father." Her smooth brow furrowed. "I always thought, you know, even when we were reading Mrs. Beecher's book, that at least the slaves have the free air and the sunlight and the warm soil to console them. I never thought about factories in the South, or that people might be locked up and enslaved to foul, noisy machines such as Flora describes . . ." Her lit-

tle head drooped and I heard a sniff and passed her my handkerchief. I smoothed the soft brown hair where it parted neatly at the
crown. Presently, she continued. "She walked six days, you know,
before they caught her the first time and dragged her back and gave
her that whipping, and then she contrived to escape again, not a
fortnight after. She is so very brave, Father, and she is bound to have
such hardships ahead of her, and Hannah says custards and so on
would be just the very thing . . ."

"My darling girl, you are quite right, and so very wise to think of
this. Tell Hannah she has a free hand with the provisions as long as
Flora is with us. Whatever she thinks the girl needs, if we can afford
it, she shall have."

Beth beamed at me, slid from my lap, and scurried off to the
kitchen. When she'd gone, I got up and paced, my mind in turmoil.
Memories I had long suppressed came flooding back: memories of a
hot day, a dark barn, and a whip biting into a young woman's bare
flesh. I went to the window and stared out on the bleak, ice-blackened
trees. Anger—at the cruelty, and at my own impotence in the face of it—
roiled within me. Without knowing I did it, I balled my hand into a fist
and brought it down, hard, on the sill. The glass rattled in the frame.

As we were obliged to follow our usual habits as closely as possible,
Marmee and I could not decline every invitation that came our way,
and so we went to luncheon one day in honor of Nathaniel
Hawthorne, who had but lately returned to our village after years
abroad. The talk, still, was of John Brown, and the ongoing hunt, led
by influential Southern politicians in Washington, to locate his co-
conspirators. This, of course, made me uneasy, and all the more so
when Hawthorne, who had been absent during the mellowing of
Northern sentiment, opined that "never had a man been so justly
hung." Every eye in the room turned to me, expecting a passionate
defense of Brown, but I remained mute.

Marmee felt my discomfort, I think, and complained of a slight headache, so that we were among the first to leave. As we walked the short way to our house I held her arm more tightly than usual, and thought of all the times we had walked this way in our years together, and I thought that I would not survive it if I were to be deprived of her companionship. When we arrived at our gate, I saw the pathway churned up by the marks of heavy boots. I hurried up to the door, and when I opened it, I saw Hannah, on all fours, wiping away the muddy tracks that led within.

"Bless us, I'm glad you're back!" she said. "That one's in a right state." She inclined her head to the parlor, where Beth was lying on the sofa, her face blotched with agitation and tears.

"Whatever is the matter!" cried Marmee, running to kneel beside her and feeling her forehead for fever.

"The constable came searching for Flora," Beth said, her voice quavering.

"I weren't here," Hannah interrupted. "I were gone to the market, so the poor child had to face it all alone . . ."

Beth's eyes were welling again, and Marmee wrapped her arms around her. "There, there! It isn't your fault! There's nothing you could have done to save her . . ."

"Ah, but she did save her, and there's the wonder of it," said Hannah, getting heavily to her feet and throwing the muddy rag into the bucket. "Flora's safe, up yonder. Our little mite here set that constable on his road right smart, she did." Hannah beamed at Beth, who was sitting up now, her head resting on Marmee's shoulder. "Who'd a thought she'd a had the courage! I'll make some hot drinks now for you all, you'll be wanting some, I 'spect."

Hannah went out and Marmee gently urged Beth to recount what had happened. In a small voice, she told how the heavy knock had come at the door.

"Flora and I had been playing with the kittens upstairs in my room, but to be safe she went to the hidey-hole while I went down to answer the door, and that was just as well, for the man barged right in, without introduction or by your leave," she said. "He had the loudest, angry-sounding voice. He said he had information that we were sheltering a runaway slave here, so I told him his informant was mistaken."

"Beth!" I exclaimed. I could barely imagine little Mouse talking to a stranger—much less a loud-voiced law officer—and uttering a bald-faced falsehood.

"It wasn't a lie, Father,"she said calmly, as if reading my mind. "I told him I had never seen a slave in this house, and that is the simple truth. Haven't you told us, many times, that there are no slaves in God's eyes? God sees everything, and if he sees no slaves in this house, how can there be any?"

Her mother and I exchanged a look over the top of the little brown head, sharing the happiness of a truly gratifying child.

"He was very rude then, and said he would see that for himself, and made to go up the stairs, but I put myself in his way, and said that before he should see anything, I should be obliged to see his warrant. He turned a strange color, for he hadn't one, and he stomped out."

"Beth," I said. "You are a marvel."

The sad truth was that though the constable would not quickly find a magistrate in Concord to provide a warrant, there were plenty of Massachusetts judges who upheld the Fugitive Slave Act, and gratified as I was by the quality of my joinery, pride in my craftsmanship did not extend to risking Flora's freedom by putting it to the test of a thorough search. So Flora had to leave us, and speedily. I sent Hannah to speak with our friends, and as soon as it was dark, Henry arrived to take her away to Edwin Bigelow, the blacksmith, who would arrange her onward journey. Jo and Meg, who had not returned from their day's employment, didn't even get a chance to say good-bye. There were tears from Beth and Amy, and Marmee and I felt close to shedding a few. Flora herself was dry-eyed, but she embraced Beth before Henry led her out, up over the hill behind our house, and through the wooded paths that threaded a private way to the smith's house.

A year later, we received a letter from the Canadian lady who had taken Flora into service. Flora herself had asked that the letter be written, as she wanted to convey to us that though her baby had not lived, she herself was well. "Despite her natural grief over the fate of her infant," the Canadian lady wrote, "she holds an optimistic view of the future and places her trust in God, whom, she says, would not have delivered her from bondage in Egypt without a plan for her, when he has left so many others in chains. She is an intelligent young woman and I know I need not tell you of her courage and resolve. I am having her taught her letters, so you may expect something from her own hand in the future. I remain, etc."

As it happened, this letter found us just one day after Jefferson Davis surrendered his seat in the Senate of these no longer United States. I read the letter, and then the newspaper, aloud to the girls as we gathered in the parlor. Before Davis's final adieu, I read that he had "told his fellow senators that he felt no hostility, and wished every one of them well. According to a Senate source, he confided that he would spend the night in prayers for peace."

Well, we all of us prayed for peace. But in my heart I expected war. As anxious winter gave way to gloomy spring, it became clear to me that John Brown was right: not in his infliction of blind and indiscriminate terror, but in his prophecy of inevitable bloodshed. For how could one turn the other cheek to this evil, when the cheek one turned was not one's own, but that of innocents, like the girl with the ruined feet and scarred back, who had cowered from the slave catchers in a hole at the top of our stairs?

War came, of course, and in early summer, the young soldiers who were to go south from our village mustered in the Cattle Show grounds. Like others of the citizenry, we walked down to cheer them on their hard road south. Many of the young men knew me, and one cried out: "Don't you have a word for us, Mr. March?" Soon, others took up the cry, and I found myself ushered through a throng of young, eager faces, and assisted onto the precarious pulpit of a fallen log. They were all looking up at me, expectantly, these youngsters who were prepared to peril their lives. I found myself wondering how many of them would return to us. My gaze stopped on a sandy-haired youth who looked pale and pensive. I recognized him. He was the son of a Quaker family. I knew it must have cost him a great struggle of conscience to be here.

"You know that even he whom we call the Prince of Peace once told his followers, 'He that hath no sword, let him sell his garment, and buy one.' Now it has come to that day for us. We did not ask that the evil of war be unleashed upon us, but it has been; and it is well, on such a day, that we reflect on why we go to war, and against what it is that we fight.

"Does not the Bible say, 'We ourselves will go ready armed before the children of Israel, until we have brought them into their place . . . We will not return into our houses until the children of Israel have inherited every man his inheritance.'

"We go because there is within this blessed country an unholy land. A land where it is become a crime to teach God's children God's word. We go, because within this country is a blighted land, where a man *may* put asunder those whom God has joined together. We go because there is in this country a land which one may, which one must, in all reverence, call a *damnable* land, and we must go forth and root out the evil that lies within." Even as I cried out these words, I felt their essential emptiness. What were words, after all, when set beside the action these young men were about to take? Action, now, was all that mattered.

I paused to wipe the sweat from my forehead, and I looked over the bent heads, and saw Marmee, her head held high, looking straight at me with tears in her eyes. She had heard a truth in my words and recognized my intention even before I knew it myself. We held each other's gaze for a long moment. I read the question in her face as clearly as if she shouted it aloud, and I nodded.

I had said "we will go." She knew, even before I did, that I meant it. She lifted her palms in a gesture of assent, as if to put wind beneath my wings. And so I cried out:

"I say 'we,' my friends, because if the army will have me, I propose to go with you." The youths raised their heads then, and made me a great huzzah. I hushed them, and went on. "We will go forth together. And together we will return, God willing, on that great and shining day, when all the children of Israel have come into their inheritance: and that inheritance will be one nation, and that one nation will be forever free!"

I stepped down from the stump, and made my way through the press to Marmee. She was so proud of me that she could not speak, but only took my hand and clasped it, the pressure of her grip hard as a man's.

The village treated me like a hero in the weeks that followed. All the great and the good of Concord came to our house. They took up a collection and presented me with a purse, and everyone wanted to congratulate me. If some thought me imprudent, at my age, to embark upon such an undertaking, only my Aunt March felt free to say so. She called me a vainglorious fool, and an irresponsible father, and predicted I would die down there and leave my family destitute. I thanked her for her honesty and asked for her prayers, if not her blessing.

As it happened, the Concord unit's commander had already assigned its chaplaincy to a clergyman of more orthodox stripe than I. So I did not depart with our own lads; but I had said I would go, and could hardly give back either the purse or the plaudits, and so Reverend Day recommended me to a unit filled with the sons of strangers from the mill towns, and I joined them that autumn, and served them as best I could, although, as I have set down, that tenure was brief. But it has led me here, to this service among the people of Oak Landing.

And now, a year has passed since I undertook to go to war, and I wake every day, sweating, in the solitude of the seed store at Oak Landing, to a condition of uncertainty. More than months, more than miles, now stand between me and that passionate orator perched on his tree-stump pulpit. One day, I hope to go back. To my wife, to my girls, but also to the man of moral certainty that I was that day; that innocent man, who knew with such clear confidence exactly what it was that he was meant to do.

CHAPTER TWELVE

Red Moon

The memory I return to, when I want to block out the images of what came after, is of a shimmering mantle of white so pure it dazzled the eyes.

We were, the Negroes said, uncommonly fortunate. It had been a season without setback, and our crop stood flawless in the fields. They said we would be done picking in time to dance by the light of the full red moon, so named for the color of the orb as it rose in the humid skies at summer's end. We were ready for a great harvest. The telltales were set up at the ends of the rows, the pickers' sacks all mended, the gin house cleaned to receive the new crop. But we never brought the harvest home.

They came even before the first thin shard of the red moon had pierced the horizon. In the silent and piceous hour just before dawn, they advanced at a slow trot, fanning out through the slave quarters and into the yard that divided the gin house, the mill, and the buildings where Canning and I slept unaware.

I think I must have heard something in my sleep, the snort of a horse's breath in the dark, the clink of a stirrup. Something, at any rate, woke me, and I smelled the ripe odor of fresh horse droppings. No horses were stabled nearby. Without pausing to think, I rolled off my pallet and scrambled into my hiding hole. I tugged at the sacking and a tumble of seed whispered into place behind me.

The shiver of breaking timber came minutes later. I heard the complaint of an old hinge giving way, and then the clump of boots on wooden boards. There was the soft shush of seed settling as someone kicked at my mattress, and then a curse.

"Bed's still warm," answered a calm voice. "Damned abolitionist can't have got far." Through the air tunnel I had made, I could glimpse the flare of a lamp swinging back and forth as they scanned the room, looking for me.

"There's a missing plank back here," said another voice from the rear of the storehouse. "He must have wormed out this way." The light danced again and was gone. The darkness in my hole was complete. I was hunched over, my knees drawn up to my chest. My hands, filmed with sweat, were clenched tightly right in front of my face, but I couldn't see them.

I heard running feet—many pairs—pounding the packed earth outside. Then I heard yelling, a pistol shot, and a scream.

They were dragging something across the yard. They stopped just by the storehouse. I heard moans and cries, and then Ethan's voice, ragged, crying "No!"

The responding voice was calm, low, almost courtly.

"I regret to say that unfortunate limp of yours will be a little worse after tonight. Please summon him, Mr. Canning. Otherwise I'll be obliged to shoot you in your good leg also."

"Damn you!" Ethan gasped.

There was another shot, and a scream so pitiful and filled with pain that it made my stomach contract and heave up its contents. The sour stink of my own vomit filled the airless hole. I was shaking. I had to go out. I had to give myself up. But fear lay on my chest, crushing the air out of me, pinning me like a rockfall. I did not move.

Through the ocean roar of my own pounding blood I heard the courtly voice continue. "Do us both a kindness, Mr. Canning. He can't get far. We'll catch him in the woods if we don't take him now."

Ethan sobbed and gasped, struggling for breath. He said something, but I couldn't make it out. There was the scrape of a saber exiting its scabbard, another scream, and then a thud.

"He's fainted," said a different, coarser, voice.

"Never mind. Tie him onto his horse and bring up the old nigger."

There was a brief moment of more scuffling. Then, "What's this boy's name?"

"Ptolemy, Major." The answer—low, calm, respectful—was not Ptolemy's ancient quaver, but the voice of a younger Negro: Zeke.

"I always did care for that name," said the major. "We used to own a Ptolemy. Now, boy, be good enough to kneel down, no, over there, that's right, near the saw logs, by that chopping block. Thank you." The major raised his voice then, to a resonant shout that filled the yard. "Mr. March, I do hope you can hear me. Because I know you love niggers. We've got one here name of Ptolemy, and I'm afraid I'll be obliged to cut his head off if you don't come on out here and greet your callers." He dropped his voice and addressed his men. "No manners at all, these Yankees!" There was laughter.

I was sweating and shivering. My mind told my body to move, to crawl, to go out and save the old man. But my sinews had turned to broth.

Then I heard Ptolemy's cracked voice crying out. "Marse March, if you there you stay put, you hear? I's all used up and I's ready to go to G—"

There was a scrape of metal, a thud as the blade bit into wood, then a dull thump as Ptolemy's body hit the earth. I felt as if a spear of ice had run me through. My cowardice had just caused the death of a harmless old man. I sagged in my hole, smacking my head against the seed sacks, sobbing like a child.

"We haven't got time for any more hide-and-seek," the major said. "You three, burn the gin house and the seed store. The rest of you, fire the fields. When you're done, muster at the nigger houses."

He must have spurred his horse then, for it whinnied, wheeled, and cantered off in the direction of the Negro quarters.

I heard a crackle, then a roar. The lint in the gin house had caught. They were coming now to the seed store. I smelled the sharp scent of paraffin. They were splashing the fuel from their lamps onto the timbers of the shed. If I did not get out I would be incinerated. Finally, my craven limbs consented to move. I was man enough, it seemed, to save my own life. I pushed my way through the scrim of seed and crawled on my belly across the floor to the loose plank the guerrillas had found at the rear of the shed. They had kicked the board free and enlarged the hole, so that I was able to squeeze through. I stayed flat, using my elbows and knees to squirm across the open ground toward a stack of sawn timbers. The fires had lit up the inky night and I would have been spotted, easily, if any of the guerrillas had turned my way. But the burning building stood between us, and their attention was upon it. I reached the timber pile. As I shifted the boards my hands shook. A long splinter drove itself into the fleshy place at the base of my thumb. I shifted the sawn fence posts and wriggled in behind. It wasn't until I was hidden by the timbers that I could look out through the slats and survey the scene.

The yard was bright now, both buildings burning fiercely. In that terrible light, I saw Canning. He was lashed to Aster, his legs dangling oddly. There was dark blood dripping from wounds where his knees had been. His head lay slumped against the horse's neck. The gelding's mane, too, was all clotted with blood from the side of Canning's head. They had cut off his ear. Aster, terrified of the fire, and of the smell of blood, was dancing, his eyes white, trying to throw off the unwanted burden.

A grimacing youth clutched Aster's reins as he struggled to keep command of his own horse. He was not much more than a boy, slightly built and very thin. As Aster reared, the reins tore at his hand. He swore, and then called to the others. "We ain't got no more to do here. Let's git the niggers and git done with this place. But throw the old nigger in the fire first." The other three—older men with line-scored faces—seemed somehow under the youth's authority. Two of them picked up Ptolemy's frail body; the other, cursing, grasped the head. They tossed their burdens into the blaze as casually as if they were feeding logs to a bonfire. I murmured the prayer for the repose of his soul.

But why would God listen now, to any prayer I offered? My heart was a black pit of hatred. For the unseen, honey-voiced commander, for the thin, cruel youth, for the hard-faced men. But most of all, for myself.

I stayed hidden in the woodpile until they were gone. Then I crawled out and lay on the ground, working my fingers into the packed earth. I had cowered in my hole and let one man be tortured and another murdered. *Why* had I done that? Why had I let fear master me so completely? Because I wanted to live. But what good was living, if one had to live with such self-knowledge? What would my life be, after this night? How could I face my wife, my children, with this shame blazoned upon me like a brand?

Slowly, through my grief and self-disgust, a sense of purpose grew within me. I forced myself to stop writhing and to rise up off the dirt. I was on my knees. I wiped my hands over my face, the dirt smearing my cheeks and the splinter scraping against my eye. I would have to redeem the work of the last hour, somehow, and if doing so cost me my life, well, that was worthless now anyway. I took stock of my condition. I was dressed for sleep in a light blouse and pantaloons. I was barefoot. My boots and jacket had been looted, or else had gone up in the blaze. What use I could be in such a state was far from clear. But I knew then that I had to follow Canning, even if all I could do was to be with him at the end. If there were any mercy left in the world, there would be time, at least, for that.

The darkness had begun to give way a little, and in the pearly grayness I moved at last, running across the yard and into the house, pausing inside to see if there was anyone still there. The place was dark and silent. I ran swiftly through the dining room, noting that the guerrillas had been through the house, with a quick and quiet efficiency, stripping away the very few effects of any value. The candlestick was gone; so was the small amount of china. The precision of their theft spoke of treachery. Zeke. All those months, and his loyalty had remained with his sons, and the Confederate spawn they served. I suppose he had nursed the grievances born of Canning's early harshness, and nothing that had passed since then had caused a change of heart.

But Zeke had not known of the hiding place, under a loose floorboard in one of the upper rooms, where Ethan had kept a small store of his personal things. He had shown it to me only recently, against just such a contingency as this. I threw open the shutter to get a little light, and then felt around on the floor for the loose board. I pried it up. There was a leather folder where Canning had told me he kept a small amount of cash. When I flipped it open, I saw that it also contained an ambrotype—a picture of a young, dark-haired girl about the same age as my Meg. Canning had never spoken of her. I brought the image close to my face and took a few seconds to study it. Since there was no resemblance whatsoever between the sweet, round-cheeked, dark-haired girl depicted and the fair, ferret-faced Canning, I couldn't think it was his sister. The possibility that Canning had a beloved, that he was working himself to a raveling in order, perhaps, to win this girl as his bride, sent a stab of sadness through me. I closed the wallet and stuffed it in the inner pocket of my blouse, where I kept the small silken pouch containing the hair of my dear ones.

I tried to force my feet into Canning's best boots, but my feet were many sizes larger than his and my attempt was futile. And yet boots I had to have. I carried them to the kitchen, found the least dull of the knives stored there, and with shaking hands made a rough job of hacking out the toes. The boots were too narrow, and squeezed me, and my bare toes protruded several inches onto the ground, but even so they would serve me better than nothing.

I ran then, out the door, across the yard, and on toward the fields. They were already ablaze. Above the roar and crackle of the fire, I heard cries coming from the Negro quarters. I changed direction and headed there, coming up through the corn patch that ran all the way to the first dwellings. The corn was high and ripe, and offered good cover.

I could see now what I took to be the full strength of the force ranged against us. There were twenty men, a ragged company, clad in a motley of butternut and homespun. Two of them were Negroes; Zeke's sons, I guessed, which probably meant that the lean youth leading Aster was the son of Oak Landing's former overseer. One of the Negroes sat his horse a little behind an older, better-dressed man, whom I took to be the major. They seemed to be consulting on some kind of sorting process. The rebels had formed a cordon with their horses, ranging themselves in a circle around the Negroes, whom they had gathered together into the yard where we had performed the shout. There were about sixty of our people. I could only surmise that the others—the swiftest—had managed to escape.

The rebels had two dozen of the Darwin's Bend Negroes—mostly women but some four or five of the men—roped together at the neck. One of the rebels rode to where the little girl Cilla, the one who reminded me of Amy, cowered behind her grandmother. He pushed the woman away, grasped the child's wrist, and hoisted her up onto his own horse. When she cried out and tried to climb off, he struck her.

The others then walked their horses into the midst of the crowd and began snatching up children. They pushed aside the parents, ignoring their pleas and cries. One of the guerrillas grabbed Jimse. I saw the little boy reach out, crying, to his mother. Zannah ran forward with her arms outstretched for her child. The rebel struck her in the face with the butt of his rifle. She got up, blood streaming from her nose, and ran at him again. This time, he pointed his pistol at the child's head, and she fell back, dropping to her knees in the dirt. This was too much. I didn't know what I would be able to do, but this time, I had to do something. I moved forward, parting the corn with my arm. A blow to the back of my knees caused me to crumple. A big hand clapped itself over my mouth. "Stay put, marse," hissed Jesse, behind me. "Now ain't no time to make a move."

Just then, the major raised his voice above the sobs and the roaring of the blazing fields. "Gentlemen, move out!" he called. "We have an appointment to keep." He turned to the Negroes. "We'll have no further quarrel with anyone here so long as you refrain from growing cotton for the enemy. Good day to you." He lifted a battered *chapeau de bras* and swept it across his body in a mockery of a bow, and turned his horse for the woods. The youth leading the still-unconscious Canning fell in behind him, followed by the other irregulars, driving the bound slaves and some six of our mules. Zeke, I noted, was mounted on one of them. I wondered when exactly it was that he had determined to betray us. Then I saw that Zannah was running after the party, the need to be with her son more powerful than her fear of reenslavement. One of the irregulars also saw her, and turned to alert the major. The major shrugged, and so the guerrilla pushed Zannah forward into line with the tied slaves and roped her by the neck.

When they had disappeared into the ragged scallop of cypress woods, Jesse grasped my hand and started after them, keeping to the corn rows. He had a trash-cutters' knife slung across his back. "If we can just keep sight of them till nightfall," he said as we advanced at a brisk jog, "then maybe when they's sleeping we just might git a chance to cut loose some of them." It was a better plan than any I had, and so we followed them into the trees.

CHAPTER THIRTEEN

A Good Kind Man

The next hours passed in a blur of effort. The ill-fitting boots flayed my feet. Since we kept to the dense scrub, the whipping branches tore at my thin blouse and raked the skin beneath it. Within hours, I was dizzy from lack of food and parched for water, but still we pressed on. Jesse moved forward, apparently insensible to pain or fatigue, and I blundered behind him. The only thing that saved me was that the guerrillas could not drive their captives beyond the pace of the slowest, and even though we came close enough at times to hear the coarse taunts and threats with which they urged on their captives, occasionally they were obliged to halt. We took care to pull up well short of them, and during each brief intermission I lay gasping in the leaf mold, willing myself to stay conscious, to find the resources to continue. When we came in reach of a slow stream, I buried my head in the silty water and drank, even though the chances of the water being wholesome was negligible.

I don't think I was ever as eager to see a sunset as I was that day. The guerrillas halted their march in a clearing, and we stayed back at first, burrowed under a fern bank, holding our breath as one of them passed within a few yards of us, scouting for firewood. Jesse pressed his mouth close to my ear, and whispered: "I set two big jars of shine by the stoop of my cabin, right where the rebs could easy find it. I's praying they got it."

An hour passed, then two. The noise from the camp waxed, and it seemed the guerrillas had indeed found Jesse's moonshine, or else come ready provisioned with their own. Under the cover of the loud voices and darkness, we crept forward to where we could see the guerrillas' dispositions. They had the Negroes bound hand and foot now, all but Zannah, whom they had set to tending the cook fire. They knew she would not attempt escape while her child was captive. Jimse was roped, like the others. They had tied them in threes and fours and bound each group to a tree.

Ethan they had not bound, because he would never run anywhere again. I could not think why they were troubling to bring him on this march when the easier course would have been to kill him outright. They had taken him from the horse and propped him against a fallen log. I could not tell if he was conscious or not, but after a while I saw Zannah take a ladle of some kind of broth to him. Cradling his head, she tried to spoon the liquid into his mouth, but I couldn't see whether she had any success or not. As I watched, I saw one of Zeke's sons, a tall lean youth of about nineteen or twenty, amble over to where she squatted and say something to her. She turned her face away and spat in the dirt. The youth drew out his saber and pressed the point of it against her cheek, then he reached down, grasped her by the hair, and pulled her to her feet. Jimse cried out, but May, the Negro woman tied up alongside him, awkwardly pulled him toward her, using hands that were bound at the wrist, and turned his face into her bosom so that he couldn't see his mother struggling or hear the inhuman sounds she uttered.

The youth pushed Zannah out toward the picket line and stopped for a word with his brother, who was on watch with one of the gaunt white soldiers who had disposed of Ptolemy. "Save some for me, Cato!" his brother said jovially, handing him a lantern. The white soldier made a lewd gesture. "Wish I could teach mine to rise up for charcoal-colored sluts." I did not hear Cato's reply as he passed his brother and drove Zannah on into the the woods. The lantern bobbed and wove through the trees and out of sight on the opposite side of the clearing. I felt Jesse, tense, breathing hard beside me. "We have to help her!" I whispered. He shook his head. "Raise a ruckus now and we's all done for," he hissed. "Zannah and that little one of hers as well." But I had already stood by through a murder; I could not lie in the dark and do nothing while that girl was violated. Using my knees and elbows, I began to ease myself back, away from our vantage point in a tangle of fallen branches. Jesse divined my intention. His great arm shot out and pinned me to the ground. "I mean it, marse," he hissed. "If you wants to help her, stay quiet now. If we mess this business, she gonna be sold on someplace where she gonna be in for a lot more'n one night like this."

"So what are we to do?" I hissed in reply.

"Wait," he said. "Wait and let the shine do half the work for us. I put a little something in there that ain't corn likker."

Laughter and raised voices came from the camp. The talk was all about money: how much would the Texas traders pay, the next day, for this Negro and that one? This was the usual, coarse banter: the likening of human beings to livestock. One of the men was making a crude joke when he stopped midsentence and cursed, pressing a hand into his belly. He blundered off into the woods, bent almost double. The other men laughed and jeered at him, and called out that he had "let a stink worse than a skunk."

Suddenly and silently, Jesse was on his haunches, unslinging the great knife bound to his back. "You stay put, marse. This one's mine. You get the next one." He passed like a shadow over the ground, making no sound, despite his great bulk. Minutes passed. I strained my ears in his direction, but I could hear nothing over the raucous camp talk and the loud wood noises—the metallic thrumming of the crickets and the deep grinding of the bullfrogs.

Within a few minutes, he was back, his big knife blood-coated.

He had the guerrilla's rifle, his pistol, and his saber. He handed the latter two to me. My hands shook as I took them. I had come here hoping to free people, but I was a chaplain, not a killer. The saber I could use: I would cut bonds with it. I handed the pistol back to him in the dark. I saw the whites of his eyes regarding me, and imagined the look signaled his contempt. But the moment was not prolonged, for another man had blundered off into the bushes, groaning and cursing his bellyache.

Jesse stalked after him, and again came back within minutes, bearing weapons. "We ain't gonna have too many chances like this," he whispered. "By 'n' by someone gonna notice no one comin' back from they's shits. They gonna miss 'em, and there gonna be a big to-do till they finds them, and then a bigger one."

But for the moment, at least, it seemed that the noisy revelry had most of the men well distracted. The talk had turned to Canning, and what he might prove to be worth. "It'll have to be a good piece to make it worth hauling his sorry self." It became clear, presently, that the major had somehow formed the crackpot notion that Canning was the scion of a wealthy Northern family. Their plan was to ransom his life.

It seemed that Canning, who had regained consciousness, also was listening to the conversation. "You've made a big mistake, gentlemen," he rasped. The others hushed each other and fell quiet, struggling to hear what he had to say. "You think I'd be down here in this filthy swamp, risking my life and working like a serf if I came from money? All I've got up north are creditors. Nobody there gives a good goddamn about my life."

I wished I were close enough to Canning to clap a hand over his mouth. He might as well be confessing to a capital crime, so effectively was he making out his death warrant.

"What if he's telling the truth?" one of the men asked the major. "Why're we troubling to drag him along with us? Seems we should shoot him now and be done with it, then when we get done selling the niggers we can have us a little furlough."

The major stood and stepped toward Canning. He ran a hand over his stubble. "Are you speaking the truth? Or is this just another Yankee lie?" He took out his pistol. "Speak, or I'm going to commence auctioning off the pleasure of shooting you."

Canning's head, caked with dried blood, was turned away from the firelight. I couldn't read his expression.

"I don't lie."

"Then I'm afraid that good soldier over there is right; we're just too pressed by events to be carrying you along with us." He cocked his pistol.

And that was when I leapt up, this time evading Jesse's grip and ignoring his hissed curse. I dropped the saber in the leaf litter and crashed out of the scrub.

"Wait!" I cried, stumbling into the clearing. "He *is* lying! He has a fiancée! She'll pay for his life."

"March!" cried Canning, his voice carrying a mixture of pain and astonishment. The guerrillas, who'd survived for months in the woods by dint of their swift reaction, were on their feet, rifles ready, even in their inebriated state. Two of them had me in a firm lock before I finished speaking.

"So, Mr. March, you decided to join our party after all," the major said. "What an unexpected surprise!" He gestured, and the men who held me thrust me forward.

"Tell them, Ethan! Tell them the name of the girl in the ambrotype. Tell them, for pity's sake, and live!"

"Pity?" he laughed, and it turned into a cough. "I doubt they know what that means." He shifted painfully to relieve the pressure on his shattered knees. "But I can tell them her name. It is Marguerite Jamison, and you'll find it on a headstone in the Elgin cemetery. She died a year ago last May. Consumption. Just six weeks before we were to be married." He turned his head and looked at the major. "Shoot me, damn you, and get done with it. You've made me a cripple and a bankrupt and not a soul on God's good earth gives a damn if I live or die." He started sobbing.

The major scratched his head with the pistol butt and turned to the men holding me. "Tie this one up," he said. "I believe I'll consider what to do with the pair of them in the morning."

They lashed me tightly to a tree near Canning, at a little distance from the Negroes. One of these, I did not see who, flung me a heel of cornbread, and I used my bound wrists to push it into my mouth. I hadn't eaten all day, and the scrap of bread just served to awaken my raging appetite. Across the clearing, Jimse was crying out for his mother. May crooned to him in a soothing voice, and told him to hush now; she'd be back directly. The child fretted for a while, but he was exhausted, and soon whimpered himself to sleep in May's lap.

Ethan moaned. One of the guards kicked dirt in his direction and said, "Shut up."

"Ethan," I whispered. "I'm sorry."

The night insects thrummed.

"I know."

Through my torn smock I felt the roughness of the tree bark scraping against my back. I ached all over and was hot, and wished they had not tied me up so close to the fire. I could feel sweat dribbling down my neck, soaking what was left of my blouse. Another man, doubled up with cramp, headed for the woods, muttering that "the black bitch must've spit in the stew."

I thought it could be only a brief time before someone noted the growing number of missing faces around the camp and set up a general alarm. I hoped Jesse had a plan for that moment. I surely did not.

Presently, a chorus of snoring—ragged, hoglike—commenced from those of the guerrillas who weren't standing watch. Cato's brother remained on guard duty, along with three others. He was slumped against a tree on the other side of the fire, and I watched him through the smoke. Once, he caught my eyes on him and glared back at me.

There was a white fog rising up from the moist ground. I was hot now, but when the fire waned, my sweat-soaked shirt would chill me through. I suppose I must have fallen into a kind of fretful doze—I was exhausted, and I could feel the familiar fever ache beginning in my joints. Whether I drifted for a minute or an hour I couldn't rightly say. A branch cracked and fell in the fire, and I jerked back awake with a start. The fog had thickened. It moved above the ground like cold smoke. When it parted a little, I saw that a thin shard of red moon had risen and that Cato had taken his brother's place on picket. I wrenched myself round as much as I could in my tight bindings, to see who remained awake, and the effort set up an aching in my head. The trees that edged the clearing seemed to be undulating. I closed my eyes, but then the whole world spun. I opened them and tried to fix on one still point. I could not concentrate. But I had to; there was something important I needed to do, to see . . . if only I could just remember what it was. That was it: count the men. I waited for the fog to shift and reveal more of the campsite. If only the trees would stop that nauseating movement . . . One sentry had slumped down into a squat by his tree. His head rested on his knees and he might have been sleeping. I wanted to sleep. My head throbbed. I started to do an accounting, but the numbers jumbled. I tried to shut out the pain in my head and closed my eyes, struggling to string my thoughts together. Twenty of them at the setting out, two dead at Jesse's hand for certain, maybe three or four. Dully, I began to wonder; if Jesse had somehow managed to waylay so many, picking them off singly, then that left only sixteen . . . and Cato's brother also unaccounted for . . .

Just then I felt the bonds around me go suddenly tighter and then slack. I did not move my head but from the corner of my eye I saw

Zannah, a saber in her hand, moving to cut the ropes of the other captives. Addled as I was, I realized that the odds were still poor, even if Jesse had somehow managed to deal with all of the missing men. Fifteen armed and hardened soldiers remained. But if Jesse could get arms into the hands of our people . . .

The crack of a branch, breaking underfoot, reported like a gunshot. Cato swung round in the direction of the noise, but a ball found him first. A piece of his skull opened and flew out, and he pitched forward. What followed was a blur of noise and bodies, shots and screaming. I leapt up. My limbs felt like lead bars. I lurched toward the fire and grabbed up a burning branch. I spun around with it and a shower of sparks flung a swirl of brightness all around me. I couldn't tell who was who in the thickening fog. I made for where Jimse had been tied, but he was gone. Zannah, of course, already had him. I saw her, crashing through the scrub, the boy clinging to her back, and May lumbering and panting in their wake. Then, through the mist, I saw a guerrilla drawing a bead on them. I tried to run, to put myself in between them, but before I had moved a step the soldier fired and May fell, face forward, her arms moving like a swimmer. The guerrilla was already biting the paper off another charge. I cannoned into him sideways, cracking the brand against skull. The weapon fell from his hand and he lunged at me. The two of us tumbled onto the ground. He twisted over on top of me. He raised a fist and landed a blow into my face. The cartilage in my nose ground against itself. I tasted blood in the back of my throat. He snatched up a rock from the leaf litter. I saw it poised over my face and jerked my head to the side. Then his grip on the rock loosened and it fell from his hand, bouncing harmlessly off my chest. He was scrabbling at his neck. The point of a saber spiked through his clutching fingers. Cilla stood behind him, her mouth open in a thin howl. She had driven the sword through his neck. He slumped forward, kicking. I pushed him off and scrambled to my feet, grasping Cilla's trembling hand

and trying to drag her back toward the shelter of the trees. But she pulled hard against me, like a petulant child resisting a parent. She reached down and laid her small hand on the hilt of the saber. When it wouldn't come free, she put a bare foot on the man's shoulder and tugged. There was a scrape of metal on bone, and then a spurt of blood, and then another, and then an uninterrupted flow. I picked her up then, although my arms felt limp as string, and tried to run for the trees.

But I was running the wrong way, right into the sights of the major, who stepped out of the smoke just a few yards from us, his rifle raised and aimed. I flinched, anticipating the blast, and turned my body to shield the child. But he uttered a curse, and staggered, and the shot went wide. In the swirling fog I saw Canning, prone at the major's feet. He had dragged himself the few yards to where the major stood and, with his last strength, struck at the man's ankle with a jagged rock. The major kicked out at him. His boot thudded into Canning's blood-encrusted head. Then he reached for his pistol, bent down, and shot Canning in the face at point-blank range.

"Ethan!" I screamed, and the major raised his pistol at me. I tossed Cilla away from me and felt a thump, like a hard punch, in my side. Then the sound of the blast. Funny, I thought, as I dropped to my knees. The sound was so late . . . I pitched forward, facedown, inches from a burning coal. I stared at the red-orange heart of it, watching it throb inside the blackened wood. I thought: this is the last thing I'll ever see. The shouting and screams seemed to oscillate with the pulse of the fire in the coal: loud, then soft, then loud, and then silence.

It was daylight, and I lay prone in the clearing. There was a buzzing. I could not raise my head. I smelled acrid smoke. Through a blur, I saw bodies. Cato's, and another of the irregulars. Ethan's corpse. May, prone in her own blood. Little Cilla, lying on her side with her knees pulled up, as if she were sleeping. Except that her gut had been laid open with a bayonet and her entrails lay in a glossy pile beside her. And on every corpse, a seething, humming mass of bluegreen flies. A deep gray wave rolled slowly across the clearing. I did not fight it. I had no wish to wake to this. The wave rolled over me and I let go, into its deeps.

Darkness. Moving. Rocking, back and forth. The ground came up at me and receded. Leaf litter. My hand touched coarse hide. Pain wracked every part of me. I let go again into unconsciousness.

Night. No more movement. Flickering firelight. I tried to raise my head. The world spun. Darkness.

Rocking again. A grassy track. Tree shadows. The rich, muddy scent of the river.

Daylight. Still, at last. Underneath me, leaves. Above, a blur of branches. My eyes focused on a single leaf, turned before its time. Scarlet and gold. The color throbbed against a sky of brilliant blue. All that beauty. That immensity. And it will exist, even when I am not here to look at it. Marmee will see it, still. And my little women. That, I suppose, is the meaning of grace. Grace.

Night. A fire. Shivering.

"Cold."

The word came out of me in a voice I couldn't recognize as my own. My nose was congested with dried blood. Zannah turned from paring at some fresh-dug root and hurried to my side, laying a coarse hand on my brow. Her face was wan and streaked with dirt. She stood and pulled the saddle cloth off the tethered mule. She wrapped the stiffened fabric round me. It smelled of sweat and stables.

Another night, or the same one. A scent of roasting grain. Zannah turned from the fire holding a small, battered pan. She fingered the mush into my mouth. I tried to swallow, but the stuff burned my raging throat and lodged there. She gave me water. It might as well have been lava.

"Where are the others?" My voice was a rasp.

She looked down and shook her head.

"Jimse?"

Tears sprang to her eyes and cut shiny rivulets down her dirt-smeared cheeks. She undid the button that held her soiled shirt tight at her wrist and drew out a cluster of tight-curled ringlets. She held them against her face and began keening. I reached for her but my body was wracked with tremors and my arms seemed too heavy to lift. She dropped her head into my lap. I laid a trembling hand on the turquoise scarf that covered her hair. I remembered the merry laughter of her little boy, the day she had first put it on. I touched the locks of hair she grasped so tightly in her hand. He had been as much a part of her as her own skin. How could she bear this loss, on top of so many others? I closed my eyes, and when I opened them it was morning. She had cried herself to sleep in my lap. When I stirred, she woke, sat up, drove her fists into her eyes, and got to her feet, heavily. Jimse's ringlets were still clasped in her hand. She was about to put them back into her sleeve when she paused, separated out a small ringlet, and pressed it into my palm. I raised it to my lips and kissed it.

Much later, I asked about Jesse. She held out her two hands, locked at the wrists, mimicking manacles.

"The others?"

Manacles again.

"You are the only one who got away?"

She nodded, her eyes filling.

"And you came back, and found me? Zannah, I . . ."

She shook her head sharply, placed a hand on my mouth, and turned to load the mule. I was watching her through the heat haze of the waning fire when the fever rose and took me away.

When I woke again I was flat on my back. The rocking movement now was gentle, like a cradle. A strong smell of lye bit at my nostrils. There was a rough gray blanket tucked tight around me. As my eyes focused, I saw a billow of gauze. There was a curtained window, and beyond, bright sky. Black embers leapt upward against the blue. Something—an engine?—throbbed. The light hurt my eyes and I closed them. When I opened them again, it was to a swirl of black fabric and a gentle noise, *click-clack,* like marbles hitting each other.

And then, that most unexpected thing, a woman's face—a white woman's face, encircled by a pale wimple—peering at me.

"There, now, rest easy," she said. I tried to raise my head but she pushed me gently back against—of all things—a pillow. "Don't try to talk. You've been very ill—you still are."

"I was shot."

"A bullet grazed you. But that's healed. It's the fever that's troubling you now."

"How . . . how did I get here? And where am I? And who are you?"

She smiled. She was not a young woman. Her narrow face was heavily lined, plain almost to the point of repulsion. But to me she looked like an angel.

"You're aboard the hospital ship, the *Red Rover.* I'm Sister Mary Adela. We are a nursing order, the nuns of the Holy Cross. We are taking you north. You're safe now."

Safe? I thought. I will never be safe. But what I said was, "How?"

"Shhh. Too many questions," she said, but kindly. She took my wrist in a gentle hand, feeling for my pulse. The dull brown beads of her rosary hung from the waist of her voluminous black habit. They rattled gently as she moved to fix my pillow.

"A colored girl—a mute, the men said she was—brought you into the federal lines. The pickets took you for her master—called you a secesh and wanted to drive you away, but she wouldn't have it. Stood her ground, even when they aimed their guns at her. She was determined to make them understand. They said she pulled off her scarf in the end and picked a bit of burned stick from their fire and wrote this upon it. We saved it for you."

My vision was blurry, and the charcoal marks on the blue-green fabric blurrier still. But etched on the filthy piece of turquoise satin I could make out the quavering letters:

> *capn March*
> *yoonyin preechr*
> *he cum from plase cal concrd*
> *he a gud kin man*

I wept then, stinging sobs that gave way to violent coughing. The sister bent over me and reached past the long rosary into a deep pocket of her habit. She held a white cloth under my chin. I raised speckles of bloody phlegm all over it. The last thing I saw was the nun's face, frowning with concern, turning to call for the surgeon.

PART TWO

—∿—

Jo read aloud, in a frightened voice,

MRS. MARCH:

Your husband is very ill. Come at once.

S. Hale,
Blank Hospital, Washington.

–Louisa May Alcott, *Little Women*

CHAPTER FOURTEEN

Blank Hospital

I told him to go. I didn't cry at our parting. I said that I was giving my best to the country I love, and kept my tears till he was gone, and shed them in private. I told the girls we had no right to complain, when we each of us had merely done our duty and will surely be happier for it in the end. They were hollow words then and all the more so now. For what happiness will there be if he dies in this wretched place? What happiness, even if he recovers?

It is quieter here, now that the bustle of the day's routines has begun to ebb. The seconds tick by, marked by the drip of the drenching water cooling the dressings of the wounded. In the sickly yellow glare of the gaslight, I gaze at his face—for what else have I to do here? I study him, and I wonder where the face has gone that I loved so much: the face that belied his age when I first saw him, all on fire in my brother's pulpit. I thought then that it was rare to hear such ferocious words issuing from such a benign visage. He looked like an angel such as the Italians sometimes paint—all golden hair and gold-bronze skin, youthful and venerable at one and the same time, his expression informed by a passionate nature that spoke of both innocence and experience.

And all those years later, as I watched him going off to war at the ridiculous age of thirty-nine, he looked young to me, still. When I caught glimpses of him, smiling and waving among the press at the windows of the departing troop car, I thought that there were boy-soldiers all around him who wore their age more heavily than he.

It was folly to let him go. Unfair of him to ask it of me. And yet one is not permitted to say such a thing; it is just one more in the long list of things that a woman must not say. A sacrifice such as his is called noble by the world. But the world will not help me put back together what war has broken apart.

Aunt March was the only one of all of us who dared to utter the truth. When I got her note, wrapped around the money I was obliged to beg of her to pay for this journey, I read it and burned it. I saw Hannah's eyes on me as I balled up the paper and cast it into the grate. She thought I was angry with Aunt March. The truth: I was angry at myself, for not having had the courage to stand aside from the crying up of this war and say, No. Not this way. You cannot right injustice by injustice. You must not defame God by preaching that he wills young men to kill one another. For what manner of God could possibly will what I see here? There are Confederates lying in this hospital, they say; so there is union at last, a united states of pain. Did God will the mill-town lad in the next ward to be shot, or to run a steel blade through the bowels of the farmhand who now lies next to him?—a poor youth, maybe, who never kept a slave?

But I said none of this a year ago, when it might have mattered. It was easy then to convince one's conscience that the war would be over in ninety days, as the president said; to reason that the price paid in blood would justify the great good we were so sure we would obtain. To lift the heel of cruel oppression from the necks of the suffering! Ninety days of war seemed a fair payment. What a corrupt accounting it was. I still believe that removing the stain of slavery is worth some suffering—but whose? If our forefathers make the world awry, must our children be the ones who pay to right it?

When I saw him stand up on that tree stump in the cattle ground, surrounded by the avid faces of the young, I knew that as he spoke to them, he was thinking that it was unfair to lay the burden so fully on that innocent generation. I could see the look of love for those boys in his eyes, and I saw also that the moment was carrying him away. I raised my arms to him, imploring him not to say the words that I knew were forming in his mind. He looked me full in the face, he saw my tears, and he ignored them and did as he pleased. And then I in my turn had to pretend to be pleased by my hero of a husband. When he stepped down, and came to me, I could not speak. I took his hand and dug my nails into the flesh of it, wanting to hurt him for the hurt he was inflicting upon me.

I am not alone in this. I only let him do to me what men have ever done to women: march off to empty glory and hollow acclaim and leave us behind to pick up the pieces. The broken cities, the burned barns, the innocent injured beasts, the ruined bodies of the boys we bore and the men we lay with.

The waste of it. I sit here, and I look at him, and it is as if a hundred women sit beside me: the revolutionary farm wife, the English peasant woman, the Spartan mother–"Come back with your shield or on it," she cried, because that was what she was expected to cry. And then she leaned across the broken body of her son and the words turned to dust in her throat.

Thank God that I have daughters only, and no sons. How would I bear it if Meg were now a soldier at sixteen, and the prospect of this war stretching into years, so that Jo, too, might come of age while it yet rages? As it is, I have had to hide my mental reservations from them, to show a strong and certain face, to spare them my despair and never let them see that I doubted their father and his choices.

What is left of him? What remains, now that war and disease have worked their dreadful alchemy? I could see the change in him, even before I heard the mutterings of his delirium. When they directed me to him this afternoon, I thought they had sent me to the wrong bedside. Truly, I did not know him.

All our years together, even the difficult ones, had succeeded in drawing only pleasant lines upon his face: the marks of laughter that webbed the corners of his eyes and etched a deep parenthesis as brackets for his smile. But the months we have spent apart have carved for him a different face entirely.

Will I ever see him smile again?

I felt a hand on my shoulder and realized that I must have murmured this last thought aloud.

"Do not torment yourself with these bleak questions, Mrs. March. It is fatigue that raises them. You are very tired; shall we not go and seek out your lodging?"

I turned, and he was there at my side, where he has been almost every hour since the arrival of that dreadful telegraph. I see that he, too, is pale and drawn from the exhaustions of our hasty journey and his efforts since our arrival, and his brown eyes are full of concern.

"I do not like to leave him . . ."

"There is nothing more you can do for him here, and the night nurse seems capable. I have spoken with her. In any case, she says, they require all visitors to leave at nine o'clock, when they turn down the gaslights."

"Well," I said, my tone plaintive, "let us stay at least until then, for it is not so very long." I lifted the hand that lay limp on the coverlet and pressed it to my cheek. I heard the thump of crutches on bare floorboards as the ambulatory patients made their way to their beds and the night nurse readied her charges for sleep.

Mr. Brooke took a deep breath, like a sigh. Poor Mr. Brooke. I am afraid my good neighbor Mr. Laurence has laid a difficult commission upon him, and he feels his responsibilities too keenly. On our journey, he confided that he intends to join the army directly his duties as tutor end next fall, when Laurie goes to college. I wanted to say, No! Serve your country as you are now, by molding young minds, not by shattering young bodies. But once again, I did not speak. I lacked the courage. It cannot be easy for him to see what he sees here, the broken boys writhing in their beds. How can he not imagine himself among them? And yet, at twenty-eight, he has had a long experience of making his own way in the world, and is a grave and silent man who thinks a good deal more than he speaks.

"Mrs. March, we would be wise to set out now. The capital and its surrounds are notorious for a lack of policing, and I am afraid that Georgetown in particular has an unfortunate reputation. I have been informed that drinking places are ordered closed at a half past nine, and they say there can be, well, a good deal of unseemly behavior on the streets at that hour. I should like to see you safely to your room."

What could I say? The young man seemed so tired and anxious. So I took a last long look at my husband and laid my hand against his hot forehead, hoping that it was tenderness I transmitted, and not this smoldering anger.

As I stood, a wave of weakness swept over me, so that I was glad for the steadying hand of Mr. Brooke. In truth, I hope never again to undertake a journey such as the one that brought us here. Meg is always saying that November is the most disagreeable month of the year, and I believe that ever after this I will be obliged to concur with her. Such a bitter, frostbitten morning, when Mr. Brooke came for me and we set out—was it two days since, or three?—after a night of sleepless anxiety. I could find no rest, but paced the house, looking at my little women as they slept—Jo's fresh-cropped head upon the pillow made her look like a boy, as she lay next to Meg, who is become so suddenly womanly. For a moment, I gasped, and realized that it might not be so very long before Meg takes her place in the bed of some young man. I wondered if, when that time came, she would still have a father at her wedding to give her away.

In the adjoining room, little Beth and Amy looked like sleeping babes, too young to be abandoned by their mother, even with sensible Hannah and our kind neighbor to watch over them. All these thoughts jostled with each other and with the overwhelming fear of what news would greet me here, and so even when I lay down I could not close my eyes. Instead, I sat up, relit the lamp, and mended hose till I heard Hannah, dear soul, long before dawn, readying a hot breakfast which I could barely eat.

My eyes ached and stung as I tried to make a composed farewell. The girls were uncommonly brave: none of them cried and all of them sent loving messages to their father, knowing very well that I might arrive at his bedside too late to deliver them. I barely knew where I stepped as we made our way from the carriage to the car, passing among children, fretting and crying, the wan-faced women and the men, smoking and spitting. I was glad to reach the boat at New London where, behind the curtain of my berth, I was able at last to give way to some private tears.

In the morning, red-eyed and unrested, we made our way to the filthy depot in New Jersey, and found our car amid the racket of truck horses and swearing porters. We rattled past the crape-decked homes of Philadelphia and on through the coal-blackened expanse of Baltimore. As we left that city, there were pickets along the rail lines and one felt the war approaching like an oncoming storm. Everywhere, troops and wagons; caissons; and tents, tents, and more tents—pale cities of them—the cold and cheerless cloth houses of our army, whitening the countryside like drifts of snow.

It was raining at noon, when we finally arrived in Washington. A cold drizzle fell from heavily swagged clouds that seemed to lower on the unfinished Capitol like the lid of an upholstered box. I asked that we go directly to the hospital, for if the news was the worst I wished to hear it soonest. Mr. Brooke had obtained directions to the place, which had been a hotel before the multiple disasters at Manassas and on the Peninsula. The wreckage of our army has claimed the city's colleges and churches; even, so they say, the space between the curiosity cabinets of the Patent Office. It was fortunate that Mr. Brooke had thought to inquire in particular detail, for the first hackman was an overbearing rogue who insisted that he went our way, and I should have believed him, had not Mr. Brooke intelligently interrogated the man and learned that his destination was the other side of the city altogether. When Mr. Brooke chided him for an attempted swindle, the hackman swore, and said how should he be expected to know, since every day a hospital seemed to spring up in some new place, and his confusion was honestly come by.

When at last we found a hackman who was bound in our direction, Mr. Brooke could not forbear from pointing out to me the president's house, from which carriages rolled forth into an avenue that was become a river of mud. All I could notice was the blight of this place: the pigs wandering the streets and dead horses bloating by the roadside. Even the live horses look half-dead, so careless are the teamsters who have charge of them. And there are so many Negroes everywhere. In Concord we are used to see but one or two colored citizens, carefully dressed and decorous in manner. But Washington is flooded by the ragged remnants of slavery, contraband cast up here to eke what existence they may. I felt a pang for the little bootblacks, crying out for trade and going without, for what profligate person would spend half a nickel to tend to his boots in this world of mud?

And all that rises from the slough is ramshackle or unfinished, so that it looks already ruined. We passed the obelisk meant to honor the father of the nation. It rises like a broken pencil, not one-third built, and beneath it the dressed stones piled here and there, grass grown up all around. The few finished buildings face each other, visions of lost grandeur, a Leptis Magna without the blue backdrop of a Mediterranean sky.

It came to me that if the fortunes of this war do not turn, then maybe the city is destined to be no more than this: ruins, merely, sinking back into the swamp; the shards of an optimistic moment when a few dreamers believed you could build a nation upon ideas such as liberty and equality.

These despairing thoughts turned to dread at the moment the hackman cried out "Blank Hotel!" and Mr. Brooke handed me down before a great pile of a building, a flag fluttering before it and a number of uniformed men milling at the door. Leaving Mr. Brooke to grapple with my heavy old black trunk, I forced my feet to mount the steps. The sentinel touched his cap with grave formality. He must see many such as I, wives soon to hear that they are widows, walking up this stair toward their news.

A Negro boy—are there no end to these people?—opened the door. The interior stank—boiled cabbage and chamber pots, rot and sweat and unwashed bodies—a hideous brew made worse by a heat like Bombay. I saw that they had nailed shut the tall windows, so not a breath of crisp air stirred the miasma. A slender Negro woman, tidy, at least, reassuringly unlike the slatterns I had noticed in the street, passed me carrying a tray of instruments.

"If you please," I said. She turned and looked at me with an intelligent attention. "Where may I find Surgeon Hale?"

"If you would care to follow me, I am on my way to him." Her voice was remarkable—low and silvery, the cadence clearly Southern, but as educated as an aristocrat. I followed her quick steps, avoiding the hallway bustle of coal hods and coal black laundresses with armfuls of soiled linens; limping convalescents bearing steaming pots of tea; and haggard civilians, like me, looking for their loved ones. We passed a ward filled with serried rows of army cots and waxy faces. One man stared at me with glassy, feverish eyes. "Charlotte? Are you come to me at last?" he said. I tried to control my trembles and shook my head, returning his frowning scrutiny a weak smile.

At the end of the hall two vast double doors gave on to an ornately corniced room, hung with chandeliers. A gilded sign above the entrance said BALL ROOM, and the name seemed a bleak joke, for inside, arrayed on the polished dance floor, lay the victims of the Minié ball, many of whom would not dance again. There were forty beds within, all handsome hotel beds with turned posts rather than humble hospital cots. Some beds were tenanted, some vacant. A muddy, bloodied group of gaunt new arrivals, slumped against the wall, awaited the surgeon's attention. Their faces proclaimed defeat as plainly as any banner headline reporting wartime's latest blunder. The black nurse approached a green-sashed, silver-haired gentleman and set down the instruments, taking up a metal bowl to receive the bloody shrapnel piece he plucked from his patient's shoulder. She inclined her head to where I stood, hesitating, by the wide doorway, and said something to the surgeon in a low voice. Then she beckoned me forward. I came reluctantly, feeling I intruded on the injured man with his shoulder bared to the probe and his pain patent upon his face.

"Surgeon Hale?" I said, my lip trembling. "I have your cable. I came as soon as I could. My husband, Captain March . . . I hope I am come in time?"

The nurse's white-wrapped head came up sharply. She looked at me with a grave regard. The surgeon did not raise his eyes from the wound. "March?" he murmured. "March?"

"The chaplain," prompted the nurse. "He arrived last week on the *Red Rover*." Surgeon Hale worried away at the wound, drawing forth another shard, which dropped with a clang into the bowl. "He has bilious fever and pneumonia," the nurse prompted further.

"Oh yes . . . March. He lives, or he lived still when I made my rounds this morning. But his condition, as I telegraphed, is very grave. Nurse Clement will bring you to him, directly we finish with this man."

"Please," I said. "Do not trouble. If you tell me where he is I am sure I can find my way. These men have needs greater than mine . . ."

The nurse continued to regard me. I read sympathy in her face, and something more that I was too tired to fathom. "You will find him in the fever ward on the second floor, to the right of the staircase," she said. "His is the fourth bed from the door on the left." She paused, as if she wanted to add something. "Is there no one with you?"

"Yes," I said. "I have an escort, he is seeing to my trunk."

"I advise you to wait for him," she said. "I fear you will find your husband very much changed."

If I had been more myself, I should have wondered at that remark. But at that moment all I wanted was to hold her directions in my addled mind long enough to bring me to my husband's side.

"Thank you," I said, and withdrew. I found Mr. Brooke almost immediately. He was in the hallway, looking lost amid the bustle, moving almost at a run from ward to ward, searching for me. I raised my hand to him and he was at my side at once. He gave me his arm and we climbed the stairs.

Had the nurse not given me explicit directions to his bed, I would not have recognized the ruined occupant as my husband. His cheeks were sunken as a death's head, his fine nose flattened and crooked, and his arm, on the coverlet, was fleshless—just bone with skin draped over it. He must have lost half his body weight. There were oozing ulcers at the corners of his mouth.

When he set out, his hair had been gold, lightened here and there by the silver streaks of his maturity. Now, what hair he had was entirely gray, and scalp showed where hanks had fallen out entirely. When I smoothed it back from his hot face, a tuft came away in my hand. His skin burned, but its normal sun-bronzed sheen was replaced by a yellow pallor, save for two hectic patches beneath the eyes. His breathing was irregular, and with each breath his chest rattled. I grasped his hand and felt the bones, fragile as a bird's, give under the pressure of my grip. I could not control myself then, but surrendered to violent weeping.

Mr. Brooke stayed by me through the storm, but when I had composed myself he asked if he might leave me to dispatch a brief telegraph home of our safe arrival, to reassure the girls that their father yet lived; and to attend to the matter of our lodging. And so I was alone when the delirious raving started. He was fretful, his hand working the coverlet, his head beating from side to side against the pillow. At one point, he cried out to someone named Silas, saying over and over that he was sorry. His voice was raw; speech clearly pained him. But later, it was other names, a whole litany of them, such as the Catholics recite. I heard him say Ptolemy, then something that sounded like Jimmy, and then perhaps Susannah. All the time anxious, all the time asking forgiveness.

There were troubling things here. Much as I did not want to hear, I knew I must listen, and sift them for what specks of fact they might yield. For a while, he muttered incoherently, and then seemed to find himself in the midst of battle, urging comrades on one minute, trying to fetch them back the next, ducking his head, clutching at my arm as if he would drag me away from an imagined shower of shot.

I had not seen a nurse in the fever ward, but as he began to cry out loudly, a stout woman with a pasty face and small, deep-set eyes bustled to his bedside. Without any word to me she threw her thick arm behind his shoulders and raised him up. He groaned, her roughness clearly causing him pain. I uttered a little cry, and she glanced at me with disdain. She prised open his ulcerated lips and forced a spoon of some viscous mixture into his mouth.

"What do you give him?"

"Laudanum," she replied curtly. "We cannot have noise in this ward. Fever patients must have quiet."

"What other medicines is he receiving?"

"You'll have to ask Surgeon Hale about that," she said, already turning away.

"I have brought with me some bottles of good old wine, and some lemons, and the makings of rice water. Perhaps I could–"

"That's all very well," she interrupted. "But you'll not give him aught till you see the surgeon."

"And when will that be?"

"When he gets here!" she snapped. "In case you haven't noticed, there's more than one sick man in this hospital." And with that she turned her back on me completely.

I was so exhausted and in such a condition of nerves that tears sprang to my eyes. I tried to tell myself that the nurse was overextended, and did not mean to be unkind. But I think if my state had not been so utterly depleted I might have followed after her and given her back a dose of her own bitter medicine. Instead, I just sat there and watched over him, as the laudanum pushed him down into a deep place, where I hoped he was out of reach of the demon dreams that pursued him. I was sitting there, still, when Mr. Brooke came to fetch me away.

A blast of icy wind hit us as we stepped outside, but I gulped it greedily after the torrid air of the hospital. Mr. Brooke was apologizing for the quality of the lodging he had secured and the fact that we would have to walk to it. I had told him that I would not permit any of Mr. Laurence's money to be spent on my account; the old gentleman had been generous enough already. I had the money I had begged from Aunt March, and the twenty-five dollars dear Jo had bought with the sacrifice of her beautiful hair, and no idea how long the modest total might have to last me. As a result of my insistence on economy, the first several tiers of lodgings were barred to us, and Mr. Brooke had found himself turned away at every affordable boarding house or set of rooms he had applied to. At last, he said, he had found us beds in a private residence, "a poor enough place, but respectable, I feel sure, and not such a very great distance from the hospital." At that point, I thought any covered corner where I could close my eyes would do.

The city, Mr. Brooke explained, was brimming with all those who might profit from the great armed camp it had become. The war seemed to have drawn hither every class of person. Accommodations were filled with correspondents and sketch artists from the newspapers of every state; by furloughed officers on the prowl for promotion; by embalmers and coffin makers, teamsters, rum-jug sellers, and, so he had heard, not a few swindlers and confidence tricksters. Although Mr. Brooke forebore from mentioning it, a few steps from the hospital door we encountered members of perhaps the largest class of war profiteers: the women's army of the Magdalenes.

Two girls waited in the shadows, hoping perhaps for trade from the convalescents. Under their hectic face paint, they looked no older than Meg or Jo. The young flesh indecently laid bare by their low-cut gowns was blue with chill. "Poor children," I murmured. Mr. Brooke colored, and said nothing. I turned my face away from his embarrassment and gazed at the Potomac, where moonlight gleamed on a white steamer, tiered like a wedding cake. Hospital ship? Troop carrier? I could not tell. We turned up an alley that led to a canal towpath, to be greeted by a reek even worse than the hospital's sour stench. The canal was lined by tiny row houses, whose occupants evidently used it as the repository of every waste product, human and animal. Just as we passed a fish peddler, he heaved a pan of bloody offal into the murk. Mr. Brooke's apologies had been, as I said, incessant, but when he stopped at one of the canal-side houses, a narrow, two-story cottage of rosy brick only slightly less dilapidated than its neighbors, my heart sank.

The door was opened to us by a pale woman with a long, angular face, plainly but respectably clad in widow's black. She bore, already, the fate I feared. Mr. Brooke introduced me to Mrs. Jamison, who greeted me in a low monotone and ushered me inside. The tiny house had no hall; we entered direct into a spare little room which might once have claimed the title "parlor," but now was converted into a two-bed dormitory, the cots separated by small, improvised screens which failed to conceal that one of the beds was already occupied. "Mr. Brooke will share this room with Mr. Bolland, who works as a copyist at the treasury. You will room with me, in the attic, Mrs. March. There is a privy in the back, if you would care to use it before you go up."

I had not eaten but a mug of broth all day, and I had no appetite, but kindly Mr. Brooke had bought some oysters and a loaf of bread, which he insisted I take, though I had to eat perched on the single ladder-back chair by the room's meager fire. There was a kettle on the hob, and Mrs. Jamison poured me a basin of hot water for my toilet. I went to the drafty little outhouse, closed the door, and, alone for what would be my only moment of privacy, gave way to sighs of self-pity.

How different my life should have been, if our fortune had not been lost so completely! I had never blamed my husband for squandering all on Brown's ventures: I had no right to do so. The money he advanced was his entirely, the product of his own labors and sage investments, and the cause, surely, was dear to us both. Yet it bit at me cruelly that he had not even consulted me in this, a matter that touched me so nearly and had such large consequences for us all. I had tried to bear the small insults and indignities of poverty, even to embrace, as he did, the virtues of a simple life. But where he might retire to his study and be wafted off on some contemplation of the Oversoul, it was I who felt harassed at every hour by our indebtedness and demeaned by begging credit here and there; I who had to go hungry so that he and the girls might eat. Oh, he gardened to put food on our table, and chopped wood for others when the larder was truly bare. And what praise he won for it: "Orpheus at the plow," Mr. Emerson hailed him. (No one thought to attach such a poetic label to me, though I might wear myself to a raveling with the hundred little shifts necessary to sustain us all.)

I had grown used to this state in Concord, where we had the help of friends and the elevation of a good name. But I could see that it would be a very great deal harder to be poor here, where I was unknown, a vagabond, and friendless, save for Mr. Brooke. Sitting in that privy, assailed by yet more evil smells, the thought occurred to me that if my husband were fated to die, I would be obliged if it happened sooner, so that I could depart this scene of squalor. The second the notion formed itself, I wished it unthought. Exhaustion was my only poor excuse.

I bathed my face and arms in the welcome warmth of the water and returned to the cottage. The treasury copyist was already snoring like a beast, and I felt a pang for poor Mr. Brooke. I made my way up the stairs to my narrow iron bed, where the mattress was the thickness of a floor mat. At least, I noted gratefully, the threadbare coverlet was clean. I barely had the strength left to undress. I was just about to lay my head on the single, mildewed pillow, when a piercing cry came from below.

"Hey-y-y-y-y, lock!"

It was a bargeman, rousing the lock tender. With despair, I realized that these cries might well punctuate the night.

Whether they did or no, I cannot say, for the thought was barely formed before I fell into the deep sleep of the truly spent, from which, I think, no sound on earth could have roused me.

CHAPTER FIFTEEN

Reunion

I will not say I awoke refreshed, but when I opened my eyes to gray daylight it was with considerably more fortitude than when I had closed them. Sleep is a great mender of spirits, and as I looked around the bleak little room, I was able to manufacture some cheer by thinking of all the ways its deficiencies might be turned to advantage. It had become a habit of mind to start each day so; I had schooled myself to do it ever since the turning of our fortune into dust. It stood me now in good stead as I enumerated the cracked panes in the casement windows, and told myself that they at least afforded healthful ventilation. The blotchy-looking glass, no larger than a handspan, would be too small and dull to reflect the frightful truth of my worn appearance. The extreme discomfort of my bed would assure that I spent every available hour fruitfully, in the waking world.

So resolved, I rose, and found my landlady and fellow lodgers already up and about their business. Mr. Brooke had left me a note stating that he had gone out early to tend to some commissions for Mr. Laurence, which he thought could be addressed in an hour or two. He asked that I wait for him, but I could not. My desire to see how my husband had passed the night was too pressing. I wrote a brief note of apology, loaded my pannier with some of the wine and tonics I had brought, and set out for the hospital.

I had to pick a careful way over the piles of unshoveled mule droppings that lined the towpath. It was cold, yet not cold enough for snow. I longed for a blizzard such as we had at home: how improved would be the prospect if the incessant drizzle could only turn to pure flakes that would bury this city's muddy imperfections under a clean white quilt.

I had not thought to inquire if the hospital had set times for morning visits, and as I approached the sentry I wondered whether I should be turned away to await a certain sanctioned hour. But I need not have worried: the hospital's corridors were, apparently, open to all comers, and staff carrying trays of bread, meat, and soup had to weave between all manner of civilians: some, haggard and anxious, evidently relatives; some, the bustling and self-important agents of relief societies and others who seemed to have no business but to gawk and weary the wounded men with all manner of tactless and impertinent inquiries.

I climbed the stairs with heart thumping, wondering in what condition I would find my husband. Few of the curious souls downstairs bothered to ascend to the fever wards; wounds, I expect, were more exciting. My husband's ward was deserted, save for the patients. I caught my breath when I saw him. He lay thrashing, all tangled in a disarray of bedclothes, his sheets smeared with the watery green excretions of his illness. On the low stool beside his bed stood a bowl of soup, untouched of course, and cold, with a thick layer of grease floating on the surface. No wonder he was so thin. If no one had been troubling to feed him in his delirium, he must have been going without nourishment entirely. There were no nurses or attendants of any kind in the ward.

It was clear that if my husband was to be cared for, I should have to do it myself. I took off my cloak and bonnet, and pushed up the sleeves of my dress. I spoke as soothingly as I could as I worked the bedclothes from around his thin limbs. As I stripped the noisome sheets and bed gown, his body was laid bare to me. I had not seen my husband's body in more than a year, and even then, never in so unprivate a manner, in the harsh light of day. The sunken chest, the pallor—all of this was pitiable. I thought of the young limbs that had enfolded me, years ago, on the pine-scented pond shore. How the strangeness of his flesh—hard and muscled from a youth of physical labor—had surprised and aroused me. Knowing almost nothing, then, of the circumstances of his upbringing, I had expected the soft hands of a wealthy pen-pusher, but his had been the roughened touch of a working man. And now here he lay, all wasted and unrecognizable, too frail even to withstand an embrace.

I realized then that I had no idea where to find clean bedding, a basin, warm water, sponge-clouts, or any of the things necessary to ease him. So I drew the coverlid, which had fallen completely off the bed and therefore was not soiled, over his poor body. Then I gathered the befouled bundle in one hand, picked up the plate of cold soup in the other, and went in search of help.

As ill luck would have it, the first person I encountered was Nurse Beady-Eyes from the previous evening's terse exchange. She saw me coming and stood in my path, arms planted on her ample hips.

"If you would be kind enough to direct me—"

Before I could finish my sentence, she began her harangue: who did I think I was, upsetting hospital routines, and putting my needs above the other desperate cases . . .

I folded my lips tight and tried to keep my composure, drawing on the years of discipline imposed by the half-dead man I sought to help. I let her say her piece, and when she had done I asked again, politely, where I might find supplies. She pursed her mouth and told me I would have to wait . . . "perhaps some hours, till the grave cases are dealt with."

"Grave cases!" I exploded. "My husband is nearly in his grave, thanks to your neglect! Kindly tell me where the linens are—now!"

"I'll not have you address me that way!" Her voice had gone up an octave. "Orderly!" she cried. "I'll have you put out on the street!"

All the times, all the very many times, I had been forced to thwart and stifle my own nature seemed to gather together then, in that hot and dismal corridor. I heard a rushing sound in my head and felt a pressure in my breast, like floodwaters rising behind a flimsy dike. Before I knew I did it, the soup bowl was rising in my hand as if elevated by some supernatural force. Then, its yellow-gray contents were running down the nurse's pudgy face.

"Wipe yourself with that!" I cried, thrusting the green-smeared sheets at her. "And then tell me that a human being should spend 'some hours' in such filth!"

"Orderly!" she was hysterical now. "Help me! I am being assaulted!"

I do not know what would have happened if some swaggering man had appeared at that moment in the corridor. But the youth who limped into view was a pale convalescent, wincing with pain at every step he took.

When he asked me, gently, to come away with him, all the anger flowed out of me, and I followed meekly.

"I-I'm afraid I will have to retrieve my cape," I said. "I left it . . ."

"Never you mind that, ma'am. I'm not fixin' to turn you out, don't you worry." He led me down the stairs and into what must have been a servery in the building's hotel days. A kettle steamed on the room's small stove and he poured me a mug of tea made of lime rinds and huckleberry leaves.

"Drink that and you'll feel better by and by," the man said kindly. "We jus' needs to git you clear of Nurse Flynn for a spell, that's all. She goes off duty shortly. We all of us knows she's a right terror, that one. All that fine talk 'bout caring for the serious hurt ones . . . Truth is, she don't care for no one t'all. Just struts round the place tellin' the convalescents what all work to do, and some of us ain't fit to be up out of our own beds anyhow." He stirred the mug and handed it to me. "Fact is, plenty people in this place gonna be right glad when they hear what you done. She had it comin', right 'nough."

The orderly, a private, wounded in his thigh during the Peninsula campaign, told me to stay quiet and that he would return for me directly Nurse Flynn went off duty. "And don't you worry 'bout Chaplain March, ma'am. I'll git someone to see to him, or I'll do it meself, if I has to."

The good young man went out and I felt the great relief that simple kindness can work. It is a salve of the spirit, surely. Then, of course, I began to repent my outburst, and hope that word of it would not come to Mr. Brooke, whose good opinion I would not lightly cast away. Just as I was beginning to fret and to pace about the confines of the little closet, a scratch came at the door.

"Come!" I said, expecting the young orderly. Instead, a sober-faced, middle-aged man clad in the black suit of a minister opened the door.

"Forgive me. Mrs. March?"

"Yes?" I said, feeling a weight of guilt descend upon me, for at that moment I was sure that the hospital chaplain had come to rebuke me, as my own husband had always done, in the aftermath of my rages, and to deliver a humiliating lecture on the proper comportment of a gentlewoman, a wife, a mother.

"I am sorry to intrude upon you, ma'am, but I have certain of your husband's things. One of the nurses who was detailed to transfer the patients from the *Red Rover* gave them to me for safekeeping–things do have a habit of vanishing in this place, you see. One might blame certain little black imps that dandle round the laundresses, but one mustn't add to the afflictions of Africa, must one?" He gave an arch look and a rather stupid grin. Apparently the man was attempting some kind of witticism. I made my face a stone to convey my disapprobation.

He cleared his throat and went on. "When I heard you had come I thought you should have them." He had a very small, brown-wrapped packet in his hand, which he held out to me. I took it with thanks.

He was already turning to go, but I stopped him. "Chaplain?"

"Yes, ma'am?"

"Can you tell me anything about my husband's condition—how he came to be evacuated on the ship? For his last letter to me gave no indication that he was ill, or in any particular danger."

The chaplain had a good face for his profession, mobile, easily able to adopt the moment's required emotion. His mouth turned down, registering sympathy. "It is so often the case, I fear: bad news comes suddenly to near kin, because those who love them try to spare them hard truths. Apparently your husband had been ailing for some time, and much weakened, before he succumbed to his present violent illness. And there *was* a skirmish of some kind, that caught him up, but of that I have no details. All I know I have from the nurse; you should speak with her yourself, for she talked about your husband's case at some length with the sisters who nurse on the *Red Rover*."

"I will do so; you are very kind. If you please, of which nurse should I inquire?" My heart sank, dreading that he would say the name Flynn.

"Clement is the name, I believe," he said. "A Negro woman from Virginia—a slave, they say, though you would not know it from her address. She is generally in the surgical wards, assisting Dr. Hale. Remarkable, really. He seems to prefer her to the gentlewomen nurses. Perhaps he finds a slave more biddable."

Ordinarily, I would have bridled at such remarks from the lips of a Union chaplain. But all the fight had gone out of me, and I was grateful for the man's small courtesies.

"Thank you, chaplain. I will seek her out directly."

When he was gone, I stared at the small parcel in my lap. My husband had left Concord with a trunk of gear; books and tracts and song sheets for the men; needful things for camp life, his ever-present journals, the lap desk the girls and I had given as his parting gift. In the months of his absence, we had sewn and knitted tirelessly, replenishing his stores of clothing. I pulled at the string, wondering what tiny part of all of it had survived.

The paper opened with a crackle. Inside was a battered leather folder, a square of filthy fabric, and a small silk pouch. Of the three items, I recognized only the latter. I closed my hand over it, thinking what its contents must have meant to him, that he had kept it close through all, and then I slipped it into my bodice. I opened the leather folder. There were greenbacks inside: how extraordinary that no one had pilfered these. Behind the cash was the hard metal edge of an ambrotype. I drew it out. The girl depicted was a stranger. Since my husband had not written to me of any white women in his acquaintance, her identity was a bafflement.

I was baffled, also, by why anyone had troubled to retain the square of filthy cloth, and was about to feed it to the stove when I noticed the hemmed edges. They were irregular in a way I recognized. Jo never could stitch an even hem; her mind was always wandering off to the plot of her latest story, so that her sheets and kerchiefs had a kind of meandering scallop to their edges. I had often teased her about her rococo needlework. I smoothed the blue-green square upon my knee and smiled. It was, surely, one of the scarves we had made for the Negroes, so many months since, from the donated remnants of old ball gowns. What a journey this little fabric scrap had made! And then I looked more closely, and the mystery deepened. I realized that the black smudges upon it were not random stains but the smears of what once had been words, written, it seemed, with charcoal. I turned the cloth this way and that, but try as I might, I could not decipher them.

Not long after, the gentle orderly, whose name was Cephas

White, came to fetch me. "Your enemy has left the field," was how he announced himself. He had a most endearing smile, despite the fact that one of his front teeth was broken quite in half. But there was a drawn look about his mouth and eyes that spoke of suffering. As we made our way back through the bedlam of the lower wards, I took the liberty of asking about his wound and, when he commenced to answer me, swiftly wished I hadn't.

"They fetched out the ball all right," he said. "I was lucky: it missed the bone and I never did bleed that much. But it tore up the muscle pretty good I guess. I was on the mend fair enough till a week or so ago, an' they had me to lift a big man what couldn't turn hisself. The flesh hadn't knit just right and it tore open. They's put a big poultice of damp bread on it, and that does seem to make the pus pour out, which they say is a good thing, though it sure don't smell so good . . ."

His words, underlined by the reeks of the ward, conspired to make me feel quite faint. But that was weakness; if he, after all, had to bear his wound, I could at least bear to hear of it. I strove to master myself. I told young Mr. White not to trouble himself by unnecessary stair climbing, wished him most sincerely a speedy recovery, and then turned to go up to the fever ward.

What a change had one brief hour wrought! My husband's bed was dressed in snowy linens, the sheets pulled crisp and creaseless. His head and shoulders were propped high on large, full pillows, so that he breathed without the terrible, labored rattle. A nurse—the tall black nurse I guessed was Clement—was bending over him solicitously. How fortunate! I thought. I should be able to ask her what she knew of my husband's history and condition. As I drew closer, I saw that she was feeding him some broth.

Her back was to me. I was about to speak, to utter my thanks for her kind attentions, when she set the spoon in the empty bowl, raised her hand, and smoothed back a lock of his pale hair. She tucked the lock, and then her hand turned, where it lay on his crown. She ran the back of her fingers slowly down his cheek, her thumb traveling lightly over his lower lip.

No. That couldn't be. I must have been mistaken. That was the gesture of a lover, not a nurse. I blinked hard and told myself to stop imagining things. But when I opened my eyes it was to an even more astonishing sight. He was raising his wasted hand to her dark one and clasping it to his lips. Then his voice: a rasping whisper. "Thank you, Grace, my dear."

I did not know what to do. Part of me, relieved at his return to consciousness, wanted to run forward, to embrace him. Part of me wanted to flee the room, the building, the city, the memory of that intimate caress.

Before I could do either, Mr. Brooke burst through the doorway with a joyous cry. "I met the surgeon in the hall and he said that Mr. March is returned to consciousness! And so it is! Sir! How wonderful to see you better! Our prayers are truly answered!"

Grace Clement had stepped back from the bed with a quick, neat movement that gave no evidence of awkwardness. She busied herself taking up the tray of broth and bread crusts and swept silently away with them.

His smile, when he recognized me, was his smile after all, despite the changed condition of his face. He reached out a trembling hand—not the hand that had touched hers—and I took it.

I had rehearsed this moment in my mind a thousand times, during the lonely nights and anxious days of his absence. I had thought that to see him again, alive, would be all I could ask for in the world. I had imagined the touch of his hand, the joyful weeping.

Well, there were tears. His, and mine also. But how could I have foreseen that the tears I shed on our reunion would not be tears of simple joy?

CHAPTER SIXTEEN

River of Fire

He was too weak for speech. The effort of even a few words sent him into agonizing spasms of coughing. I told him to hush, but he fixed me with his fever-bright eyes. "So much to say . . ." he whispered.

All I said was that we would have plenty of time—"a lifetime, to speak, when you are better."

"Seeing you makes me better . . ." he rasped, and then the coughing fit seized him. Mr. Brooke had left us alone, in his tactful way, saying that he would go directly to send a cable, as the girls should not have to wait an extra minute to learn the good news. Another nurse, neither Clement nor Flynn, but a sensible woman of about my own age, came at last to administer his medicines. To my inquiries, she replied civilly that he had been on a course of calomel, which she gave me to understand was a powerful drug made with mercury and quinine, both of which were standards in the treatment for fever and pneumonia, and also laudanum "to ensure rest and help to bind the bowels."

I sat with him, watching the drug work quickly in his depleted body. His eyelids were closing. There was a terrible agitation within me. There were things I had to know. I was aware that I should exercise forbearance. But as I watched him slipping again out of consciousness, it came to me that perhaps I would not get another chance. And I could not live without the truth.

I leaned close to him then, and whispered: "That nurse, Grace Clement. There is something between you, isn't there?"

His eyelids fluttered but did not open. "Something..." he repeated. His words were a sibilance. I had to bend close, so that I was just inches from his face. "Long time..." Suddenly, his eyes opened fully. He stared at me, and yet through me. His pupils were dilated, so that I looked into an immense, empty darkness. "My love," he murmured.

His eyes closed again. There was no more. The drug had pulled him far away. I shook him gently, then roughly. I heard his teeth, loose in his inflamed gums, chatter in his head. Realizing what I did, I fetched my hands back like a guilty child and thrust them behind me. I stood up. I had been holding myself so hunched and tense that, as I straightened, the muscles in my neck and shoulders protested. I paced to the end of the ward and back again, and then sat down and drew out the small silken pouch. The touch of my girls' hair, I thought, would soothe my troubled spirit. The first curl I recognized as my own. Then Amy's golden cornsilk fell into my palm. Then Beth's, Meg's, and Jo's–dear, generous-hearted girl, who no longer possessed a single curl on her head as long as this one– I smiled, but the smile died on my lips. For another curl had fallen from the bag. It lay in my hand: a tight-sprung ringlet, black as night. Negro hair. Her hair.

I am not an innocent. I know how people can be tempted. Adultery is a most commonplace sin. Did I not watch, for years, and from too intimate a vantage, how Henry Thoreau and Lidian Emerson were tortured by their desire one for the other? Even the best of us can fall. I know all this. And therefore I had to know the truth of my own situation. What had he meant: *My love?* Was he addressing me? Or did he mean, as I feared, that *she* was his love? Only two people in the world could enlighten me, and since one of them was incapable to do so, I should have to apply to the other, no matter how awkward the encounter.

But as always happens when one sets out with an absolute necessity of locating someone, Grace Clement was not to be found. I walked the surgical wards, then climbed again to the fever wards, but no one had seen her, no one knew where she might be. Eventually, I applied to Cephas White, whom I found carrying away spent dressings from the wounded wards.

I explained that the chaplain had recommended I speak with Nurse Clement, since she had been in the party that brought my husband from the hospital ship. He regarded me over his grisly bundle and shook his head. "The white nurses, now; I could tell you where to find 'em." He winked at me, and gave me another snaggle-toothed grin. "There's dormitories for them up in the attics here. But I'm pretty sure there ain't none of the dusky ladies up there and I ain't at all sure where they rooms is . . . Maybe you could ask the laundresses? They'd surely know."

Mr. White hobbled with me down the hall and pointed out the laundry. It stood across a cobbled yard at the rear of the hospital and announced itself by billows of steam that hung low in the chilly outside air. I had not fetched my cloak and so I shivered as I hurried across the courtyard until the humid heat of the laundry enveloped me as I stepped inside. What I had not reckoned with was finding myself in a dead house. The laundresses' duties evidently included washing the bodies of those soldiers whose battles had finally drawn to an end, and the first room of the laundry was set up for this purpose. One corpse—a double amputee, I noticed, before I turned my eyes away—lay naked on a trestle as an elderly Negress plied a cloth over his abbreviated body, carefully cleaning around the stitches that had failed to hold the life within him. Two more ravaged bodies lay waiting for her attentions. She was singing as she worked, which struck me as unseemly, until I realized that what she sang was a hymn. Her voice was deep and resonant. In the clouds of steam that issued from the coppers beyond, I thought she seemed like a large black angel, serenading the man to heaven. Beside the table gaped thin plank coffins, waiting for their cargo. She looked up from her work and smiled at me, and asked how I did. In truth, I did badly, and could not stand there and banter across the bodies of the naked dead. I wished her a good day and pressed on, holding my skirts high off the wet floors, to the room behind, where several women toiled over washboards and mangles while their infants tumbled about like puppies, sliding on the spilled suds that slicked the floor.

The women looked at me curiously and so I blurted out my query. "That one?" replied an older laundress, straightening up and pushing a fist into the small of her back. "That yaller woman don't bide with the likes of us." The woman working the mangle caught her eye and the pair of them laughed.

"I worked here since this place was a hotel, and them days we roomed up in t'attics. But they needs them rooms for the white nurses now, so we's all got give the shove, and we has to sleep down in the boiler room, yes'um. But that yaller girl take a look down there and wrinkle up her itty-bitty nose." The woman pinched her own broad black nose and tilted it into the air, provoking general hilarity. "Not good enough, no ma'am, never mind she come direct from being a slave on over the river. So the doctor done give her a place in his own house, big ol' red mansion on up the hill a piece. And way dat ol' man looks at her, we reckon she ain't sleeping in the servant quarters, if he let her sleep at all!" The other women convulsed with laughter.

I felt the color drain from my face. What manner of a woman was my husband entwined with? I was trembling with anger as I strode back into the ward, retrieved my cloak and bonnet, applied for directions to the doctor's residence, and set out to find it.

The drizzle had turned to a drenching rain. The fallen leaves, rotted into a wet brown mash, slicked the soles of my boots so that I slid and skidded as I toiled up the hill. Water sluiced off my bonnet until I could not see my way. I tore it off impatiently and pressed on bareheaded, regardless of propriety. I had been careless pinning up my hair, in my haste to be at the hospital, and now I felt the sodden skeins unloose and dangle about my shoulders. By the time I reached the top of the hill and mounted the steps to what I deduced must be the doctor's mansion, I was soaked.

The liveried Negro who opened the door was so appalled by my appearance that he took an involuntary step backward. My manners made no better impression than my looks.

"I want to see Nurse Clement!" I blurted angrily.

He was a good servant; his impassive face betrayed distaste only in a swift downturn of his lips. "One moment," he said, and closed the door on me.

When it opened again, a tiny, silver-haired woman regarded me. She was richly clad in mahogany silk trimmed with a pale lace tippet. "Good gracious!" she said. "You are soaked through! Do come in and get out of the rain.

"Markham, please take Mrs.–I'm sorry; what is your name?"

"March," I said.

"Please take Mrs. March's wet cloak and bring her the robe from the Chinese room. And be kind enough to ask Hester for some tea."

"Very well, Mrs. Hale," the Negro said, holding my dripping garment as if it offended him.

"Do step in here, Mrs. March, and warm yourself."

The parlor was very fine, with swagged velvet draperies and a marble mantelpiece surrounding a deliciously hot fire. I stood there, dripping onto the wine-colored carpet.

Mrs. Hale waited until the robe had arrived and been reluctantly accepted, and the tea set down by Hester upon a low table of polished marble, before she turned a direct green gaze upon me and asked, firmly but not unkindly: "Would you be good enough, Mrs. March, to say what has prompted this extraordinary call?"

I set down my tea dish and stared at my hands, which were blue with cold and trembling. "My husband is very ill. We had a telegraph from Dr. Hale; he summoned me to Washington. I arrived yesterday. Today, the chaplain told me that Nurse Clement knows the history of my husband's condition. I-I am anxious to learn of it. That is all." I looked up. The cool green eyes regarded me steadily.

"And you did not think it could wait until Nurse Clement, who works with my husband for sixteen to eighteen hours every day, was on duty at the hospital? You had to invade the privacy of her dwelling and intrude upon her few scant hours of respite?"

I felt the sting of her words as an errant schoolgirl feels the slash of the ferrule. My voice, when I answered her, was small. "My husband's condition is very grave. I have to know the truth so I might be better able to help him."

"I think it is you, Mrs. March, who is withholding the truth. Grace Clement has been working with my husband and living in this house for half a year. Today, for the first time, she left her duties early, saying that she felt unwell. And now you arrive . . ."

Her eyes traveled from my wet head to my sodden boots. "I do not think I shall disturb her unless you care to be more frank with me."

I looked down at my boots. Scuffed, muddy. A piece of rotted leaf clung to the left sole. The right had a hole in it, and the water had wicked up my stocking. Mrs. Hale would not speak to me so, I thought, if my attire did not so plainly cry out "Poverty."

I felt the fury rekindling itself. How could my husband have set me in this humiliating situation? I raised my head. But the sharp words died on my lips. Grace Clement had come in, soundlessly. She stood just inside the doorway, clad in her simple nurse's dress of dove gray wool, her hair tied up in a spotless white rigolette, her hands clasped calmly before her.

"It's all right, Emily. I am quite prepared to receive Mrs. March."

The silver head turned sharply. I saw that her chignon was held in place by a diamond clasp.

"Grace, my dear, are you certain? It is not necessary that you—"

"Please, Emily. It is really quite all right."

"If you say so, but—"

"Really, it is better so. I should like to set Mrs. March's mind at rest."

"Very well, my dear. But call me if you need anything."

They spoke to each other like equals, like sisters. This was hardly the manner of a gentlewoman dealing with her husband's fancy piece. I flushed, ashamed. I would not have listened to envious, malicious gossip from the mouths of white washerwomen. Yet I had been willing to hear and believe it from black.

Mrs. Hale rose and excused herself. On the way out, she took Grace's hand in hers and pressed it. Grace, who was much taller than Mrs. Hale, leaned down and kissed the older women's cheek.

She took Mrs. Hale's place on the sofa and poured tea into the dish Hester had set for Mrs. Hale, but which had remained unused. Her back was straight as a ramrod, her gestures elegant and unhurried. It might have been her drawing room, her bone china tea service. She took a sip of tea, set the dish down, and folded her hands in her lap. Now the unwavering gaze to which I was subjected came from eyes of honey gold.

"Mrs. March, I have known your husband since he was eighteen years old."

Her words struck me like a fist. I had to dig my fingers into the chair to keep myself upright. "I will tell you the whole of it," she said. She began with her own history in the Clement household, and then disclosed in full what had passed between her and the callow Connecticut peddler. Then, she recounted, in detail, their reunion after the battle of the bluff.

When Meg was little, someone gave her a kaleidoscope filled with shards of colored glass. For a long time, it was her favorite toy. She loved the way that the gentlest turn sent the pieces cascading into new patterns. I felt, as I sat there, that Grace Clement had shattered my marriage into shards, and every sentence she spoke shifted and sorted the pieces into something I did not recognize.

How he had lied to me! I had been proud, when I read his words from Harper's Ferry, telling of the inspiration that had led him to quit his unit and go south to teach the contraband. Now I realized the demeaning truth of it: he had been caught by a fellow officer in a compromising position with this woman and been driven out by the threat of a ruinous scandal. I felt the blood beat in my head. I called on years of discipline to keep my composure as her mellow, uninflected voice went on.

"Two months later, when my father died, I did as your husband had urged me. I wrote to the colonel, and he in turn recommended me to Surgeon Hale. It has been a most fortunate situation for me. Dr. Hale has taught me a very great deal, and Mrs. Hale has been kinder than I could have conceived possible. They have become my family. In return, I do what I can to lighten Dr. Hale's many burdens. About three months ago, Dr. Hale delegated to me the duty of meeting the hospital ships and selecting which patients should be transferred to his care at Blank Hospital. That was how I happened to be at the docks the night your husband's vessel, the *Red Rover,* came in."

She described the scene to me, and once again she spared nothing. The ship was full beyond its large capacity; it had picked up a great number of burn patients, scalded when the steam boiler in their ship had been hit by a shell. Men were laid on every inch of boat deck, even on its stairs and gangways. Stretcher bearers carried them off the boat and placed them on the wharf. She worked by torchlight, moving carefully among the mass of groaning men, laid out like merchandise, and felt herself watched by hundreds of imploring, worried eyes. "They are afraid of being stepped on, you see, for they have been: by soldiers running over them as they lay helpless on the battlefield; deckhands treading on them aboard the boats. So they fear boots in the dark."

Her concern was with the surgical cases, but one of the nurses from the *Red Rover*, a nun, had watched her work and, deeming her competent, asked her to take note of a fever case, a chaplain who had been much beloved for his efforts among the contraband. The nun told Grace the story of the Negro mute who had brought him into the Union lines, of the scrawled words on the turquoise scarf. But my mind was on fire now. Had this mute woman been his lover, too? Why else would she have trekked dangerous miles to bring him to safety?

Grace Clement seemed to have no conception of the turmoil her words were creating within me, for she went calmly on with her narration. The nun had written a new tag: "Captain March of Concord," which she had sewn onto his blouse. When Grace read the name, she knew him: "Though without it, I assure you I would not have recognized him, in the uncertain torchlight, changed as he was.

"I saw to it that he was transported in our ambulances. When I looked in on him at the hospital later that night, he was muttering in his delirium. I leaned over to adjust his pillow and called him by name. He came very close to consciousness—as they do, sometimes— and he recognized me. He thought we were back on Mr. Clement's plantation, and that I was bringing him coffee, as I had done, the morning after the bluff defeat.

"I spent the night with him, once the surgeries were done. He talked a great deal. Ravings, mostly. But amid the babble, he told me things . . . hard things . . . about the bluff battle . . . things that he had not confided in me at the time. He blamed himself for the death of a soldier named Stone. It seemed that the boy couldn't swim, and he was helping him across the river. He said he kicked him away in midstream, to save his own life, and watched the boy die when he could have rescued him.

"The next day, he had lost all memory of me. He confused me with another slave, perhaps the one who saved his life. He wept, asking pardon for the death of a child; for other deaths he thought he should have prevented, for captives carried back into bondage." She sighed, and looked down at the still hands folded in her lap. "I tell you all this not because I wish to lay burdens upon you. But if you are to help him, I believe you need to know what troubles his heart. He has been dipped in the river of fire, Mrs. March. I am afraid that there may not be very much left of the man we knew."

I had held myself in check until that point, absorbed by the effort of fitting her narrative to the fragments of what I thought I had known from his letters—his pathetic, dishonest letters! But this reference to "the man we knew" snapped my trance. How dare she couple herself with me in relation to my husband!

I stood up, pacing. All this false candor was nothing but a sham. I had asked him about her and he had said "my love." I knew now that when he said those words, he had not meant me.

"He loves you," I blurted.

"You are wrong, Mrs. March." She stood then, so that we were face to face, her gaze as level as if she merely told me I was mistaken about the time of day. "He does not love me." She turned away and walked to the window, looking out on to the rain-drenched street. There was a bowl of greenhouse blooms on a polished table near the sill. Absently, she plucked at a stem of orchids, improving the symmetry of the arrangement. "He loves, perhaps, an idea of me: Africa, liberated. I represent certain things to him, a past he would reshape if he could, a hope of a future he yearns toward."

She turned to look at me. "Am I wrong to suspect that he lives for ideas, that he builds his whole world of them, and that it is you who are left to deal with the practical matters of life?"

That she knew him so well only kindled more suspicion in me. Her composure also was irksome. Who was *she,* a jumped-up housemaid born of lustful indecency, to tell *me* the truths of my marriage?

"You have been lovers! Admit it! Why else does he keep a lock of your hair–" and here my voice failed me. I pulled out the little silk bag and tore at it with wild fingers, dropping the curl onto the marble table top. She frowned and looked at it, and then her frown relaxed. She sat down again upon the sofa, reached up, and commenced untying the complex knot fixing the scarf around her head.

I imagined him watching her do so; watching her, by candlelight, as she bared her body for him.

"Don't," I said.

But it was done. The white fabric fell away from her brow. And then I blushed. The hair that tumbled from beneath the scarf was thick and black, but it fell in loose, heavy waves–nothing at all like the tight-sprung ringlet lying upon the table.

She raked a hand through the fall of her hair as if considering it for the first time.

"I have my father's hair, you see."

"Then who . . . ?"

She took up the ringlet and ran it between her long fingers. "Who can say? But my guess is that it is the hair of a child. See the ends? They are so fine. It appears like a lock one might retain from an infant's first haircut."

It was a few moments before I could trust my voice.

"I don't know what to say."

"Then say nothing." She tilted her head on that slender neck, first to one side, then the other, half closing her eyes as she did so, and breathing deep as if to release an inner tension. It was the first sign she had given that this conversation had cost her something; that the composure she seemed to wear so easily was a garment put on with a hard discipline. She rose.

"They were drying your cloak in the kitchen. I will see if it is ready. The rain seems to be easing now; I will bring some more tea, and perhaps it may stop entirely while we take it."

"Please, no; I have imposed here long enough."

"Not at all. I am very glad you came. I do not think many women would have done so."

She went out, and I turned to the fire, storing up the warmth for my cold walk back down the hill. Despite her words, I felt sad and very foolish and, yes, belittled by the morning's revelations. There was so much I had not known. So much that he had not seen fit to share with me.

When she returned, her hair was bound up again in a fresh cloth. As she bent close to me to set down the teapot, I caught a sharp scent of starch and a hot iron. As I sipped the scalding tea, anxious to be done with this encounter, she asked where I was staying. I replied civilly, trying to make light of the vicissitudes of my situation. But she knew Georgetown, and the squalor of the canal, and she knit her brow. There was an irony here that at other times would have made me laugh: an ex-slave, feeling pity for my hardships. She wouldn't let me leave until the rain had entirely abated, and then she walked with me out the front door and some way down the street. She would, she said, look in on me at the hospital when she returned later in the afternoon.

As I picked a careful path down the hill, I knew I could forgive my husband for his momentary weakness regarding such a woman. What manner of man–adrift and lonely, far from home, emotionally ravaged–would not be drawn to Grace Clement?

But I did not know if I could forgive him for the years of silence, and the letters filled with lies.

CHAPTER SEVENTEEN

Reconstruction

He did not wake again that day, even when the laudanum might have been expected to have lessened its grip, and even though his fever had abated somewhat.

Grace Clement looked in, as she had promised, felt his pulse, sounded his chest, and, when she had done, her concern was clear in her face. "His spirit is like a guttering candle," she said. "I believe the torments of his mind are acting on his body, preventing it from healing. I have seen like cases, and I have seen their opposite. When the mind wills it, sometimes a patient pulls himself back from the very brink of the grave. But when the mind is troubled, as his is . . ." Her words trailed away. "His pulse is feeble, his chest—it is not yet the death rattle I hear, but very like."

I will not say it did not chafe my heart, watching her touch him and tend to him with skills I did not have. But even as I felt the hot pangs of jealousy, I knew they were unworthy, and strove to subdue them, asking, as humbly as I could manage, for her counsel.

She smoothed the coverlid and lifted his hands so that they lay pale against the white sheet. "If—when—he returns again to consciousness, I think you must find a way to speak with him that will diminish the guilt he feels about the past. He must be brought to care about the life—the future—that awaits him. I think you have daughters?"

"Four of them," I said.

"Speak to him of them, remind him of their needs, his duty. That girl—woman—whoever she was—who saved him: she was right in what she struggled to set down about him: he *is* a good, kind man. But I don't think he sees himself that way anymore. It will fall to you to convince him of it, if you want him to live."

After she went to her other duties, I thought about her words. There was wisdom in them. But to do as she asked would not be easy. As a mother, I often had asked my girls to forgive each other; "Don't let the sun go down on your anger," I had instructed them, when the small and great slights of childhood set them against one another. Now, I would be tested. I would have to follow my own preachments. He had failed me in so many ways. He had not provided the material life I had expected, but I had adjusted to that long ago. He had not considered me, in deciding to go off to war, but I had feigned acceptance of that and held my peace. Now he had subjected me to a wound even more profound. He had betrayed me in the deepest, most personal way, harboring secret feelings toward another woman. And though I understood how it had come to happen, still it hurt me. Others had known truths about my marriage that he had kept hidden from me.

Somehow, I would have to unpack the anger and humiliation I carried in my breast, put it away, deep in an imaginary box, and store it somewhere on a high shelf of my heart, where I would deal with it much later. I was not sure if I had the discipline to do it. Even to save him.

How easy it was to give out morsels of wise counsel, and yet how hard to act on them. Before I left home, I had advised my girls to lessen their worry by being about their work—"Hope, and keep busy," I had said. Well, that advice, too, might be as good for the mother goose as the goslings. So in the hours that followed, I tried to find solace by making myself useful to some of the other men in the ward. I wrote their letters or adjusted their pillows or fetched fresh water. They were touchingly grateful for these small attentions, and the doing of them provided a distraction from my own concerns and raised my spirits a little.

Mr. Brooke joined me in the waning afternoon and said that he would keep vigil at the bedside if I wanted some respite. Since there were still no signs of returning consciousness, I said yes to his offer, as the strains of the day had fatigued me. When I reached the cottage, Mr. Bolland had returned from his employment. A fire smouldered in the grate and he sat close by, engrossed in a newspaper. There was only the one chair, and as he did not offer it, I proceeded upstairs to sit upon my bed. I wanted to write something to the girls before I lay down to rest; I had, until then, left it to Mr. Brooke to convey the details of our situation. I fetched out my writing things, but found myself shivering. Generally, I tolerate cold very well. But there was a damp chill in the stoveless attic. An icy wind fingered its way through the cracked window panes. So I returned downstairs— a mean fire better than no fire at all—and upended the empty kindling box to serve as a stool. I returned my attention to my writing things. I inscribed my greeting.

But it was not so easy to go on from there, and not only because of the distraction caused by Mr. Bolland's constant and apparently ineffective throat clearing. The young man had a dreadful case of catarrh. Every three or four minutes, he would cease his reading, snap his newspaper, and begin a painful effort to loosen the phlegm in his throat. I tried my best to block out the disagreeable sound and focus on what I wished to convey to my girls.

But what *did* I wish to say? My news was cheerless. What could I say of their father's condition? That his apparent recovery may have been chimerical; that he had relapsed and remained in grave danger. And what of myself? An honest accounting of my hours would hardly make fit reading: that I had thrown soup over one nurse in the morning, and spent the subsequent hours interrogating another as to their father's secret past. That I was lodged in a miserable slum by a reeking sluiceway, cheek by jowl with a stranger who had egg stains on his waistcoat.

The ink dried on my nib as I searched for a style of truth that would not completely dishearten its recipients. And then I realized that this was exactly the dilemma *he* had faced, day following dreadful day, in camp or on battlefield: the lies had been penned, the truths unwritten, because he was ashamed, yes, on occasion; but also, and more often, because he had wanted to spare me from the grief that an accurate account would have inflicted. How he must have toiled over those pages, denying himself the satisfactions that come with unburdening the heart, censoring his every sentiment so that I could continue to think only the best of him and cast his situation in a tolerable light. And I had been ready to condemn him, for what had been, perhaps, a daily act of love.

I sat there as the light faded and Mr. Bolland folded away his broadsheet. I became aware that he was staring at me, my dry nib, my blank pages. When I returned his gaze, he looked away, embarrassed. I felt constrained to speak.

"Have you been in the capital very long, Mr. Bolland?"

"Too long, Mrs. March. It will be a year in January."

"But surely the city affords some pleasures to a bachelor such as yourself?"

"I am not a bachelor. My wife and child reside with my parents at their farm on the Delaware, and I miss them grievously. The salary I make as a copyist is insufficient to allow me to relocate them here. No, Mrs. March; apart from the occasional improving lecture at the Smithsonian, there is little here to enjoy, if you set it beside the domestic happiness one might possess."

Mr. Bolland's words dropped unanswered into the bleak little room. My attempt at a natural exchange between strangers had misfired. Somehow, the thought of this man, also sundered from his family, was a final weight laid upon my depressed spirit, and I found I could not go on. What kind of life could one have, after all, if a family allowed itself to be torn apart—by war, by necessitous circumstances, or by a wedge driven into the heart by a crisis of trust? I knew then that whatever it cost me, I would bring my husband home. With my emotions suddenly stirred, I did not have it in me to make any answer to Mr. Bolland. Certainly I had no reserves from which to draw polite words of cheerful consolation. So I folded away my abandoned attempt at a letter, excused myself, and climbed up to the attic where I could at least lay my throbbing head upon a pillow. I drew my cloak around me, as well as the thin coverlid, and put gloves on my icy hands.

I fell asleep, though I had not intended to. When I awoke it was fully dark, and the waning street sounds told me the hour must be very advanced. I rushed down the stairs, anxious to return to the hospital, but Mr. Brooke was waiting for me by the fire.

"Do not fret yourself," he said kindly. "I stayed till 'lights out' and that very capable Negro nurse spooned him some of the rice water with lemon that you had left with him, and also a little beef broth."

I colored a little at the mention of Grace, troubled again by the thought of her attentions. But I knew my husband well enough to understand that he would not thank her if he knew she was feeding him animal fare. I smiled, thinking that such an abomination might very well be enough to rouse him into a conscious rage, he who had insisted on being a vegetable product almost his entire life. Yet I would not raise any objection. He needed strengthening, and if meat "medicine" might help to make him well, he would have to take that bitter pill along with all the others.

Kindly Mr. Brooke had bought me a pie, which he had kept warmed by the fire, and I ate it gratefully, although he had to stand so that I could use the kindling box to sit down upon. Mrs. Jamison had brought a kitchen stool for her own use, and was darning a sock.

Mr. Bolland had turned his attention to a book. They shared the light of a single candle.

Mr. Brooke had two letters for me, a slender envelope inscribed in a small, precise, and unfamiliar hand, and a fat packet from home. This I opened eagerly. It contained cheering dispatches from each of my girls, and reassuring notes from Hannah and the two Laurences. I was obliged to hold these almost over the fire to get light to decipher the words—especially Jo's chaotic, ink-blotted scrawls. I read them through once quickly, and then again, savoring each reassuring word, and sharing some of the contents with Mr. Brooke, who seemed especially attentive to what Meg had written. I turned then to the other envelope, and drew from it a lavender-scented note.

> *Dear Mrs. March,*
>
> *Miss Clement has made known to us the details of your situation. Dr. Hale and I would be pleased if you would accept the hospitality of our home for whatever period is necessary.*
>
> *Assuming the offer is acceptable to you, I will send a carriage to fetch you and your effects at eight in the morning.*
> *Awaiting your arrival,*
> *Very cordially yours,*
> *Emily A. Hale.*

This unlooked-for kindness—and from a perfect stranger!—brought a blush to my face. It was yet another testimony to the goodness of Grace Clement, that she had sought this invitation for me. Mr. Brooke looked questioningly, but was too polite to interrogate me. How I longed to accept the offer of a quiet and dignified retreat, away from this squalid, unprivate cottage. But how could I, and leave Mr. Brooke behind?

"I did not know you had any acquaintance in the city," he said at last.

"Very recent; acquaintances made today only." I could not bring myself to elaborate in the crowded confines of that room. "I-I am afraid I must beg another kindness, Mr. Brooke–"

"I think it is time you called me John," he interrupted softly.

"John, may I ask you to accompany me to the post? I must reply to this note, and I am afraid it requires an answer tonight."

"Of course I will," he said, immediately fetching his coat and helping me into my cloak.

As soon as we stepped out into the cold air, he said: "I would have carried the letter for you willingly, but I wanted a private word. I, too, had a letter today, from Mr. Laurence. He is appalled at what I told him of our accommodations. He admires your scruples but insists that we relocate at once to Willard's Hotel. He says that since I am representing his interests, I must be able to present myself properly to his associates, and that you do him no kindness by, as he put it, 'insisting on fetching up like a pair of beggars'– Well, forgive me, but you know how very direct he can be. I do not see how I can flout his will in this. Please, what answer shall I make him?"

I felt gratitude toward the generous old man, and relief that I would be able to gracefully decline his charity without inflicting hardship on John Brooke. "Tell him thank you, but that it will not be necessary for him to extend himself any further on my account. I have unexpectedly received an offer of a room at a most comfortable and convenient Georgetown home. If you go to the Willard's, then I shall be perfectly free to accept it and I need not post this letter after all."

"You were going to decline, for my sake? You are too good."

"Not at all."

He shook my hand and then walked on alone. I turned back and went, for the last time, to my meager bed.

·   ·   ·

In the morning, the carriage arrived as promised, and waited for me at the bottom of the steep hill where road met towpath. Mr. Brooke carried my trunk for me as I paid Mrs. Jamison and wished her well. The woman's face looked pinched and pale in the early morning light. I saw her carefully finger the bills I handed her, and felt a pang that our departure was depriving her of income she so clearly needed. I reached into the small pouch where I kept my money, and pressed several more notes into her hand, without counting them.

The carriage ride was so brief as made it barely worth harnessing the horses, but as the way was all uphill I was glad of the conveyance. The Negro servant, Markham, was waiting for me at the gate and handed me down most civilly. Mrs. Hale met me at the door. She was attired to go out, plain but elegant in a camel-colored cloak, calfskin boots, and a becoming, feather-trimmed bonnet.

"I am so sorry, Mrs. March, that I cannot stay to see you properly settled, but it is my day to assist at the contraband home in Alexandria, and I do not want to keep the driver waiting. You must use the house as your own. If you can dine with me, that would be delightful: I should like to hear more of your work with the Underground Railroad–Miss Clement mentioned your family's long involvement– but I will not expect you, and do not feel obliged. If you need to remain at the hospital I quite understand, and cook will send you up something on a tray. The household keeps 'doctors' hours,' which always are irregular, so feel free to call for something at any time. I have asked Markham to put you in the Chinese room; do not hesitate to let him or Hester know if you need anything–anything at all– to make you more comfortable."

She laid a gloved hand on my arm and gave me a kindly look. "I do hope you find Mr. March improved today."

I started to convey my thanks for all her kindness, but she cut me off. "Not at all, my dear. From what I hear from Miss Clement, he is a most remarkable man and the two of you deserve every consideration. And you would do the same for me, I daresay."

Well, Mrs. Hale, I thought, when Markham closed the door and left me alone in the Chinese room, perhaps I might have done the same for you at one time, but it was long since such grand hospitality was in my gift. The room was beautiful. Light poured from two tall windows onto a red lacquered bed hung with heavily embroidered silk. Fresh-cut flowers in a T'ang vase spilled a jasmine scent that spoke of a distant springtime. There was an armoire inlaid with mother-of-pearl and a writing desk with ornately carved legs. On the back of a matching chair lay the warm, quilted robe I had borrowed on my previous visit. I felt like falling onto that soft bed, cocooning myself in its silkworm luxury, and sleeping for a week. Instead, I set my few things in the armoire and hurried off for the hospital.

Miss Clement had clearly mobilized all the resources of the Hale family. I had dreaded finding Nurse Flynn on duty and when I reached the top of the stairs and saw her just leaving the ward, my impulse was to shrink out of sight until she passed. But her pebble eyes missed very little. She recognized me at once, drew in her brows, and strode purposefully to where I stood. She nodded curtly. "Surgeon Hale asked to be told when you arrived," she said, in a voice that was surly but also a little awed. "I shall let him know you are here."

She had evidently just seen to my husband, for his bed was freshly made and there was greenish salve on the ulcers around his mouth. His color seemed better. I lay a hand on his brow and found his fever only slightly elevated.

Presently, Surgeon Hale arrived. He made me a most civil greeting and apologized for his brusqueness at our earlier meeting. "I am not as young as I was, Mrs. March, and I have a deal of trouble keeping the medical cases straight in my mind. The surgical cases—now, that's another matter. Plunge a knife in a man, you remember it; but one fever or flux is much like another, wouldn't you say?"

I did not know what to say, so I held my peace. Surgeon Hale was a small, delicate man, in his middle sixties, with a soft cadence to his voice that spoke of Southern origins. This need not have surprised me, for until the outbreak of war, and indeed even after, Washington had been more of a Southern town than a Northern one. But Mrs. Hale had a crisp Yankee diction, and I wondered how the two of them had come together.

I have no idea if the doctor had troubled himself much with examining my husband when he had first been admitted. I could not think so, given the demands of the surgical wards. But now he made a most thorough investigation: sounding every inch of the chest, laying hands on the abdomen, raising eyelids, and probing in the mouth. It was difficult to watch; impossible to turn away. When the surgeon had done, I hastened to adjust the gown over my husband's withered nakedness and return him to the privacy of his coverlid. Surgeon Hale had turned his attention to some notes that Grace Clement had given him. He shook his head. "According to this, your husband's bowels have moved eighteen times in the last thirty hours. This is incompatible with any hope for recovery. The calomel—that is mercurous chloride—targets his fever, and has reduced it, but it is a strong laxative, and the opiate tincture is not binding him sufficiently. I propose that we make a trial of discontinuing both drugs, and see how he does on quinine alone. If you will see to it that he gets fluids—barley water, rice water, broths—every hour, without fail, we will watch his condition and see if we can turn the tide here."

"Will he—will he recover?"

He shook his head. "I cannot say. His age is against him. The bodies of the young are more resilient and can bear more insult. Hope, Mrs. March. That is all we can do."

• • •

Hope, he said. So I hoped. I hoped so hard that Hope seemed to take corporeal form, my thoughts and wishes reaching out to him and wrapping themselves around him, as avidly as my body had wrapped around him when we both were young. I wanted to transplant my vivid spirit within his depleted one, to root out the memories that troubled his sleep and sow in their place a vision of every good moment we had spent together. So I sat by his bed, all day and into the evening, whispering reminiscences of sunlit days and crisp fall apples, of girlish laughter and great minds brilliant with new ideas.

It took two days for the change of regimen to show a result. On the third morning, Hope triumphed. He awoke to the world, took my hand and held it, and would not surrender it, even when I required it of him so that I could help him eat a little custard—the first solid food he had taken in weeks. By the end of that day, he was able to sit, supported, and the next to stand for a few moments. By the end of a week, he could make his way, on an orderly's arm, to the privy. We talked then, of all that had befallen him, and I tried to make him turn his face from the ashes of his endeavors, and to look at the sparks of hope that still flickered, here and there, for the greater cause he had served. Sometimes, it seemed he listened. Other times he became weary and I let be, thinking that there would be time to mend his spirits as his body continued to heal.

By then, the weather, too, had changed, and on Sunday morning I walked to church with the Hales and Miss Clement through falling flakes and a city suddenly made lovely to me. On the mornings that followed, I would wake in my warm chamber and look out on a clean, sparkling world. It seemed that everything in my life was being made fresh and restored to me.

I was able at last to write good news to the girls, and they replied with merry mock dispatches and songs to cheer the invalid.

I sat by his bed, reading from the latest parcel of missives. Jo had included a "pome," a "silly little thing" that she had entitled "Song of the Suds," about her struggles to master domestic arts, which I read to him:

> *And I cheerfully learn to say,*
> *"Head, you may think, Heart, you may feel,*
> *But, Hand, you shall work away!"*

"And see? She signs it 'Topsy Turvey Jo.'"

"How I miss them!" he sighed.

"You will see them, soon enough," I said brightly. Now that his needs were less pressing, I had taken to bringing a basket of needlework to his bedside, mending clothes for the convalescents. I bent down to put the letters away and took up a shirt with a torn seam. I was examining it to see the extent of the rend and did not look up until I heard his breath catch in a sob.

"Why, whatever is it?" I said, laying the shirt aside and reaching over to stroke his cheek.

"I can't go home to them," he said. "Not yet."

"Well, of course," I said, soothingly. "Dr. Hale says we must not think of moving you while the snowstorms persist. But he says there is every good chance that if the weather eases, we may have you home in time for Christmas."

He shook his head. "No. I cannot go home. I am not discharged from the army."

"But that's only a formality–Dr. Hale says it can be effected in a matter of a day or two . . ."

"I am not prepared to seek a discharge."

"What are you saying? Are you still delirious?"

As soon as the words were out I wished them unsaid, for I did not wish to recall to him the cruel torments of those hours.

"My work," he said in a whisper, "is not finished. The efforts of the past year, all of them bore rotten fruit. Innocents have died because of me. People have been dragged back into bondage. I cannot go home–to comfort and peace–until I have redeemed the losses I have caused."

"And how," I said, my voice grown cold, "do you propose to do that? When you set out a year ago, you were merely too old for the venture. Now you are both too old and a ruin. Who, precisely, do you think you can help? You, who cannot make his water without assistance?"

He winced, and I bit my tongue. He needed my understanding, not my anger.

"Not all you did went for naught," I said gently. "The education you gave to so many, that cannot be taken away. Why, the letters you taught that girl–you said her name was Zannah–saved your life. Had you not taught so well, you would in all probability be dead now. How can you doubt the value of that?"

He waved a hand weakly, as if to dismiss the hard effort of so many months. "What good are letters to a woman who has lost her only child? Or to a man who has lost his liberty?"

"You did not kill that child, a Confederate did. As for the captive Negroes, the war does go on without you, you know. There are others whose efforts might have something to do with liberating those people–all of them–your friends included. It is pride that makes you think like this, that makes you feel as though you are indispensable."

"Pride?" he said, smiling weakly. "How could you accuse me of pride? I have no pride left to me. I despise myself. I-I did not always act bravely. I left wounded men behind at the battle of the bluff. I let go of Silas Stone in the river . . ."

I cut him off, for once his mind turned to these matters it began a cascade: weeping led to coughing, which gave him pain, which caused him to lose his appetite, which arrested the essential daily increase in his strength.

"You must stop this. Think of your girls and how their hearts lift at the thought of having you home . . ."

"How may I revel in thoughts of my own homecoming, without reflecting on those who will never get home? Those wounded I left, crying; young Stone, drowning? They will never go home, because I was not brave enough."

"Brave enough! How brave do you need to be to satisfy yourself? I said pride, and pride it is, when you speak so. For it is not enough for you to be accounted commonly courageous. Oh no: you must be a Titan. You must carry all the wounded off the field. You must not only try to save a man, you must succeed at it, and when you can't, you heap ashes on your head as if all the blame were yours—none to spare for the generals who blundered you into that battle, or the stretcher bearers, who also fled for their lives; or for Stone's own panic, or for the fact that he never troubled to learn to swim, not even a modicum of blame for the man who shot him . . . You did not kill Silas Stone, or Zannah's child. The war killed both of them. You must accept that."

"But I *might* have saved them. There was a man, Jesse, he handed me a gun, and I handed it back to him. I valued my principles more than I valued their lives. And the outcome is, they are slaves again, or dead."

"You are not God. You do not determine the outcome. The outcome is not the point."

"Then what, pray, is the point?" His voice was a dry, soft rattle, like a breeze through a bough of dead leaves.

"The point is the effort. That you, believing what you believed— what you sincerely believed, including the commandment 'thou shalt not kill'—acted upon it. To believe, to act, and to have events confound you—I grant you, that is hard to bear. But to believe, and not to act, or to act in a way that every fiber of your soul held was wrong—how can you not see? *That* is what would have been reprehensible." And even as I said this, I knew that if I stood again in the cattle show ground, and heard him promise to go to war, I would hold my piece, again, even knowing what terrible days were to follow. For to have asked him to do otherwise would have been to wish him a different man. And I knew then that I loved *this* man. This inconstant, ruined dreamer.

He closed his eyes, his brows drawn. His breathing had become labored from the strain of our exchange. I fetched a cloth and made to bathe his forehead, which was beaded with sweat. He submitted for a moment or two, and then he pushed my hand away.

"Leave me now," he said. "I need to sleep."

"Yes," I said, trying to school my voice so as not to reveal my hurt and confusion. "Yes, that would be best."

I leaned down and kissed his brow. He did not open his eyes or respond in any way.

I gathered my things and walked toward the exit of the ward. Before I passed through the door, I turned back. His eyes were wide open, staring at the ceiling. He did not see me go.

CHAPTER EIGHTEEN

State of Grace

I kept my eyes closed till I thought she had gone. I lay there, listening, as the click of her heels on the wooden floorboards receded into silence. But I made a mistake and opened them too soon. She had paused, merely; turned in the doorway to look back at me. So she saw I was awake. I felt the power of her troubled gaze, but I did not turn my head. I could not bear to talk of it anymore; there was no way to make her understand.

I lay there, sleepless, and let the ghosts come. I offered myself up to the torment of their visions and their accusing whispers. And when exhaustion finally claimed me, just before dawn, I let them inhabit my dreams. It was the least I could do.

I had grown used to waking and finding her beside me, ready with warm cloths and a bowl of oats or grits which she coaxes me to eat. But she wasn't there that morning, and I was glad of it. How could I explain to her that all her kindly ministries were a torment? That her warm cloths seared me and her oatmeal caught in my throat like ground glass? For I did not wish to be clean and fed when others lay cold and hungry in their filth.

The morning wore on, and except for some perfunctory attentions from the nurses, I was left mercifully alone. I dozed fitfully for a time, and when I opened my eyes, the young man, John Brooke, was sitting in her accustomed place, and still I was glad, for he at least would not presume to tell me that I had done enough.

He wished me a civil good morning, and asked if I wanted anything. I shook my head. Only then did I notice that he had a rather gray cast to his features, and his dark eyes, always grave, were sunken and somber. He had a paper scrolled up in his hand. He kept twisting it nervously.

"Is there something you must tell me, John?"

"Sir, I-I do not wish to lay a burden upon you, but I'm afraid I have some grim news. Laurie—my pupil—sent a telegraph yesterday evening. It—it appears that young Beth has had scarlet fever for some days, and Mrs. Mullet bade the girls conceal it from Mrs. March, knowing she was bound here with you. But Teddy—young Mr. Laurie, I should say—became increasingly alarmed, and convinced his grandfather that the little girl's illness was such that Mrs. March must know of it. The short of it is, she left last night, and should be there by the early hours of tomorrow morning. She left a note for you. She said it is but a line. She did not have time to write more."

Brooke handed me the scrap of twisted paper. I could barely read it through the blur. *Now you must see the need to be together. Remember that we are a family. Hope with me, and come to me as soon as you can.*

I fell back on my pillow. "Pray God she arrives in time!" I barely heard Brooke as he recounted what he had learned from quizzing the nurses on the course the fever takes. I knew enough: we had sat up, fretting, when Meg and Jo had contracted it, but they were strong girls, tough in the fiber and robust. Beth was delicate. Her whole short life had been marked by illnesses whose journeys took her out to the very edge of existence. Sometimes it seemed to me that her hold on this world was no firmer than the petal's to the blown rose. And yet she was the best of all of us. Was I to have another ghost to join the reproachful throng at my bedside? Already, I heard the reedy whisper that would haunt my dreams: "Papa, why did you leave your little Mouse? If you had only stayed with us . . ."

I felt my chest tighten, and then the spasm, and I surrendered to it. I let the coughs wrack me, thinking that my heart might burst. Indeed, I hoped for it. At that moment, the idea of oblivion seemed to me no more than the promise of a sweet release.

When I had surrendered all belief in mercy, so mercy was granted me at last.

I will not say I woke to the good news, for I kept vigil with my distant child that night, and did not sleep. But in the first gray stirrings of morning, I turned to see Mr. Brooke enter the ward, his face stamped with manifest relief and joy so complete it did not need the elaboration of the telegraph's few words. Marmee had arrived to find our Beth recovering: the fever had turned as she traveled northward, so that our little daughter awoke from her long struggle to the sight of her beloved mother's face.

The letter that followed in due course stated the simple obvious: that she would remain with our small recovering invalid and not return to Washington. She wrote that she proposed to entrust my recuperation to the capable supervision of Mr. Brooke, and that all at home awaited the easing of the weather in the confident expectation of our speedy reunion.

But what she expected was not possible. I did not know how to judge her letter; whether it was calculated, in that she reasoned if she pretended to assume a certain course of events, I would become more pliable to her vision, or whether her obtuseness was unfeigned, and nothing I had said to her had pierced the carapace of her obstinacy.

The fact was this: I could not go home. I had not earned the right. My service was not completed. If I struggled now to speed my convalescence, it was because I was anxious to set my feet on the path of atonement, and find some niche in which a diminished man could be of modest use. Mr. Brooke, of course, misconstrued my new willingness to accept food and take exercise. He naturally assumed that my redoubled efforts were born of a desire for reunion with my family. Since disabusing him would be too complicated, I let him think what he would.

Slowly, I regained the strength of my limbs and was able to take my place for a few hours each day with the other convalescents, the corps of the feeble, who tried our best to sweep and scour, fetch and carry for those sicker than ourselves, and so relieve the nurses of such routine burdens. And if these duties more often took me downstairs, to the surgical ward, than to any other place, then I will not apologize for that. For I took satisfaction from any small effort I could make that lessened the tasks of Grace Clement, whose skills at nursing were become as prodigious as those of many who claimed the higher titles of healing.

Grace herself was not in favor of using convalescents as attendants, or so she told me one day as she taught me how to drench the stump of a boy named Cephas White. "He should have walked out of here on two legs, had they not overburdened him with heavy tasks before his injury was fully mended," she said. The boy was still unconscious following his surgery, which was fortunate, for the poison had spread so far from his wound that, as well as taking off the leg, the surgeon had been forced to debride the flesh of his thigh and groin so that it looked raw and disgusting as beef on a butcher's block. He would wake to certain agony.

As Grace directed me, I slowly poured the cold water on his dressings until they saturated, and then adjusted the oilcloth beneath his bed to catch the falling drips. He had developed a fever, so she laid a cold compress upon his brow. "It will be remarkable now if he leaves this place alive," she said. She looked at me across his ruined body. "You would do well to consider your own strength, and not exceed it, or you, too, may be here longer than you need to be."

"And what would that matter? I must find some way to be of use. Here, at least, I can be a little help to you."

She raised an eyebrow. "Maybe, but not for many weeks more. They are forming a medical corps to serve the planned colored regiments, and Dr. Hale has agreed that I should join it."

The jug handle slipped in my hand as she said this, and water splashed onto the oilcloth. I had not realized how much store I set in being of service to her. To be deprived of her company, so soon after our unlikely reunion—this seemed a cruel prospect.

"I had planned, that is, I had hoped, that we might work together, that I might learn some basic skills that would be of use to you, as you are of use and learn from Dr. Hale . . ."

"You should think instead about going home, and growing strong again," she said. "There is no way you can make a full recovery here. Most likely in your weakened state you will succumb to some hospital malady. And even if you do not pick up any new affliction, you know the nature of your fever. It is bound to recur."

"But I do not look for hearth and healing! How can I seek comfort when others—like this boy here—suffer still? My conscience will not let me rest idle at home." I dropped my voice then. "You know there are grave matters—mistakes, failings—for which I need to make amends."

"You are not the only one who has to live with a troubled conscience," she said. "There are many of us who bear guilt for what we have done—what the circumstances of our lives have led us to do."

I grew impatient with her. "You!" I said. "You can know nothing of this. You are the noblest person I ever met. Your choice, to care for that man, your so-called father, when you could have abandoned him and no one to blame it—"

"This is no place to speak of such things," she said sharply. She dropped her voice. "But you are quite mistaken. Walk with me if you will, this afternoon. It is milder today. If it remains so, I believe a short walk in the full air might be beneficial to you. I will wait for you, a little after three o'clock, by the ruins of the French minister's house. There was a fire there; the building was quite gutted. Anyone will be able to direct you. It is not far."

She turned away then, and instead of going on to the next bed, whose occupant also was unconscious, crossed the ward to change the dressings of a man who was quite alert. There was no way to continue our conversation, as she had clearly purposed.

So I swept the floor and then went to lie down so that I would have the strength to walk. At three o'clock I borrowed a greatcoat and some gloves from an orderly. Just before I set out, I thought to look in on the poor boy, White, and see if he had regained consciousness, and if so, to ensure that he had been given something to ease his suffering.

When I got to his bedside, it was evident that suffering, for him, was over. I went looking for an orderly to take the body to the dead house, but everyone was occupied just then, transporting wounded from newly arrived ambulances. So I returned to White's bedside, thinking to remove the pillow beneath his head before the rigor set in. As I did so, a paper fluttered to the floor. I bent to retrieve it. Upon it was a verse, scrawled in an uncertain hand.

> *I am no longer eager, bold & strong.*
> *All that is past;*
> *I am ready not to do*
> *At last, at last,*
> *My half day's work is done,*
> *And this is all my part.*
> *I give a patient God*
> *My patient heart.*

The boy had written this before the amputation. I expect he had seen enough by then to know his likely fate. *I am ready not to do.* The line burned me. How could an unlearned youth such as White write with such wisdom and resignation, while I, brimful of philosophy and book learning, was unable to still my heart into patience?

I set the paper carefully with White's few effects and left the hospital. The cold air hit my face like a welcome slap, breaking me out of morbid reverie. I stretched my legs, feeling pleasure as the muscles once again answered to my will, and allowed myself the luxury of anticipation. There was so much I wished to say to Grace; all of it impossible in the close confines of the hospital.

It was, as she had said, easy to find the blackened shell of a mansion that she had appointed for our meeting. The ruined house abutted a little wilderness of cedars bisected by a narrow, silvery brook where Georgetown's black washerwomen gathered to do their clients' laundry. Since my pace was slow, Grace had reached the place before me. I told her about White, but did not mention the poem. She nodded gravely. She had not expected him to survive; that he had passed without further suffering was, she said, a mercy of a kind.

When we had passed into the trees and away from eyes that might be scandalized, she took my arm as any nurse might do, to support my still-unsure steps over the uneven pathway. When we had gone a little distance, she turned to me and addressed me with an abrupt severity.

"You have to stop wallowing in this notion that you are somehow at fault in all the ill things that have happened this past year. War is full of misfortune. Cannot you see? It is folly to let this self-flagellation shape your future."

I was angered by her tone and by her obtuseness—she, who had never seemed the least obtuse. "You do not know what you are speaking about," I said, abrupt in my turn. "You have always done the highest and best thing; the self-sacrificing thing. What can you possibly know of a conscience ablaze with guilt? What can you know of sin?"

Her reply came like a whisper, or a hiss.

"Is not incest a sin? Is not murder?"

"What?"

I stopped still on the path. The cedars sighed above us.

She let go of my elbow. She held herself stiffly, as if some struggle were under way within. Her lips were drawn tight and her hands were balled into fists. She pressed them together, and pushed them against the underside of her jaw. She breathed in deeply then and rubbed her hands over her face, flexed her shoulders, and began to speak, her voice low and measured.

"I told you Mr. Clement's son died when his fowling piece discharged in his face. I told you he tangled his boot in a thicket of honeysuckle. I did not tell you—I have not told anyone—the full account of that accident, and I do not propose to tell it now." She gave me that assessing look that I remembered from years earlier. "But you are not the innocent who arrived at the Clement house that long-ago spring. I think you have seen enough of evil now to understand very well how things stood. All I will say is this: that he, knowing the truth of my parentage, knowing he was my brother, committed a sin whose magnitude has ever been understood, even by savages. And do you know what the worst violation was? That I realized my father had intended just such a thing. That I had been kept, perchance, for just such a purpose, to be used in my turn as my mother had been used. What happened to him was, in part, an accident. But only in part. I don't believe I meant to kill him, but I rejoiced in his death, Mr. March."

For a moment, there was a blaze in her eyes that looked like exaltation. The images came to my mind, unbidden. I cannot know, I will never know, if I saw aright. An unexpected encounter in an autumnal field. A youth giving way to a moment's base lust or a year's corrupt longing. A scuffle amid the yellowing honeysuckle, a fall, a gun discharging, a face exploding like a shattered watermelon. And another face, lovely and pitiless, hurrying silently away.

Grace had dropped her head, and her voice, when she spoke

again, was even lower than before. "The remorse—that came later. When I saw the loss in my father's eyes, and in the eyes of Mr. Harris. When Mr. Harris left, because of my brother's death, and I watched the plantation come slowly undone, and saw everyone suffer on account of it. Prudence and Justice sold, Annie drowned. All of it, all of it, because of my actions.

"So, do not presume that I have no experience with a conscience that flays me alive, every waking day."

"Whatever it was that you did—" I stumbled, and began again. "Whatever misadventure happened as you sought to defend yourself—" But there she cut me off, waving her hands impatiently as if to clear a noxious mist.

"I do not ask your absolution. I simply ask you to see that there is only one thing to do when we fall, and that is to get up, and go on with the life that is set in front of us, and try to do the good of which our hands are capable for the people who come in our way. That, at least, has been my path."

"Well, then," I said, a little querulous, "that, too, is what I purpose. When I am a little stronger I could work with you: there will be needs, great needs, when colored troops are enlisted at last—"

She cut me off again, angrily this time.

"We have had enough of white people ordering our existence! There are men of my own race more versed in how to fetch and carry than you will ever be. And there are Negro preachers aplenty who know the true language of our souls. A free people must learn to manage its own destiny."

She had raised her voice and her eyes glared. I looked away, astonished by the vehemence of her rejection. "Go home, Mr. March," she said. Then her voice softened. "If you sincerely want to help us, go back to Concord and work with your own people. Write sermons that will prepare your neighbors to accept a world where black and white may one day stand as equals."

"But I don't know if I can preach at all anymore . . ." My voice broke into a high whine, like a boy on the cusp of manhood. I imagined it would break, just so, if I ever again mounted the steps of a pulpit. For me, silence had become more eloquent than any sermon.

She moved toward me and laid a hand on my arm. "Go home. Be a father to your daughters. That, at least, you can do. They are the ones who need you."

She didn't say it, but the unspoken words hung in the air between us. *They* might need me: she, most definitely, did not.

CHAPTER NINETEEN

Concord

You go on. You set one foot in front of the other, and if a thin voice cries out, somewhere behind you, you pretend not to hear, and keep going.

But some steps require more effort than others. As I set my foot upon the path leading to that little brown house, I felt like an impostor. Surely, I had no business here. This was the house of another man. A man I remembered. A person of moral certainty, and some measure of wisdom, whom many called courageous. How could I masquerade as such a one? For I was a fool, a coward, uncertain of everything.

Had I been alone, I might have turned back then, melted away like the snow on that bright, mild morning, become a particle lost in the vast spate flowing through the landscape of war, so that my daughters could live with the unsullied memory of that other man, and not be obliged to know this inferior replacement.

But I was not alone. John Brooke had a firm grip upon my arm and the young Laurence boy pranced brightly ahead of us, barely able to contain his excitement. He was carrying on as if he brought some bright-wrapped, welcome Christmas gift. If only he knew for what shoddy goods he was the forerunner. I pulled my muffler up high around my face, so as to hide the trembling at the corners of my mouth. Truly, walking up that path was an act of courage greater than any asked of me at war.

The boy burst into the house ahead of us, opened the door to the parlor, and vanished behind it. I leaned against the hall table. John Brooke, thinking my weakness a product of the journey, clasped a strong arm around my back. Thus encompassed, he propelled me forward whether I would or no.

The door opened. My eyes, snow-dazzled, registered only a blur. Brooke tried to say something, but his words disappeared under a general uproar. There were soft arms flung around my neck. Someone tripped over a footstool and did not even trouble to rise, but set about embracing my boots. I looked down on golden curls. My Amy. And Jo—hand to her head—her cropped, curly head—as if she were about to faint. Meg—could it be Meg, this womanly figure?—touching heads with Brooke in the confusion and adding to it with blushes and mumbled apologies. Meg and John—so that was the way of it—I hadn't realized—and Marmee, serene in the center of the maelstrom. Her face weary but smiling. I felt the grip of her will like a gaff plunged deep in me: she had been determined to see this day. She would have me back in the boat, she would keep this craft, our family, afloat, together, no matter how damaged my state, or her own, no matter how uncertain the seas.

She raised her hand in a calming gesture.

"Hush!" she said. "Remember Beth!"

But Beth had heard the commotion, of course. How not, in that small cottage? My little Mouse, her red gown flying, ran toward me on unsteady legs. Instinct opened my arms and I caught her—frail wisp that even I, depleted, could hold without effort.

I fumbled through the next hours feeling somehow swaddled like a mummy, or wafted away on the fumes of an ether-soaked rag. At times, I knew I was being touched, but I could not feel the contact on my flesh. I knew I was being spoken to, but I could not quite make out the sense of the words. Oh, I made some reply; I know this, for I sensed that my mouth shaped words, and I must have said reasonable things, as the faces that regarded me remained calm, and no one looked startled or taken aback. But I cannot tell one word of what passed as I made my way from those parlor greetings to the Christmas dinner table and finally to an armchair by a twilit fireside.

The temperature dropped sharply as evening came on, and a little snow flurried outside. Had someone, walking in the white street, looked in at our window, he would have seen in the family tableau a simulacrum of domestic joy. Beth sat on my knee, Meg beside, her hand resting on the arm of my chair, Jo opposite, and Amy on the cricket at my feet.

Some turn in the conversation made me glance down at Meg's hand. The flesh was puckered and burned. Suddenly, it was not Meg's slight stove burn that I saw, but Jimse's melted flesh, healed into the white cobweb that would not allow his little palm to fully open. I had been concerned that the hand would trouble him, later in his life. And now there would be no later life.

But even while this thought filled my mind and clouded my heart, somehow, my mouth was uttering small encomiums about Meg and her diligent housework, and how her scarred, workworn hand seemed finer to me than the unblemished one of which she had used to be a little vain.

Beth, her small face pressed close to my ear, asked me to say how I thought the year had changed Jo, and so I did, speaking in praise of her newly dignified bearing and of her careful nursing of her little sister. And all the time I spoke, my heart ached for the dignified bearing of that other nurse, who would soon march off to care for the colored fallen, and whom I would likely never see again.

"Now Beth," demanded Amy, leaning against my knees. I said something about finding my Mouse less shy, and then a real emotion pierced my rote recital, as I recalled how nearly I had come to losing her. I held her close. "I've got you safe, my Beth, and I'll keep you so, please God."

And I looked down, and began to speak of the change in Amy, and how I perceived, by her forbearance at the dinner table, a new-found consideration for others. But when she looked up at me, lit by my praise, the tilt of her head and the light in her eyes recalled my pupil Cilla. That poor little girl, whom I had not been able to keep safe. My mind reeled with the memory of her terrible wounds, the buzz of the flies, the stink . . . I felt my gorge rise and knew I would not be able to continue to speak. So this was how it was to be, now: I would do my best to live in the quick world, but the ghosts of the dead would be ever at hand.

Fortunately, Jo asked something of Beth at that moment, and the conversation turned from me. Beth slid from my lap, went to her little piano, lightly touched the keys, and began to sing:

> *He that is down need fear no fall,*
> *He that is low, no pride . . .*

All eyes were on her then, before anyone had thought to ask their father how a year at war had changed *him*. I hid my face in the gathering darkness until Marmee came in with a taper, and bent over the lamp. The wick caught. There was a tiny clink as she settled the glass. As she turned the screw to adjust the flame, light flared. For an instant, everything was bathed in radiance.

Afterword

March is a work of fiction that draws its inspiration from one of the great American families of the nineteenth century, the Alcotts of Concord, Massachusetts. For its scaffolding, I have borrowed from Louisa May Alcott's iconic *Little Women,* among the first novels to deal, albeit glancingly, with the Civil War. But it is to Alcott's father, the transcendentalist philosopher, educator, and abolitionist, A. Bronson Alcott, that I am most indebted.

Readers of *Little Women* will remember that the novel opens on a rather bleak Christmas Eve in the home of the March family. The father of Meg, Jo, Beth, and Amy is absent: he has gone south to minister to Union troops. In a dramatic moment two-thirds of the way through the narrative, a telegram arrives, urgently summoning Mrs. March to Washington, where her husband lies gravely ill. The crisis is resolved when Mr. March appears unexpectedly on the following Christmas Day, so that the year, and the novel as it was originally published, both close with the family reunited. Alcott's story is concerned with the way a year lived at the edge of war has worked changes in the characters of the little women, but what war has done to March himself is left unstated.

It is in this void that I have let my imagination work. In attempting to create a character for the absent father, I have followed Alcott's lead, and turned for inspiration to her own family. Alcott modeled the March girls on herself and her sisters: she, of course, was Jo, the aspiring writer. Meg was modeled on the dutiful Anna, who married young; Beth was the delicate, doomed Elizabeth; and Amy was her youngest sister, May, who achieved early success as an artist in Europe before dying of childbirth complications. So it seemed natural to turn to the journals, letters, and biographies of Alcott's father, Bronson, for inspiration of my own.

Bronson Alcott was a radical, even by the yardstick of nineteenth-century New England, where all manner of new ideas, from a reappraisal of the nature of God to the dietary benefits of graham crackers, found eager adherents. He recorded his own life in sixty-one journals and his letters fill thirty-seven manuscript volumes in the Harvard College Library. He is the subject of an 1893 two-volume memoir by Franklin B. Sanborn and William T. Harris, and a 1937 biography by Odell Shepard. Warm references to Bronson Alcott—often as mentor and inspiration—appear frequently in the letters and journals of Ralph Waldo Emerson and Henry David Thoreau, who were among his closest friends.

I have drawn heavily on this material in creating a life and a voice for March. Occasionally I have borrowed snatches of Bronson's own words: for example, the expressions of affection for his family in Mr. March's first letter home, or the physical description of John Brown. I have also, in places, used the actual words of Emerson and Thoreau (readers of *Walden* will recognize the rant on Flint's pond), though I have taken large liberties with their context.

Bronson Alcott grew up with barely literate parents on a hardscrabble Connecticut hill farm. In his late teens he went south as a peddler of notions and books to wealthy planters. His early journals seem blind to slavery's cruelties, so swept up was he in the leisured life of the mind that the slaves' labor made possible for their wealthy owners. Yet years later, back in New England as a middle-aged philosopher, he risked his life by stepping into the line of fire to protest the repatriation of a runaway slave.

His radicalism took many forms. A vegetarian, he founded a commune, Fruitlands, so extreme in its Utopianism that members neither wore wool nor used animal manures, as both were considered property of the beasts from which they came. One reason the venture failed in its first winter was that when canker worms got into the apple crop, the nonviolent Fruitlanders refused to take measures to kill them.

The Mr. March of *Little Women* departs from Bronson Alcott's biography in many important respects. Bronson was an educator, not a minister of religion (he is credited with inventing the concept of recess, and also for attempting one of the first racially integrated classrooms). Also, since Bronson was already sixty-one when the Civil War broke out, he did not go south with the troops as does Mr. March, who is portrayed as more than a decade younger. So I have imagined a war for a Union chaplain of Bronson Alcott's transcendentalist and abolitionist convictions.

The first problem I encountered was temporal. What year of the Civil War are we dealing with, anyway? Louisa May Alcott takes a novelist's license here. The one anchoring date in *Little Women* comes quite late in the book, and is the November 1861 inscription on Amy March's last will and testament. This puts the novel's opening on the prior Christmas Eve in 1860. Since the first shots at Fort Sumter weren't fired until April 1861, Mr. March could not have been "away down south where the fighting is" during that Christmas. So I have taken the liberty of moving the action forward a year. I chose to put Mr. March at the battle of Ball's Bluff simply because the terrain of that small but terrible engagement lies just a few miles from my Virginia home, and because many soldiers from Massachusetts first "saw the elephant" there. For details of that battle I am indebted to the wonderful interpretive work of the National Park

Service, to John Coski at the Museum of the Confederacy in Richmond, and to the book *From Ball's Bluff to Gettysburg . . . and Beyond: The Civil War Letters of Private Roland E. Bowen, 15th Massachusetts Infantry 1861–1864,* edited by Gregory A. Coco.

I consulted two fine books on Civil War chaplains: *Faith in the Fight* by John W. Brinsfield et al., and *For Courageous Fighting and Confident Dying* by Warren B. Armstrong. But I have drawn most heavily on the 1864 memoir, *Chaplain Fuller: Being a Life Sketch of a New England Clergyman and Army Chaplain,* by his brother, Richard F. Fuller. Chaplain Arthur Buckminster Fuller was known to Bronson Alcott; the chaplain's brilliant elder sister, Margaret, had worked for a time as an assistant at Alcott's Temple School in Boston.

It was in researching the role of New England clergy that I became intrigued with the story of the contraband and the North's mixed record of high idealism, negligence, and outright cruelty. During the war, three-quarters of a million African Americans—one in five of the Confederacy's black residents—came within federal lines. Though the Sea Island experiments at Port Royal have been studied extensively—*Letters and Diary of Laura M. Towne,* edited by Rupert Sargent Holland, and *Rehearsal for Reconstruction* by Willie Lee Rose, were particularly helpful—the ad hoc situations on individual, privately leased cotton plantations are less documented. I have relied on Thomas W. Knox's *Camp-Fire and Cotton-Field,* a remarkably honest first person account by a Yankee war correspondent who turns cotton planter in an attempt to make a quick fortune. In creating a world for March, I have hewed very closely to Knox's record. The tragic outcome at Oak Landing is based on Knox's account of the harrowing end to his own venture. Two other books were helpful here: Louis S. Gerteis's *From Contraband to Freedman* and Elizabeth Hyde Botume's 1893 memoir, *First Days Amongst the Contrabands.* For those who care about such things, I freely confess that I have taken a small novelist's license with the time frame, because plantations on the Mississippi would not have been leased to Northerners quite so early in the war.

In deciding how a man like March would render African American speech, I have followed the conventions in the writings of Knox, Towne, and other Northerners who went south in that period. Though the character of Grace Clement is entirely fictional, her voice is inspired by Harriet Ann Jacobs's elegant and painful 1861 autobiography, *Incidents in the Life of a Slave Girl, Written by Herself.*

I am grateful to the expertise of Dr. Norman Horwitz, who introduced me to Sickle's leg and other gruesome Civil War medical relics in the National Museum of Health and Medicine at Walter Reed Army Medical Center. The work of the historian Drew Gilpin Faust on the handling of the dead during the Civil War provided many useful details. For a picture of hospital life in Washington I was able to turn to Louisa May Alcott's *Hospital Sketches,* the memoir of her brief service as Civil War nurse. Alcott served at the Union Hospital, a converted hotel in Georgetown, and wrote vividly of its shortcomings. That short work preceded *Little Women* and was her first real publishing success. The poem attributed to Cephas White was composed by an unnamed patient of Alcott's; she transcribed a copy of it in a letter to her aunt that is held among the rare manuscripts in the Library of Congress.

For the fine bookstores, new and used, and the many fascinating museums of Concord I am also extremely grateful. The memory of its illustrious former residents is well served by the proud sense of historic stewardship that pervades the town. A short distance away, just outside the town of Harvard, Bronson Alcott's Fruitlands dream lives on in a way he could not have imagined, as an intriguing museum and a place of exceptional beauty.

I would like to thank my editor, Molly Stern, and my agent, Kris Dahl; my early readers, Darleen Bungey, Linda Funnell, Brian Hall, Elinor and Joshua Horwitz, Sophie Inwald, Graham Thorburn, and

William Powers. I must also thank Maritess Batac and Amanda Levick, my indispensable supports.

As with so many things in my life, this book owes its being to my mother, Gloria Brooks. I was about ten years old when I read *Little Women* for the first time, at her suggestion. Though she recommended the book, she also counseled that I take it with a grain of salt. "Nobody in real life is such a goody-goody as that Marmee," she declared. In that, as in almost all things, she was correct. Louisa May Alcott's real family was far less perfect, and therefore much more interesting, than the saintly Marches.

Lastly, I should like to take a flyleaf from George Eliot's *Middlemarch*, which she dedicated to her "dear husband . . . in this nineteeth year of our blessed union." In the nineteenth year of our own union, I retract unreservedly my former characterization of my husband, Tony Horwitz, as a Civil War bore. Further, I would like to apologize for all the times I refused to get out of the car at Antietam or whined about the heat at Gettysburg; for all the complaints about too many shelves colonized by his Civil War tomes and all the moaning over weekend expeditions devoted to events such as the interment of Stonewall Jackson's horse. I'm not sure quite when or where it happened, but on a sunken road somewhere, I finally saw the light.

A PENGUIN READERS GUIDE TO

MARCH

Geraldine Brooks

An Introduction to
March

With her critically acclaimed and bestselling novel *Year of Wonders*, Geraldine Brooks was praised for her passionate rendering and careful research in vividly imagining the effects of the bubonic plague on a small English village in the seventeenth century. Now, Brooks turns her talents to exploring the devastation and moral complexities of the Civil War through her brilliantly imagined tale of Mr. March, the absent father from Louisa May Alcott's *Little Women*. In Mr. March, Brooks has created a conflicted and deeply sensitive man, a father who is struggling to reconcile duty to his fellow man with duty to his family against the backdrop of one of the most grim periods in American history.

October 21, 1861. March, an army chaplain, has just survived a brush with death as his unit crossed the Potomac and experienced the small but terrible battle of Ball's Bluff. But when he sits down to write his daily missive to his beloved wife, Marmee, he does not talk of the death and destruction around him, but of clouds "emboss[ing] the sky," his longing for home, and how he misses his four beautiful daughters. "I never promised I would write the truth," he admits, if only to himself.

When he first enlisted, March was an idealistic man. He knew, above all else, that fighting this war for the Union cause was right and just. But he had not expected he would begin a journey through hell on earth, where the lines between right and wrong, good and evil, were too often blurred.

For now, however, he has no choice but to press on. He is directed to a makeshift hospital, an old estate he finds strangely familiar. It was here, more than twenty years earlier, that he first met Grace, a beautiful, literate slave. She was the woman who provided his first kiss and who changed the course of his life.

Now, he finds himself back at the Clement estate, and what was once the most beautiful place he had ever seen has been transformed by the ugliness of war. However, March's sojourn there is brief and he finds himself reassigned to set up a school on one of the liberated plantations, Oak Landing—a disastrous posting that leaves him all but dead.

Though rescued and delivered to a Washington hospital where his physical health improves, March is a broken man, haunted by all he has witnessed and "a conscience ablaze with guilt" over the many people he feels he has failed. And when it is time for him to leave he finds he does not want to return home. He turns to Grace, whom he has encountered once again, for guidance. "None of us is without sin," she tells him. "Go home, Mr. March." So, March returns to his wife and daughters, and though he is tormented by the past and worried for his country's future, the present, at least, is certain: he is home, he is a father again, and for now, that will be enough.

A Conversation with
Geraldine Brooks

1. In your afterword, you make an amusing apology to your husband, a well-known writer and Civil War afficionado, for your previous lack of appreciation for his passion. Although you say you're not sure "when or where" it happened, would you talk a bit about your change of heart and what led to your new and profound interest in the American Civil War and eventually to the writing of March?

In the early 1990s we came to live in a small Virginia village where Civil War history is all around us. There are bullet scars on the bricks of the Baptist church where a skirmish took place; we have a Union soldier's belt buckle that was unearthed near the old well in our courtyard. The village was Quaker, and abolitionist, but in the midst of the Confederacy. The war brought huge issues of conscience for the townsfolk, a few of whom sacrificed their nonviolent principles to raise a regiment to fight on the Union side. It was thinking about the people who once lived in our house, and the moral challenges the war presented for them, that kindled my interest in imagining an idealist adrift in that war. I am gripped by the stories of individuals from the generation Oliver Wendell Holmes so eloquently described when he said: "In our youth our hearts were touched with fire." I'm still not all that interested in the order of battles, I still drive Tony crazy by failing to keep the chronology straight, and offered the choice between a trip to the dentist and another midsummer reenactment, it'd be a hard call. But sometimes, alone on a battlefield as the mists rise over the grass, I feel like a time traveler, born back by the ghosts of all those vivid, missing boys.

2. Grace Clement is such an extraordinary character and is pivotal in shaping March's life. You tell us that her voice was inspired by an

1861 autobiography, but what inspired you to create a romantic relationship between Grace and March? Were there any historical hints that Alcott had had such a relationship?

The idea of an attraction between March and Grace is entirely imagined and not at all suggested by Bronson Alcott's biography. It grew naturally out of the narrative: they are young and attractive when they first meet, he is an idealist, she is a compelling person in a dramatic and moving situation. It seemed inevitable to me.

3. A year after March enlists he says, "One day I hope to go back. To my wife, to my girls, but also to the man of moral certainty that I was . . . that innocent man, who knew with such clear confidence exactly what it was that he was meant to do." Do you think he can go back? Is it even possible? Would you discuss how you think March changes by the end of the novel and what parts of him remain intact?

I don't think he can go back. Nor do I think it is necessarily desirable. Moral certainty can deafen people to any truth other than their own. By the end of the book, March is damaged, but he is still an idealist; it's just that he sees more clearly the cost of his ideals, and understands that he is not the only one who must pay for them.

4. Your book Nine Parts of Desire *deals with the issues of Muslim women.* Year of Wonders *had a female heroine, Anna Frith. How was it different writing principally from a man's point of view this time?*

I have always believed that the human heart is the human heart, no matter what century we live in, what country we inhabit, or what gender we happen to be. This is a book about strong feelings: love and fear. I can't believe there's much difference in how a man or a woman experiences them. And then, I had the journals and letters of Bronson Alcott, which are perhaps as complete a record of a Victorian man's interior life as any you could find.

5. It is quite a surprise to suddenly hear Marmee's voice in Part Two. Can you talk about how and why you decided to change the point of view here?

The structure of *March* was laid down for me before the first line was written, because my character has to exist within Louisa May Alcott's *Little Women* plotline. That meant March has to go to the hospital gravely ill and Marmee has to arrive to tend him. The alternative to switching voices would have been to continue the narrative in March's voice, disoriented by his delirium. But giving Marmee a voice seemed like an opportunity to me to better explore some of the themes of communication, and miscommunication, in a marriage. Also, the book was written against the tumult of my own feelings about the war with Iraq, and as I started to write in Marmee's voice I found that she could naturally articulate a frustration, grief, and confusion that seemed in common between us.

6. The American Civil War was enormously complex with different political, social, economic, and psychological factors all playing a role. What did you learn from your research that may have surprised you and, other than your obvious newfound interest, is your opinion of the war any different now than when you started?

Nations inevitably fall into the trap of romanticizing their militaries and are always astonished when the truth of awful atrocities is revealed, as it inevitably is in almost every war. There were plenty of hate-filled racists in Lincoln's army, fighting side by side with the celebrated idealists. March's growing dismay as he learns this in a way reflects my own journey to a more complete understanding.

7. Would you talk a bit about how your past work as a foreign correspondent informs your current writing? What do you think historical fiction can achieve that nonfiction cannot? Would you ever entertain the idea of writing a novel about current events?

Write what you know. It's the first advice given to writers. I did draw on some experiences of war from my correspondent years. You see things during war, and you can never unsee them. The thing that most attracts me to historical fiction is taking the factual record as far as it is known, using that as scaffolding, and then letting imagination build the structure that fills in those things we can never find out for sure. And to do that you use all the experiences you can. While I love to read contemporary fiction, I'm not drawn to writing it. Perhaps it's because the former journalist in me is too inhibited by the press of reality; when I think about writing of my own time I always think about nonfiction narratives. Or perhaps it's just that I find the present too confounding.

8. What are you working on now?

Another historical novel based on a true story, but one where the truth is not completely known, and so there are intriguing voids for the imagination to fill. Like *March* and *Year of Wonders* it has a lot to do with faith and catastrophe.

QUESTIONS FOR DISCUSSION

1. Throughout the novel, March and Marmee, although devoted to one another, seem to misunderstand each other quite a bit and often do not tell each other the complete truth. Discuss examples of where this happens and how things may have turned out differently, for better or worse, had they been completely honest. Are there times when it is best not to tell our loved ones the truth?

2. The causes of the American Civil War were multiple and overlapping. What was your opinion of the war when you first came to the novel, and has it changed at all since reading *March*?

3. March's relationships with both Marmee and Grace are pivotal in his life. Discuss the differences between these two relationships and how they help to shape March, his worldview, and his future. What other people and events were pivotal in shaping March's beliefs?

4. Do you think it was the right decision for March to have supported, financially or morally, the northern abolitionist John Brown? Brown's tactics were controversial, but did the ends justify the means?

5. "If war can ever be said to be just, then this war is so; it is action for a moral cause, with the most rigorous of intellectual underpinnings. And yet everywhere I turn, I see injustice done in the waging of it," says March (p. 65). Do you think that March still believes the war is just by the end of the novel? Why or why not?

6. What is your opinion of March's enlisting? Should he have stayed home with his family? How do we decide when to put our principles ahead of our personal obligations?

7. When Marmee is speaking of her husband's enlisting in the army, she makes a very eloquent statement: "A sacrifice such as his is called noble by the world. But the world will not help me put back together what war has broken apart" (p. 210). Do her words have resonance in today's world? How are the people who fight our wars today perceived? Do you think we pay enough attention to the families of those in the military? Have our opinions been influenced at all by the inclusion of women in the military?

8. The war raged on for several years after March's return home. How do you imagine he spent those remaining years of the war? How do you think his relationship with Marmee changed? How might it have stayed the same?

For more information about or to order other Penguin Readers Guides, please e-mail the Penguin Marketing Department at reading@us.penguingroup.com or write to us at:

Penguin Books Marketing Dept.
Readers Guides
375 Hudson Street
New York, NY 10014-3657

Please allow 4–6 weeks for delivery.
To access Penguin Readers Guides online, visit the Penguin Group (USA) Web site at www.penguin.com.

Year of Wonders

When an infected bolt of cloth carries plague from London to an isolated mountain village, a housemaid named Anna Frith emerges as an unlikely heroine and healer. Through Anna's eyes we follow the story of the plague year, 1666, as her fellow villagers make an extraordinary choice: convinced by a visionary young minister they elect to quarantine themselves within the village boundaries to arrest the spread of the disease. But as death reaches into every household, faith frays. When villagers turn from prayers to murderous witch-hunting, Anna must confront the deaths of her family, the disintegration of her community, and the lure of illicit love. As she struggles to survive, a year of plague becomes instead *annus mirablilis*, a "year of wonders."

Inspired by the true story of Eyam, a village in the rugged hill country of England, *Year of Wonders* is a richly detailed evocation of a singular moment in history. Written with stunning emotional intelligence and introducing "an inspiring heroine" (*The Wall Street Journal*), Brooks blends love and learning, loss and renewal into a spellbinding and unforgettable read.

"The novel glitters . . . a deep imaginative engagement with how people are changed by catastrophe."   —*The New Yorker*

"*Year of Wonders* is a vividly imagined and strangely consoling tale of hope in a time of despair."   —*O, The Oprah Magazine*

"Beautiful . . . [a] deeply involving story."   —*Newsday*

ISBN 0-14-200143-0